PRAISE FOR *THE HEIRESS GETS A DUKE*

"A delightfully entertaining read, rich with romance, glamour, and lush Victorian detail. Harper St. George truly captures the spirit of the era."

— Mimi Matthews, *USA Today* bestselling author

"A sexy, emotional, romantic tale . . . Harper St. George is a must-buy for me!"

— Terri Brisbin, *USA Today* bestselling author

"Wit, seduction, and passion blend seamlessly to create this deeply emotional romance. St. George weaves an intriguing plot with complex characters to provide the perfect sensual escape. There's nothing I didn't love about *The Heiress Gets a Duke*, especially its lush, captivating glimpse into history."

— Anabelle Bryant, *USA Today* bestselling author

"Rich with period detail, *The Heiress Gets a Duke* brings to life the Gilded Age's dollar princesses in this smart, sexy, and oh-so-satisfying story."

— Laurie Benson, award-winning author of
The Sommersby Brides series

The
HEIRESS
GETS A DUKE

HARPER ST. GEORGE

JOVE
New York

A JOVE BOOK
Published by Berkley
An imprint of Penguin Random House LLC
penguinrandomhouse.com

Copyright © 2021 by Harper Nieh
Excerpt from *The Devil and the Heiress* by Harper St. George
copyright © 2021 by Harper Nieh
Penguin Random House supports copyright. Copyright fuels creativity, encourages
diverse voices, promotes free speech, and creates a vibrant culture. Thank you for buying
an authorized edition of this book and for complying with copyright laws by not
reproducing, scanning, or distributing any part of it in any form without permission.
You are supporting writers and allowing Penguin Random House to continue to
publish books for every reader.

A JOVE BOOK, BERKLEY, and the BERKLEY & B colophon are
registered trademarks of Penguin Random House LLC.

ISBN: 9780593197202

First Edition: January 2021

Printed in the United States of America
1 3 5 7 9 10 8 6 4 2

Cover design by Rita Frangie
Book design by George Towne

To the thirteen-year-old me who didn't think this was possible. And, especially, to all the girls who are wondering if it's possible for them. Yes, you can do it.

Prologue

I feel sure that no girl would go to the altar if she knew all.

QUEEN VICTORIA

NEW YORK CITY
SEPTEMBER 1874

A feminine wail floated through the crowded ballroom of the Bridwells' newly built Fifth Avenue mansion. The soft cry hovered beneath the notes of the waltz, its ghostly fingers touching everything it passed. The efforts of an army of musicians did nothing to drown out the sorrow inherent in the sound. It settled like a fog of despair over the glamorous evening, dusting it with melancholy. August Crenshaw shivered as if the icy fingers had stroked down her spine.

Before her eyes, the engagement party continued in full swing, not the least bit concerned with the rather unremarkable fact that the bride-to-be was not a willing participant in the festivities. There was a momentary hitch in the happy amusement—a brief pause in conversation, a minute hesitation in the steps of a few of the couples twirling on the dance floor—but not one of them stopped. No one appeared willing to acknowledge the cry. In fact, they all seemed livelier, propelled forward by a new purpose to appear as joyful as possible with the intention of hiding the depth of the sadness upstairs.

August glanced up at the frescoed ceiling as if she could see Camille in her bedroom, but instead a bright-eyed cherub stared back at her, a silent witness to the atrocity that was about to occur. The champagne went flat on her tongue and slid down her throat to settle heavy in her belly. The sad fact was that no one cared about Camille's reluctance. New York Society thrived on financial and social matches made in marriage, and one unwilling bride wasn't going to change anything. A hundred unwilling brides wouldn't change anything.

August's stomach churned, so she set her unfinished champagne on the tray of a passing servant. There was something unspeakably disturbing about the scene. A compulsion to do something to stop it pushed her forward, but a sharp bark of laughter pulled her up short. Camille's fiancé, Robert Emerson, seventh Duke of Hereford, stood inside one set of open balcony doors, glass of champagne in hand, his gray whiskers impeccably groomed in the muttonchop style. The apples of his cheeks were pink as he laughed at something Camille's father had said.

The two had been thick as thieves the entire evening. The impoverished duke stood to make a fortune on his marriage to Camille, while Mr. Bridwell gained a much-needed social ally. Rumors were that the duke would be given one hundred thousand dollars outright on the marriage, with an annuity of ten thousand dollars. It was hardly surprising that he was in such good spirits. He probably hadn't noticed that his fiancée had yet to make an appearance. She was the least important aspect of their agreement. Camille was the only one who stood to suffer from the arrangement. She was also the only one who'd had no say in the matter. There could be no mistaking the anguish in that wail.

Turning from the maddening scene, August made her way through the crowd to the wide hallway that bisected the house and led to the front rooms, nodding to the small groups of people she passed. An insistent sort of panic had begun to claw at her as she walked, pushing her forward until she was almost running. At the mansion's elegant front doors, she turned abruptly, grabbed a handful of her silk skirts, and took the wide marble staircase to the second floor.

The mahogany-paneled doors to Camille's bedchamber swung open when August reached the top of the stairs, revealing the debutante in full evening apparel. She was gorgeous in pale pink silk embroidered with golden thread. Her gold curls had been arranged atop her head with elaborate diamond-encrusted combs, and a few curls had been left to cascade over a partially exposed shoulder. Her neck and fingers dripped in diamonds, making her look every bit the American princess her parents wanted her to be. But the comparison ended there. From her red-rimmed eyes to the sallowness of her complexion, it was obvious that she'd been crying for hours . . . maybe days.

This was madness.

August opened her mouth to speak, to offer some objection on her friend's behalf, but Mrs. Bridwell stepped out from behind her daughter, her expression dark and forbidding. Three maids along with August's younger sister, Violet, spilled out of the room behind them to arrange her skirts. Camille looked as if she was only held together by the strength of her corset, ribbon ties, and grim determination. The last thing August wanted to do was to say something that would break down her composure.

"Come, my darling," her mother was saying. "Make me proud tonight, and we can go over to Tiffany's tomorrow and pick up that emerald you've had your eye on." As if that alone could make up for selling her daughter's future to a man who offered her nothing beyond social standing.

Unable to hold herself back a moment longer, August said, "Camille—" Mrs. Bridwell's stern glance cut off her words.

Speechless, August stepped to the side as they shuffled past. Camille did not glance her way. She walked as if she were made of stone, spine rigid and gaze focused straight ahead. Violet followed close behind their lifelong friend, her hands out as if she wanted to help but had no idea how to go about it.

"August?" Violet's voice was a harsh whisper as she paused at the top of stairs, her face ashen and her wide eyes brimming with concern as mother and daughter descended.

"It's a travesty." August mouthed the words, so that no one would hear.

August slid an arm around her sister's waist, and they both watched solemnly as Camille glided gracefully toward her fate. The girl had not yet reached her nineteenth birthday, but her future had been sealed. A future that would see her ensconced on some estate in the English countryside, far away from her family, friends, and everything that she knew.

Aware of the maids who had lined up at the railing to observe their mistress, August made eye contact with one of them. She could not have been older than Camille, but her eyes reflected pity. The maid, who was forced to work for her living, pitied *them and their Society marriages*. August could not maintain the eye contact.

"It's horrible of me, but I cannot help but be grateful that Mother and Papa would never do such a thing to us," Violet whispered as the pair turned at the bottom of the stairs and disappeared from their view.

August tightened her arm around her sister's waist, but she couldn't forget that pitying look. She turned her head to discreetly look at the maid again, but the trio had disappeared back into Camille's room to tidy up.

She told herself the maid had no reason to pity them, but a niggling doubt in the back of her mind refused to go away. Their grandfather, Augustus Crenshaw, had made the Crenshaw fortune in the railroad and iron industries. Their family would want for nothing for generations to come, so they would never be forced to marry for money. But status was something else entirely. Railroad money—*new* money—closed more social doors than it opened.

The Crenshaws, like the Bridwells, had never set foot into Mrs. Astor's ballroom, the only ballroom that mattered to the Knickerbockers of old New York. No matter how much money one family possessed, dirty money recently earned wasn't welcomed in those established social circles. Augustus's ostentatious reputation had further confirmed their family's status as outcasts. He'd been rumored to be a drunkard and a philanderer. His most renowned fete had involved a traveling troupe of French dancing girls clad only in petticoats for entertainment. If there had been any spark of hope for the Crenshaws to achieve respectability after that, he'd extinguished it when he'd married one of those dancers.

A duke in the family could open up doors that had been sealed tight for decades. Mrs. Bridwell had confided in them only last week how Mrs. Astor had paid a surprise call and discreetly hinted at an invitation to the engagement ball. In fact, the woman was downstairs now with everyone else, blissfully ignoring the atrocity. It wasn't very often that a duke presided over a Fifth Avenue ball, social classes be damned. That revelation had created a gleam of interest in her mother's eye that August couldn't forget.

But would their mother do *this* to them? Would she marry one of them off to a stranger old enough to be their father? August knew very little about the English aristocracy, but she knew there weren't very many dukes among them. The odds were that they would all be as old as Hereford, or worse.

August glanced at her sister's pretty face, for if one of them would be forced to that fate, it would be Violet. She was everything August was not: charming, graceful, biddable . . . a lady.

Sensing an underlying meaning in her hesitance to answer, Violet glanced over at her. "Our parents would never do that . . . would they?"

For the first time in her life, she lied to her sister. "The Crenshaws have no need for a duke in the family."

If August said it with enough conviction, it was bound to be true.

Chapter 1

Independence is happiness.

SUSAN B. ANTHONY

LONDON
APRIL 1875

Sneaking out for a late-night assignation had not been on
August's London itinerary. Yet here she was in a hired
carriage being whisked through the dark streets of the city
at midnight.

"Don't look so vexed . . . please?" Camille managed to
appear contrite from her side of the hansom cab. Her wide
brown eyes took on a faintly desperate glow that went a
long way toward soothing August's temper.

But, really, how could Camille expect her not to be irritated? She had arrived unannounced at the Crenshaws'
rented townhome off Grosvenor Square not a quarter hour
ago, looking fairly pitiful as she'd pleaded with August to
come with her. The entire time she had refused to say
where they were going, only that August must come this
instant. August had only agreed to put away the financial
reports she had been poring over because the girl had appeared so wretched and dispirited. Now she found herself

traveling at a breakneck speed through the streets of a city she barely knew while hoping for the best.

"That's asking a lot," August said.

The brightness of Camille's smile shone through the murky darkness. "But you'll do it because you're such a good friend."

August rolled her eyes and settled against the lumpy seat. The streets were growing noticeably darker. The cheerful and dependable gas lamps that lined the lanes of Mayfair had long since disappeared. Streetlamps here were spaced farther apart, and most of them didn't work anyway. The buildings appeared to be actively crumbling before her eyes as they passed. Worse, down the alleyways she caught glimpses of open fires with shadows huddled around them. Wherever they were going, it did not appear to be in a safe area. She'd been naive to assume that Camille wouldn't take them off to somewhere dangerous.

"Very well." August sighed. "But please tell me where we're going. And why am I wearing this?" Camille had presented August with a black cloak identical to her own as she'd ushered her out the servants' entrance. She had assumed it was to hide them as they made their escape; now she wasn't so sure that was the only reason.

"Never." Her friend's mischievous smile returned, reminding August of the child that she still was in many ways. Despite her misgivings, August was relieved to see it.

When the invitation had come from Camille, Duchess of Hereford, requesting the Crenshaws join her for a few weeks in London, August and Violet had seen it for the plea for help that it had been. Camille had been lonely since her wedding in November and needed her friends around her for the Season. They had arrived to find her thinner and paler than she had been in New York. It was plain to see that marriage had not agreed with her. She was friendless in a foreign country with a husband who seemed to spend all of his time elsewhere, though possibly that was for the best. He had not seemed very pleasant company the few times August had met him. Thankfully, Camille's disposition had slowly improved in the fortnight since they had arrived. Tonight was the first time she had shown a spark of her former mischievous self, so August resolved to try to humor her and her adventure.

"You'll have to tell me at some point." A grin tugged at her lips. "Where are we now?"

"We're near Whitechapel." Camille made the declaration with all the enthusiasm of a child who saw only an adventure with none of the danger.

"Whitechapel!"

"Trust me, August, you won't be disappointed."

"It's not my disappointment I'm concerned about." Thank God she had come along. Someone had to keep Camille from her own self-destruction.

"I brought a footman along for protection."

Not comforted in the least, August reached up to rap on the trapdoor to direct the driver to take them back home but the vehicle came to an abrupt halt before she could. They were in the middle of a dark, nondescript street surrounded by deserted buildings. A huge warehouse loomed across the road. One of its large doors had been thrown open to reveal a crowd of rough-looking people mingling beneath a swirling cloud of cigarette smoke. Some of the men had their shirtsleeves rolled up as if they had come in from a day of labor, while the few women she could see were wearing gowns that were less than respectable. She had the sneaking suspicion that they had arrived at their destination. "Are you mad? We could be killed in that crowd."

Camille shook her head. "We'll be fine. You've been sheltered too long. Besides, I said *near* Whitechapel." August knew she looked stunned when Camille laughed and continued, "On this side of town I am not a duchess and you are not one of the Crenshaw heiresses. We are no one. Make up any name you'd like. I'm partial to Delilah. Only, please, pick something that's not boring. No Annes, Marys, or Sarahs."

August had no intention of assuming any identity. If it were found out that she had traipsed across town in the middle of the night, her reputation would be ruined. Not that she cared much for that—marriage was not in her immediate future—but Crenshaw Iron Works could suffer. However, before she could respond, the carriage door was opened by Camille's footman. He cut a lithe figure in a dark suit with strong shoulders, a kind face, and light brown hair. He'd helped them into the carriage back in Mayfair before taking his post. His gaze gentled when it settled on Camille, whose face lit up when she saw him, her eyes lingering on his as she gave him her hand. He looked at her as if no one else existed, and in that moment, August was certain that no one else did exist for him. He was obviously smitten. Despite how inappropriate it was, August felt a twinge of longing in the pit of her stomach. No one had ever looked at her that way. No one probably ever would.

Once he helped Camille out of the carriage, he managed to pull himself away long enough to offer his hand to August. The pungent odors of fish, damp earth, and decay indicated they were near the river. This was a terrible idea, but they were here, and Camille wouldn't be dissuaded. Sighing, she took his offered hand and disembarked. "Have you been here before?"

Camille shook her head and stood on the tips of her toes as if to get a better look into the large brick building across the crumbling road. "No, but doesn't it look exciting?"

It didn't look exciting at all. In her work with her family's company, she was often charged with evaluating the possible rewards of taking on a particular new investment. She was very good at identifying risk, and this had danger written all over it. If this were a business proposal that had crossed her desk, she would have written R-E-J-E-C-T in block lettering across the top and underlined it twice.

The footman turned and pulled out a small drawstring purse from inside his coat to pay the driver. August took the opportunity to lean in to Camille. "Are you and he . . . involved?" The idea seemed far-fetched, but that look had been full of things August shouldn't have witnessed.

Camille laughed, but it lacked humor. Her hungry gaze roved over his athletic form in admiration as she spoke, "Henry? Not like you mean. Hereford made it quite clear that I must give him a child before he'll tolerate anything like that."

August gaped. "You spoke with the *duke* about this?"

"On the contrary. He spoke to *me* about it on our first day home when he informed me that he planned to carry on with his mistress regardless of my feelings on the matter. He said that I was free to do the same discreetly, but only after he had his child." At the blank look August gave her, she shrugged. "It is how things are done here."

August drew back in shock, not so much at the words but at the bitterness in Camille's eyes. It had been clear from the beginning that theirs would not be a love match, but to have her feelings so callously disregarded by her husband had to smart. August understood then what this outing was all about. It was Camille's way of rebelling against the unfairness of her fate. It was irresponsible and dangerous, but it was all she had. At least she'd had the foresight to bring her footman for protection.

In many ways, this reinforced August's own views toward marriage. It wasn't worth the loss of independence. She worked with her brother and father running Crenshaw Iron Works, and she wasn't yet willing to give that up for what Camille described. No husband on earth would be willing to allow her to keep working like she wanted.

"I am so sorry, Camille. How horrid that sounds."

"It's not that terrible." Her friend waved away her concern and glanced back toward the warehouse. "So far he's only been able to complete the act a handful of times. It was over quickly."

No matter how she tried, August could not stop her mouth from dropping open. No one had ever so openly discussed sexual activity with her before. Was that too little? It seemed to be—the couple had been married for over five months—but she honestly didn't know. Her brother, Max, had dinner with his mistress every Thursday, though what happened during those *dinners,* she did not want to know. "I . . . Only a handful?"

Camille grinned and leaned closer to whisper, "He's

tried more than that, but he has issues . . . staying upright."
She giggled. "I am told that happens with age, but I think
it's due to the amount of scotch he drinks."

August had no reply to that. To have a marriage forced
on you was bad enough, but to have it come in the form of
an aged groom, she could not countenance. She struggled
to put voice to another meaningless, benign word of comfort when Camille nodded toward the warehouse. "Say
you'll come inside with me. Please?"

Knowing how badly her friend needed this small rebellion, August found it impossible to deny the request. They
should be able to hide their identities easily enough—she
couldn't imagine any of the aristocrats she had met fre-
quenting a place such as this—so no one would be the
wiser. Her parents and Violet weren't due to be home from
their party for hours yet. The irony of the fact that she had
begged off to enjoy a quiet evening alone was not lost on
her.

"Fine. We will stay for a quarter hour."

"But that's no time at all," Camille complained. "The
brawl won't have started yet. I daresay it'll last longer than
that."

"Brawl? Where on earth have you taken us?" But Camille didn't answer, because Henry came over and offered
her his arm. The two of them walked toward the crowded
building as if they were a couple, leaving August to follow
as she would. The driver called out to his horse, and the
vehicle pulled off. Left wondering how she, a woman who
was capable enough to assist her father and brother in the
daily operations of Crenshaw Iron Works, had come to this
unlikely pass, August had no choice but to follow them
across the damp cobblestone road and through the entrance.

The place was a mass of sweating bodies as the crowd
of men and women pushed closer to some unseen space
farther into the open ground floor of the building. The
sharp scents of gin, sweat, and cheap cigarette smoke
tinged the air. People yelled to be heard over the cacophony
of a hundred different conversations. Brick pillars trisected

the space, while wooden crates stacked to the high ceiling lined the massive room, indicating that it was a working warehouse—at least during the daytime hours.

"Ho there, Henry, didn't think you were going to make it." A burly man who spoke in a distinct East End accent stopped them inside the door. He wore a wool coat that had seen better days and scuffed boots. The rough skin on his face was lined in a permanent scowl, only emphasized by the countless scars thickening his brows.

"Evening, Jim, had to make another stop." Henry's words were spoken in an accent tinged with a hardscrabble inflection that wasn't present when he wore the Hereford livery.

The older man's gaze drifted past Camille to August. Apparently, she was the extra and potentially unexpected stop in the scenario. "Good evening," she said, giving him a smile.

His colorless eyes lit with amusement as he tipped a hand to the brim of his flat cap. "An American." His assessing gaze roamed over her, as if trying to figure out who she was. August felt a moment of panic that perhaps it wouldn't be as easy to hide her identity as she'd thought, so she gripped the cloak's hood closed under her chin. Finally, he said, "Come on, then. Room for you lot on the riser."

August followed the group around the edge of the room. Without even looking at him, the crowd seemed to be aware of the mysterious Jim and made way for their small group. The few times they were too slow to move, he didn't mind shoving the men out of his path. Soon they stopped at a wooden platform raised knee-high off the ground. There was already a score of people milling about on top of it. Unlike the crowd on the packed-dirt floor, these people wore dress coats, and a few colorful evening gowns could be seen among the black. This set had much finer attire than the rest of the crowd, which was obviously made up of laborers and factory workers. Henry stepped up and helped first Camille and then August up.

"A word of warning, miss." She turned back and found herself eye to eye with Jim.

"'Tis tempting to stand close to get a better view, but best to keep your distance." He seemed to be putting effort into enunciating so that she wouldn't mistake him. "That is if you're concerned about blood spattering on your pretty silk dress."

August gasped as she saw that the cloak had parted and the rich navy of her skirt had shown through. Jim chuckled and left her there to arrange her clothing while wondering if that had been a genuine warning or if he was toying with her. A brawl couldn't be as gruesome as that. Could it? She hurried to catch up to Camille and Henry, who had moved farther onto the platform. Where the hell had Camille brought her? Surely, she realized that she was risking her own reputation by coming to such a place.

Between the shoulders of the mostly male group crowding the riser, August could make out an open area of dirt floor before the platform. Eight stakes were firmly planted in the ground with a double line of rope stretched tight between them to form a square of roughly fifteen feet on each side. This was a real-life prizefighting ring. She had heard that these fights happened back home in New York, but she'd never even thought about attending such an event. They must certainly be illegal.

Henry had muscled his way through to the front so that they had an unobscured view down to the fighting area. August wasn't entirely certain that she wanted one. Jim's gory warning was in the forefront of her thoughts and had her imagining all sorts of grisly scenes. "Is this prizefighting?" she asked Camille to be sure.

Camille was all excitement again as she took in the energy of the crowd. The whole space seemed to be alive with the anticipation of the coming brawl. Voices called out bets, while others derided their choices. A boy with pale skin who couldn't be more than ten stood on a barrel on the other side of the roped-off area pointing at whomever called out the loudest. Then he'd repeat the bet along with the caller's name, yelling it out to a young man with brown skin who stood on the ground next to him scribbling away in a notebook.

Camille nodded. "Henry's told me all about it. He knows because he participates sometimes. It sounded like great fun, and I knew that you'd come with me. Violet is a dear, but she doesn't know the way of the world yet."

There had been a time when August would have put Camille in the same category as her sister. Perhaps Camille had been once, but that had been before her world had been uprooted. Before August could respond, the roar of the crowd intensified until hearing anything that was said became impossible. A side door near the ring had swung open, and a very striking man appeared. Shirtless and wearing nothing but breeches and boots, he could only be one of the fighters. He was surrounded by three formidable men who, though very well-dressed, she assumed were there to keep people away from him. His appearance drove the crowd into an almost frenzied state. If it was possible, they became louder and pushed closer to the clearing. As the fighter walked through, bouncing on the balls of his feet, his guards were forced to push back the men who tried to reach for him. The man himself seemed unfazed.

He sauntered with his shoulders back and his chin held high. There was an arrogance painted across his face that she both admired and detested, as if he knew before the fight even began that he'd walk away the victor. She recognized it for what it was, a necessary ruse needed to intimidate his opponent. Her father had taught them all about swagger, and she'd participated in enough business meetings to see it in practice. The fighter wore the expression well. Even though he couldn't have yet reached the age of thirty, the confidence made him seem decades wiser. His looks were unabashedly handsome: dark hair slicked back artfully with pomade, cheekbones and a jaw that could have been carved from granite covered in a close-cropped beard, and clear blue eyes with just enough brooding to be remarkable. His chest and arms were roped with muscle, but rather than making him appear common, the effect was startling to her. She found that she couldn't quite bring herself to look away from him.

His gaze inspected the crowd on the riser as if he were

looking for someone in particular. It passed over her but then came back immediately. She caught her breath as a flicker of awareness tightened in her belly. It almost seemed as if he had recognized her, but she knew that couldn't be true. She'd only met a seemingly endless series of aristocrats in her fortnight in London. August would remember meeting this man. A slender woman stepped out from behind his strong, wide shoulders, her hand on his arm in a proprietary manner as she drew his attention. She wore a fine gown in a lustrous black that showed off her lithe frame.

"He's the favorite." Camille leaned close to be heard. "And that's Gabrielle Laurent, the ballet dancer."

August had seen her dance the role of Juliet only last week. Madame Laurent was a gorgeous dancer. She didn't know why she was so surprised to see the woman here. Perhaps it was because this seemed like a base pastime for a woman of such refined talents. However, the man was handsome and obviously popular. It stood to reason that they were a couple.

"What's his name?" Her gaze jumped back over to the man, who gently stroked the back of his knuckles across the side of Madame Laurent's face as she backed away from him with a smile. Her own cheek tingled in a phantom touch.

Henry must have caught part of their conversation, because he leaned over. "No one knows his name. They call him the Hellion. He started fighting about a year or so ago and hasn't been beaten yet."

She nearly laughed aloud at the ridiculous name. There was no time for a follow-up question, because the cheers started again as his challenger made his way to the ring. The man was at least a decade older, and he seemed harder somehow. His frame was thicker, with bulging sinews of muscle roping his chest, and his eyes were tougher. His appearance didn't seem to faze the Hellion, who beckoned the older man to step through the ropes and join him in the center of the fighting area.

Everything that happened next was a blur in the excitement going on around them. The moment Madame Laurent joined them on the riser, the crowd exploded in another cheer of excitement. Apparently, this was the indication to those in the back that the fight would officially begin now. A man with an air of authority stood between the men, but his words were lost in the noise. The fighters listened intently, nodding when he finished speaking. He hadn't even stepped out of the ropes yet when the older man lashed out, catching the Hellion unaware with a fist to his jaw. The younger man absorbed the blow, pulling himself together and swinging his right fist in an impressive blow that staggered his larger opponent. He followed it up with a series of punches that demonstrated his athleticism. The muscles in his back and arms bunched and flexed beneath his smooth skin as he advanced. August was mesmerized by the beauty of it. She had never seen a man move like that before, so in control of every movement. He swung around, stalking back to his side of the area and giving her a clear view of the blood smearing the older man's face.

"This is barbaric." She thought she'd mumbled the words under her breath, but the gentleman standing next to her gave her a harsh glare as if he had heard and taken personal offense. A cigarette hung loosely from the side of his mouth, and his gaze was hard with censure. A mild panic seized her as she took in the impeccably groomed dark hair and cold gray eyes that belonged to none other than the Earl of Leigh. Violet had whispered about how striking he was when they had seen him at the opera last week. It was a beauty stained by wickedness, though *enhanced* might be the word many would choose. She imagined Lucifer himself would take his exact form if he decided to mingle with mortals.

Since they hadn't been introduced, she hoped he wouldn't recognize her. Offering him a conciliatory nod of her head, she tightened her grip on her cloak and looked away. This had been a horrible mistake. She quickly did a skim of the other people on the riser but did not recognize anyone else.

Meanwhile, the drama in the ring continued to unfold; the fighters circled each other, feinting right and left and exchanging blows. It was becoming clear that the Hellion had the advantage as the larger man huffed and puffed with exertion. Despite his lead, the younger wasn't without injury. A drip of blood from his left brow ran down his face. It did nothing to hinder his look of cocky assurance. In fact, it somehow enhanced it. He'd taken his punches, and he still moved as if he hadn't been touched. There was something surprisingly attractive about that. She found herself silently urging him to win the match.

She faintly registered the sound of a whistle of some sort, but it was off in the distance. It had nothing to do with the fight before her. The Hellion swung and the large man grimaced, taking a solid punch right in his gut. The look of anger and grim determination he'd worn in the beginning had given way to resignation. Still he fought back, but the Hellion blocked his swing and landed a blow to the other man's jaw, sending him backward. The crowd roared.

"He's done it!" Camille squealed, caught up in the excitement. The thrill was contagious, because August smiled despite herself. The crowded riser quaked beneath her feet with the celebrations of the people all around her. They must have all wagered on him, because not one of them seemed to be upset with the way the fight was turning out.

She couldn't pull her eyes from him. He walked around the perimeter of the roped-off area with his hands in the air and a smile that lit his entire face. She didn't precisely know if he'd won yet, but the larger man was lying still on the ground with someone bent over him. Behind her a man yelled to a friend on the other end of the riser. The friend yelled back happily, causing the man to push his way through the mass of bodies, and the crowd swelled and contracted around him. A beefy hand landed solidly in the middle of her back. Unfortunately, August had been too caught up watching the fighter to pay close attention to where she was, so when the crowd swelled outward, she was pushed dangerously close to the edge of the platform. Her shriek was swallowed up in the excitement. She turned to reach for Camille, or Henry, or even the earl, but her fingers closed on air as her heeled boots scrambled for purchase on the wood and she fell back. She was dimly aware of the harsh scrape of the rope against the cloak on her shoulder as she closed her eyes to brace for an impact that never came.

Strong hands caught her under her arms as her back leaned into a solid chest. When she would have fallen to the straw-covered floor, a man had saved her just in time. He half supported her until she could get her legs under her and find solid footing on the ground. Then he turned her to face him with the ropes between them, his arms around her waist to hold her indecently close to him.

She stared up into a pair of deep blue eyes that looked down at her with humor and a proprietary glint that she might have found disturbing under different circumstances. Right this moment she felt too much relief to care about that. His hair had been displaced in the fight and hung down heavy over his brow and on each side of his face. It should have softened him up a bit, but instead it made the angles and planes stand out, making his handsome looks even more striking as a drop of blood trailed down the side of his face from his brow.

"Thank you." To her utter shame, her voice came out soft and barely discernible.

He grinned, revealing even white teeth and a smile that could have only been born from sin. "I hope you won." His voice was smooth and deep with a cultured inflection.

She smiled, strangely quite willing to stand here with him. His scent surrounded them, sweat, certainly, but mixed with a faint cologne so that it wasn't pungent. Her heart pounded in her chest. He was holding her so tightly she wondered if he could feel it. No man had ever made her heart pound before.

"I'm afraid I did not wager." Her voice rose slightly so that he would be sure to hear her.

"A pity. I assumed you were the gambling sort."

"Why would you assume that?"

His sensually formed lips made a perfect bow as he smiled. His eyeteeth were pointed, lending his smile a particular wickedness. "Because you're here, Miss Crenshaw."

An icy heat prickled down her spine. How did he know

who she was? Was it so obvious? She glanced at the crowd above them on the riser, but no one seemed to be watching them; they were too busy either congratulating one another or yelling at the downed fighter to get up.

"You Americans are said to be risk-takers. Is it true?" he asked.

She could only nod as movement behind him caught her eye. "Behind you," she warned as his opponent began to get to his feet. He didn't loosen his grip, only glanced over his shoulder to watch the big man swaying on his knees.

"Kiss me for luck," he said as he met her gaze again.

Her eyes widened. How could he demand a kiss now, when his very large and very angry opponent was coming to his feet at this very moment? "He's almost on his feet." Fear for him made her voice rise.

"Then hurry." He spoke the words very near her mouth. His breath—smelling of brandy and peppermint—warmed her skin, bringing nerve endings to life. His hands had loosened at some point, settling on her waist in a casual way that branded her through the layers of her clothing far more effectively than if he still held her tight against him.

"You don't need luck," she said through the thickened air between them. He half bent his head over her. When he shook his head, the tip of his nose brushed hers, making the air catch in her lungs.

"No, but I want it, Miss Crenshaw."

One glance showed the larger man coming toward them. Her heart pounded against her chest like a crazed bird flinging itself against a window. She wanted to push him away and tell him how ridiculous he was being, demanding a kiss right now, but most of all . . . she wanted to kiss him. She closed the short gap between them and pressed her mouth to his. His lips were warm and surprisingly soft against hers. A groan vibrated from deep in his throat, moving from him to settle deep in her own chest.

She moved her lips in response to the gentle pressure of his and felt the slightest moisture trace along her bottom lip. She gasped, but instead of leaning into the kiss, he pulled back and released her. His eyes were bright with satisfaction at the success of the game he'd been playing with her, but it was mingled with something else. Some new awareness that hadn't been there before. Something that cut through the teasing, hinting at more to come, except there was no time. The opponent's large chest loomed right behind him.

"Go!" he yelled, and she wasted no time in scurrying away as he turned to spar with the man.

Back against the riser, she watched his opponent plant a boot into his muscled thigh. The Hellion grunted in pain. When the man pulled it away, the thigh of the Hellion's breeches was dark red with blood. August brought her hands to her mouth to stifle a cry of dismay. The last thing she wanted to do was cause another distraction. A flash of light glinted on a metal spike embedded in the sole of the opponent's boot.

"No!" she yelled along with many others in the crowd. That had to be against the rules.

The sharp metallic sound of the whistle came again, only this time it was much closer and accompanied by panicked shouts.

"Bloody hell!" Henry yelled near her ear. He must have jumped down from the platform when she'd fallen. "Someone's called the bobbies."

"Come on!" Camille pulled on August's arm, tugging her to the wall and toward the side door.

"What is happening?" August asked, reluctant to leave the man hurt.

"The police are coming!"

"He's hurt!" August cried.

"We have to go. We cannot be caught here. He has people to help him." Camille continued to pull her along.

She was right. Already the men in suits who had accompanied the fighter had gathered around him, and even Leigh had jumped down to attend to him. Knowing there was nothing she could do, and very aware of the need to protect their reputations—if that was even possible at this point—she followed Henry and Camille out the side door and down the dark alleyway, hoping they knew where they were going.

Chapter 2

If he made it through the next hour, Evan Sterling, Duke of Rothschild, planned to reward himself with a bottle of Lochnagar and an evening in bed with a woman. The festivities would have to commence in that order, unfortunately, because his thigh was on fire after climbing that flight of stairs. He would need the whisky to dull the pain from the injury he had sustained last night before enjoying any other entertainment. Clenching his jaw against the agony, he tightened his grip on the silver hawk's head of his walking stick and made his way to the study on the second floor of Sterling House, his mother's London residence.

Decades of stale cigar smoke mixed with bay rum assaulted him as soon as he stepped into his father's antiquated lair. The man had been dead for over a year, and yet the smells lingered, soaked up by the wood paneling and Persian rugs. Habit, born over a lifetime of disappointing his father, caused Evan's stomach to churn uncomfortably as soon as he entered the room.

"Apologies for my tardiness."

His solicitor, Andrew Clark, came to his feet with almost military precision. "Good afternoon, Your Grace. No apologies necessary." The apology had been for his mother, but Evan inclined his head to Clark anyway. The man was young as solicitors went, but he'd come highly recommended. Evan had let his father's longtime solicitor go shortly after he'd come to understand the full scope of the debts the estate had amassed. Much to his chagrin, the situation had not improved since he'd inherited.

"Morning, Mother." Evan leaned down to place a kiss on his mother's cheek, grimacing as he transferred weight onto his leg. She cast a quick look at his cane; that look was equal parts disapproval and concern as she murmured a greeting.

"Don't say one of the stallions got the better of you again, Your Grace." Clark smiled, causing his lips to twitch with nerves.

Evan cursed inwardly. Clark had overcome his nerves when dealing with Evan and his mother months ago; the fact that they had made a reappearance indicated that this meeting would go even worse than Evan had previously feared.

"That is precisely what happened." The lie fell stiffly from his lips. Apparently, Evan had used the errant horse excuse to explain away an injury too many times. One of many he had been forced to utter over the past year to explain his unusual ailments. "The heathen threw me in a turn, but I will tame him yet."

Wilkes had disappeared in the chaos of the police arriving, but Evan had vowed to find him. Not only to answer for the damned spikes on the soles of his boots, but he owed Evan for not finishing the fight.

"If you don't mind me saying, perhaps you should stick with betting on horses at the track. You seem to have the devil's own luck when it comes to the races."

Evan gave a slow nod as he took his seat behind his father's desk, indicating that Clark should sit. A lance of pain seized his thigh, and he briefly debated starting the whisky early. "Sage advice."

"Indeed," said his mother, reaching for the teapot to offer him a cup. He shook his head, and she grasped her own cup and saucer.

Evan suspected her tea had been heavily laced with brandy. She despised these meetings almost as much as he did. He resented that she had to endure them, but she insisted. If his father hadn't spent the two years previous to his own death locked away while mourning William's premature death, perhaps the family might not be in this mess now. Or even if he had listened to his sons and invested in manufacturing, they might have something left to sustain them.

"Go on, Clark. Let us have the monthly report of our accounts." He could not help the acerbic turn of his tone any more than he could stop the constant hemorrhage of their coffers.

"Of course, Your Grace." Clark spread open the leather-bound account book and in a strong, precise voice began to read out where they stood.

The numbers changed by the month, a little up, a little down, but the end result was always the same. Foreign grain could be imported cheaper than their farms could produce it. Drought had only worsened the predicament. His mother had cut back her expenses as much as she was reasonably able to without appearing a beggar to her friends. Evan had given up his London terrace and had a small suite of rooms at Montague Club. Residing here with so many memories of his father lurking about wasn't an option.

They had no funds. The little he was able to bring in with fighting, gambling, and investments only went out again to keep the creditors at bay. To make matters worse, his sisters—twins!—would have to make their debut next year. He hadn't a clue how he would afford the gowns and accoutrement necessary for the occasion, not to mention the eventual trousseau that would follow for each of them.

Evan rubbed the ache that was starting to build between his temples. Their circumstances were impossible. Bankruptcy for him and social ruin for his family lurked on the horizon. Evan had not a damned thing to do with its cause, but he would be the one to shoulder the burden and shame. He could almost feel the weight of his father's self-righteous glare from the other side. Of course, Evan would be the downfall of their family's honor. It stood to reason that *he* would be the one to fall in disgrace.

"I am deeply sorry the numbers are not better, Your Grace." Clark kept his eyes lowered as he closed the ledger.

"You have done what you can." Which amounted to borrowing from Peter to pay Paul. There was no creating coin out of thin air.

"Have you had no luck in finding Lichfield?" His father's solicitor had promptly disappeared after Evan had begun asking tough questions, leaving more questions than answers behind.

"Not yet, no," said Clark.

After a moment, Clark cleared his throat and seemed to finally summon the nerve to meet his employer's gaze. "There are options." His voice came out a nervous squeak.

Yes. Options. Evan was afraid of those.

His mother set down her cup and saucer on the spindly table next to her with finality. "It is past time that we consider our *options* seriously."

"*Our* options?" Everyone knew bloody well that *he* was the one who would be called on to make the noble sacrifice.

"Very well." Her blue eyes focused on his intently in that way that had always let him know that the time for arguing had come to an end. "We have tried things your way for a year now. Elizabeth and Louisa must have a coming-out next Season. Their futures depend upon it."

The fact that she was willing to speak this way with Clark present let him know just how concerned she truly was.

"If I may add, Your Grace, the situation has become even direr than it was a year past. With no signs of the agricultural market improving, Crandall and Mercer are threatening to call their loan if we are not caught up."

Evan ground his molars together. His father had been a fool to fall in debt to those vultures. "How long?"

The man's Adam's apple bobbed before he said, "If a marriage were announced within a fortnight," and at Evan's expression, he hurried to add, "possibly a week more, it might hold them off."

"A fortnight!" Evan's voice burst out of him, thundering through the room.

"Come now, Evan, we have spoken of this possibility for months," his mother said. " 'Tis hardly a surprise."

The idea of marriage was no shock, but the haste with which it needed to be accomplished was. The need to pace brought him to his feet, but pain like darts of fire spread through his thigh. Moaning aloud, he fell heavily back into his chair, which groaned in protest.

"Oh, for the love of—" His mother bit off the unladylike curse and forced a smile for the solicitor. Evan had always admired how easily she was able to retain control of her composure. "That will be all for the day, Mr. Clark. We will send word to you tomorrow. I'll have Hastings show you out." She rang for the butler, giving Evan time to stew as Clark gathered his things and said his goodbyes.

Once Hastings had wisely pulled the door closed as he led Clark out, Evan's mother gave him a stern once-over. "What in heavens have you done to your leg? And do not tell me it was a riding accident. You were riding before you could walk."

Evan stared at her, torn between furthering the lie and telling her the complete truth. As it turned out, he did not have to decide. Her astute gaze took in the cut on his brow line and then dropped to his bruised knuckles. The temptation to hide them like a child caught doing something wrong was strong, but he managed to fight it back.

"You are engaging in fisticuffs again? For money?"

Fisticuffs. The understatement of the word made him smile. He let out the breath he had been holding and flexed his fingers, enjoying the ache that throbbed in his knuckles. Ice had worked wonders for the swelling, but experience had taught him that they would be sore for days. Not that the pain mattered. He deserved the small discomforts. It had been over a year since his father had died. Surely, that was long enough to change their fortunes, and yet no matter what Evan did, the family only sank deeper into debt. Evan might not have been the sole reason that worried crease had appeared on his mother's brow, but he had done nothing to take it away.

"I do instruct on the skill at Montague Club, yes." He hedged.

"I meant prizefighting. Do not lie to me."

"The earnings keep us afloat in a sea of debt."

She winced as if he had wounded her, and he sucked in a sharp breath to hold back the apology on his lips. He *was* sorry. Sorry that he was not the son she deserved, that he was not William. When Evan had played pranks on his tutors, William had excelled in every subject. He had been the heir, the one suited to this role, not Evan. The family would have been better off if Evan had been the one to die. An ache swelled like a balloon in his chest, squeezing his lungs and making it momentarily difficult to breathe.

She shook her head, her hands falling to disappear into the black skirts of her mourning gown. "Do you think I want to see another of my children die before his time?"

The question, coupled with the red rim of her eyes, moved him to kneel at her side, heedless of the pull on his thigh injury and the immediate agony. Finding her hand amid the plethora of skirts, he said, "That will not happen. I may get bruised, but I will not die."

One finely plucked eyebrow shot upward. "Do not patronize me, Evan. I have heard of the dangers. A man could bring a knife in, and there are instances of men being so concussed they never recover. Men have died."

"What men?"

"Simon Byrne. William Phelps."

"Someone spoke to you of Byrne and Phelps? They both died decades ago." Evan could hardly imagine any of her society matron friends knowing their names.

She blinked and procured a sudden interest in the chair

he had vacated as she refused to meet his gaze. "The point is that deaths happen."

It would be a lie to claim otherwise. Though it was not a prominent worry in his mind, there was always the risk that someone like Wilkes could take losing badly and retaliate outside of the match. Instead of addressing it, he asked with a smile, "Did Lady Dragonbottom tell you about them?" He used the name he had invented for the surly matron in his youth. The lady in question was one of the most straitlaced and boring of his mother's generation. While only in her mid-fifties, she could easily pass for a woman bordering on seventy-five, primarily due to her expression of perpetual disappointment. "Does she have a secret gambling habit that she confessed to you?"

The corner of his mother's mouth tipped up in a reluctant grin, which is exactly what he had hoped would happen. "Her name is Lady Diginbotham, as you well know, and no, it was not her, more's the pity." She sobered as she continued, "If you must know, I had a footman explain the rules to me and, when pressed, he admitted that death was not out of the question."

Evan resisted finding out which footman had told her that. It was not the servant's fault. His mother could be quite forceful when it was called for. "You needn't have worried yourself. Rules have changed since their day. Besides, I have men who go with me for protection. They make certain things do not progress so far."

"And the eleven previous men who held the title Duke of Rothschild roll over in their graves to see one of their rank brought so low. Every night I ask why your father left us this way. After William died . . . he seemed to give up." She touched his hair, brushing it back from his forehead to soften the words. "None of this is your fault. You do know that?"

Rising to his feet as gracefully as his leg would allow, he hobbled over to the window to escape the tenderness in her gaze. The day was gray and dreary, and a light rain fell onto the cobblestones. Appropriate given his mood. "It hardly matters who is at fault, nor does it change the fact that I have done nothing to improve things."

The silk of her gown rustled as she rose and walked up behind him. "You are right. The fault does not matter when we are the ones cleaning up the mess." Her hand came to rest on his back, and she rubbed a small circle between his shoulders. He closed his eyes, remembering how she would visit the nursery every night to give them a kiss. William was always asleep, but Evan would lie there until she came so that she could rub his back.

"Believe me when I say that I understand how it feels to have a marriage arranged for you. I hardly knew your father. It was like marrying a stranger."

He remembered the often-strained silences between his parents. They had not been enemies, but neither had they been friends. The Duke of Rothschild had been a forbidding man in the best of times. "And, yet, I will have a stranger for a bride," he muttered.

Her hand came to a stop, but she kept it in place. "I am so terribly sorry. Your father should have done better, but . . ." Her voice drifted off. What was there to say? There had been no money set aside anywhere. He should know, because he had looked. Clark had looked. There was nothing. "If you choose not to marry now, then the task will fall to your sisters. Only, I shudder to think of the offers they shall receive next Season with no dowries."

Evan shook his head. Once the extent of their debts, along with their inability to pay them, became publicly known, there would be no offers. Hell. There were already rumors. It was no secret his terrace had been sold. Had he allowed his sisters to come out this year, he had no doubt their only offers would be from scoundrels and perverted lechers. He had spent the past year in denial, but it was time to face the future. He had to marry to save his family.

He had grown up naively assuming that the task of marriage to form an alliance with a noble family would fall to William. His older brother would have faced the duty with honor and selected a woman capable of becoming the next duchess. He would have married her gladly and spent the rest of his life dutifully begetting children with her all the while continuing to write his papers dissecting Aristotle's

Nicomachean Ethics or the finer points of Hellenistic astronomy. And he likely would have never so much as looked at another woman.

When faced with the same prospect, Evan was fighting a knot in his belly the size of his fist. Swallowing against the thickness of his throat, he turned to face his mother. "Who did you have in mind?"

"Have you met the Crenshaw family of New York City?" He was not surprised that she already had someone picked out for him; he was only surprised that he knew her. An image of the Crenshaw heiress as he had seen her last night sprang to mind. Evan had been shocked to see her at the fight. Her wide eyes had held an intriguing mix of sharp-witted integrity and questioning innocence. She had clearly been both dismayed and scandalized by the brutality of the fight, but she had also been curious. Curious enough to stay.

Curious enough to kiss him.

"Not formally. I saw the family at the ballet last week." Everyone had been talking about the wealthy American family who had been making the social rounds. They had shared a box directly across from his, which is how he had recognized Miss Crenshaw at the fight.

"Did you by chance notice their daughter Violet?"

Violet. He vaguely remembered other people with the Crenshaws in the box, but she had to be Violet. "I saw her," he said.

"She is the prettiest young woman I have seen this Season. While I have yet to meet her formally, she appeared very mannered. Not quite as brash as that other American, so obviously from quality stock. I spoke with Mrs. Crenshaw extensively about her and have concluded that she will make you a perfect match." *That American* was how many had begun to refer to the Duchess of Hereford; the poor woman had barely stood a chance when she had made her debut in society. The matrons had eaten her alive.

"You do realize that you could be describing a horse?"

She gave him a sharp glare. "I would prefer grandchildren who refrain from running wild across Hampshire, but your father did not leave us much choice, so we have to make do. If we have to become involved with an American heiress, then I would prefer it to be a woman of a fine disposition." Hurrying over to his desk, she opened a drawer and pulled out a piece of parchment. "We will have to come up with a way for you to meet formally . . . a dinner, I think, and if all goes well, a ball to formally announce your intentions. Of course, you will have Clark investigate their actual holdings, but I have heard that the Crenshaws have a net worth that far surpasses the Bridwells'. We have to move fast before someone else latches onto them."

"You've heard that as well, have you? Perhaps you missed your calling and should look into a position at Scotland Yard."

She waved him off and started scribbling on the paper. "Miss Crenshaw may very well have other offers in hand already. But I guarantee you they will not be from a duke."

Evan nearly laughed as he watched his mother come alive with excitement for the first time in years. "No, fortunately, we have a title to recommend us."

And little else.

Chapter 3

Women are the real architects of society.

HARRIET BEECHER STOWE

M arriage?" Violet's voice was a high-pitched screech that might have come close to peeling the wallpaper in the sitting room of their mother's bedroom suite. August was too stunned to investigate. Their mother had delivered the surprise announcement with all the aplomb of a woman blissfully unaware of its unwelcome reception.

Her smile was so bright that August was certain they must have misheard. She was simply overly tired from accompanying Camille to the fight last night. "Pardon me, Mother, but did you say *marriage* and something about a *duke*? That Violet is to receive a proposal of marriage from a *duke*?"

Their mother paused, preening in the glorious aftermath of her news. Shifting on the settee, she tucked a curl of chestnut hair only lightly touched with silver back up under the silk turban she wore to bed every night. August suspected she was savoring the moment, and her mouth went dry at the implication that she had indeed heard correctly.

"Oh, if I must say it again, then I will." Another maddening pause for effect. "The Duke of Rothschild will attend the Ashcroft dinner later this week. If he finds favor with Violet—and I am certain he will—then I have hope that we can expect an offer of marriage to be forthcoming."

Violet had gone pale. The announcement had pulled her to her feet, and she stood speechless there before the settee she had shared with August opposite their mother.

August took it upon herself to ask the pertinent questions on behalf of her sister. "Forgive me, but I am having a bit of trouble putting together how this came about. We have never met this family, much less the duke."

"The Ashcrofts have been very good to us this Season. Lord Ashcroft has a fondness for your father and has introduced him around to his men at the clubs. As luck would have it, Lady Ashcroft is very friendly with the duke's mother. They grew up together. We met at tea several days ago, and Her Grace implied that her son is eligible and in need of a wife."

"You mean that she asked you for Violet?" August asked.

Her mother looked heavenward before shaking her head. "Not in so many words, no. They *are* civilized people, August." Her eyes flashed a warning, before softening as she transferred her gaze to Violet. "But Her Grace expressed an interest in making Violet's acquaintance. She's heard nothing but good things about you, my dear."

Violet had yet to recover her ability to speak and covered her mouth with her fingers. When it became clear that she had nothing to offer, their mother continued with her explanation. "After Her Grace departed, Lady Ashcroft was kind enough to explain the situation to me. No one knows, you understand, but rumors are that when the elder duke died last year he left them without so much as a penny."

"How can that be?" Violet asked. Her voice was soft and faraway. Whether she meant the Rothschilds' financial state or the proposed marriage, August couldn't say.

"It hardly matters," their mother continued. "The important thing is that they need funds no matter the currency, because they have very little of their own. I suspect their debts are going to be called soon, since the duchess was being a bit forward in her interest. They need us." There was a distinct gleam in her eye that made August uncomfortable. "Oh, do say something, Violet. This is wonderful news."

Violet shook her head slowly and, with a hand on her forehead, made her way to the darkened window that looked out over the garden.

"Why do the Rothschilds' financial woes have to involve Violet? Can't they and Papa work out some sort of arrangement? An investment?" asked August. "Or better yet, if the Ashcrofts are their friends, they can lend them money."

"Because that is not how it is done here, August." Her mother's voice was sharp again with impatience. "The duke needs an alliance with a powerful family."

"A *wealthy* family, you mean."

Her mother's glare matched the severity of her tone. "Very well, if you insist on mercenary terms, then yes, he needs an alliance with a wealthy family. We are a wealthy family."

"This is because of Camille, isn't it?" August had been wary of the covetous look in her mother's eyes as Camille had shown them around her manor in Sussex. Now she knew why. It wasn't the wealth that the manor represented that had caught her mother's attention. It was the history of the estate and the family. The stench of new money could not linger in a home that had existed for centuries.

"You have to admit things have worked out quite well for her."

Camille was miserable. Anyone could see that. Anyone who cared to look could see that, August amended. "Financially, perhaps, but do you truly think Camille is happy?"

"Happy?" Mother's laugh grated as it climbed the ridges of her spine. "Of course she's happy. She has everything a young woman could ask for."

Before August could challenge that, Violet's voice interrupted what was quickly promising to escalate into an argument. "I still don't understand. We never came here with the intention of arranging a marriage. The Season was for fun. We were going to return home soon."

Their mother smiled. "And aren't we fortunate that this

opportunity arose? Why, it's nearly been presented to us on a silver platter."

"I am sorry, Mother, but to be perfectly frank, I still do not understand how this arrangement benefits us." August rose and paced around behind the settee, trying her best to work this out. Years of analyzing decisions for Crenshaw Iron Works had taught her to look at every deal from every angle. No matter how she turned it over in her mind, the benefit lay only with the Rothschilds. They would be given a fortune, while the Crenshaws would lose Violet.

"How can you not see it, child? It's a golden opportunity for us. Violet will become a duchess. That is very nearly royalty." She said it as if that were enough. As if Violet marrying a stranger and giving up her entire future to a man they knew nothing about was worth a title.

"What if Violet doesn't want to become a duchess?"

"August, dear, you have to see the opportunities this could bring our way. This could open up doors for us that were previously locked. Why, we are only friends with the Duchess of Hereford, and look at what has already happened. Crenshaw Iron Works could benefit far more than we could imagine."

August hated the way her mother referred to Camille by her title now. Despite the fact that Camille had spent hours upon hours playing with August and Violet as children and running the halls of their home, she wasn't even allowed to be herself anymore. She was a figurehead, a name . . . *a wife*. Ever since August had learned how much women had to give up when they attained the title of wife, she had been wary of the position. Now she had even more reason to be suspicious of it.

"I believe that Crenshaw Iron Works is doing fine. More railways are being built every year. Max has our projections increasing annually."

"One can hope, but one must not underestimate the value of social connections. If we were to be accepted by some . . ." Her mother's voice trailed off, and her expression hardened. "We all know that there are places where the

Crenshaw name is not welcomed. If that were to change, then we would not have to worry about the Astors of the world making things more difficult for us. This is an investment in our future, our name as a family, as much as it is about Violet."

August swallowed thickly, feeling stupid and naive that she had never guessed the depth of her mother's embarrassment. As *new money,* there were many families that did not include their name on the guest list. August had always known that this was a sore spot for her mother, but she had never allowed herself to believe that it would come to this. Even seeing Camille walking down the aisle, her shoulders shaking as she had cried silent tears beneath her veil, had not made August seriously consider that this could happen to her or Violet. She had been a fool to ignore her initial misgivings. As a result, anger heated her next words.

"You are manipulating this arrangement, forcing Violet to marry this man so that you can impress Mrs. Astor." It wasn't a question. Her hands clenched into fists so tightly that her fingernails threatened to cut into her palms.

Her mother nodded. "I am doing what is necessary to secure this family a solid future."

"Have you spoken with Papa about this?" She hoped that he would see reason.

"Your father agrees with me." Her mother's usually sparkling eyes had gone glacial.

A hollow opened up in August's belly at the betrayal. She had assumed that she and Violet would have his full support. Perhaps her mother was stretching the truth about his agreement.

Violet made a noise from the window. It seemed she had finally come to some conclusion, or perhaps she had been holding out hope that their father was not in accord on this. "But have you both forgotten about Teddy?" Violet's voice shook.

Theodore Sutherland was a darling of their social circles in New York, except he and his family had several fatal flaws. First, his family came from St. Louis and not New

York. Second, his family had earned their money in breweries. Third, they, too, were new money, but even newer than the Crenshaws.

Although nothing had been made official, Teddy and Violet had been close for a while now. Everyone had assumed he would offer for her once he graduated university. Now August understood that her mother had never intended anything to come of the match.

"What do you mean? What about Teddy?" asked their mother in a tone that seemed deliberately obtuse.

Violet stomped her foot in a rare demonstration of pique. "We are to be married."

This finally brought their mother to her feet. "Violet, dear, that is most certainly not true. The boy is only twenty years old. It will be years before he's ready to settle into marriage."

"It *is* true. Everyone knows it." Violet's eyes were bright with unshed tears when she looked to her sister. "Tell her, August." Without giving August time to respond, she looked back at their mother. "He's told me that he loves me."

"It's true, Mother. Everyone knows that he wants to marry Violet."

Their mother shrugged. "Well, I do not know this; your father does not know this. Apparently, everyone does *not* know."

"It's true." Violet stepped forward, seizing on this misunderstanding. August had to close her eyes against the desperate hope on her sister's face. "You have but to send a letter. I am certain he'll respond and tell you everything."

Their mother was already shaking her head. "There isn't time for that. A letter would take weeks to even reach him."

"A telegram, then," said Violet, but their mother pretended not to notice as she took her daughter by the shoulders and gave her a gentle smile.

"Besides that, dear, it hardly matters. Mr. Sutherland is no duke. Furthermore, he hasn't a penny that his father hasn't given to him."

"That makes no sense, Mother. If what you say is true,

the duke hasn't a penny, either." Violet huffed, shrugging out of Mother's grip.

"True, but the duke has a title. It's not such a bad exchange, that. A tiny pittance of our good fortune for a title." The woman kissed Violet's cheek and gave August a nod. The bliss on her face was nearly blinding. "Good night, my dears. I am off to bed. Tomorrow will be an exciting day. Violet, dear, we need to go through all of your gowns. We'll select a Worth gown for the eventual ball, of course, but maybe something more reserved for the dinner. I can hardly fathom it . . . a duke! And our Violet to be a duchess." With those words, she disappeared in a swirl of lavender silk into her bedchamber.

August wasted no time in rushing over to her sister and embracing her.

"What am I going to do?" asked Violet. "I cannot marry this stranger. You've seen Camille. You know how wretchedly her husband treats her. I cannot . . ." She gulped in a deep breath, nearly overcome with emotion.

"No, you cannot marry him. I don't know what they're thinking trying to marry you off like this." Without letting go of Violet, August leaned back to look her sister straight in the eye. "We'll stop it."

"But how? You heard her. She seems set on the marriage."

"I'll talk to Papa in the morning." August wondered if she would get anywhere with him. He was well-known for his pragmatism. If Mother had already convinced him that this would help their business, then there might be no changing his mind. But there was no sense in sharing her concern now, when her sister needed reassurances.

Violet nodded. "I'll send Maxwell a telegram tomorrow. I have no idea if this duke will actually offer, or when this damned wedding is meant to take place. Max won't let them do this."

While August knew that their brother would take Violet's side in this, she just didn't think there would be time. There was little hope that a telegram from their brother would sway her parents. He'd have to come here, and before he could leave, he'd have to arrange things with Crenshaw Iron. It could take weeks. No, they would have to take care of this themselves.

As if reading her thoughts, Violet said, "Dear God, will he have time to get here? How soon do you think they want this marriage to take place?"

"I have no idea. That's why we cannot wait for Max."

"And what if Papa doesn't relent?"

August stared down into her sister's dark eyes, wide now with genuine terror. "If Papa doesn't help, then I'll talk to the duke myself. I am certain he can be persuaded to see reason. After all, who would want to marry an unwilling bride?"

It was hardly a reassurance. Violet's brow crinkled as they both remembered the sight of Camille walking down the aisle. She hadn't wanted Hereford, but no one had cared.

"I won't do it, August. I won't give up Teddy."

August pulled her sister in for another hug and did her best to soothe her.

"He's said he loves me." Violet sobbed.

"Shh . . . You won't be forced to marry anyone. I promise." As she made the vow, that vision of Camille refused to leave. She would go through hell to make certain that did not happen to Violet.

Very early the next morning, August made her way to the library, where her father would be drinking coffee and catching up on the news he had missed the day before. London hours had not changed Griswold Crenshaw or his habits. He still awoke at dawn to prepare for the day ahead. The only minor concession he had given to staying up until all hours of the night to imbibe in social events was the addition of an afternoon nap.

A pang of affection made her smile when she saw him. He sat in a large wingback chair with his reading glasses perched on the end of his nose as he flipped through the pages of the *Times*. A pot of coffee sat on the spindly table at his side, and a fire danced merrily in the hearth. Something about the way the morning light splashed warm color over the otherwise darkened room reminded her of the times she would invade his morning routine as a child. He never spoke harshly to her. He would simply smile and ask her how she thought the market would perform that day.

"Good morning, Papa." She walked over and dutifully gave him a kiss on his clean-shaven cheek before taking the chair opposite the table. He had never approved of facial hair on men, so his well-groomed mustache was his compromise to the fashion of his generation.

"Morning, darling." He gave her the charming smile that had gained him many business deals and set his newspaper aside to pour her a cup of coffee. "How do you feel about the market today?"

She smiled at his continued loyalty to their routine. "New York will be fine. In recovery and getting stronger every day." Stirring in the cream, she grimaced when she realized the tray did not contain sugar. Her father never took his coffee sweet, so it hadn't been included. She had a weakness for sweets.

Taking up his paper, he held it in front of him so that she was treated to a view of an article detailing the declining market for pigs in Nottingham.

"Lord save us from another Jay Cooke and Company fiasco shutting down the exchange again," he said.

"I do believe we all learned a valuable lesson about the dangers of speculation."

He gave a mirthless chuckle of agreement and grumbled something unintelligible into the newspaper.

Staring at his hands—the very hands that had held hers many times as they danced at various functions and only weeks ago had patted her shoulder to congratulate her when the investment in a factory she had recommended had paid a tidy dividend—she found herself suddenly very nervous. To cover her anxiety, she took a sip of the bitter coffee, letting it roll around her tongue before swallowing.

What if Mother turned out to be right and Papa was in complete agreement with her? What then? It would be a rarity, but not completely unheard-of. Hadn't he sided with their mother when Maxwell had wanted to move into his brownstone? They had both decided that bachelors should live at home until they were married. Not that their displeasure had stopped him. He had moved out and life had gone on. Surely, this could be resolved as simply. Only this was marriage and so much more permanent.

"Papa?" Her stomach churned, so she set the cup and its saucer on the table, afraid the smell would make her more nauseated. "I have come to discuss something very important with you."

He glanced at her from behind the paper and must have noted the seriousness of her expression, because he opted to set it aside again. Before his frown could become a question, she said, "Mother spoke with us last night. She mentioned the idea that Violet might marry the Duke of Rothschild."

To her horror, he smiled and took up his cup and saucer as if the idea were something to be mulled over and entertained with intelligent conversation. "I sometimes believe that I don't give Millie the credit she deserves. She's hopeless when it comes to business, but she has proven very shrewd in other areas."

A chill started in her face and made its way down her entire body. "Are you saying that you agree with Mother? That Violet should wed this man we know nothing about?"

"It's a fine idea, August, and he isn't some stranger. True, we do not know him personally, but he's a duke." He shrugged as if the title alone should be enough. When that didn't get a response from her, he added, "He and his family are well-known. Several gentlemen I know, including Hereford, have vouched for him."

"Do you mean men you have only met since we arrived?" She could hardly keep her voice from trembling with her fury.

His infuriating smile stayed in place as he inclined his head. "I concede your point. However, I have known Hereford for nearly a year, and most of them are his friends and acquaintances. Rothschild counts the Prince of Wales among his friends. What more of a recommendation do you need? I have it on good authority that the Prince of Wales himself will approve the match."

"How on earth could you know that? How long have you been planning this?"

"Only recently, darling. The prince speaks highly of Americans, as you know. It stands to reason that he will welcome more of our girls. He approved Camille, didn't he?"

August could hardly believe what she was hearing. While it was true that the Prince of Wales had sent Camille and Hereford a wedding gift, and his love of Americans had been written up in various papers, she could not fathom that extending to Violet. Not because her sister didn't deserve his esteem, but because it all seemed so unbelievable.

"The prince doesn't concern me. I am more concerned with losing Violet and having her married to a man she doesn't love or even know."

"You've always had a soft heart for her. Violet is not like you or me. She doesn't know her own mind. She needs a husband who will take care of her, nurture her as her own family has. She needs an environment where she will be protected from some of the harsher realities of the world."

How was this man she knew to be perfectly rational willing to marry his daughter to an aristocrat he barely knew? Did Violet mean so little to him? "But she does know her own mind. She knows that she doesn't want to marry this duke. She knows that she wants to be a writer."

He gave a quick shake of his head. "I am certain her husband, whoever he may be, will indulge her penchant for writing." He took a sip of his coffee and stared into the fire as if Violet's future was of no consequence.

He said it as if her writing was a mere hobby and not something to be considered a serious pursuit. But then far more insidious thoughts crossed her mind. Was this because Violet had been born a daughter? Did she have no other worth to him than something with which he could barter? If he was willing to part with Violet so easily, did that also extend to August?

August had always believed that he found her advice to

be genuinely helpful. He had always taken the time to include her in his work, marveling at her ability with numbers. Had she . . . Had she been little more than an oddity to him? A female who could add a column of numbers faster than his best clerk? No. She gave a shake of her head, refusing to believe it.

"But how do we know this man will nurture her—"

He raised his hand in an effort to quiet her. "August, please. We do not know him yet, but we will. There has been no announcement. We are still very much in the preliminary stages of discussing a possible union. From all appearances, he will be a suitable husband for her, but if we meet him and do not like him, we can certainly reevaluate. Give me a little bit of your confidence. I do not plan to marry my youngest child off to an ogre." He grinned at his jest.

As long as she had known him, her father had never raised his voice. He was stern when it was called for, and he had a way of speaking that was very quiet while still managing to resonate. It was how he addressed a crowded room of stakeholders at Crenshaw Iron Works. It was how he spoke at important functions. His voice could sneak inside her head and calm her even when she wanted to be angry. He just sounded so completely reasonable about it all.

Willing to push her earlier fears aside, she asked, "But what of Teddy?"

"Who?"

She fought the urge to roll her eyes. Not quite sure if he was being deliberately obtuse, she said, "Theodore Sutherland. He and Violet have been practically inseparable the last two summers at the cottage."

It wasn't completely out of the realm of possibility that he didn't remember, because he did not spend the entire summers with them in Newport. He tended to spend long weekends and travel back for work during the week. Even her own attendance at the cottage was sporadic, unlike Violet and their mother, who lived there for the summer months.

"Ah yes, I remember now," said Papa. "You must admit the Sutherlands are not so well established as the duke."

"Of course I admit that, Papa. That isn't the point. I mention Teddy because Violet fancies that he is in love with her, and they will marry after his graduation."

"I have never indicated that I will give permission for that particular union. In fact, I believe he is a poor choice. Is he even twenty years old yet? He's too young. Besides, his father mentioned that he has an interest in studying the law. If he attends law school, that could be another several years before they marry. She'll be too old by then. No. Absolutely not."

"She'll barely be twenty-five. I'll be twenty-five in two years. That is hardly too old for marriage."

He gave her a look that was filled with more compassion than she was comfortable with. His mustache drooped further at the corners as he quickly gave his attention to his coffee.

A mild sort of fright clawed its way up her throat, and the words were out before she could stop them. "Do you think I'm old?" Or at least too old to marry. Did they view her as a spinster to be humored and placated?

Without looking at her, he placed his cup and saucer on the table and retreated to the safety of his newspaper. "Of course not. One day you will find a fine man to marry. We were discussing your sister. Violet will have wasted her youth waiting for Theodore, and he might very well decide he wants another after law school. Let us entertain the notion of the duke for a bit and see what happens."

"Papa, must we even—"

The paper crinkled as he glanced at her. "Enough with this, darling. Nothing has been carved in stone."

When he hid behind the newspaper again, she knew this was as far as she would get with him today. Still, she couldn't help but sit and stare at the typeface as she took in shallow breaths. She wanted to ask him about her own future. Would they consider a marriage for her if it would further the family name? Would he be so willing to give her up, and all that she had brought to Crenshaw Iron Works, if it would give them social standing? She opened her mouth to ask, but a moment of cowardice kept her silent. Part of her didn't want to know. What would she do with the information anyway?

As always, reason would have to prevail here. While she disliked the idea that he was almost as excited about the plan as Mother, she was gratified that he was at least willing to discuss the situation rationally. Perhaps the Duke of Rothschild would turn out to be the very ogre he would not want Violet to marry and all of this would prove moot.

Or, if her parents couldn't be made to see reason, perhaps the duke himself could be dissuaded. Camille had been an unwilling bride, but no one had ever discussed it, preferring to keep that fact hidden in niceties. Perhaps if she confronted Rothschild with Violet's unwillingness, he would back down.

Really, who would want an unwilling bride? This wasn't the Middle Ages.

Chapter 4

*But the cloud never comes in that quarter of
the horizon from which we watch for it.*

ELIZABETH GASKELL

E van and his mother were the last to arrive for dinner at
the Ashcrofts'. As they followed a footman from the
mahogany-paneled entryway, Evan glimpsed gilt-framed
paintings on the walls of the rooms that they passed. He
recognized at least one Rembrandt and two Titians. A
twinge of guilt drew his mouth tight as he thought of the
paintings he'd had Clark sell only last month. A minor concession to the creditors clamoring for his throat. Not
enough to cure their bloodlust, but enough to assuage them
for a time. His mother had not returned home to Charrington Manor yet to notice, and if his sisters had written to
her about them, she had not mentioned it.

"Please try to smile," she whispered. A glance at his
expression had her amending her request. "Or at least stop
scowling. You will frighten the dear girl."

To her credit, she had her graceful half smile in place. It
was the one she pulled out for formal events such as this. It
said that she was appropriately interested but elegantly benign about what was happening around her, and that everything was absolutely satisfactory in her world.

"How can you sound so cheerful?" he asked.

"I have faith that it will all work out well. She is a lovely girl who will make you a lovely bride."

It hardly signified that he did not want a bride, lovely or otherwise. He wanted the basic dignity of being able to provide for his family like any man. Unfortunately, his father had robbed him of that. Now this woman, barely more than a girl, would be responsible for saving them. Perhaps bankrupting the dukedom to see Evan flounder had been part of Father's plan all along.

"You'll make it through this. I promise." His mother patted his cheek and moved ahead to the door a footman was opening. The music of a quartet of stringed instruments wafted out of the drawing room.

A flicker of excitement sparked to life in his belly, only partially dampened by the gloom of the forced marriage ahead of them. Miss Crenshaw was in that room. She had been brave to attend the fight. Braver still for taking what she wanted and kissing him. The fact that she was his intended bride was the only thing that made this situation tolerable for him.

When they approached the door, Lord and Lady Ashcroft crossed to greet them. The room was filled with several people, and his gaze flicked from one to the next trying to find her. Hereford was present, as was an older couple he recognized as his mother's friends, Viscount Ware, and a middle-aged couple he vaguely recognized as the Crenshaws. They were elegantly dressed, even if Mrs. Crenshaw did appear a bit too ostentatious in her jewelry choices. The large diamonds at her neck and ears were a bit overwhelming taken altogether. An attractive young woman stood beside them, but there was no sign of the woman from the fight.

"How wonderful to see you, Rothschild. Margaret, you are glowing with health." Lady Ashcroft fawned over his mother, while Evan swallowed his dismay and greeted Lord Ashcroft. The man had been a friend of his father's but lacked the elder Rothschild's austerity.

After pleasantries were exchanged, Evan found himself again searching for her. She had to be present. He refused to accept the niggling doubt that said he might be mistaken. A door to the garden had been left ajar, and gaslights flickered beyond the windows to encourage guests to explore it. Perhaps she was out there.

Impatient to see her again to discover if that same spark would be lit between them, he made a move in that direction, but, as if she suspected his intent to leave, his mother took his arm and guided him toward the others.

"Rothschild. Good of you to join us." The Duke of Hereford had also been a friend of his father's, though unlike Ashcroft, he tended to view Evan with the same disappointment as Evan's father. The man inclined his head in the barest echo of a bow.

Evan returned the gesture, hating that he was now Rothschild. In his mind it was his father's name and not one he had ever planned to associate with himself. "Hereford."

"Have you met our American friends yet?" asked Ashcroft.

And here it was, the reason they were all gathered. His chest tightened as he looked past Hereford to the couple who were watching him with interest. "I have yet to have the pleasure."

Hereford turned toward the couple. "May I present Mr. and Mrs. Crenshaw of New York City."

"Your Grace, it is an honor," said Crenshaw, a handsome man of medium build who happened to be his future father-in-law.

Evan managed to breathe out and offer a cursory greeting. His mother mumbled something, but Evan barely registered the conversation. Taking Mrs. Crenshaw's hand out of rote protocol rather than conscious thought, he bent over it. "Madame, it is my sincere pleasure to meet you."

The woman had dark hair that was only starting to show strands of gray. She was pleasing enough to the eye, but her manner was more forward than his own mother would have found appropriate. She did not lower her gaze as was proper when he greeted her. Instead, she gave him a smile and stared at him as if she might be gazing upon the second coming of her savior.

"You are even more handsome than your mother suggested, Your Grace," she said.

He offered her a benign smile and caught a flash of disapproval in his mother's eye before she managed to hide it. "I am shocked. Typically, there's no end to her exaggeration."

The disapproval in his mother's gaze was back, but this time it was directed at him. Her smile firmly in place, she said to Mrs. Crenshaw, "I am pleased to see you again."

"This is our Violet." The woman turned to present the young woman standing beside her.

It took a moment for his brain to catch up with his eyes and ears. *This* was Violet, but this was indeed *not* the woman he had kissed. His heart moved into his stomach where it settled with a nausea-inducing plummet.

Like her mother, she met his gaze without flinching. However, she did not seem quite as enchanted as the older woman. Raising her chin a notch, she appeared to be fighting to keep a hard glint from her eyes.

"Hello, dear," said his mother. "It is lovely to meet you. Miss Violet, may I present my son, the Duke of Rothschild."

Evan's good manners had deserted him in the face of this turn of events. He had been well and truly prepared to meet the woman from the fight, the one who'd challenged him and kissed him. This was not her. This woman was her sister and had been sitting beside her that night at the theater.

"It's a pleasure to meet you." He forced the words out. "How are you enjoying your time in London?"

For the barest fraction of a second, her eyes flashed fire, and he found himself expecting—hoping?—that she would dare to lash out. It was clear to him and probably everyone else that she had been informed of his intention and she was not as flattered as another young woman in her position might have been. He was too disappointed still to take offense. Why the devil were they offering the younger sister to him? Everyone knew that the older daughters were married off first.

With the fire successfully banked, she discreetly withdrew her hand and said, "I am enjoying it very much, thank you. You have a lovely city."

Before he could respond, Mrs. Crenshaw launched into a lively discussion detailing their time in the city. From the exhibits at the British Museum to the opera to the shops on Bond Street, she made certain to drop the names of at least a handful of the aristocracy she had met along the way. To her credit, Violet did not join in; she simply muttered an agreement when necessary all while staring at him in disapproval.

Bloody hell, this was to be his mother-in-law. Visions of endless holidays filled with her constant boasting stretched out before him. Perhaps bankruptcy would be worth it to avoid that fate. Another glance at his mother disabused him of that notion before it could take root. She still wore a deep mourning gown trimmed with crape as was customary, but she had refused to have new ones made this year. He had noticed as they disembarked the carriage that the lace along the hem in the back had frayed. The expense was the true reason for her refusal. What right did he have to not perform his duty?

An ache developed in his jaw, and he realized that he had been gritting his teeth. He forced himself to relax and noticed Violet watching him with curiosity, her head tilted slightly to the side. Perhaps marriage to her would not be so terribly unbearable. She was very pretty. With her slight frame, her rich dark hair pulled up in an elaborate twist, and a stylish, rose-hued gown, she was the image of a lady. The flashes of fire in her eyes gave him hope that she had more in her head than visions of a title.

Still, when he opened his mouth to speak to her, he asked, "Is your sister joining us this evening?"

Violet brightened for the first time that evening. "My sister is here. She's stepped into the garden with Her Grace." Her voice was soft with just the right amount of husk to be pleasing. It should have enchanted him. Instead, his pulse pounded with the anticipation of seeing the elder Miss Crenshaw again. Her gaze went past his shoulder, lighting up pleasantly as it rested on whom he assumed would be her sister.

He whipped his head around to look for her before he could think better of what it might reveal about his eagerness. The woman he had kissed stood framed in the doorway, her eyes wide in shock as they roamed from her sister to him. She was as striking as she had been that night, except instead of a cloak, she wore a sapphire blue gown that revealed the right amount of bosom. In the light of the lamp overhead, he could make out the striking shape of her cheekbones and the tilt of her chin. Even across the room, he could see that her eyes had hardened in determination.

He did not think she would recognize him. The pomade he wore in his hair when he fought darkened it from blond to brown. He also made certain to have a few days' growth of beard for each match, and now he was clean-shaven. The anger alighting her eyes as she made her way into the room was most certainly from the position they found themselves in and not recognition. Apparently, neither of the women welcomed his suit.

Instead of waiting for him to approach her, as any proper English girl was raised to do, she strode across the room with her shoulders back, her gaze never wavering from his. She walked with purpose and a confidence that was very attractive. Upon reaching him, she did not bother to wait for a proper introduction; instead she held her hand out to him.

"I am August Crenshaw," she said, as if she were not causing a scene before the entire room.

Momentarily startled, he stood for a moment, staring at her glove-clad fingers. Her hand was offered to him with her fingers stacked in a line, thumb on top. She was not holding it out, palm down, for him to kiss or bow over but offering it in a handshake. Yes, she truly meant for him to shake her hand.

Deciding to take up her challenge, he recognized it for what it was, and he took her hand, savoring the heat of her palm against his own. Obliged to answer her direct manner, he said, "I am Evan Sterling, Duke of Rothschild." Then, with wicked amusement, he added, "Marquess of Langston, Earl of Haverford, Viscount Blackwell, Baron Clifford."

Without missing a beat, she said, "That's quite a mouthful." Her tone was dry, but her lips quirked upward in the most fascinating way.

Someone coughed. Someone else made an odd choking sound. Evan genuinely smiled for the first time since the meeting with Clark when the question of marriage had been finalized.

Mrs. Crenshaw rushed forward to her eldest daughter and took up a position beside her as if to somehow guard him from her brazenness. "This is . . ." Her mouth opened and closed again as if at a loss to explain the creature standing so proudly next to her. Color had risen to her powdery cheeks. "This is August, our eldest daughter."

"Yes, so she has said." His gaze drifted back to her.

August. The name floated in his head, uncertain where it should land. It was unusual for a woman, but somehow it suited her. There were sun-kissed highlights in her hair, and the hazel of her eyes was swirled with grass green. Her creamy skin had a glow that showed a defiance of parasols. From now on when he thought of summer, he would think of her.

"It is a pleasure, Miss Crenshaw."

There was the barest hint of a moment when he thought she might actually give him a set-down. The words were there, flickering behind her eyes, which very clearly said she did not appreciate his intention. However, she finally lowered them, no doubt in response to her mother's clasp on her arm. When she raised them, the fire had been momentarily banked, but they were no less livid in their intensity.

Would she dare confront him here? He found himself leaning forward with anticipation when she parted her lips. Unfortunately, he did not get a chance to find out, because the butler announced that dinner would be served.

"Your Grace?" Lady Ashcroft's voice floated into his consciousness, making him realize that he was still staring at the impertinent Miss Crenshaw.

"Yes?" he asked, struggling to remember that they were in the middle of a drawing room and not somewhere private. What he would not give to have Miss Crenshaw to himself in the garden for five minutes. He wanted to hear the storm she obviously longed to unleash on him.

Lady Ashcroft gestured politely to where the butler stood in the doorway. As the duke with precedent, Evan would lead the party to the dining room. No one could leave until he did. He *wanted* to offer the elder Miss Crenshaw his arm simply to watch the fireworks in her eyes. However, etiquette demanded that the lady of the house go in on his arm.

"Shall we?"

Inclining her head, Lady Ashcroft took his arm and he led the way.

The duke was not an ogre. He was arrogant, entitled, and overconfident, but he wasn't an ogre. In fact, he was at least twenty years younger than August had been expecting, and even with her immense aversion for him and the situation in which he had placed them, she could admit that he was handsome. Handsome if one liked the proud, aristocratic type, which she did not. Unfortunately, that dislike did nothing to stop her from appreciating his good looks.

It was annoying, and she had spent the entire meal trying *not* to look at him. Not an easy feat since the meal had seemed to drag on for hours with at least ten courses. She had lost count somewhere between the lark pie and the chaudfroid of chicken. To complicate things, Violet had been given the seat on his far side. August kept checking on her sister to make certain that she wasn't too upset. So far, Violet had kept her composure and carried on a constant, if subdued, conversation with both the duke and the gentleman on her other side. However, since they were both opposite August and down a bit, she had to look past him to see her sister, so she couldn't help catching glimpses of him.

Also, there was something about the duke that kept drawing her attention. Something about the shape of his face that looked familiar. She had caught him smiling once at a comment, and it, too, had seemed familiar. Though she was certain that she had never met the Duke of Rothschild before, she felt as if she had seen his smile. And then there was the particular way he said her name that threatened to jar some unknown memory.

"Miss Crenshaw?"

She blinked, realized that she had been staring at the duke again, and glanced down to see that a new course had been set before her. Blancmange. *Please let this mean that this meal is coming to an end.*

"Miss Crenshaw?" The gentleman next to her raised an eyebrow expectantly. "Do you enjoy sweets? I confess I can hardly abide them."

"I do enjoy them, yes." She took a small bite of the dessert and let the mild almond flavor melt in her mouth.

The gentleman next to her was a perfectly presentable young man whose name she kept forgetting. He was a viscount, or perhaps an earl, which made her assume her mother had had a hand in the seating arrangement. All she knew was that he had more than a passing interest in her bosom, and he slurped his soup. He tended to gesture as he spoke, so her gaze kept catching on his hands. They were so pale that she could easily trace the blue veins on the backs of them. Not that there was anything wrong with pale hands; it was more that she kept imagining how little of the outdoors he must have seen. How little work those hands had accomplished.

On her other side sat the Duke of Hereford. His hands, while neat and tidy, were not nearly so pristine. The backs were peppered with liver spots and wiry gray hair. She knew from Camille that he rode daily, but she very much doubted those hands had seen a day of work in his life.

Before she realized her intention, she found herself looking at Rothschild's hands across the table. From this distance and between the artfully placed candelabras, it was difficult to tell much, but they seemed lightly tanned and well-formed. They were broad, but not boorish, and appeared strong. Of course he would have handsome hands to go with his handsome face. The long, graceful fingers elegantly held his spoon as he brought a bit of dessert to his lips. Candlelight flickered across his knuckles, turning them gold and highlighting a healing gash that spanned across the middle two. Interesting. Those were not the hands of the typical nobleman.

"Have you visited the Royal Botanic Gardens yet, Miss Crenshaw?" Lord Earl-or-Viscount said to her as he found a way to slurp the pudding. "It is still early in the season yet, but I find that to be the best time to tour them. The buds are only starting to show their promise. It is when you can truly see the beauty that Mother Nature has in store."

His eager gaze had hardly left her. She wanted to gently let the man down, but dinner did not seem to be the proper place for such a discussion. Instead, she murmured that she had not and turned her attention to the Duke of Hereford. Thankfully, he was engrossed in conversation with the woman beside him.

Camille snickered and decided to save her. "Lord Ware, you must tell me the places you believe Miss Crenshaw should visit before she returns home. I will personally make certain that she sees them all."

Lord Ware, that was his name, though August still couldn't remember if he was an earl or viscount. She caught Camille's eye and gave a brief nod of thanks.

"Your Grace, you must deign to visit our fair city sometime soon." Her father's voice rose over the conversations at the table. "I am certain a man with your enthusiasm for entertainment will find much to enjoy in New York."

"Perhaps I will," Rothschild answered. "I have heard it said that you Americans are quite bold. I am sure to find your city entertaining."

There was that voice followed by his distinct smile and a tilt of his head. Combined, they made her think of the fighter. She hadn't let herself think about that man very much. He had hovered there in her memory because of the kiss, but she tried to move her thoughts along when they would have lingered. She would rather forget that she had kissed a stranger, not that Camille would ever let her forget. But now that the memory had been evoked, every second of her time with him came back to her.

Her father responded, but it was lost on her as she remembered the stranger's hands on her waist, and his smile as he looked down at her. The duke laughed, raising his wineglass in a mock toast to Papa. That smile. It was the eyeteeth that were so similar. Again, the distance worked against her, but she thought they were pointed, like the fighter's. Before he drank, Rothschild made eye contact with her, inclining his head a little and smiling again. This time for her, as his lips made a perfect bow.

"Would you agree, Miss Crenshaw?" he asked.

That voice. Her name with that same inflection that she couldn't articulate. The fighter had said it just that way. She hadn't followed the rest of the conversation, so she said, "That we are bold? Yes. But I am afraid you would find our city terribly boring. There aren't very many amusements for a man of leisure."

August did not have to look at her mother to know that she would be displeased with her. The duke, however, only widened his grin. "Then I will endeavor to find amusements where I can." With that, he drank, never taking his eyes from hers. Something about that—him slaking his thirst while focusing his attention on her—seemed too intimate for the dining room table. Her face burned in a response that she couldn't control, and a thrill of interest tightened low in her belly. Despite her intention to meet him head-on, she looked away first. Her breath caught in her throat as she stared at her barely touched dessert.

When she looked up again, he was back in conversation with her father, who was busy assuring him that he would be well amused in New York. A small strand of hair had fallen to his temple, and he absently brushed it back. The movement drew her gaze to his knuckles, which were indeed bruised, and a minor abrasion sitting along his hairline.

She gasped aloud as she remembered the older fighter,

Wilkes, landing a particularly brutal blow there. The fighter's head had flung to the side, making her grit her teeth as she waited to see if he had been very badly injured. He had responded by doubling up his attack, coming at Wilkes in a fury.

Could it be him? He smiled again, and again she noted it. The perfect bow of his lips. The divot below the center of his bottom lip. The devilish pointy teeth. It was him! That smile was familiar because she had seen it before. Had kissed the lips that framed it.

No, it couldn't be. A duke couldn't participate in prize-fighting. Even as the denial pulsed through her, she could not take her eyes from him. Rothschild's gaze dashed back to her. Something in her face must have told him that she suspected. He took a long, lingering look from her eyes to her mouth, perhaps remembering their kiss, and back again. Finally, he raised his glass and said, "A toast to risk-takers." He gave her a wink before taking another sip of the dark liquid.

It *was* him! Against all odds, the man known as the Hellion was here in the Ashcrofts' dining room, and her parents were offering Violet up to him on a silver platter.

Perhaps just as bad—worse—*she* had kissed him!

Chapter 5

*The secret of success in life is for a man to be
ready for his opportunity when it comes.*

BENJAMIN DISRAELI

August Crenshaw had finally recognized him. There
was no mistaking that gasp, or the blush that had accompanied it as she remembered their kiss. A kiss he had
never believed would happen when he had taunted her. She
had surprised him then, just as she had surprised him tonight.

Dinner had ended, and he sat forced to endure smoking
and cognac at the table with the men. He despised the cloying smell of tobacco, as it always reminded him of his father's disappointment. The cognac was excellent, so he
endeavored to savor it, while Mr. Crenshaw did his best to
court him from behind a wall of smoke. The man had
boasted about the family's extraordinary success in the
years since the American Civil War, all but divulging the
figures on their balance sheets. Now he was lauding his
ambition in expanding their operations to the European
market.

Evan wanted to tell the man that a marriage was very
nearly a foregone conclusion, so there was no need to come

on so strong. His lack of wealth and the Crenshaws' excess of it having sealed the deal. Mr. Crenshaw's constant attention and deference was making Evan feel like *he* was the wealthy heiress being courted by a titled aristocrat. Is this what peeresses had gone through all these centuries? It was a wonder they had not broken ranks and started their own colony, free of needy men.

Evan's gaze kept going toward the door, remembering how August had looked back at him before she had disappeared through it. Her gaze had been full of contempt with the slightest hint of confusion. He wanted to ask her father if he would be willing to switch the daughters, August instead of Violet, but the idea sounded crass even to Evan. Before he even thought of requesting something so outlandish, he needed to talk to her. He needed to see if she truly was as he remembered her.

Before he could stop himself, he rose to his feet. The men all stood in response, looking startled with their half-finished cigars and drinks in their hands.

"Stay and finish. I need to . . ." Not accustomed to explaining himself, he floundered for an excuse for his sudden departure. He stopped himself before he could say "go speak to Miss Crenshaw" but only barely. That would have been disastrous.

"Are you feeling well, Your Grace?" asked Lord Ashcroft as Evan hurried from the room.

Ignoring the footman outside the door, Evan walked to the back of the house, turning a corner that would lead to the garden. He did not want to go directly to the drawing room, as that would invite comments and conversation, when he simply wanted to see her alone. Perhaps if he made his presence known in the garden, she would come out to him. It was not the least bit proper, but she had already proven she did not care a whit for propriety, and she was itching to speak with him. That look of recognition had told him as much.

Opening a door he thought bordered the garden, he found a little-used sitting room that had a narrow window facing out. As quiet as an intruder, he made his way across the darkened room, and his heart gave a start of satisfaction when he saw the window was actually a door with a latch. Turning his body to the side to slip through, he stepped outside to find that he was on the opposite end of the garden from the drawing room. Feminine conversations wafted out a partially open door, and one of the violins in the drawing room played a haunting tune that floated in the cool night air.

Quietly, he made his way toward the bright lights of the drawing room along a gravel path that meandered among the rosebushes and hedges. The last thing he wanted was to get cornered by Mrs. Crenshaw; her husband had been bad enough. No doubt she would demand a proposal and a wedding date that very night. He peered around a corner and saw the slim figure of a woman standing beneath a gas lamp. It seemed too easy to assume it was the appropriate Miss Crenshaw. She wore a shawl covering her shoulders, but the light caught the blue skirt of her gown.

August.

His heart kicked against his ribs. She was stunning in the low lighting. She stood in profile, gazing at something he could not see in a rosebush. The light caught the soft curve of her cheekbone, highlighting the graceful contour up to her hairline. She was a brunette, but the same sun that had delicately burnished her skin had lightened portions of her hair so that some strands shone gold. Her lips were full enough to be enticing, but not enough to take away from the rest of her. When her breasts rose on a sigh, he could not help but take them in. They were fuller than her frame suggested they should be, and he found that he very much liked that.

"Good evening, Miss Crenshaw."

She turned toward him as if he were a burglar intent on stealing from her. Perhaps that is exactly what he was.

"Your Grace," she said, lifting her chin a notch and crossing her arms over her chest. "I'm glad you're here," she continued. "I believe you and I should talk."

He loved how direct she was. No one in his entire life had ever said what they meant. His father had never called him a disappointment, but the sentiment had been implied. No one had ever said that he was less capable than his brother, William, but everyone had believed it to be true.

She was honest, and honest was refreshing. He was ready for the fury she was only barely holding back from releasing on him. Was it so wrong to want to bask in the blaze of her righteous wrath? Probably, but he was going to do it anyway.

He approached her slowly to stand outside the circle of light cast by the lamp. Trying to appear at ease, he pretended to be intrigued by the flames flickering behind the glass as he said, "I thought you might feel that way. What shall we discuss?"

"I believe you know." Her gaze bore into the side of his head harder than Wilkes could have ever hoped to land a punch. She was not retreating. Almost everyone retreated from him in one way or another.

Before he had realized it, he was moving closer to her, drawn by her intensity. "Come now, Miss Crenshaw. You have been refreshingly direct all night. Why stop now?"

"All right. I want you to give up your pursuit of my sister. She does not want to marry you."

The words, the tone, they were all angry and harsh, so why did they feel like a balm to the ragged ache in his chest? This was madness. He was mad. It was the only explanation for why he continued to taunt her. "She has only met me tonight. Are these the types of conversations that go on between ladies in drawing rooms after dinner?"

"She didn't have to meet you to know. Contrary to almost everything else in your life, this isn't about you. We have a very nice life back in New York, and we intend to return there after this visit. As a family," she added for extra emphasis.

Anger and the chill in the night air had added spots of color to her cheeks. She was beautiful. "One of you is bound to marry eventually. What then?"

She shook her head, annoyed with him. "Of course Violet will marry eventually, to a man of her own choosing. Not an aristocrat or even an Englishman."

Biting back a smile, he said, "I believe I am beginning to see the problem. Do you have an issue with Englishmen specifically, or is it more anyone who is not American?"

He had said it to fan the flames of her anger, and he was not disappointed when she burned hotter. "How dare you? This has nothing to do with your nationality and everything to do with your entitled way of gaining a wife. You think every woman should bow down to your title and offer herself up for you. Well, that is not how the world works." She frowned and seemed to think better of it, because it was most definitely how his world worked.

Until now. Until her.

"Not my world, at any rate," she added. "Violet has a perfectly respectable fiancé back home. She has no use for you or your suit. If you would leave off and find yourself another heiress, then I would be most appreciative."

If Evan had been expecting her to hold back even a tiny bit, he would have been disappointed. Fortunately, he had been expecting a set-down, and she more than delivered. She was magnificent. And if Violet did indeed have a fiancé back home, then his problem would be solved. Too bad she was lying.

"You have my apologies, Miss Crenshaw. No one told me that Miss Violet was already betrothed. It is an oversight by your parents that I will take up with them right away. Obviously, she is not free to wed."

She had not been expecting him to be reasonable. Her lips stayed parted for a few seconds before she managed to bring them together again. Her hand made a loose fist against her chest as if she were very literally trying to still her beating heart.

"I . . . Thank you. I expected more of a—"

"If you will excuse me, Miss Crenshaw, I am off to speak with your father now." He gave a polite bow of his head and turned, but he only took one step before she stopped him.

"Wait, Your Grace."

He smiled. In the days since he had decided to pursue this plan of his mother's, Clark had investigated the Crenshaws to determine if the suit was worthwhile. It was, and the investigation had thus far turned up no mention of a fiancé. He need not have asked, but he did because he could not walk away from this sparring session with her. "Yes, Miss Crenshaw?"

She nibbled her bottom lip and then seemed to come to some decision. "I'm afraid it's your nature as a gentleman that I must call upon."

"The very nature that you abhor?" He scoffed.

Her lips pursed together so hard that a tiny pale line appeared around the edges. "Violet is expecting to marry a family friend. Nothing has been announced yet, but an engagement will be forthcoming."

"And your parents have agreed to this match?"

"Not yet." She said the words like they had hurt her on the way out.

"Ah . . . then your sister is indeed free to marry me."

"I suppose that depends on your definition of *free*. If you can live with yourself knowing that the woman you are wed to wants someone else, then yes."

He laughed at that. "Miss Crenshaw, I am the twelfth Duke of Rothschild. My family line can be traced back to the Norman Conquest. In the countless unions between then and now, I am unaware of a single one where the parties involved desired the marriage for reasons that were not mercenary. Historically, it is very low on the list of requirements in a suitable match."

"You mean you never actually intended to look for a woman you want to marry?"

He shrugged. "Hundreds of families are depending on me to save my estates. I have four houses that are threatening to crumble down around me. I have two sisters who must be launched into society next year, and a mother who must be cared for. Finding a woman I *want* to marry is a luxury I do not possess."

She seemed a bit stunned by that admission. Her eyes widened the slightest bit, and she sat back on her heels. Her thoughts were nearly visible as they spun in her head. Had she believed that he was wife hunting because he was simply inconvenienced by his lack of funds and needed a new suit of clothes? God, if only things were that simple.

"All right." She took in a breath. "I can see things are direr than I anticipated."

He nodded, remembering when he had had that same realization, though his had involved considerably more alcohol.

Her color receded, and she blinked up at him. "With that in mind, I am very sorry to say this." She paused, and a hint of pity passed across her eyes before she stomped it out. "But I know who you really are."

He could not help but grin as his gaze automatically fell to her lips and that kiss played across his mind. "The Duke of Rothschild?" he teased.

She took another breath, and the words rushed out of her. "I know that you are the prizefighter they call the Hellion."

Her eyes had gone fierce again, though she kept the fire contained. He wanted to see what would happen when she let it loose, so he said, "Why do you think that?" A coil of anticipation tightened low in his gut.

"Do you have the audacity to deny it?"

"That is a strong accusation. How would you know such a thing?" Did she think of that kiss like he did? His gaze dropped to her lips, wanting to taste them again and be allowed to take his time. His blood heated and thickened just imagining it.

"Do not tease me." Her voice shook, but it had lowered an octave. She was not quite bold enough to have the entire dinner party know of her attendance at that fight, it seemed. "Your hair is lighter, but you have the same strong nose, the same smile. The way you speak is the same. And your hands." She gestured to his right hand, which had yet to heal completely from the last fight.

His thigh still pained him, as well, but he could walk without a limp when he needed to. Oddly moved that out of all of that she would find his smile noteworthy, he asked, "Not that I am admitting to anything, but why are you accusing me of this?"

She crossed her arms over her chest again and glanced toward the drawing room. They were around a hedge, but it was not so far away that someone could not easily come upon them. Satisfied that they were still alone, she met his gaze with the solemnity of someone condemning a soul to the gallows and said, "Because if you continue in this pursuit, then I will be forced to explain your true nature to my parents and anyone else who will listen. You will only have yourself to blame for pushing me to it. Leave Violet alone, and I am willing to keep your secret."

"I ask you again, how would you even know about this fighter?"

She sighed in exasperation. "I was there, you dolt. I nearly fell into the fighting ring, and you caught me, and then you . . . then we . . . well, *you know*."

Never in his life had anyone called him a dolt. They might have thought it a time or two, but even at Eton, being the son of a duke came with a few privileges. Her honest rage soothed away any anger that her words might have evoked. He instinctively knew that he would always get the truth with her. His palms itched with the desire to hold her again, so he fisted his hands to stifle the impulse.

"And you would tell your parents this?" A crease formed between her eyebrows. Ah, she had not considered how she would explain her knowledge of him. "You would tell them that you attended this dangerous fight, nearly injured yourself in the process, and this prizefighter came to your aid, after which you . . ." He allowed his voice to trail off as she began to understand what he meant. A flush worked its way up her chest to her face. Perhaps he should be smiling in victory, but pressure tightened his chest instead as she came to her realization.

She could not out him without implicating herself. Some in society already suspected his prizefighting. Those close to him already knew it. There had been whispers in broader circles, but nothing was confirmed. The truth was that they did not care. At most it was a minor scandal. At worst, it would close a few doors to him. Unfortunately for her, the people who would care about his prizefighting were the same people who would look down on her even more for attending such an event.

He knew the exact moment she came to that same conclusion, because she stepped back and turned as if in revulsion. Whether that distaste was reserved for society or if he was included, he did not know. He only knew that he did not want to be included. He wanted the woman who had seen him at the fight and kissed him. Her truth and her fury.

Bloody hell. He was making a mess of this conversation. He had meant to let her know that her plan to blackmail would come to naught. Instead, he had very nearly crushed her with the awful truth of the world in which they lived. Reaching out to touch her shoulder, he let his fingers close into a fist and fall back at his side. There was no way in hell she would welcome his touch.

"Miss Crenshaw . . . understand that I am not—"

She whirled to face him, but instead of tears as he had expected, her face was livid. "You will not force my sister into marriage. I do not care if I have to risk my reputation to see it done." With those words, she turned away from him in a whirl of skirts and stormed off toward the drawing room. A soft orange blossom–scented cloud floated behind her, prickling his skin as it settled over him.

His heart pounded with the aftermath of her fury, and he could only watch her go. "Bloody hell," he whispered, raking his fingers through his once-perfect hair and leaving it mussed.

No one had ever spoken to him that way outside the fighting ring in his entire life. Why did he find it so appealing coming from her? He was not . . . He had heard that some men liked to be bound and dominated by their lovers. There were whispers that a couple of high-ranking members of Parliament kept women specifically for that purpose. It had sounded ludicrous to him. He was not one of those men.

But her fire was something special. Instead of burning him, it warmed him deep down in a way that he had not words to explain. It soothed him. He wanted it. He wanted *her*.

A rustle of fabric behind him had him whirling to see a

woman in a rose-colored gown standing at the corner of the hedge, watching him. How much of that had she heard?

"Miss Violet."

"August can be strongheaded at times, Your Grace." Her voice was soft but firm, and she held his gaze as she stepped toward him. "I would apologize for her, but it seems you knew what you were getting into."

He liked her at least ten times more in that moment. There was a softness about her, but he now saw the strength he had not bothered to notice before. Her chin was held firm like her sister's, but her eyes held a mischievous spark.

"Indeed. There is no need for you to apologize. I admit I provoked her needlessly." He would have done almost anything to be singed by the fire burning in August.

Her lips tightened into a line as she seemed to accept that. Finding her courage, she opened her mouth, and her words came out in a rush. "Was it true?"

Dear God, she *had* heard the whole thing. Sweat broke out on his brow as he thought of a way to explain it to her. He did not believe the fighting would break the deal, but he had hoped to have a betrothal contract in place before confronting that.

"Do you really have hundreds of families depending on you?" she continued.

Stunned out of his internal debate, he stared at her and wondered how that would be the most important question on her mind if she had overheard their conversation. "Yes, many of them tenant farmers. We need to modernize with new equipment and techniques. Most are still using field labor. I hope to introduce stock raising." His voice trailed off as he realized he was explaining far more than necessary.

"That's why you need an heiress, then?" She cocked her head to the side and looked up at him through narrowed eyes. "It's not for yourself?" There was far more going on in that head of hers than she wanted people to think.

"Not *only* for myself." He would be a liar if he did not confess to being accustomed to the comfortable lifestyle he enjoyed. "I will benefit, of course, but if these families are to survive, we have a lot of work to do. Unfortunately, modernizing is expensive."

"And you can promise that? Will you put in writing exactly how you intend to utilize a dowry?"

He took in a sharp breath. Was she negotiating with him? Was she about to say yes to a question he had not even asked yet? A mild roar began in his ears. He should be damn near ecstatic. Instead, he glanced toward the drawing room door where Miss Crenshaw had disappeared. He did not want to bind himself to this girl. Not when he wanted her sister.

"Do you or do you not have a fiancé, Miss Violet?"

The corner of her mouth twisted in a rueful smile. "I do not, Your Grace. Not yet."

"Then why—"

"Good evening, Your Grace." Her voice was as soft as ever as she walked past him, following the same path her sister had taken moments earlier.

Set down by not one but two Crenshaw heiresses. It was damn near inconceivable. He would not have believed it had he not witnessed the entire debacle. He needed to sit down and absently felt his way across the gravel to a bench tucked against the house. His earlier inkling had been correct. He was mad. He wanted August more now than he had before. He should accept the younger one. She was everything a duchess should be, and by all appearances the match had nearly been made. And she was right. This should be about more than his personal preference. Families were depending on him to do right by them. His own father had neglected them for far too long. It was up to Evan to set things straight.

Still, everything in him resisted walking along like a lamb being led to slaughter. He wanted August. The need for her fire and honesty pounded through him with the persistent beat of fists against a sandbag.

He wanted August, and he would find a way to have her and save his estates.

Chapter 6

No man chooses evil because it is evil; he only mistakes it for happiness, the good he seeks.

MARY WOLLSTONECRAFT

Violet, you seem to have got on well with the duke." Their mother wasted no time in bringing him up once they were in the carriage. Their father was still settling himself in the seat beside her when she made the comment. Clearly, she had been champing at the bit to hear Violet's impression of him. Next to Violet, August gritted her teeth but managed to keep her thoughts about him to herself.

"He was . . . well, a gentleman," Violet offered mildly.

"I'd say he was every bit a gentleman as he was handsome." The carriage swayed as the driver took his seat. Light from the gas lamp outside shifted over Mother's face, revealing her shrewd grin and the calculation in her eyes as she watched Violet for her reaction. "I haven't seen a man so handsome since your father in his day."

August clenched her jaw harder. As if Rothschild's looks were the most important thing when they were talking about Violet's future.

"He is handsome," came her sister's unrevealing reply, but August felt her stiffen in the seat beside her.

Not satisfied that Violet was sufficiently enthusiastic, Mother glanced at August. "Even August will admit he's very handsome, won't you, dear?"

To be able to unclench her jaw, August was forced to tighten her hands into fists in her lap. "Of course he's handsome." The words tasted bitter, because she knew that Mother was really attempting to court her agreement in this travesty.

The admission earned her a bark of laughter from Papa. "Even *I* can admit he's handsome. Not much of an ogre, huh, August?"

The jab was meant to be lighthearted, but it stung with betrayal in a way she didn't understand. Rubbing the heel of her hand as if to soothe the invisible pain, she said, "People can be ogres in ways that do not include their looks."

"But he's the perfect gentleman," Mother said, her voice taking on a lilting tone.

"We still don't know anything about him." It seemed irresponsible that her parents did not care about that detail.

Mother scoffed. "What more is there to know?"

Papa, who sat across from August, reached over the short distance to fondly pat her knee. "August is right, Millie. She has a good head for business. I've taught her that no business deal should ever be entered into without reviewing it from all angles." To August, he said, "I have people investigating his assets and liabilities, of which there are many of the latter. The reports are as you'd expect. Debts from some bad investments his father made. Properties that need a good deal of refurbishment. The young man needs a significant influx of cash to address his debts, and he needs it fairly soon."

August took a breath as the tension started to drain from her, allowing her to sink into the plush upholstery. This was language she understood. At least one of her parents was thinking rationally. "And you are not at all concerned that giving him this influx will only lead to more debt eventually? More loss?"

"Oh, for heaven's sake, August, really," said Mother.

"How could *more* money lead to more debt? It doesn't work that way."

"Millie, now, she is right. When you have a business that's been floundering, and you suddenly pour in money, well, sometimes it goes right through whatever drain they've created." To August he said, "We're still looking, darling, but so far it doesn't seem that His Grace has been the problem. He inherited extraordinary debts. Once they are all paid off, the financial drain should close substantially."

That wasn't enough of a reassurance, and she leaned forward to say so. There would likely still be a hole, and whether it took a year or ten years for the money to drain away, Violet could be left penniless. "But there's the upkeep of all those estates. That could be an enormous sum alone for each of them. Will those estates draw in enough income to be profitable? Have you looked into his tenants? How many of them are able to pay their rents? How much of a deficit is he running annually? How can we be assured that Violet will control her own money?"

To her surprise, her father patted her knee and sat back against his seat. "I appreciate you being so concerned for your sister. We are still looking into his estates. I expect to have completed reports next week."

If he'd had a newspaper, she was quite certain he would have flicked it up between them and stuffed his nose inside it, effectively shutting her out. Her mother nodded as if all had been settled and smiled fondly at Violet across from her. She was probably imagining her in a wedding gown and thinking of her as the Duchess of Rothschild. Didn't either of them care about Violet's future beyond her wedding?

Violet met August's gaze in silent rage.

August knew that she had to tell them about the prizefight and damn the consequences to herself. They were both too enamored of him to think clearly. No, it wasn't even him they liked so much. They were seduced by his title and his position in this society. They knew nothing about who he was as a person. He had been charming enough, but he hadn't spared either Mother or Papa any more attention than he had given anyone else. Her parents had spent all of a few of hours in his company and were ready to hand over their daughter to him. She had to break their illusion of him, because this was about saving Violet.

"Has your investigation uncovered his prizefighting activities?" she asked.

The carriage was completely silent for all of five seconds while that sank in. Finally, Mother asked, "What are you talking about?"

Not quite as brave as she had thought, August hedged a bit. "I've heard that he fights for money. Bare-knuckle brawling, I believe it's called." Shifting in her seat, she ran her palms over the velvet upholstered bench. Violet touched her hand in silent support.

"Brawling?" Mother mimicked the word as if it were foreign and she didn't know what it meant. "But he's a duke, a gentleman, not a street person. Why would anyone invent such a terrible rumor?"

Papa seemed less affected. "It's a rumor," he said with a shrug.

"You've heard it!" August gasped, appalled that he would not have mentioned it to them before now.

"Yes, I've heard it. He belongs to a club . . . Montague, and they have fights there. Pugilism, they call it. Earlier this year I heard that Van Alen has taken up boxing." He sighed, and the newspaper would have come up again had he had it. Instead, he glanced out the window at the passing sites of Mayfair. "I have even been thinking of taking it up."

"You? Boxing?" Mother's laugh filled the night air.

"It's a perfectly acceptable activity. With all the hours I spend at my desk, I could do with some physical activity," said Papa, taking offense.

"Wait a moment. Do you mean James Van Alen?" Mother asked when she had stopped laughing. August wasn't surprised that she had caught on the name. "He's going to marry Emily Astor." The tone of her voice indicated that she might view the once-distasteful sport in an entirely new light if Van Alen had taken it up.

To Mother, Papa said, "Yes, that Van Alen." To August, he said, "Mind you, it's only a rumor I've heard about the duke, which is why I haven't repeated it." Turning back to face his wife, he asked, "And why, may I ask, is it laughable that I would want to take up a new sport? I *am* a sportsman. I enjoy a good hunt and the occasional fishing excursion."

Mother shook her head with an indulgent smile. "Griswold, the last time you went hunting was when Violet was still in knee-length skirts."

Papa guffawed. "That is not true. The last time I went was with George . . . When was that?" His gaze drifted to the ceiling of the carriage as if the answer could be found there.

August watched the entire exchange in disbelief and mild irritation. Sometimes talking to them when they were together was like wrangling young children. Was she the only one concerned with the potentially disastrous turn this could all take? Violet and her future children could be destitute, and all they cared about was how fashionable boxing was at the moment. "What do boxing or Mr. Van Alen have to do with anything?"

In response to the frustration in her voice, Violet reached over and placed a supportive hand on her arm. Even that annoyed her. How could Violet be so calm when they were discussing her entire future like it was a sport? Why was she the only one in this family who managed to see the destruction that almost assuredly awaited her sister?

Both her parents looked at her as if she had taken leave of her senses. August forced herself to inhale a steadying breath. It wouldn't do to have them accuse her of hysterics when she was making perfectly rational arguments.

"I only mean to say that boxing is not the sport in question. The Duke of Rothschild is a bare-knuckle prizefighter. He fights for money in Whitechapel. I don't know how often or to what extent, but he is known as the Hellion, and he associates with questionable characters."

Papa frowned and was silent as the carriage rocked with the final turn that put them onto their street. "That isn't the rumor I heard. Boxing or bare-knuckle"—he gave a wave of his hand as if the difference were negligible—"he fights at his club. A fair number of young men are taking it up. The other day someone mentioned French footfighting. Have you heard of that? It has another name that escapes me at the moment."

August stifled a sigh of frustration. "I'll concede that perhaps some of these events take place at his club. However, he also fights in Whitechapel. These are public fights with dangerous men." A shiver ran down her spine every time she thought of Wilkes. His eyes had been cold and dead and almost as vicious as those spikes on his shoes.

"How do you know this to be true, August? As your father said, it's only rumor, and obviously one only you have heard. It cannot be true. He likely only fights at his club as Papa believes. He is a duke." She said the last as if that were all the reason she needed to disbelieve it.

August knew then that she absolutely had to tell them the complete truth. Bracing herself by gripping the edge of her seat, she said, "I know because I was there at the fight. I don't want to get into specifics, but I saw him with my own eyes."

The carriage fell silent as they came to a stop. The groom opened the door, but her father held up a hand, and it discreetly clicked shut again.

"You were at a fight in Whitechapel? When was this, August?" Papa's voice had taken on the cold tone she had only heard in the most demanding business meetings.

"I cannot say."

"How do you know it was the duke?" he asked.

"His hair was darker, but it was him. I know it was him."

"Did he admit this to you?"

"No, of course not." She hadn't expected him to admit it, and he hadn't. However, he hadn't seemed particularly concerned that she might expose him, which was galling to no end.

Papa let out a long breath. "Then you might have been mistaken."

Her shoulders stiffened, and she found herself sitting straighter. "I am *not* mistaken. It was him."

"The bigger issue here is that you were in Whitechapel. How did this happen?"

She opened her mouth to explain about Camille, but she no longer trusted her parents to understand. What would stop her father from running off to tell Hereford? She could only imagine the sort of punishment the man might mete out to Camille. When once she had told her father everything, she found herself unwilling to discuss this with him. "I cannot say. I can only tell you that I was there with a friend."

Her father pursed his lips as he often did when discussing a disagreeable subject and opened the door himself. The groom came forward to hold it as Papa reached back to help Mother disembark. Together they marched up the steps to their rented townhome, leaving the groom to assist her and then Violet. Anxiety knotted August's belly as she followed them inside.

Papa's strong steps could be heard ascending the stairs, but their mother stood in the entry of the front parlor, where she was handing off her gloves and hat to a waiting maid. "August, Violet, come and attend me a moment."

They both followed without pausing to take off their outerwear. Violet kept her composure; the only clue to her anger was the stiffness of her shoulders.

"This will take but a moment. I wanted you both to know that it has been brought to my attention that we are in need of a chaperone." She raised a hand when August opened her mouth to object. "This is not because of your shocking revelation, though it does prove that there is a need."

August crossed her arms over her chest and decided not to point out that a chaperone would not have stopped her from sneaking out of the house alone at night.

"Lady Ashcroft has been such a dear in helping us acclimate here. She helpfully suggested that young ladies of quality do not take walks to the park or the shops without a chaperone, and your father and I aren't always available to go with you."

Now August could not stay silent on the matter. "But that's ridiculous, Mother. I am twenty-three years old, and I have managed my walks in the park just fine all these years on my own."

"Of course you have, dear, but we are in London now. They do things differently here. When in Rome, as they say."

At home she had frequently dashed out to the dressmaker's or milliner's without anyone accompanying her. August could not help but feel that London was quickly becoming nothing but a great gilded cage from which she couldn't escape. Would they actively try to pawn her off on a husband as well?

"I really do think this is unnecessary, Mother." Violet finally spoke.

"We are heading into the high point of the Season, and there will likely be scheduling conflicts. Since I am certain you and August will not bother yourselves to wait for one of us to be available, this step is necessary. Besides, I am under the impression that the contacts of the women I have in mind will be as beneficial as the actual duties the woman will provide. To that end, I have a list of names of perfectly respectable ladies ready to offer their services. We can go over them in the morning." With a gentle smile, she stepped forward and kissed them both on the cheek, but she gave August a look she knew all too well. It always came with a gentle shake of her head, and it meant—Why can't you be like your sister? Why can't you be different?

August shifted under the familiar weight of the look, feeling exactly as she had as a gangly fourteen-year-old more interested in her father's ledgers than her mother's fashion plates. She had no answers for those questions. Giving August's hand a gentle squeeze, Mother told them both good night and left.

All of the strength seemed to leave August's legs, and she sank down onto the sofa. Violet sank down beside her, and this time she was the one offering support. Violet's reassuring presence was so calming and antithetical to her own state of mind that it was almost abrasive. When she spoke, August's words were harsher than she intended. "Why are you not more upset about this? You met him. Do you really want to marry him?"

"No, I do not want to marry him, and I don't intend to," Violet said calmly.

"Then how do you plan to stop it? You can see they're not being reasonable."

Violet raised a brow and shook her head as if August were the difficult one. "They're not reasonable people. You can't make rational arguments with them and get anywhere. You of all people should know that by now. You heard them in the carriage."

There was sound logic in Violet's words, and it only served to further depress August's mood. "Yes. I don't think they can be swayed. Then what do you plan?"

Violet shrugged, and worry creased her brow. "I don't know yet, but I do know that only I will be charged with speaking vows to him, and if I don't do it, then there can be no marriage."

The first genuine smile of the night curved August's lips. Violet was difficult to rile, but once it happened, she was the most stubborn person August knew. "So that's it? You'll simply stand there and refuse to repeat your vows?" She could already see it now. Mother would be livid, and Papa would offer her a pony to say them. The scene had her letting out a small laugh.

Violet didn't seem as amused. "I hope to stop it before it goes that far. I telegrammed both Max and Teddy but haven't heard back yet. Do you think they're holding on to the response?"

"I didn't even think of that possibility. "August groaned and leaned to the side until her head rested on the back of the sofa, but then she sat back up almost immediately. "I haven't tried reaching Maxwell yet. I naively—and absurdly, it seems—believed that we could get past this ourselves. I'll also send him one in the morning. Perhaps if he contacts Papa, he can set things to rights again. If not, then perhaps he can come to London, and we have to simply hold off a wedding until he can get here." But just in case, she would come up with some other way to dissuade the duke. She had no idea how yet, but there was still time.

They were both silent as the enormity of the situation settled over them. After a moment, Violet spoke as she pulled off her gloves, revealing the near-constant ink stains that marred her fingers. "I overheard you and the duke in the garden."

That explained Violet's silence in the carriage. August wracked her brain to remember if she had mentioned the kiss aloud. How awkward it would be if the man she had properly kissed turned out to be her sister's fiancé.

"What happened between you . . . at the fight?"

"I fell and landed near the roped-off section where they were brawling. He caught me before I could hit the ground, thankfully."

Violet watched her with knowing eyes. Sometimes she saw far too much. "And then?" she prodded when August fell silent.

Unable and unwilling to lie to her sister, August said, "We kissed. It was very brief, I assure you, and not an experience I plan to repeat." She fell silent as she waited for Violet's judgment.

Her sister fell silent, as well, and she got that pensive look she would sometimes get. August could never figure out if it was disappointment or some other sign of distress, so she babbled to fill the silence. "I am sorry. I swear to you that I had no idea who he was. It happened so fast that I barely had time to think about it."

"August, you have no need to apologize. I don't want him. I only . . ." A crease formed between her brows, and she stared at August as if she were the older one and August the younger. "You've never been so reckless. I know you've kissed men at a dance or dinner, but never a stranger."

All of those thoughts had tumbled over and over in August's mind ever since that night. It was why she had tried so hard to make herself forget him, and she'd come close to succeeding. Oh, she had relived the pleasure of the kiss more than she wanted to admit, but guilt had always followed. He could have been anyone that night. Married. The leader of a street gang.

A duke.

"I don't know how it happened." She glanced down at her hands folded in her lap, because she could not meet her sister's questioning gaze. "I still can't explain why I did it. He asked me to and so I did." It sounded inane and impulsive, which was so unlike her.

But when she looked up, the hint of a smile curved Violet's lips. "And you liked it."

It wasn't a question. Apparently, it was obvious. She had kissed the duke and had liked it. What was happening to her?

"A little." August stood, preferring not to dwell on that. "It hardly matters. I'm allowed to take leave of my senses every now and then, aren't I?"

"Of course," said Violet, but humor lurked in the depths of her eyes.

"So you don't hate me? Even if you end up engaged to him?"

"I don't hate you, and I will not end up engaged to him."

"Good. Then I'm going to go to bed. It's been an exhausting evening, and I need to telegram Max in the morning."

"I suppose we'll find out if the duke approves of our family soon," said Violet, standing. "Mother says it's likely he'll make his intentions known at Camille's ball."

Bother! It was as if this plan was moving forward at the pace of a runaway train, and she was powerless to stop it. Since it was obvious her parents were not going to see reason, she had to get busy coming up with ways to make the duke see that marrying into their family would be a poor decision.

Evan settled himself against the plush interior of the Rothschild carriage and stretched out his legs as much as he could. As far as evenings went, dinner at the Ashcrofts' had not been terrible.

His mother sat next to him and waited for the carriage to lurch smoothly forward before she gave him a brief glance. "Well, what did you think of Violet?"

"She was lovely. She'll make an excellent duchess."

Mother let out an audible sigh of relief. "Yes, I believe she will. She has a bit to learn, being American, but she seems bright and mild mannered. Both virtues will do her well."

But she was not who he wanted. It was entirely likely that August would not settle into the role of duchess nearly so easily, but she would suit the role of his wife. He waited a heartbeat as the enormity of that thought washed over him. His wife. August Crenshaw would be his wife.

He turned the thought over in his mind like a new frock coat. Running his palms along the hemming to check for rough edges, smoothing out the lapels, and savoring the rich feel of the fabric before trying it on for comfort. It was snug like all new things could be before they became supple with time and familiarity, but the fit was good. Yes, this could work.

He waited the space of two heartbeats before he said, "I want August Crenshaw, not her younger sister."

The steady clip-clop of the horses emphasized the silence that had fallen. His mother was a quiet person, rather like the younger Miss Crenshaw. He was not at all certain how she would take having the elder Miss Crenshaw for a daughter-in-law. He wanted August regardless, but he also hoped his mother could find peace with his choice.

She finally turned to him. "Do you have any idea what you'll be facing with her? She's not the least bit biddable or conventional." Despite her words, her voice was gentle.

He smiled as he remembered the bold way August had approached him in the drawing room. Then again in the garden. Then his thoughts went further back to the kiss. "Yes, I know. That's rather why I like her."

His mother stared at him for so long that he was taken aback and uncertain of her thoughts. It had never occurred to him that she would say no. Hadn't he agreed to this scheme of hers and Clark? The final choice of his own wife should be his.

"You oppose August? Is that why you chose Violet instead of her even though she's the eldest?"

"Mrs. Crenshaw made the choice. She seemed to think that Violet would make a more suitable wife, and I had no reason to disagree. Everyone knows the elder one is a bluestocking."

"And bluestockings make terrible wives?"

"No." She sighed and raised a hand to place it against his cheek, much like she had done when he had been a child. "You never wanted to take the path laid out for you." She smiled and gave his face a pat before lowering her hand back to her lap. "She is more spirited and stronger willed, but it is your choice, dear boy. I would welcome either of them as long as they can help us out of this tangle you inherited."

He frowned at the reminder that they were not in the clear yet. When the carriage turned at Curzon Street and stopped before Sterling House, he disembarked to help her out but climbed back inside.

She turned on the pavement and raised a brow at him. "This is your home, Evan. Your suite is ready and waiting for you."

He shook his head, still not ready to live in the house he considered his father's domain. He kept rooms at Montague Club. With only a few precious weeks of freedom left, he intended to embrace them. "Thank you, but no. I've promised to meet up with friends."

The evening had been a full day of honest work as far as he was concerned. Now that they were one step closer to restoring the dignity of the title, he planned to go celebrate.

Chapter 7

> *Remember, all men would be tyrants if they could.*
>
> ABIGAIL ADAMS

To: Maxwell Crenshaw, Crenshaw Iron Works, New York, NY

Papa is determined Violet will marry a peer STOP She is distraught STOP Please intervene STOP Letter to follow STOP

From: Miss August Crenshaw

To: Miss August Crenshaw, 12 Upper Grosvenor St., London

Appalling STOP Have demanded explanation STOP I look forward to your letter STOP

From: Maxwell Crenshaw

August stepped into the foyer of Hereford's townhome and was nearly overrun by a maid carrying an arrangement of lilies larger than she was. The poor girl wobbled and might very well have fallen over from the impact if the housekeeper had not swooped in behind her and steadied her.

"Apologies, miss." The voice came from somewhere behind the lilies, and the girl tried to bob a quick curtsy, but the movement sent her wobbling again.

"No harm done," said August as she took in the chaos around her.

The housekeeper shooed the maid away along with a trio of others who came trailing out of the front parlor, each of them bearing identical arrangements as they marched up the curved staircase. The ball was tomorrow night, so August had no doubt they were bound for the ballroom. The footman who had accompanied them to the fight, Henry, stood at the curve in the staircase tying garland to the banister, while another directed him in the proper draping from below. He had looked up when she first entered but now pretended absorption in his task.

"Well, everything looks marvelous," August said to absolutely no one.

The butler appeared justifiably put out by her arrival in the midst of such chaos, while her chaperone—the Honorable Mrs. Harold Barnes—shook her head at the madness.

"Her Grace is expecting you." Keeping his nose well in the air, the butler began to lead them to the drawing room, but a voice from above stopped him.

"August! August, is that you?" Camille appeared at the first-floor landing, her face alight with happiness. Upon seeing August, she hurried down the stairs far too quickly to be considered proper for a duchess.

Mrs. Barnes sniffed in disapproval, but August hurried over to meet her friend at the bottom step. Camille had all but disappeared since the Ashcroft dinner, and that had been days ago. "I came as soon as I received your note. I hope I'm not interrupting."

Camille took her hands once she reached the bottom and said, "Of course you're not. I am so glad you're here."

It was only now that Camille was close that August could see that her friend's eyes were almost unnaturally bright, and her grip was hard. Desperate. Her gaze was so fixed on August that she had yet to even acknowledge Mrs. Barnes. "Camille, are—?"

The question was destined to go unasked as another voice screeched, "Lilies? Who ordered lilies? I specifically requested roses!"

Footsteps warned of an approach seconds before two women appeared at the landing. August immediately recognized Lady Russell, Hereford's sister, and her friend Lady Fawly. She had met them both at dinner her first week in London and had found them very similar in disposition to Hereford. Self-important and vaguely condescending.

"Miss Crenshaw. I did not hear your arrival," said Lady Russell, her lips pursed in disapproval.

"I invited her for tea." Camille took her arm and practically dragged her toward the drawing room, calling over her shoulder, "And it was I who ordered the lilies. Roses are so overdone, don't you think?"

A silence colder than the bitterest New York winter descended from the upper floor. August tried to ignore it, but the glacial stillness followed them into the depths of the house. She felt that she should call out a greeting, but it seemed disloyal to Camille, so she kept quiet and let her friend lead her away.

Camille was all smiles again as she opened the door to her private drawing room. The tea service was already set up near the sofa and matching chair. "Mrs. Barnes, I presume?" Camille asked as the woman followed August into the room.

In the chaos, August realized that she had forgotten to properly introduce them. "My apologies. This is Mrs. Barnes. Mrs. Barnes, please forgive my error. Her Grace, the Duchess of Hereford."

After pleasantries were exchanged, Camille went to close the door. However, the butler stood there in the opening and gently pushed it back so that she was forced to let go. "His Grace prefers the door open."

Camille stiffened, her shoulders held firm. Instead of saying a word to him, she addressed Mrs. Barnes. "Would you care for tea?"

August only barely kept her jaw from dropping open at the impertinence of the servant. To be fair, he had been courteous, but she could not imagine any of her own servants in New York or London contradicting her wishes so openly.

"Thank you, Your Grace, but if you do not mind, I shall set myself up over here by the window." She indicated the carpetbag she carried, which held her knitting. As chaperones went, August had to admit Mrs. Barnes wasn't intolerable. She typically kept out of the way.

The butler's footfalls could be heard retreating as she settled herself. Camille took a seat on the sofa beside August and served them both tea. August stole glances at her friend's face, but it was impassive as she focused on the task. Shifting in her seat, she noted the accompanying tray was practically bare, holding only a scone for each of them with the tiniest pots of clotted cream and jam she had ever seen. The room itself was comfortable enough, done in what was once a tasteful lemon and gold scheme, but the colors had faded until they were nearly indistinguishable from the other. The front rooms with their fresh wallpaper and new furnishings were ostentatious by comparison. Evidence of the fortune Hereford had needed to restore his estates.

An awkward silence heavy with all the things they longed to say but couldn't in the presence of others filled the space between them. It was only broken by the clacking of knitting needles and the clink of the cups against their saucers.

"I am sorry your mother and Violet were unable to come."

August tried to ferret out Camille's mood, but she kept her gaze focused on the china. "They send their regrets. Mother insisted on yet another fitting for Violet. Despite the fact that all of our ball gowns are new, she wanted to make absolutely certain the gown was perfect for tomorrow night."

"And how is Violet feeling about . . ." Camille glanced at Mrs. Barnes, who appeared happily absorbed in her task. It seemed she was making a scarf with the questionable color choices of an alternating pattern of brown, mustard yellow, and puce. Lowering her voice, she continued. "You know-who and the likely proposal?" She mouthed the last word.

"As you would expect. She has vowed to not go through with it."

"And your parents?"

"Still praising him as if he is a saint." August took a sip of her tea so that she would have something else to focus on besides Rothschild.

It wasn't easy. The man had hardly left her thoughts since the dinner party. He had been rude, sarcastic, and utterly arrogant. Mother kept going on about his looks and titles, as if those alone could make up for so little else to recommend him. Yes, the man had an acceptable bone structure and lips that promised kissing him wouldn't be the worst part of a girl's day. And, yes, she could admit that when his gaze focused on her it made her feel . . . something. However, she was also intelligent enough to know that it was the practiced look of a libertine and meant entirely nothing.

"I've asked Papa to share the reports he's gathered on the d—" A quick glance at Mrs. Barnes assured her that the needles were still going at full steam. While rumors were already flying since the dinner, there would be no use feeding the rumor mill until things were publicly known. "The information about the gentleman in question, and he has agreed to share it with me, but so far he's found countless reasons to put it off. I currently have a pile of reports on my desk related to a factory in York. I'm to read them all and write up a recommendation on whether to purchase it or not, and then we will discuss"—another glance at Mrs. Barnes—"the other situation."

Setting her cup down with a slightly harsher rattle than intended, August asked in a low voice, "Can we not have a discussion without a chaperone? Or at least with the door closed?" As if awaiting the cue, a crash sounded from the front entryway as what sounded like a ladder toppled over.

"I am sorry." Camille's face fell seconds before she covered it with her hands. "I should not have asked you over with the preparations under way."

August scooted closer to her friend and took her in her arms. "Nonsense, I'm not upset about the noise, merely the lack of privacy." Through it all, the click-clack of the needles could be heard from the direction of the window. "How have you been? It's been days since we've talked. Have you been too busy with the ball, or is it something else?"

"It's Hereford," Camille whispered. "He found out about our outing, and he's livid."

August's face went cold, and the numbness crept down her body, where it settled in her belly, drawing forth a ball of dread that settled as heavy as iron. "Please forgive me, Camille." Keeping her voice to a whisper, she took her friend's hands. "It's my fault. I told Papa about that night. I had to admit that I went with a friend, but he must have assumed it was you. I'm so terribly sorry."

"Why, August?" Twin spots of color appeared in Camille's cheeks.

Papa's betrayal stung more than she could face right now. There had been a time not so long ago when Papa would have listened to her and taken her side in the scheme. Why had he hurried off to Hereford like a schoolboy running off to tattle to the headmaster? "I had to tell him because . . ." The knitting needles continued their clacking, but she lowered her voice even more just to be certain. "Do you remember the fighter from that night?"

Engrossed in the tale, Camille seemed to have forgotten her anger and leaned in closer. "You mean the one you—" She placed the pad of her forefinger against her lips in place of the word *kissed*. August's cheeks flamed—if only she could forget that had happened—and Camille grinned. "I remember him."

"Well, he is none other than the gentleman in question."

"No!" Mrs. Barnes jolted at Camille's screech and gave them both a sharp look. Sobering from her shock, Camille whispered, "That's impossible."

"I assure you it's not. I confronted him with it in the garden, and he all but admitted it. Same cheekbones, same nose and eyes." *Same lips.* "Same height. Think about it, Camille. Only his hair was darker, and that could easily be a cheap dye, and the growth of beard, which a shave can fix. If you noticed, the gentleman had nicks on his forehead and his knuckles."

"I confess I did not examine him that closely." Although she raised a brow and commenced studying August very closely. "Why were you?"

August shifted under the scrutiny, fearing that her corset must have been laced too tightly after all. She kept feeling hot, and there didn't seem to be enough air in the room. "I wasn't . . . I didn't . . . They were fairly obvious, I thought."

"Not to me. And why would he participate in such a dangerous activity?"

"For coin, of course. He's willing to marry a stranger for it. Why not fight for it, too?"

Camille raised her hands. "Because it's absurd and he's a d—well, you know what he is."

"It's true. I saw him and I know that it was him."

Camille smiled again as belief made her eyes widen. "Oh my, that's remarkable. I never would have caught on. Do your parents believe you?"

"No, it hasn't stopped their plotting at all."

Nodding in understanding, Camille said, "I think the prospect of someone of his stature in the family is enough to make them disbelieve anything they don't want to acknowledge."

That was an understatement. "Agreed, but we've gone off track. Please understand that the only reason I said anything was because I hoped that it would save Violet. I kept your name out of it, naively assuming that the omission alone would keep you safe. I'm sorry."

Camille nodded. "I understand. I would have done the same. The last thing I want is for Violet to suffer a similar fate to me." Just like that, the spark of intrigue was gone from her eyes to be replaced by sadness.

Guilt tore at August's heart. "Has he punished you? Has he harmed you?"

"He hasn't hurt me, but yes to the punishment. I am not allowed to go anywhere, nor am I allowed an ounce of privacy. I cannot be alone with anyone. Doors must always stand open, and my meals are served to me in my room. I am married and a duchess at that, but I might as well be a child who has displeased her father."

Anger burned a fiery path through August, but she swallowed down the bitterness that rose in her throat. Her anger, no matter how justified, wouldn't help Camille, and it might only make her feel worse. "I am so sorry for my part in that."

"No, please don't. He would have discovered eventually. It was not the first outing or the first punishment. Besides." She flashed a smile that didn't reach her eyes. "His sister is always here, and she falsely believes that planning for the annual ball is still her domain. If I were not here constantly, then I couldn't prove her wrong."

A not-so-discreet cough from the open door caught their attention. The butler stood there with vague contempt on his face. August glanced at the clock on the mantel and confirmed that precisely fifteen minutes had passed. Apparently, it was the only amount of time allotted to Camille for a social visit. August would have complained, but she supposed she was lucky that Hereford allowed her to visit.

"I should be going," she rushed to say when an embarrassed flush rose in Camille's face. "I have a lot of reading ahead of me."

They both rose, and Camille followed her out with Mrs. Barnes on their heels.

"Please say that you are coming to the ball?" asked Camille.

"Yes, of course." She wouldn't miss it now if for no other reason than to see her friend again. "Can you confirm that the gentleman in question is due to attend?"

Camille smiled. "Confirmed, yes."

"Good, I will endeavor to keep him far away from Violet."

Her friend laughed, as August had intended, and said, "Then the entertainment is sorted. I'll turn my attention to the decorations."

Chapter 8

❦

*Action may not always be happiness; but
there is no happiness without action.*
BENJAMIN DISRAELI

Evan smoothed down the lapels of his tailcoat and
checked the length of his sleeve again. Both were fine.
Stewart was an excellent valet who would have thrown
himself bodily across the threshold before allowing Evan
to leave without every stitch of clothing in place. Knowing
that, however, did not stop him from checking his bow tie
in the gilt-framed mirror they passed. Perfectly straight as
expected, but the silk felt as if it was about to choke the life
out of him. Perhaps sharing that he would be selecting a
bride tonight had pushed Stewart toward fastidiousness that
bordered on desperation.

"You are fidgety tonight, as if it were your first ball."
Christian Halston, Earl of Leigh, gave him a cold once-over
with a raised brow before turning his attention to the couples twirling on the dance floor below them. They stood
along the gallery above the open room, where Evan had
hoped to catch a glimpse of his intended bride before approaching her.

"No, but this *is* my first bride." When his finger slid easily between his collar and throat, Evan was forced to admit the tailoring of his suit was not the problem. It was the woman dancing somewhere below.

Taking one last look at his bow tie, he turned to try to find her. It did not take long for his eyes to make their way to the golden-clad woman dancing a quadrille with several couples around her. She moved gracefully and with confidence, an easy smile on her face. A tasteful collar of diamonds set in gold glittered at her throat, with a matching bracelet encircling her gloved wrist. She dressed with the extravagance of a seasoned duchess, not the demure pearls and semiprecious stones of a young, unmarried woman. But that was to be expected when her family was wealthier than most peers.

Her partner, a young viscount who was heir to an earldom, was no match for her. His movements were practiced and lacked her natural grace, and he kept stealing glances at her as if he were saving them up for later. Finally, he leaned over and said something near her ear that made her laugh. A polite laugh that lacked enthusiasm, Evan noted with satisfaction. Nevertheless, the melody of that sound reached him through the music of the orchestra and the din of the crowd. Surprised to find that he wanted her laughter for himself, his hands tightened on the balustrade as she leaned in and replied, making the man lose his rhythm as he joined in her laughter.

"Where is she?" Leigh's straightforward voice broke through his jealous stupor.

"She's there. Dancing with Atherton." The gold fabric fell artfully off her shoulders and dropped to a low bodice that emphasized her narrow waist before draping elegantly in folds that cascaded like liquid waves down to the floor. The gown was almost definitely a Worth original. The cost of one of those alone could keep Charrington Manor afloat for several months.

That was the goal and what he should be focusing on. And while the thought was there, lurking in the dark and decidedly mercenary recesses of his mind, it had been shoved to the side by a much more pressing and visceral consideration. He wanted *her*. He wanted her laughter, her sharp tongue, her quick mind, but even more urgently, he wanted to strip the gown from her body and feast on the lush curves hidden beneath. And to find all the places the honey tones of her skin turned to cream.

"The one in gold?" Leigh interrupted his thoughts again as he brought himself closer to balustrade to peer down at her. "But that is not the young Miss Crenshaw."

"No, it is her older sister. She's the one I have decided to take as my bride."

"Ah, well, lucky for you she is not mannish at all, despite what they say."

"Mannish?" It was likely the only word that would have removed his attention from the woman and put it on Leigh.

Leigh shrugged and continued to stare at her. If he'd had opera glasses, he probably would have used them. "She sits in business meetings with her father, she reads financials in the *Times*, and she belongs to one of those women's clubs in New York. They call the younger one the pretty one and the elder one the . . . well, the mannish one." His sharp gaze turned on Evan. "Surely, you have heard this?"

Evan had not heard that. "No, but I am hardly surprised. Our group never handles differences well, do they?" He regretted the words as soon as he had said them. Leigh knew better than anyone how flaws were not tolerated among most.

Leigh gave no indication that the words had bothered him. "I confess, it never occurred to me to not imagine her with a square jaw in need of a shave."

"But you saw her at the ballet."

"Did I?" Leigh looked up toward one of the two chandeliers hanging above as he searched his memory. "I only remember the younger one at the ballet. Are you certain the elder Miss Crenshaw was there?"

"Yes. It is how I recognized her at the fight."

"Ah yes, she *was* at your fight. I thought she was familiar." Sardonic humor was evident in Leigh's tone. "Does she know that it was you she kissed?"

"She does."

"And what does she think of that?"

"I believe she has tried to forget it happened." Evan smiled. Despite the way he dreaded a forced marriage, he was quite looking forward to sparring with her again.

She whirled one last time to the fading notes of the song, smiling up at her partner. He dearly hoped she was not getting too fond of the boy. Something along the balcony caught her attention, drawing her gaze up, and their eyes met. The smile faded from her lips. Even across the great distance between them, an awareness of her pulled at him.

She glanced away but looked back just as quickly. There was no doubt in his mind that she felt the attraction between them as well. After tonight she would be his and everyone would know it. There was a satisfaction in that he had not felt in a very long time. It was even better than brawling an opponent into submission. As he watched, she raised her chin and intentionally gave him her back as she allowed Atherton to lead her into the crowd until they both disappeared.

Having watched the exchange, Leigh gave a soft grunt that was as close to a laugh as Evan had ever heard from him. "I am glad now that I decided to come along with you. I will have a front-row seat to the moment when you make your intentions known. Should be interesting."

Interesting was one way to view it. Evan half expected to come away with his eyes scratched out.

"She seems to have a mind of her own," said Leigh. "How do you intend to gain her cooperation in this marriage?"

"I am not certain her parents will give her much of a choice. In time, she will come to understand that I will hardly make the worst husband."

"That leaves much to chance. What if she decides on the young viscount there?"

"Her parents prefer a duke." Evan had seen their eyes glaze over in pleasure when he was introduced to them. He knew the type enough to understand that it was his title they were after. A mere viscount would not do when one was in search of a duke.

"Sterling." Leigh and his brother were the only ones who still called him that. Leigh had been two years ahead of him at Eton, and despite the lame leg that had him using a cane, he had managed to wrangle control as head student of his class. Much of that was to do with the tone he was using now. "Do you remember the first rule I taught you in fighting? Never, under any circumstances, underestimate your opponent. That includes women, perhaps especially women. You cannot leave this up to her. We already know she has an independent streak. She ostensibly snuck out to attend the fight, so she is not above a bit of impulsiveness. If you do not take control, then she could very well find someone else ready to snatch her out from under you."

The heat of suppressed anger prickled through Evan's chest, swelling it with ire at the very idea of someone taking her from him. "What would you have me do? Abduct her?"

"That's one way to handle things. However, the logistics would likely get in your way. Without a special license, you would need to get her across the border and married as soon as possible, and you do not have an estate in Scotland to satisfy the residency requirement."

The stillness of his features suggested he was entirely serious. Stunned, Evan said, "I see you have given this a disturbing amount of thought. I was jesting."

Leigh shrugged. "I like to win, so I consider all angles. Have you considered ruin?"

"She does not care a whit for her reputation."

"Be that as it may, her father is trying to secure some fairly major deals while in London. Having a daughter with a scandalous reputation would not help him, nor would it help her younger, unmarried sister. We all break to pressure at some point. The question is, where is Miss Crenshaw's breaking point?"

"I do not care for the idea of ruining her." He did, however, like the idea of kissing her. Of having the time alone with her to properly explore her, having her open beneath him, all soft and warm. Perhaps a gentle reminder of the passion that flared between them would be enough to convince her.

"Sometimes I wonder why you and I are friends. You're not nearly ruthless enough in your ambition," Leigh said in a wry tone.

"That is because you are ruthless enough for both of us." Giving his friend a grin, Evan made his way to the couple below, ready to claim his bride.

August had known to expect Rothschild at the ball, but the reality of seeing him again was far different than what she had imagined. She had anticipated she would feel self-righteous anger and a renewed commitment to keep her sister safe from him. And both of those were there. Yet, as much as she wanted to, she could not deny the fluttery anticipation in her belly when she had met his gaze.

She hated to admit it, but it was because she was as attracted to his looks as any other woman. Perhaps it was because she had seen him as the Hellion, before knowing him as the duke who meant to take Violet from them. Despite their argument in the garden, there had been a tiny seed of a spark even then. How unlucky that the one man she found more appealing than all others was the one man she most despised. August had once thought herself above such base emotions, but it appeared that she was not. Not one of the men back home whom she had kissed had managed to rouse her interest half so well.

Damnation!

Lady Helena March waited for her with two glasses of champagne in hand. August had met the young widow at a small dinner party her first week in London where they had bonded over their mutual love of sweets and their distaste for small talk. Ever since, they managed to seek each other out when they attended the same events. The sight of a friendly face—no matter how recently the friend had been made—in the midst of her turmoil was enough to make her knees weak with relief. Thanking Lord Atherton for the dance, she sank down onto the edge of a chair. Her gown was not made for sitting and pulled across the bodice. To be fair, it was not made for much other than standing and the occasional dancing. The silk fabric was temperamental and prone to wrinkling, but August couldn't bring herself to care about that at the moment. Now was the time to get her thoughts in order, because Rothschild's expression had left no doubt that he had come prepared to do battle and win.

"Where is Violet?"

"Your mother intercepted her on the dance floor with the intention of introducing her to Lord and Lady Hampford." Lady Helena sank into the chair beside her and pressed a coupe of champagne into her hand. "I have danced with Lord Atherton enough to know that look on your face. Here, you need this."

August smiled as she brought the glass to her lips and drank deeply, hoping to settle her nerves. "It's not Lord Atherton. He was perfectly charming."

Lady Helena tilted her elegant blond head and pursed her lips thoughtfully. "As a child, he once coaxed me into the woodshed with the promise of a nest of baby rabbits, only to pull a lizard from his pocket, toss it on me, and run away. *Charming* is not a word I would use to describe him."

August laughed. Despite the fact that Lady Helena was the daughter of an earl, she had an easygoing manner about her and was always ready with a smile and a jest. Older than the debutantes surrounding them, August found her to be charming, intelligent, and generous.

"How horrible of him. I'll remember to take him to task on the matter the next time we dance."

"No need. The trick was on him. I happen to like lizards and took the poor, frightened thing home where he lived out the rest of his days in peace." Lady Helena's eyes softened in concern as she asked, "If not Lord Atherton, what has you looking so pale?"

"The duke has arrived."

There was no need to explain which one. After the Ashcroft dinner party, everyone seemed to know that he was interested in acquiring one of the "Crenshaw heiresses," as they had been named. *Acquiring* one of them. It was the exact phrase August had heard an elderly lord use in reference to the situation. As if they were objects or exotic oddities to collect and admire on a shelf. The temporary good humor Lady Helena had roused in her vanished as anger roiled in to replace it.

Her friend nodded in understanding, her expression turning grave. "He rarely attends these sorts of events. Since he is here, I expect he has come to make his intentions known."

It wasn't a question, but August nodded just the same. "That is what Mother and Camille believed would happen tonight."

"Being seen dancing with your sister would cause quite an uproar, especially if he does not dance with another partner. Everyone will know that he has chosen her."

"Yes, that's what Mother believes."

Lady Helena chewed gently on her bottom lip, looking uncomfortable and as if she had more to say on the matter.

"Is there more? There's more. Please tell me. You've been such a help to me with customs and manners; please don't mince words now." It was true. Lady Helena's subtle advice and cues had saved August making a social gaffe more than once.

Leaning toward her, Lady Helena said, "Forgive me if I am overstepping, but it seems that your sister does not welcome this particular match." She waited for August to nod in confirmation before continuing. "Then am I correct in assuming that she would intend to turn down an offer should one be made?"

August nodded again. "Perhaps." She was genuinely frightened that somehow Mother and Papa would figure out a way to goad Violet into accepting. She did not like to believe it would go that far, but it was not out of the question. The carriage ride home after the dinner party had revealed as much. And then what? The only man she had ever desired in a physical sense would become her brother-in-law? They would be expected to carry on as if nothing had happened? The very idea of it had her feeling nauseous and unsettled, as if her skin was being pulled too tight. How would it feel to know that ultimately he had chosen her sister?

"If the duke were to dance exclusively with her and a

betrothal announcement were not forthcoming, then many would view that negatively." The other woman's voice pulled her out of those dark thoughts. "Unfortunately, Miss Violet would bear the brunt of their speculations, no matter if she was the one to turn him down."

"Oh dear." August understood exactly what she meant. It would not be as terrible as a broken engagement, but people would wonder, and Violet would become fodder for gossip. August rose to her feet, scanning the crowd for some sight of her sister. While she was certain the family could weather any sort of scandal that would arise from the nonengagement, it would be best to avoid that situation entirely. "Please excuse me. I have to find Violet and try to intervene." If she could only somehow help Violet avoid Rothschild, then the whole thing could simply go away, at least for one night.

"Of course. Please let me know if I can be of assistance. I have thwarted my share of would-be grooms." Lady Helena took the coupe from her, now empty of champagne.

Laughter welled within her despite the gravity of the moment. She knew that without a doubt she would invite Lady Helena over soon to hear more details of that particular story. "Thank you for your help."

August whirled and struggled to make her way through the crush. More people came every hour, it seemed, until there was hardly room to walk around the perimeter of the dance floor. She had barely moved six feet when she was brought up short by a group of several older couples chatting in front of her. With the wall to one side of the group, she was stuck unless she darted through the throngs of people heading to the center of the room to dance.

"Pardon me." She made one last attempt to move through the group and smiled at a matron who regarded her with a severely raised brow. "If you would be so kind as to . . ." The man to her left moved back, and he was followed by the fellow at his elbow. "Oh, thank you so much. I must—"

The words lodged in her throat as the group parted to reveal the Duke of Rothschild standing on the other side.

He wore the same wolfish smile from earlier. She understood immediately that he was the reason the couples were so obliging of her predicament. They had been parting for him, not her.

"Good evening, Miss Crenshaw." His voice was smooth and rich, and some part of her she couldn't face directly thrilled at the way it massaged its way down her spine.

He was so striking in his black-and-white evening wear that it was a moment before she could find her tongue. "Good evening, Your Grace. I am afraid my sister is not here." It wasn't precisely a lie. She wasn't there in the immediate vicinity. "She left early." Fine, that was a lie.

He appeared impassive, except for the fact that his eyes still held a devilish sparkle. "How unfortunate." Perhaps he was putting on an act for their small audience, but he genuinely did not appear to care that his plan had been thwarted. There was the briefest of pauses before he gestured toward the dancers. "I would hate to waste a good waltz. Perhaps we could dance instead."

He might as well have said perhaps we could row a boat down the Thames. The possibility of dancing with him had never crossed her mind. Should she accept? Honestly, she wanted to spend as little time in his company as possible. It seemed safer that way. Would it be unbearably rude to decline in front of their audience? The group seemed very concerned with their exchange.

The opening notes of "The Blue Danube" started playing. "I promised the next waltz to Lord Ware." She had forgotten. The poor man had probably come to collect her, and she had been nowhere to be found. She started to turn and stopped when she realized that leaving him would leave the duke free to go find Violet. As if he sensed the internal battle in her head, he offered his arm to her.

"I do not think he would object." When she glanced up, he inclined his head toward Lady Helena, who was graciously accepting Lord Ware's arm in her absence. Lord Ware gave August a tight smile as he led her friend to the floor.

Left with no other choice to make, she lightly pressed

her fingertips to Rothschild's arm and allowed him to lead her. The crowd swirled out of their way like Moses parting the Red Sea. Rothschild had not uttered a single word, only held his gaze straight ahead as if their opening a path for him was his due. And it was. This was his world.

It was not until that very second that she understood the power this man held. He might not have inherited wealth, but he had inherited something even more valuable to those who traded in that currency. Respect. Reputation. Standing. Whatever word it was known by, it all came down to power. He held the power here.

When his arm slipped around her waist and his hand settled on her back, she felt the strength in his loose hold. Restrained power. As she rested her hand upon that arm, she could not help but note the flex of the muscle beneath the light touch of her fingers. She remembered the strength of that arm with its unrestrained power as it had landed a blow to his opponent. A strange flutter moved through her belly when his gloved fingers closed gently around hers as he swept them into their first turn. His strength was evident in every movement and touch. Much to her dismay, she understood now that she found it very attractive on him.

"Are you all right, Miss Crenshaw?" Genuine concern shone in his eyes, and she realized that her breathing had increased to match the pace of her heart.

"I . . . Yes." The blue of his irises was the exact shade of a Newport summer day. How had she not noticed before? Perhaps it was the lighting. Or perhaps it was the odd way the room whirled around them as he took her into another turn, making her more aware of him as everything else blurred. Her fingers tightened reflexively, indecently on his, but he only smiled in response.

Tipping his head forward so that a lock of hair threatened to drop down over his forehead, he asked, "Are you quite certain? You are flushed."

Dear Lord, why now? Why was she only understanding at this most inopportune moment the depth of her attraction to this man? Despite the fact that both of their hands were gloved, her fingers tingled from the heat of his. She tried to hold on to her anger, but it floundered like a fish in her grasp. This is why some girls became foolish in the arms of a handsome man. She had never understood before, had in fact believed herself immune to the silliness, but now felt the urge to write letters of apology to every childhood friend who had borne the brunt of her judgment.

"I'm fine." The words came out sharp and clipped as she tried to disguise the crisis of awareness crashing through her.

"I am not your enemy, Miss Crenshaw."

"But neither are you my friend, Your Grace. We both know that."

"I could be."

"Impossible. We have opposing goals. I want to save my sister from you, and you want to marry her. Why, that almost does make us enemies."

He released a breath on a laugh. The not-at-all-unappealing fragrance was brandy laced with peppermint, the same as when she'd kissed him at the sparring match. His lips were curved in a slight smile, reminding her of how warm and surprisingly soft they had been beneath hers. She also remembered something she had tried to make herself forget. The moist stroke of his tongue against her bottom lip right before he had pulled away, and the dismay that had rampaged through her in the immediate aftermath that she had been cheated of more.

"You are remembering that night." His voice was low and entirely too sure of itself.

She pulled back with a gasp, and while he didn't resist her, his calm hand on her back kept her from making a scene. "I didn't . . . I only thought . . ."

"Would it help if I admit that I think of it as well?" His eyes were not mocking but gently solemn and filled with longing as they slipped down to her mouth and back again.

A whole flock of butterflies took flight in her belly. "This is not appropriate conversation for a dance." Despite her best intentions, she could not look away from him. Something in his face held her transfixed.

His hand flexed at her back. She shouldn't have been so aware of it, given the layers of fabric and boning of her clothing, but she could feel the press of each finger. "I think of it far more often than I ought to admit," he said.

Before she could stop herself, her gaze flicked back to his lips. Would kissing him again feel as interesting as it had the first time? What was wrong with her? He was a fortune-hunting duke intent on marrying her sister. There was no way he thought of that kiss. If he did, it was purely for reasons of using it to blackmail her.

"You need not think you can hold that over me. I told my parents about that night." There. He was for vanquishing, not for kissing.

"Did you?"

She gave a single proud nod as he led her into another turn. "Yes, they know about you and your pugilistic tendencies."

He laughed again. This one a deep laugh that started down in his chest and garnered them curious looks from the couple gliding past them. "I am intrigued. What was their reaction to that bit of gossip?"

She tried to scoff, but it was difficult with the smile she had plastered on her face. It would hardly do to feed the gossip mill by arguing with him in front of the entire ball, no matter how much she might want to. The music called for a twirl, so she waited until she was back in his arms to say, "It is not gossip if it's true, and I was a party to the situation. Do you intend to deny it happened?" He smelled pleasantly of citrus and bergamot as he had that night in the garden.

"Very well. What was their response to that bit of news?"

"That hardly matters." She was not going to admit to him that they did not care one whit if their potential son-in-law brawled for money. His smile told her that he knew. Damn him.

"I am going to guess that you did not mention our kiss." He said it loud enough that anyone dancing by them could have heard.

"Shh . . . We hardly need to share that. It was once and ill-advised at that." Her face flamed at the memory, so much so that she could not bring herself to see if any of the couples around them had heard.

"I do not think it was ill-advised at all." His voice lowered a hair.

"Stop talking about it." She spoke through clenched teeth because it was the only way to keep her temper in check. Had he lured her into this dance to make a fool of her? Was this his way of keeping her unbalanced so that she would not intervene when he went for Violet tonight?

"All right," he said easily. Too easily. "I will not mention it anymore during our waltz. You have my word."

Since he was being agreeable, she decided now was the time to appeal to him. "Please reconsider your plan for tonight. Or at least postpone it."

"What do you believe my plan to be, Miss Crenshaw?" The area between his brows furrowed attractively. For heaven's sake, did every expression the man made have to be so attractive? It wasn't fair.

"I think you plan to let your intentions for her be known tonight. I would like for you to wait, at least until we can talk more."

He did not smile or put her off in any way as she had expected. Instead, he became thoughtful as the dance continued. His eyes deepened somehow, the pupils expanding ever so slightly as he led her into another twirl. When she came out of it, he pulled her into his arms again, and his pleasing scent washed over her. He made her want to step closer into the circle of his arms, to savor his warmth.

"As I see it, Miss Crenshaw"—his voice was husky and deep when he finally spoke—"I have only two options before me and must make a choice."

As she waited for him to elaborate, the waltz came to an end. Always the gentleman, he bowed to her and placed her hand on his arm as he walked her back to her family. The crowd parted as it had before, only this time she noted that everyone they passed seemed to be watching them both, and whispers followed behind them. Perhaps they had been too obvious in their sparring. She probably shouldn't have stared at his mouth the way she had. People would have noticed. People seemed to notice everything about him, which undoubtedly extended to the shadow he cast.

Her mother and Violet stood watching them with silent eyes at the edge of the dance floor. She tried to signal that Violet should leave so that Rothschild would have no opportunity to ask her to dance, but all too soon he was greeting both of them in turn. Her mother smiled and returned the greeting, while Violet seemed a bit stunned. Her mouth fell open slightly, and her gaze kept going back and forth between them.

Finally, he turned to August and brought her hand to his lips. "Thank you for the dance, Miss Crenshaw. If you will excuse me."

He was the embodiment of decorum as he inclined his head to both her mother and sister before taking his leave. He walked away as if nothing of note had happened on the dance floor. Had anything happened? Maybe not for him. Was she alone in this strange need to see things settled between them? Why wasn't he asking to claim the next dance with Violet?

It was unseemly, but she couldn't stop herself from calling him back. "Wait."

He paused and turned, and every eye in the vicinity seemed to turn with him. Aware of their intense interest, she kept her voice light. "You mentioned options. What are they?"

He grinned, the wolf back to play with its prey. "It hardly matters. I have made my choice." Turning, he made his way through the crowd. It was easy to follow his progress as the people shuffled like waves in his wake.

"August?" Violet's voice seemed to come from far away as August tried to regain her equilibrium. She felt as if she had just returned to herself from an odd dream.

"Miss Crenshaw?" Lady Helena moved in front of her, fixing her with an urgent stare.

"Yes?" August looked back and forth between them, and then became aware of the rising murmurs around them. She had expected the attention to follow Rothschild, but it seemed that at least some of it had stayed with her. "What is happening?" she whispered.

"Oh, my dear." Lady Helena shook her head and glanced

to the large open doorway where Rothschild had disappeared. "The duke never comes to these balls. He never dances with anyone, especially single women."

"Yes, I know, we discussed this. He was coming to dance with Violet, to establish his interest." She was a little annoyed that they had to go through this again.

"He did not dance with Violet, though, did he?" Her brows rose as if August should be able to formulate the rest.

August looked to Violet, who was staring at her as if she had sprouted another head. Mother gasped and covered her mouth to hide the unladylike sound.

"No, he danced with me because I told him Violet wasn't here."

"That's right," said Lady Helena. "He danced with *you*."

August nodded, growing impatient when it really was her own fault for not explaining. "You misunderstand. I asked him to not make his intentions known to Violet until we could talk about things."

"What did he say?" Violet asked.

"Well . . . I'm not sure." Already everything about that conversation was blending together. He had answered questions without really answering them at all. What did it mean that he had two options and he had made his choice?

Had he chosen *her*? The knowing look on Lady Helena's face seemed to suggest as much. August's heart sped up, and her lungs seemed to shrink. "Do you think . . . ?"

No! It wasn't possible.

But Lady Helena was nodding. "He chose you, dear."

Everything inside her screamed that it wasn't true. That he hadn't meant to choose her. That he'd only danced with her out of courtesy because Violet wasn't available. But none of that explained why he had only offered the mildest greeting to her sister.

The room had become stifling and the air too thick. August took in a breath, but it did nothing to stop the spinning of the room. "Excuse me."

"You poor thing," said Lady Helena as she clucked her tongue softly. "Shall we go to the dressing room?"

August nodded but waved both her and Violet off when

they moved to come with her. "Please . . . I need a few minutes alone." What she actually needed was to find Rothschild and make certain Lady Helena was mistaken. He had only not asked Violet to dance because August had requested it.

"That's fine. We'll be along in a little while," Violet said as she watched her with worried eyes.

The crowd had filled back in the swath he had cut through them, making the journey to the entrance slow and tedious. Everyone paused to watch her as she passed, the weight of their gazes seeming to make the trip even longer. She cursed them, but she cursed him more. If there were any justice in the world, Rothschild would find his carriage caught up in the snarl of traffic outside and still be waiting. If she was lucky, she would be able to catch a moment alone with him.

Her heels echoed off the oak floors between the Persian carpets as with each step toward the front stairs she rediscovered the anger that vanished when he had held her. Losing her head to him wasn't a mistake she would allow herself to repeat. She would find him and give him a taste of that anger. How dare he presume to single her out? How dare he presume that she would accept this betrothal? If that's even what he had meant.

"Looking for me?"

She whirled to see him lounging against the doorframe of a darkened room off to the side. His ankles were crossed as if he had been waiting for her this whole time. Satisfaction that she had found him warred with her displeasure that she had fallen into his trap so easily.

"Yes." Her voice was sharp as a whip, and she silently congratulated herself on that accomplishment. She would prove to him that she wasn't some simpleton who turned to mush at a smile from him.

He pushed the door beside him open further to reveal the spines of leather-wrapped books set into a bookshelf and flashed a grin at her before he disappeared inside. It was an obvious challenge, one she was eager to accept. Stiffening her posture, she made it all the way to the door before hesitating. Fingers of trepidation tickled their way down her spine. Somehow, she knew that her life would be irrevocably different after this conversation.

But knowing him had already changed her in ways she couldn't articulate. It was too late to turn back now. Taking one last look around to make certain that no one saw, she followed him into the room and pushed the door closed behind her.

Chapter 9

It is always incomprehensible to a man that a woman should ever refuse an offer of marriage.

JANE AUSTEN

The very air in the room altered when she entered. She was simply stunning wrapped in her Worth gown and her confidence. She pulled the door closed behind her, her chin parallel with the floor and her shoulders squared to face him. It was almost as if she had been born to be a duchess.

"You are angry with me." Noting the way her small hand kept a secure hold of the doorknob as if she intended to leave at the first sign of trouble, he stayed where he was so that he would not frighten her. He wanted many things from the woman before him, but her fear was not one of them.

Eyes bright with her fury, she said, "Of course I am. Do you have any idea what you have done?"

Even though he knew that it would only goad her, he could not stop the smile from twisting his lips. "I presume you mean the waltz?"

"You know precisely what I mean. Everyone thinks that you intend to propose to me now instead of Violet."

It was terrible of him, but he could not resist himself when it came to her. Smiling widely now, he leaned a shoulder against a shelf and said, "You did ask me to not dance with her tonight, if I recall."

She violently let go of the doorknob, if such a thing was possible, and crossed her arms over her chest to pace the short distance to the low-burning fireplace. The library was a small but comfortable room with dark oak paneling and a seating area with several overstuffed chairs and low tables set before the fire. Aside from the bookcases framing the mantel, and the row of them at his back, they were the only furniture in the room. Had she kept the chairs between them because she feared being alone with him? A twinge of guilt made itself known that she was probably right.

"I should have realized you would make this into another sparring match. Whatever your reasoning, you have made everyone believe that you intend to propose to me. Why would you do that?"

She could not look directly at him when she asked that. Her gaze had settled somewhere along his ear. Interesting. Also of note, the color on her cheeks was higher than when she had walked into the room. Partially due to her anger but, he would be willing to bet, also because she was as attracted to him as he was to her. Watching the myriad of expressions on her lovely face during their waltz had made him suspect as much. Now he knew for certain.

Tipping his head slightly to attempt to force her to meet his gaze, he explained, "Perhaps because I do mean to propose to you. Have you considered that?" He was surprised to find that his heart was pounding with those words.

Breath lodged in her chest as she jerked to meet his gaze. "What? No." Her lips parted as she appeared to struggle to form her next words. "I . . . I do not accept."

Not yet, but she would. "I have not proposed to you, yet."

Having overcome her apparent shock, she drew herself up. "That hardly matters. I won't accept when you do, so you shouldn't bother."

"Thank you for the fair warning, but I rather hope to change your mind."

She laughed at that. Laughed as if he were a lowly servant asking for her hand rather than a duke. "Impossible."

For the first time that night, a glimmer of anger burned in his chest. "I am a respected peer with four estates and—since I lack the requisite excessive weight and want of hair of others in my position—more than a passing attractiveness."

She took in a breath and closed her eyes briefly before catching him with that directness he found both enticing and unsettling. "The fact that you believe those are the only things that recommend you as a spouse is both troubling and sad."

He could only stare at her, taken aback by her opinion. "As troubling and sad as they may be to you, they are very sound reasons for marriage. Why would you not want to marry me?"

Crossing her arms over her chest again, she asked, "Why on earth *would* I ever marry you? You truly cannot fathom a woman turning down your offer of marriage, can you? I do not intend to marry you, because I like my life as it is now. You have absolutely nothing to offer me."

He swallowed thickly as he silently acknowledged that she was right. If she was not to be swayed by his title, estates, or handsome face, what else was there? If she were a proper aristocratic girl, the title alone might have been enough. He had never considered having to work so hard to secure a marriage, so he was momentarily flummoxed in the face of her logic.

Was Leigh correct that coercion of some kind was the only way? Evan had hoped to avoid that, but the stakes were too high to simply hope for the best. The town house was the only unentailed property left. Without a betrothal in place by the end of the month, Clark had hinted there would be no choice but to sell it. Evan would be fine with that, except his mother would be crushed. All notion of politely sidestepping the obvious downfall of their family in society would be gone. Their fall would be gossip for the tabloids as well as the dining rooms across Mayfair and Belgravia. Louisa and Elizabeth would have no hope of a stable future.

"Nothing is such a strong position." He heard himself saying the words and moving forward without ever consciously thinking of what he was saying. "You like kissing me. The marriage bed will be no hardship for either of us."

Her lips parted, and this time he heard her gasp. As he wove around the chairs separating them, she took a step back until she came up against the bookcase. The soft flames of the fire lit up the rose of her cheeks and the interest in her eyes. They had fallen to rest on his mouth, much as his own gaze was eating up the sight of her soft lips. It was amazing how the simple reminder of their kiss had changed them both so fast.

Dear God, to have her in bed beneath him would be one of the greatest accomplishments of his life.

"That is hardly . . . That is no reason . . ." Her gaze moved back and forth between his eyes and his mouth as he came to a stop in front of her. Near enough to touch, but he did not dare take that path yet. "Are we like horses to you, then? Choose the mare you would prefer to breed and we all simply go along with your choice?"

He managed to swallow down his laugh, even as her words made heat pulse in his veins. "That is not at all how I see this, and it is hardly fair to assume as much when I am willing to negotiate."

"Not fair?" The softness that had crept into her eyes was burned away by a new wave of anger. "You have some nerve speaking to me about fair play. None of this is fair. You decide you need money and then decide to marry to get it. Now you've decided that I will be your convenient bride, no matter how I feel about it."

This time he could not hide his laughter. "I assure you that you are anything but a convenient bride. You are the most stubborn and infuriating woman I have ever met. None of this up to now has been my decision."

Amazingly, she seemed mollified by that, and her posture relaxed by the slimmest degree.

Capitalizing on the moment, he added, "Until you."

"Me?"

"The debts are my father's. The family honor rightfully

belonged to my dutiful brother. My mother is the one who chose Violet." He took the final step to reach her, closing the distance between them. The heat of her body warmed him as the fire could not. "I would have one thing that is mine. I would choose my own wife. I choose you."

"Why me?" Her voice was quiet.

"Because I have never met anyone like you. Because I want to know you. Because you challenge me. People in my world marry for much less. For money, land, a name. I want you for you, Miss Crenshaw. That is far more than most people get."

It was as honest as he had ever been with anyone. Her wide eyes stared up into his, and for a moment he thought he saw mutual understanding. As much as he had never thought of marriage before, now that it was before him, he wanted to share it with her. To spend the rest of his life learning her.

"Those are fine words, Rothschild. The only problem is that you are only saying them because I am packaged with the funds you so desperately need."

He would have given his eyeteeth in that moment to deny that was true. "Nonetheless, they are true words."

"Be that as it may, I will not be a pawn manipulated for money. When I do marry, it will be with a man who respects me for me and whom I can respect for his mind." She pushed past him, and he closed his eyes at the jolt of attraction that tore through him.

"Did you not hear me, Miss Crenshaw?" He turned to follow her progress toward the door. "I very much want you for your mind. You will challenge me in ways no other could."

She paused and glanced at him over her shoulder. The corner of her mouth turned up in a coy and infinitely attractive smile. "Yes, I understand that. Did you not hear me, Rothschild? I said that *I* require someone whom *I* can respect for his mind."

He stared at her, unable to decide if she had just called him unintelligent. He was aware that his mouth opened and closed several times, but he could not seem to stop it as he searched for the right words. No one had made him speech-less before.

Taking advantage, she came back to stand before him. "You were right about one thing, though." Her blush covered her entire face now, and she glanced down once before steeling herself to meet his gaze. "We are very good with kissing, and I would very much like to do it again."

The sentence rattled around his head, trying and failing to coalesce into a coherent thought. Every time it tried to make sense, he would rearrange it again, unable to believe that she had said what he thought she said.

"To do what?" he finally asked, rather daftly, which rankled after her previous statement. "You want me to kiss you?"

If it were possible, her face became redder, but she stood her ground. Somewhere in the periphery of his vision, he became aware of her hands fisting the fabric of her skirts in nervous anticipation. She rolled her eyes and nodded.

"Why?" Was he really belaboring this? It was foolish and it was merely his ego needing to be assuaged, but he wanted to hear her reason.

"Oh, for heaven's sake," she said on a breath. "Kiss me." She took hold of his head, her fingers tightening in his hair as she pulled him toward her. Her breath was warm with the faint scent of champagne when he covered her lips with his. It was a soft press of their mouths, hardly enough to be a proper kiss, but he could feel her trembling. He drew back enough to see her long lashes fall against her cheeks as she closed her eyes, and her lips parted in silent invitation for more.

It was an invitation he was powerless to resist. His mouth covered hers, this time molding to her lips with relish as his hands swept down her back to draw her to him. Her smaller frame fit against him perfectly. She made a soft mew of pleasure in the back of her throat and kissed him back. The soft and wet heat of her tongue answered the stroke of his, lighting a fire of need within him so strong that it raged out of control before he realized it was even there. Fierce desire swept down his spine, tightening his groin and settling low in the pit of his stomach. His mouth took everything she offered. Seconds, minutes, hours might have passed as he savored the sweetness of her mouth.

Drawing back to take a breath, she whispered breathlessly, "We should stop." Her gaze was drunk with need as it met his, and her lips were slightly swollen and wet from the kiss.

"Why?"

A crease formed between her brows, and her eyes darted down to his mouth. Slowly, he leaned down, closing the distance between them as he took her lips again. Another soft groan vibrated in the air between them. This time she pressed herself more tightly along his front. Even through the layers of her skirt, he was quite certain she must feel how much he wanted her.

Overcome with the need to feel more of her, he lifted her against him enough to walk her backward to the bookcase by the door. Kissing her felt lush and extravagant. Her mouth was hot and wicked, demanding and indulgent. She was obviously inexperienced but eager to learn from him. When his teeth scraped against her bottom lip, she sighed in pleasure and then did the same to him. When he sucked at her tongue, she returned the favor, making his cock throb with the echo of what it must feel like to be inside her.

His hand moved over her waist and up to cup her breast; the hard pebble of her nipple pressed into his palm through layers of fabric. She arched into his touch, and his mouth watered to lick the salt from her skin. His thumb moved over the sensitive peak, which had her hips pushing against him.

"This shouldn't go further," she whispered, covering his hand with hers. She was breathless and not at all in control of herself. Gratification welled within him at how kissing him affected her. If nothing else, she could not deny that she wanted him.

"No." He agreed. It was one thing to kiss her at a ball. It was entirely too much to take anything more, yet he could not seem to listen to reason when it came to her and kissing. "You should go." He took her mouth again in an endless string of kisses, his hips pressed against her of their own accord. It was exquisite torture when she moved, grinding his erection between them. "Tell me to stop," he whispered against her lips.

"Maybe one more minute."

He groaned. Her hand stayed over his, but she pressed his palm against her. Jesus. This woman set him on fire. His fingers skimmed the edge of her bodice, hoping there was enough give to touch her, and there was. He nearly fell to his knees in thanks when the fabric gave way the slightest bit so that his fingers could slip inside. She made a sensual gasp when he found her erect nipple, catching it gently between two fingers. He dipped his head and pushed the silk aside as his mouth found her, his tongue torturing the rigid nub before sucking it into his mouth.

She arched into him and gave a cry of surprise and pleasure. She grabbed onto his shoulders, holding him tight against her. "Rothschild," she whispered against his ear.

Something wild and elemental came over him. He imagined her beneath him and crying out his name. The tight clasp of her body welcoming his cock as he took her over and over again. A rough groan escaped him as he took her mouth again, her naked breast in his palm as he ground his cock against her hip. His thigh found its way between hers, pressing against the heat he knew he would find there. If the way she moved against him, all but riding him, was any indication, she was as aroused as he was. He wanted to feel her on his fingers and started to pull up her skirts.

If he sat in one of the chairs and pulled her onto his lap, he could open her thighs and bring her to pleasure. He pulled back to stare down into her face. Her eyes were glazed over and dilated, and he realized that she had given herself completely over to him. She trusted him. His fingers fumbled in their intent, touching the smooth silk of stocking at her knee. Gently and reverently, he placed a kiss at the base of her neck above her pulse. Somewhere in the background a very unwelcome and indistinct voice penetrated the fog of his arousal.

He broke off, his breath coming in harsh gasps. She stared up at him bewildered, but then she heard it, too.

". . . believe I left it here. I read it again only last week." This was followed by a laugh that was much closer. Right outside the door.

Her eyes grew wide before narrowing on him almost immediately in suspicion. Crushing hurt and betrayal took over as she hurried to put distance between them and pull up her bodice. The door handle rattled, and both looked at it as if it had suddenly come alive.

If he let them be discovered, then the question of marriage would be settled. But she would hate him, and he doubted she would give herself over to him as sweetly as she just had ever again. Without thinking it out further, he grabbed the knob, releasing her to hold tight with both hands when whomever was attempting to open it tried more force.

"It seems quite jammed." Hereford knocked on the door. Evan was certain Leigh must be with him. "Hello? Is anyone inside?"

"Let me give it a try." Leigh's voice confirmed his suspicion. *Bloody hell.* There was a shuffle of bodies outside before a renewed attempt to open the door.

Evan held his jaw taut as he kept the handle from turning and set his shoulder against the doorframe. What had been a half-thought-out plan at best had become a nightmare. It was one thing to conceive of forcing her hand; it was another to see the terrible accusation cross her lovely features. He could not live the rest of his life knowing that he had taken her hard-won trust and hurt her so irreparably. He wanted to win her on his own merit.

"The handle is broken," said Leigh. "It will not turn."

"Come on, then. I . . ." The words faded away as suddenly as they had appeared.

Evan waited a moment more to make certain they did not return before he let go of the knob. He turned slowly, uncertain of her reaction. She had a chair between them again, and her gaze was on the front of his trousers. He glanced down to see that the drama had done nothing to ease his desire for her. It was clearly outlined against his trousers.

"August," he said. Meaning to go make certain she was all right, he took a step in her direction.

"Oh no," she said, her eyes wide again as she backed up. "We are finished with kissing."

Drawing several gulping breaths, he turned toward the bookcase wall and counted backward from twenty in his head as he forced his need for her to go away. It was not in the least bit easy. He could still smell her on him, and her sweet taste lingered on his tongue. Cursing softly, he watched her watching him with wariness as she adjusted the pins in her hair. She did not look nearly as disheveled as he felt.

"That was a mistake," she said, smoothing her palms over her skirts.

"Was it?" It had not felt like a mistake to him. Perhaps the venue had been ill-advised, but not the kissing.

"We were lucky. I have to go before someone comes back to repair that door."

He did not think Leigh would allow that to happen, but he did not dare mention it. Instead, he nodded and stepped aside so she had free access to the door. He thought she might walk right out, but she paused next to him with her hand on the knob.

"Mistake or not, thank you for that."

Inclining his head, he said, "I will pay you a call soon, so we can discuss how to proceed."

"This changes nothing. I will not marry you, no matter how skillful your kisses."

"You admit that I am skillful?" he asked, grinning like an idiot.

"I am leaving, Rothschild. If you intend to pursue this ridiculous betrothal, then I'm afraid you're declaring war."

He took her arm before she could disappear. She stared at his hand, and then her fierce gaze held his. "Then why kiss me?"

The slightest grin tilted her lips. "Because I knew it would be my last chance." With that, she was gone.

Chapter 10

*I shall not change my course because those
who assume to be better than I desire it.*
VICTORIA CLAFLIN WOODHULL

August did not dare stop outside the library door in case
Hereford and the other man came back. Even though
her knees were trembling, she hurried through a series of
rooms that would take her to the ladies' dressing room. She
forced measured steps and did not stop until she slipped
inside the door.

The room was vacant of guests, and the strains of a waltz
coming from the ballroom assured her that it would stay that
way for the next several moments. The walls were covered
in pale green watered silk, with clusters of settees and spindly chairs upholstered in a darker jade. A maid in the corner
of the room came to attention, but August smiled and waved
her away. She needed to think, and she did that best alone.
She darted to the safety of one of several dressing screens
scattered about. Delicate, hand-painted silk stretched across
four panels to complete an elaborate scene of lotus blossoms
floating on a lake. August could not help but wonder at the
expense of the obviously extravagant item when Camille's
own sitting room languished in faded disrepair.

Sinking onto a padded stool, she touched her swollen

lips. Her other hand went to her bodice, making absolutely certain that she was covered. What had she been thinking? Following him into the library had been completely foolish. Kissing him might have been the most irrational thing she had ever done. If anyone had discovered them alone together, it would have been devastating. *Worse!* The entire course of her life would be altered.

Dropping her head into her hands, she contemplated the sheer foolishness of her actions. Max had always teased her that her boldness would get her into trouble someday. He had meant it playfully, not like this. Neither of them would have suspected she would do something so foolish. When faced with the prospect of never having the opportunity again, August had decided to kiss Rothschild. Her spur-of-the-moment reasoning had been that it would be a quick test to prove to herself that it wouldn't be as notable as she remembered. She had half convinced herself that their first kiss had been so exhilarating because it had been at the fight. The night had been alive with drama and violence. It was that, and not the duke, that had made it so exciting.

How could she have known that it would get so out of hand, or that she would be so completely naive and unprepared to deal with the feelings he ignited in her? That he possessed an uncanny power over her? That she would still feel alive with sensation even after leaving him? Her pulse still seemed to throb throughout her entire body.

A soft and unwilling laugh escaped her. Who would have known that Rothschild was the one who could unravel her so easily? No amount of analysis would have made her accept that finding had she not experienced it for herself. Now that she knew, what did she plan to do with that information? She shook her head at her own foolishness. The most important thing was that she now knew to be very careful to avoid being alone with him in the future.

Catching sight of herself in the small oval mirror on the wall, she set about pinning the strands of hair that had become mussed with their kisses. If one good thing had come of it, it was the knowledge that such kisses were possible, so when she decided to find a husband, perhaps she could find one who would kiss her like that.

"I, for one, was surprised she knew how to waltz," said a voice as a pair of women rushed into the dressing room, completely disrupting August's solitude. Thank goodness for dressing screens. "I thought dancing was forbidden to Puritans." The proclamation was punctuated by giggles and the rustle of skirts.

August paused. While the woman might have been talking about Camille or even Violet, August *knew* she was speaking of her and the waltz with Rothschild. A lump settled in the pit of her stomach.

"Now, Cecilia," came the voice of her friend. "You know her grandmother was a *stage dancer*. It runs in her blood." Both women let out peals of laughter as the muted click of their heels led them across the room to a seating area.

While many of the women she had met in London had been kind and accepting, there were a few who openly disliked the Crenshaw sisters, like Lady Cecelia. The daughter of an earl, she had snubbed both August and Violet from the beginning. Whether she felt her marriage prospects were threatened, or if the aversion ran deeper than that, August hadn't been able to tell. She had been too busy with Crenshaw Iron Works business and social engagements to allow it to concern her.

"Indeed. Did you know that her mother is called Millie, *like a chambermaid*?" Another giggle.

"I heard that her mother *was* a maid."

Lady Cecilia tittered before adding, "Then the duke should not be too surprised when his children prefer polishing the furniture to learning Latin. Blood will tell."

Blood will tell. It was a phrase that had haunted August most of her life. The first time she had heard it had been as a child in a Broadway department store happily enjoying a piece of stick candy while her mother shopped. An elderly, refined woman had taken one look at August and murmured the phrase to her friend with a nod. Then they had both given her mother a scathing look. Lady Cecilia and her unknown companion were exactly like the old New Yorkers who thought that because their money had been earned a century or two earlier than the Crenshaw fortune, it somehow made them better. Impotent anger burned through her veins. Confronting them would not change their minds; she had learned that lesson the hard way.

The rustle of skirts told her that another woman had entered the dressing room. As if someone had closed the lid on a music box, the giggling stopped. She peeked around the screen to see the yellow-gold of her sister's skirts and breathed a sigh of relief.

Violet caught sight of her and hurried over. "I am so sorry it took me so long to come find you. I was on my way, but Lord Leigh detained me." She whispered so that no one would overhear.

"Lord Leigh?" August had seen him talking to Rothschild earlier and knew they were friends. Rumors claimed that he was a part owner of Montague Club, but that wasn't what disturbed her. He was a known cad, and all self-respecting unmarried women knew to stay away from him. "What did he want? You haven't been properly introduced."

Violet gave a mirthless laugh. "You know he cares nothing for propriety. He merely said hello, and then Lady Helena offered the introductions. It was a bit odd, because we had only begun to exchange pleasantries before he remembered an engagement and hurried off."

"Well, I suppose that's fine." Though August preferred that he stay away from Violet altogether. "Don't worry, I only just arrived myself."

"Did you talk to Rothschild, then?"

August bit back a smile. Of course Violet would assume she had talked to him. "I did. He needs an heiress, and it appears he has chosen me." She made certain to gauge Violet's expression for any hint of regret, but there was none.

"Oh dear." Violet's dark eyes widened. "Tell me what happened."

August gave her an abbreviated account of the conversation minus the kissing. At the end her sister merely nodded and asked, "And you are certain that you do not wish to marry him?"

Of all the questions Violet might have asked, that was not one August had considered. "Of course!"

Violet gave her a half smile, the mischievous one that seemed to say she saw more than she let on. "I only wanted to make sure. He *is* handsome. Perhaps he wouldn't be the worst choice for a husband if you wanted one." At August's incredulous look, the smile dropped and she became serious again. "What will we do? You know that Mother and Papa will want this match."

"I don't know." August didn't know, but she was not planning to simply go along with a fortune hunter, no matter how skillfully he kissed her. "Do you think you could make my apologies to Mother and Camille? I cannot return to dancing any more tonight. I have to go home." She had to think her way out of this.

"Of course," Violet said as they rose. She reached out and carefully arranged August's skirts, before tucking a stray lock of hair that August had missed back into a pin. Her eyebrow rose in pointed curiosity that it would have come loose, and for one horrifying moment August was certain she would know that Rothschild's hands had been in her hair as he had kissed her. But Violet simply said, "Go home and rest. You've had a terrible shock."

"I'll send the carriage back."

August hugged Violet and made her way to the front of the house. She was sure that Rothschild must have left by now, but that did not stop her head from being on a constant swivel. Whether she was hoping to catch sight of him or was dreading the prospect, she did not care to examine. What she did observe were the countless eyes that turned toward her as she passed. People had noticed the Crenshaws ever since they had arrived in London. Their attention wasn't anything new. What was new were the questions lurking on their faces now.

Why did he choose you when everyone knows your sister is the one being offered to him? Or, *How much does it cost, precisely, to purchase a duke for a husband?* There were also a few sneers among them. They were easy to interpret. *You might buy yourself a title, but you'll never be one of us.*

Had August been in the market for a noble husband, she wasn't at all certain that she would be up to the task of handling his peers. No, it would be best to return home to New York as planned and put this all behind them.

E van had almost had her. If he had simply allowed the door to open, Hereford would have discovered them, and Evan would now be ensconced in a room, perhaps in the Crenshaws' townhome, discussing the particulars of a marriage contract with her father. Instead he was at the gymnasium in Montague Club hours after the kiss, punching a sand-stuffed burlap sack.

Still without an heiress.

The fine moldings and paper that plastered the wall, along with the grand chandelier hung with hundreds of crystals, marked the room as a ballroom. It had not seen any dancing in years and had been refitted with gymnasium equipment: an incline with cables and pulleys to exercise the abdominal area, a standing machine with straps for pulling that exercised the arms, several machines intended for leg repetitions, and a wall hung with slats and bars for climbing. Perhaps he would get to them all before the night was done. Physical exhaustion seemed to be the only way to calm his frustrations lately.

As his fist made solid contact with the sack, a welcome pain vibrated through his knuckles, reminding him that he should have had someone bind his hands for him. The batting strips he had hastily wrapped around his fists were too loose and already slipping. Another blow thudded dully, sending the bag reeling backward on its tether and twitching as if alive with electric current. A left hook checked its progress so that it flinched and trembled. None of the punches brought the satisfaction he sought.

Again, he asked himself why he had done it. The worst that could have happened was that August would be furious with him. Fine, it was a certainty that being caught with him in the library and forced to marry would have sent her into state of fury so intense she might have tried to kill him. He was confident in his ability to handle that. He handled two lively younger sisters all the time. While August was a different type of woman altogether, he would have survived. Given time, she would have adjusted to life as a duchess. Their marrying was inevitable; he had no doubt about that. So why had he blocked Hereford's entry?

The only answer he could settle on was that the kiss had thrown him off. What had started as a very straightforward attempt at seduction had gone off the tracks. How had kissing her so overwhelmed him? One moment he had been in control, and the next he had had her up against a bookcase with his hands under her skirts. He never lost his restraint like that. Certainly not in a library at a ball.

Growling, he unleashed a fury of blows on the battered burlap until a pleasant burn developed in his arms. The only thing he could command in his life was his training. It was the one thing he did daily, and it grounded him as nothing else could. Unfortunately, it was doing nothing to ease the fury coursing through him. Fury with himself. With her. With his father and the situation that had made her so necessary to him. He had lived his life until now with no restraints, and now that was all he seemed to have.

Bloody hell. When his lungs desperately needed more air than he could pull in, he let his hands fall. His fists pressed into his knees as he leaned over and tried to draw air into his lungs. A telltale hint of red bonded a strip of batting to his knuckle. Despite the pain and discomfort of his body, her expression still haunted him. The mild confusion that had turned to emotional pain when Hereford had come to the door. Lips swollen, she had been as lost in the kiss as him, but when the voices had penetrated the fog of passion, she had believed that he had betrayed her. Not only had she believed it, but she had been hurt by it.

Up until that moment, or that kiss to be more precise, Evan had viewed his extraordinary courtship of her as a game. Winning her hand would be the prize at the end.

Knowing that the future of so many lay on his shoulders had helped convince him that winning by any means was not as unconscionable as it might have been. Yet, a bizarre mix of her expression of painful betrayal and his own conscience rearing its head at the very last moment had made him put his hands on the latch. As he had held it tight, something had become clear to him. He wanted to win her on his own merit. He wanted her to *choose* him. And, more importantly, he did not want to hurt her.

Letting loose a roar of frustration, he attacked the sandbag again, wishing it was the long-buried sense of honor that had reared its ugly head at the wrong time.

"Ha!"

Honor had nothing to do with it. His conscience would not allow him to hide behind such a noble lie. It had been pure selfishness. Wanting her to choose him would be a way of proving to himself and everyone else that he had won. That he was capable of holding her esteem on his own merit. It was most definitely not rooted in any sense of honor. That particular sentiment had not been present in his decisions for a long time.

He had not wanted to cause her pain, but what right did he have making that decision when the far nobler one would be to secure the future of the families who depended upon him? One door had stood between him and the right decision. One door, and he had let them down. Again.

"It appears quite dead." Leigh's voice filled the cavernous room from the doorway.

Evan let his arms drop to his sides when he saw the tear in the burlap. Sand rained down from the bottom corner as if through an hourglass to create a miniature dune on the floor. Leigh came farther into the room still dressed in his evening finery minus his hat and gloves. Beside him stood Jacob Thorne, the earl's illegitimate half brother. The three of them owned Montague Club with Evan holding a lesser share. Thorne was also dressed in his evening finery, but his coat and waistcoat were made of velvet and were a deep blue in color as opposed to the traditional black and white of the aristocracy.

THE HEIRESS GETS A DUKE   129

Despite the different hues of their skin—one was pale and the other golden brown—the two were obviously brothers to any onlooker who cared to make the connection. They were the same height with the same breadth to their shoulders. Though their features were slightly different, they were clearly defined by the sharp angles that had been distinct to the earls of Leigh for centuries. The same devil lurked in their smiles, though Leigh's was more rapacious while Thorne's carried a devil-may-care buoyancy.

Gesturing to the area marked off with ropes where they held their mock fights—and sometimes real fights if gambling was involved—Evan asked, "Are you offering to spar with me, Leigh?"

Leigh smiled, his limp more pronounced than usual as he came to a stop and leaned heavily on his silver-topped cane. "Not in your current mood. It may not appear this way at times, but I do value my life."

"Thorne?"

Thorne shook his head and grinned as he made his way to the lounge area in the corner of the room. Pouring himself a finger of brandy, he said, "I have a later engagement that's a damn sight more appealing than fighting with you tonight, Sterling."

Evan's own name. It was such a simple thing, but it reminded him that there were people in the world who did not view him by only his title. There had been a time when he had simply been Lord Evan Sterling. God, he missed that.

"Only one?" Evan adjusted the batting around his knuckles and flexed his fingers to test for comfort. Still too loose.

"Two if she brings a friend," said Thorne, folding himself into the sofa.

Evan shook his head. If only a woman would cure the deep well of frustration lodged within him. Ironically, one woman could. His arms ached, but the irritation persisted, so he moved to the next sandbag hanging from the ceiling, catching Leigh eyeing his current attire skeptically. Evan had shrugged out of his coat, waistcoat, and tie when he had walked in but still wore the rest of his clothing from the ball. He knew the questions would come, but he could not help but wince when Leigh spoke.

"You blocked the door."

Evan gritted his teeth and gave the sandbag a series of one-two punches. "I did."

Leigh waited, and when it was evident an explanation was not forthcoming, he sighed and leaned back against the wall, crossing his arms over his chest. "Did you even kiss her?"

Glaring at his friend, Evan stopped to pull the cloying linen of his shirt away from his neck. When that failed to ease it clinging to his shoulders and back, he cursed and ripped away the first couple of buttons. Pulling the offending garment over his head, he used it to wipe the sweat from his chest and neck and then tossed it aside.

"I did." Oddly, he was reluctant to elaborate. The kiss had been far more heated and exciting than he had expected. August was attractive, and he had never considered kissing her to be a hardship, but he had not expected the strength of her response. Nor had he anticipated the intensity of the passion it would ignite so quickly. It was a singular experience that he did not want to ruin by talking about it.

Leigh waited again, as if expecting more. Evan went back to pounding the sandbag. His thoughts of August were so convoluted, he knew that talking about her would not help.

"I assume it was enjoyable?" prompted Leigh, clearly amused.

Evan remembered the soft little moan she had made in the back of her throat when he touched her nipple and gritted his teeth as blood started to flow to his cock.

From his place on the sofa, Thorne added, "You were kissing your heiress in a room alone and barred the door when you could have been discovered?"

"Correct," Leigh answered for him. "He refused to give us entry to discover them."

"Had you already gained her agreement to marry you?" asked Thorne.

"No." Evan paused and gave voice to the idea that had been taking shape all this time. "If the past year has taught me anything, it is how to be a good negotiator. I shall find out what she wants, what she finds important, and give it to her if she agrees to my terms."

The room was silent as the men pondered this. No one asked why his change of heart, which was for the best, because he did not want to discuss it.

"What do you think she wants?" Leigh looked thoughtful as he straightened.

"Freedom. To be treated as an equal. I need to figure out how that translates to marriage."

Thorne rifled through the newspapers and periodicals scattered on the table before him. The papers crinkled and fluttered until he found the one he was looking for and pulled out the long sheet. Walking over to Evan, he handed it to him and said, "Middle of the page."

Evan's gaze quickly went to the illustration of a disgruntled and unattractive woman wearing a top hat bearing stars and stripes reminiscent of the American flag. SUFFRAGE DEALT A BLOW was typed in bold lettering beneath it. A quick skim of the article informed him that the Supreme Court of the United States recently had cause to decide a case that had been brought before them. They had found that the Fourteenth Amendment of the Constitution did not guarantee citizens, including women, the right to vote.

"What is this?" asked Evan.

Thorne shrugged. "Figured your bluestocking might be on the side of women's suffrage."

Was she? Evan was dismayed to find that he did not know. It was a fair assumption, but it only emphasized how little he knew of the woman he was planning to make his wife. If she were an ordinary aristocrat and this an ordinary marriage, it would not matter. He doubted his own father had known or even given a damn about his mother's political thoughts when they had married. He likely had been unaware that she might possess any. But this was a new world, and August was a different type of woman. Evan was not in any way guaranteed her hand.

He had been going about this all wrong.

Thorne stared at him. "Have you never once courted a woman?"

Evan laughed. "No. Have you?" He had spent his life avoiding the matrimony trap.

"No, not courting for marriage at any rate, but it is very simple."

Leigh ran a hand over his hair in exasperation and said to his brother, "You forget that as a son of a duke, he has never had to use charm."

It was true. Most people went out of their way to court his favor.

To Evan, Thorne said, "You have to find out what she likes and pretend to like it, too. Talk with her about this." He pointed toward the paper. "Express your deep sorrow for the ruling."

Evan was skeptical, so his voice was laced with sarcasm when he asked, "And then she will fall down on her knees and agree to marry me?"

Leigh gave a dramatic sigh before saying, "No, but it will soften her to you. It is your only option given your abhorrence of entrapment. Find a way to use it to your advantage."

Wiping a hand on the back of his neck, Evan slung the hair out of his eyes. "For centuries, wealthy heiresses have been lining up to marry dukes. Why am I the one who has to go crawling on his knees to one?"

"Because you are the one who has chosen a difficult bride," Leigh pointed out.

Evan grumbled inwardly and changed the subject, tired of talking about himself. "What of Wilkes? Have you found him?"

Leigh smiled. "Jacob found him."

"In Rochester," answered Thorne. "Has a woman there. He has been persuaded to pay five thousand. Says he does not have the rest, but he will fight you again. This time without shoes. The match should generate the rest he owes you and more. You keep the pot, of course, if he wants to keep his life."

"Good. When can we do this? Tomorrow?" Evan was ready to fight the bastard right now.

Thorne shook his head. "Likely a week, maybe more. No broken bones, but he took some persuading before he agreed to hand over the five thousand." He flexed his fingers, drawing Evan's attention to the scabs on his knuckles. "You will want him healthy first."

"Where is he?"

"Somewhere safe where he won't run off again," Leigh answered.

Leigh had been running this bare-knuckle boxing league since before he and Evan had finished school. He had contacts and hideouts that Evan knew nothing about, and Evan wanted to keep it that way. He did not ask any more questions.

"So we have a little time," said Evan.

The five thousand would have to pacify the creditors for a bit. He would have to figure out a way to get August's agreement during that time. Clark seemed to think that the creditors would not be held off much longer.

"Do you plan to hold Violet Crenshaw as a reserve?" Leigh's question was quiet, his face still.

"No. I will have August." After a beat, Evan added, "One way or the other."

Leigh nodded as if something had been decided. "Good. Then I will start my plan for the sister."

It took a moment for him to comprehend Leigh's intention. Even then, he thought he must be mistaken. "What plan?"

Shifting his shoulders, Leigh spread his fingers on the hawk's head of his cane. He was prevaricating, as if reluctant to say more. Disquiet caused a prickling sensation to travel up the back of Evan's scalp.

"I have decided that it is time to take a wife. Why not an heiress?" Leigh gave him a bitter smile.

Evan thought of the girl he had met at the Ashcrofts' party. She was young. Was she even twenty yet? Her eyes had been innocent even in her anger with him, and there had been a gentleness about her that was missing in her older sister. The wave of protectiveness sat uneasily inside him, but he took up the role it cast him into anyway. "But why?"

Leigh shrugged, his gray eyes glittering with interest. "She is beautiful, and she pleases me. Why not?"

Evan had known Leigh since their days at Eton, and while they were nearly the same age, there was something about Leigh that made him seem decades older at times. But it was not the age difference that bothered Evan so much as the depths the man would stoop to get what he wanted.

"She is too innocent for you."

Though Leigh's expression did not change, he squared his shoulders and his jaw hardened. "What precisely do you mean by that?"

Evan frowned, struggling to articulate the unexpected protectiveness within him. "I mean you will run her over and make her miserable. She has been sheltered and is not bold like her sister."

"I've met her. She can hold her own with me." The corner of Leigh's mouth kicked up in a smirk.

"When did you meet her?" asked Evan.

Leigh's smirk widened into an actual smile. "Earlier tonight. I appreciate your concern for your soon-to-be sister, but she will not come to any harm with me. She will be kept in luxury and given a child or two to dote over. Is that not her fate regardless of who the husband is?"

Before Evan could answer, Leigh turned and made for the door, his limp slightly more pronounced than it had been earlier in the evening. "I will leave you to your frustrations. I need a drink."

Leigh was right. Her fate would be set either way. Until now Evan had assumed that marriages simply happened. Families had discussions, arrangements were made, a date was set. Never once had he considered the actual *convincing* of a bride. It was almost demeaning. Perhaps it might have been demeaning had the bride not been August Crenshaw. Earning her acceptance and respect filled him with anticipation. It was a precise goal, when all of his goals seemed to be moving targets lately, that he was confident he could reach.

Chapter 11

❧

Be bold, be bold, and everywhere be bold.
EDMUND SPENSER

August sat at her dressing table staring at herself in the mirror. She had allowed Mary, her startled maid, to stay only long enough to strip her of her ball gown and help her into her nightgown and wrapper before bidding her a good night, preferring to unpin her hair herself. However, she couldn't concentrate on the chore because oddities in her reflection kept distracting her. First it was the color high in her cheeks that wouldn't seem to leave. Then it was the way her eyes shone. They seemed almost vivacious in the muted tones of the oil lamp. Now, while it seemed unlikely, her lips appeared to be still swollen from his kisses.

Pausing in her task, she dropped the hairpins into their dish and touched her mouth. Yes, they were definitely fuller than usual. Her fingertips drifted down to the small bit of skin exposed above the high neck of her nightgown. The touch ignited an ember slumbering in her belly. It was a faint echo of the flame Rothschild had brought to life in her. Moving her hand down lower, she tentatively touched the nipple he had stroked. It stood up beneath her touch, round like a gumdrop caught beneath the linen.

Before Rothschild, she had kissed precisely three men in her entire life, not counting the chaste kisses on her forehead given by her father or Maxwell. The first had been a hastily stolen kiss at a dance when she was eighteen. The man, a son of her mother's friend, had pressed his lips to her cheek and turned seven shades of red when she had pushed him away. The next kiss had happened a year later at a summer party at the cottage in Newport. More curious about kissing at the worldly age of nineteen, she had encouraged a childhood friend to kiss her on the mouth. His lips had been dry when they had brushed hers and had left her feeling awkward and relieved when it was over.

The third kiss had been a couple of years later. Also in Newport over the summer, this one had been by a son of Papa's business associate. The family had visited from Chicago, and August had liked him right away. Handsome and intelligent, he had been the first man she had ever tentatively begun to imagine a future with. Uninvited, he had kissed her rather roughly on the beach one night. She had been both stunned and appalled. When she had managed to push him away, he had sneered and said that it was a good thing her family had money because she was too cold for any man to want.

To her everlasting shame, the words had cut deeply. Everyone knew that Violet was the desirable one, while August was the bluestocking. The one who, while pretty enough, would only marry when she found a man who could overlook her many shortcomings. She was too opinionated. Too intelligent. Too mannish.

Too cold.

It was the last one that had haunted her most. What if she was too cold for any man to want?

The puckered nipple reflected in the mirror seemed to suggest otherwise. She moved her hand to her other breast and cupped the small mound, allowing her thumb to play over her nipple as Rothschild's had done. It tightened under her touch, and if she kept her eyes closed tightly, she could almost imagine that it was him touching her. A dart of pleasure moved from her nipple to her belly, burrowing so deeply that she had to press her thighs together. She pinched the little nub of flesh as he had done and was gratified when another pulse of desire shifted through her. She remembered how he had whispered her name, and the thrillingly rough sound he had made deep in his throat.

Flattening her hand to her pounding heart, she opened her eyes to her reflection. With her hair in careless waves around her and eyes wild with arousal, she almost didn't recognize herself. Her skin prickled with gooseflesh, but she was anything but cold now. He had proven it. If nothing else, she could thank him for that.

No, that wasn't true. He had given her something else. When he could have had Violet—Hadn't he said that his mother had chosen her? Hadn't her own parents offered Violet up on a silver platter?—he had *chosen* August.

I would have one thing that is mine. I would choose my own wife. I choose you.

The memory made a smile curve her lips. The words were so simple, but they had settled down inside her like warm whisky and softened her hard edges. Almost no one had ever wanted her for her. Her mother wanted her to be more like Violet, and her father—while encouraging her business-minded pursuits—had marveled at her, like an eccentric he didn't quite understand but was willing to humor. Was it possible that this man, this *duke*, was willing and able to see her and accept who she was?

Charlatan. Trickster. Fortune hunter. All of those could be applied to him. She understood that it was in his best interest to get her on his side, and he'd likely say anything to make that happen . . . but what if . . . what if he meant it?

Shaking her head, she reminded herself that whether he meant the words or not, he only wanted to marry her because of the money that came along with her. He was an impoverished nobleman who had figured out that marrying an heiress would solve all his problems, and he wasn't above seduction to get what he wanted. It would serve her best to simply focus on the physical. His kisses might have been tinged with coercion, but the thick length of manhood swelling against her thigh had been genuine desire, if the anatomy books she had devoured as an adolescent had been correct.

It was a small victory, but it proved that she was neither cold nor unable to stir a man. She would take that victory and still figure out a way to beat Rothschild at his own game, because she *was* opinionated and intelligent, too.

The next morning, needing to savor her time alone before dealing with the almost certain ambush of her parents as soon as she stepped out of her room, August slept late. After a distressing night of tossing and turning, the extra sleep that morning was just the thing to set her to rights again. She awoke feeling refreshed and eager to take on the challenge of thwarting a fortune-hunting duke.

It wasn't until Mary brought her a breakfast tray that she realized things were odd. For one, her maid seemed far more devoted to her duty than normal. A pretty woman only a few years older than her mistress, Mary tucked August's napkin across her lap and added two lumps to her coffee as if she were taking care of a most treasured child. Her dedication, combined with her knowing glances, were undeniably more than her usual need to please.

"Thank you, Mary."

Mary curtsied and mumbled, "Yes, miss."

It seemed that news of her waltz with the duke and its significance must have made the rounds downstairs. Fine. Gossip was inevitable, and she was prepared to ignore it. Things would die down when she made it clear that his interest was not returned.

Next, the distant peal of the doorbell kept ringing through the house. It happened once while August was eating and scanning a contract from Papa's secretary that had arrived yesterday, and two more times as Mary helped her into her corset and then while pinning her hair. Papa had a meeting that afternoon that she planned to attend. There were hours yet before the meeting, and no one would call before three in the afternoon. Would they? Suddenly afraid that she had missed something important, she hurried through the rest of her toilet and out her door.

The doorbell had gone silent, leaving the corridor quiet. Too quiet. Usually, her mother would be up and ordering the maids to make some last-minute alteration to Violet's planned costume for the evening. Had Mother gone out this early in the day?

Rare sunbeams cast golden rays on the carpet through the panes of leaded glass at the end of the corridor. Perhaps the sun had lured her mother outside into the garden. Giving the maid polishing a brass lighting fixture a smile and a nod as she passed, August glanced out the window to find the garden empty.

"Pardon me, but have you seen my mother?" she turned to ask the maid.

The girl nearly fell over herself in her haste to straighten her skirts and bob a curtsy. "Yes, miss. Mrs. Crenshaw is taking breakfast in the garden parlor with Miss Violet, miss." She curtsied again at the end for emphasis.

The Crenshaws tended to run a more casual household than their English counterparts, or so August had been led to assume when the maids and footmen had all shown extreme reverence to the family the first several days after they took up residence in the townhome off Grosvenor Square. The reverence could have been because August had insisted the family pay higher wages to compensate for the positions being of a temporary nature. After a few gentle dissuasions, the servants had treated them with slightly less formality, and everything had settled to rights. Strange that the overly abundant display of deference had returned. August stared a moment at the top of the maid's lowered head before muttering, "Thank you."

"Yes, miss." The girl curtsied again and waited until August was well away down the corridor before turning her attention back to the fixture.

The strangeness did not end there. Reginald, the butler, stood at the top of the stairs, directing a maid on what to do with an armful of folded linen, but he shooed the poor woman away toward the narrow servants' corridor leading to the back as soon as he caught sight of August. He brightened immediately, as if he had been waiting for her. She had only ever seen him upstairs in the housekeeper's domain when he was ushering a guest to Papa's study. He didn't tend the maids. It wasn't his job.

"Good morning, Miss Crenshaw." The man had never stood so straight. It was as if a broomstick had been slipped down the back of his coat. "Your father has requested you join him in his study at your earliest convenience."

How long had the poor man been posted there waiting to relay the message to her? The one day she had slept late, and everything was off. "Thank you, and good morning, Reginald."

He bowed as she passed. He had never once bowed to her. To be sure, the man was cordial and respectful, but this was much more than that. If she hadn't been certain before, August now knew that there was talk belowstairs about the waltz. The servants must all assume that she was to be the next Duchess of Rothschild. The talk must be all over London by now. She did not dare read a gossip column to see what might have been written about the previous night.

Politely rapping her knuckles on the study door, she opened it at Papa's entreaty. It was time to put an end to the needless speculation. She would tell him that the waltz had not swayed her in her intentions to keep the Crenshaws firmly away from Rothschild. Papa would likely grumble, but, in the end, he would let Rothschild down. It would be unseemly in the extreme for Rothschild to then move on to Violet, so hopefully he would find some other heiress entirely—one of the unwed Jerome sisters, perhaps—and leave the Crenshaws alone.

She did not hear the other male voices until she opened the door. Two men sat across the desk from Papa, and her heart gave a start when she thought one of them might be Rothschild. But no. While the man was blond, upon closer inspection his hair was fairer than the duke's and his shoulders were not as broad. He rose, along with the older man at his side, when she entered the room. She recognized them both as soon as they turned to face her as Lady Helena's father and elder brother.

"Good morning, darling." Papa was dressed for business in a smart coat and tie. Rising from behind his desk, he walked around and took her hands as he kissed her cheek. "Did you sleep well? You look stunning."

She did not look stunning. She knew for a fact that there were faint blue smudges under eyes because it had taken her a long time to fall asleep. "Yes, thank you."

His attention had already returned to the two men in the room as he put a hand at the small of her back and presented her proudly. "I believe you have already met the Earl of Farthington and his son Viscount Rivendale. Gentlemen, my daughter."

She had met both men in passing at various functions but had never held a conversation with either of them. They both greeted her politely but seemed far too preoccupied to entertain pleasantries for long. The fact that Lord Farthington held a prominent seat in the House of Lords made the meeting even more auspicious.

"Come join us, darling," said Papa as he walked back to his leather chair.

The earl, an older man with brown hair liberally mixed with gray, appeared flummoxed with his creased brow, and the younger one gawked at her openly before gathering himself to stare at the edge of her father's desk. Fixing a placid smile on her face, she walked to her Chippendale desk near the window, a compact piece of furniture with a hinged door. Taking up parchment, pen, and inkwell, she carried the tray to her place at the end of her father's desk. A carved rosewood side chair was already there for her, as it was where she normally sat during meetings so that she could easily keep notes of the discussion.

"I apologize if I am late, Papa," she said as she settled herself and the men resumed their seats. "I did not have this meeting on my schedule."

"Their visit is a pleasant surprise for me as well."

Lord Rivendale cleared his throat and gave her a bemused glance before addressing her father. "Yes, as we were saying, the issue is of some discretion. Perhaps it would be best if we continue in private." His gaze slid to August in case there was any question of his meaning.

"My lord, although Miss Crenshaw is my daughter, she is also a trusted employee of Crenshaw Iron Works. I trust her discretion and her advice implicitly. You did say that this was a business issue?"

Lord Rivendale paused before nodding a bit reluctantly. "Yes, very much so." The words were slow to come, as if he were weighing the benefit of proceeding against the obvious drawback of her presence. Fixing a smile on him that could only slightly be construed as spiteful, she waited.

He shifted, his shoulders twitching as if the perfectly tailored coat encasing them had been fitted with the pins left in it. Despite having met him in passing, she only now observed that he was one of those self-important people who somehow lacked self-assurance. Being important was his birthright, so he had never earned his place and had never bothered to acquire the knowledge of self that earning *anything* would give him. It was why he tended to look around things rather than directly at them. Much as he was looking around her now.

Not all noblemen were that way. Rothschild wasn't. A pleasant heat stole over her face as she remembered how he had looked right at her and seen her. Lord Farthington also did not seem similarly afflicted. He sat with his shoulders back, comfortable with himself, his gaze on Papa.

Papa smiled. "Then I would very much like that she attend."

"If you prefer, I will not write down notes." She slid the tray several inches away from her on the desk.

Lord Rivendale glanced to his father, whose expression had not once changed from the befuddled grimace he wore when she appeared at the door. Lord Farthington gave precisely one nod, his lips in a firm line of disapproval.

"Very well," said the son. "But there can be no written record of this meeting."

Again, he spoke directly to her father and only deigned to shoot her a glance out of the corner of his eyes. She wondered if that was how he spoke to his sisters. Or perhaps he did not speak to them at all, preferring to give orders through the servants. August held up her fingers in a show of her intention not to touch her pen.

"Of course not. Whatever is said here will be certain to stay within the confines of this room," Papa assured him in his smooth negotiation tone. The voice that was never flustered no matter how disagreeable the adversary.

"The matter is of some urgency," Lord Farthington began. "What do you know of the Indian subcontinent?"

Papa smiled. "Not nearly as much as I am about to learn, I assure you."

The earl nodded as if he had assumed as much. "Britain holds roughly one million square miles in India. Population estimates claim that is approximately two hundred million people. In contrast, England has a population of a mere twenty-two million souls but spread over fifty thousand square miles." He raised a hand. "Give or take."

August leaned forward slightly, afraid to believe that this conversation could be going where her intuition believed it would lead. He could not be here to discuss railways in India. Those contracts had been notoriously difficult to obtain, given only to a select few firms based in Britain. But why else would he be approaching them? She found herself holding her breath as she waited.

Papa inclined his head to indicate he understood. "Yes, yes, quite a difference in size."

"As can be expected, the railways in the empire have lagged behind those here in Britain and even your America," Lord Farthington continued.

August nodded in agreement. "I have read that your rail works have laid over fourteen thousand miles of track here. For contrast, the people in India are making do with a mere four thousand miles." August could not pretend to understand all of the problems facing the people in India, but she knew that four thousand miles was not nearly enough to help ease the effects of drought and the subsequent famines sweeping through the country.

The earl hesitated, but to his credit he did look at her.

"Four thousand at the beginning of the decade," he confirmed. "At that time we pledged to have ten thousand miles in ten years."

"You're nearly five years in, then. Are you on path to meet your goal?" Papa leaned forward, his fingers laced together on top of his desk.

Lord Farthington's brow creased, and his voice lowered almost imperceptibly, as if what he was about to say was confidential. "If you ask publicly, you will hear much boasting and swagger, but the truth is that we are lagging behind, which is why I am here. We need more railroad companies. Men who know how to get the most out of their labor. Men who are efficient and knowledgeable."

"It sounds that way. What exactly are you suggesting, my lord?"

The earl paused, and his nostrils trembled the tiniest bit as he took a breath. "Privately, I would consider it a personal favor if you would submit a proposal from Crenshaw Iron. Your reputation with your own transcontinental railroads precedes you, and since your arrival on our shores, we have found you to be a man of substance. You and your company are who we need in India."

The viscount let out a breath as if in relief. "Yes, someone of your expertise might find it a welcome challenge to expand your investment portfolio. If you could be persuaded to take on this project, then you are certain to not only find financial profits, but you would also gain favor with many."

"India." Despite his many years of playing at subterfuge and practiced nonchalance, Papa could not keep the wonder from that one word. He had always been an adventurer. Stories of his travels as a young man had become legend in their family. But then he had married and started a family, and his father had died, leaving him to run Crenshaw Iron, and that had been that for his adventuring. She could almost see the memories of his exploits running through his head.

"What would such a commitment require of us, my lord?" August asked, sensing that while the allure of the Indian railway system was hard to resist, accepting would come with its own price.

Lord Farthington reluctantly pulled his gaze away from her father to her. "Crenshaw Iron Works would be required to open an operation here in Britain. We cannot open the doors to all of America, you understand. Having an operation here would help perception, and I am given to understand it aligns with your own goals for expansion." When she nodded, he turned his attention back to Papa. "Of course, you will find that many of the restrictions that might have prevented an earlier attempt will be eased for you."

"I am afraid that we must insist on autonomy, if we agree to this," August said, drawing attention back to her. "We control our own operation, and that includes our relationship with our workers. We pay them a wage that we determine to be fair." Max had begun the work of making certain their laborers were compensated fairly when he had entered the family business nearly a decade earlier. She had supported him in that, even though some of their contemporaries had bristled at the move, preferring a standard of depressed wages to control competition.

Lord Farthington appeared to be on the verge of arguing, but then he gave a nod of agreement. "Your contracts are your own to negotiate."

She let out a quiet sigh of relief that she hadn't needed to fight harder. The ethical and fair treatment of the people she employed, be they laborers or servants, was important to her.

"How extensive of an operation do you mean?" asked Papa.

Lord Farthington shrugged. "All details that can be arranged later and that I am certain will not pose an issue. You will find your investments here very lucrative." Sensing that victory was close, Lord Farthington's gaze narrowed in assurance. "After all, the Duke of Rothschild clearly believes you are someone with integrity and honor. How could we believe any less?"

August only barely managed to hide her gasp. To disguise it, she looked down at her hands clasped firmly in her lap and swallowed. These men were here because of the betrothal they assumed would be forthcoming. She would bet her last dollar on it. Had it truly meant that much to everyone?

"Well." Papa's smile was in his voice. "We are looking forward to becoming better acquainted with His Grace."

"Now, Papa, I believe it is far too early to—"

Both father and son looked at her. The earl with gleaming speculation, and the viscount with faintly veiled disdain. Perhaps he was thinking that he could not possibly conceive of lowering himself to marry a common woman for money. He himself had married a marquess's daughter, a nod above his own station.

Wishing only to wipe the smugness from his face, she said, "The duke is a good friend to us."

The older man gave a nod and seemed to relax, while the younger turned his attention away from her. The conversation continued for the next few minutes as Papa gleaned pertinent details about the potential deal. As far as the men were concerned, August was attentive and an active participant, but inside she was quaking. She had severely misjudged the reach of the duke's influence, and now walking away from him did not seem nearly so straightforward as it once had.

Finally, the viscount turned to his father and said, "We must be leaving if we are to make our next appointment."

Although nothing was remotely settled and there were far more details that begged to be discussed, Lord Farthington nodded and made to stand. Everyone else in the room followed suit. "I trust we shall be hearing from Crenshaw Iron soon."

"We will certainly consider the opportunity, my lord. I look forward to communicating with you further." Papa walked around his desk and crossed to open the door.

Both the earl and Lord Rivendale offered a murmured good day to her before turning away. As the earl approached, Papa held out his hand to offer a handshake. The earl paused and only after a brief hesitation offered his own hand. Lord Rivendale did the same. Father walked them out and returned moments later wearing a wistful smile.

"Well, that was . . . unexpected." His eyebrows rose.

Her stomach roiled in agitation. "It certainly was. Max had petitioned for a contract several years ago. Perhaps now that they have fallen behind schedule, they have deigned to open things to American companies," she said. It sounded like a lame justification even to her own ears. Lord Farthington had all but said it was because of their ties to Rothschild.

Papa's gaze narrowed in doubt. "Something tells me that Crocker and Huntington will not be receiving similar offers. Neither of them are acquainted with the Duke of Rothschild."

The palms of her hands began to sweat, making her fight the urge to wipe them on her skirts. "Then it is a good thing we have made his acquaintance." Perhaps the friendship would be enough. There had been no formal announcement of a marriage, and already this offer had come. Lord Farthington wouldn't revoke it. Would he?

Turning abruptly, she went back to her desk and rifled through the papers there until she found the ones she sought. She sensed Papa's gaze on her the whole time. Hoping to avoid a further discussion about the duke's intentions, she turned the conversation to preparations for their meeting later that afternoon. "Have you had a chance to read my summary on the textile factory? They managed to turn a small profit last year, but I found inconsistencies in their depreciation reporting."

"Your summary was well done, and yes, I made note of that and it is something to discuss with them. Their equipment would cost a fortune to refurbish as it is. It's clear that they never built it with innovation in mind."

He started to walk back to his desk, but a brisk knock stopped him. "Yes, Reginald?"

The butler opened the door. "Lord Holloway has asked to see you."

"What a surprise," said Papa, though he did not actually sound surprised. "Show him in, please."

A charged silence descended when Reginald left to retrieve Lord Holloway. Another earl, he was also a well-known member in the House of Lords, most notably for having the ear of Benjamin Disraeli. This visit was most definitely prompted by their association with Rothschild. While Papa had entertained callers over the past weeks, none of them had been so prominent in Parliament. August hardly dared to meet Papa's gaze, but when she did, it was knowing and triumphant.

He gazed at her with a pride that was almost frightening in its intensity. He had certainly had cause to look at her with approval and happiness over the years, and he often had. This, however, was beyond approval. It was made even more worrisome by the fact that she had done absolutely nothing to deserve it aside from catching Rothschild's interest. Is this what it had come to? Her earlier intellectual accomplishments would be wiped aside in favor of her ability to attract a duke?

A deep hollow of dread tinged with anger opened up within her. How did one go about fighting back against a sentiment that had its roots so tangled in visceral emotion? She worried that she might not be able to outrun Rothschild's clutches. Not when he so easily fed the Crenshaw appetite for acceptance and success.

It seemed as if she was destined to lose either way. If she married, she would most certainly have to give up her place in Crenshaw Iron Works. Duchesses most definitely did not work. If she refused, then she might very well lose her place anyway. What if her refusal so angered Papa that he declined to allow her to continue to hold her position? She wanted to believe it was impossible, but she couldn't.

There was only one solution. If she could not convince her parents that a match between them was destined to fail—and her previous conversations on the matter indicated that would be impossible—then she would be forced to make Rothschild understand that having her as his duchess would be so disastrous that he would give up his ridiculous notion. The trick would be doing that while keeping from disparaging the Crenshaw name. It wouldn't be easy, but she was willing to try anything.

Chapter 12

*Opportunity, sooner or later, comes to all
who work and wish.*

EDWARD SMITH-STANLEY,
14TH EARL OF DERBY

To: Maxwell Crenshaw, Crenshaw Iron Works, New
York, NY

Please come to London STOP Am afraid betrothal is
imminent without your intervention STOP Papa has
gone mad STOP He sees only the benefit to the company
and the family with no regard for my feelings on the
matter STOP Hurry STOP

From: August Crenshaw

\- - - - - - - - - - - - - - - - - -

To: Miss August Crenshaw, 12 Upper Grosvenor St.,
London

Itinerary to follow STOP

From: Maxwell Crenshaw

Evan waited before approaching the Crenshaws. There were a few reasons that this tactic seemed prudent. The first was that an inherited mountain of debt had taught him that it was not beneficial to appear too eager in a negotiation. Not only did it appear desperate, but it gave the other party the impression that they were in control. To negotiate successfully, one had to maintain control.

Second, Miss Crenshaw—August, as he thought of her more and more—was under the impression that she was in control of her own future. As such, she would need time to come around to the practicalities of marriage to him. His presence would not help that along, given how he seemed to agitate her. He could lead her gently and hope she made the right decision. If she did, then their transition into marriage would flow more smoothly. If she did not, then they would still marry, but he would have a bigger obstacle to overcome.

Finally, he quite enjoyed *not* being married. If he could hold his creditors at a distance for a short time while they awaited his betrothal, without actually having to be betrothed, then he would. However, he would have to be betrothed eventually, so he found himself calling at their Grosvenor Square townhome two days after the ball.

Instead of being shown to Crenshaw's study, Evan awaited the man in a finely appointed drawing room deep inside the house. It appeared less formal than the one off of the entry hall at the front of the house, but no less elegant. The furniture was comfortable and stylish in creams with touches of navy and gold. His gaze was caught by two oval portraits set in gilt frames on the mantel. August's likeness stared back at him with a slight tilt to her lips, as if she held a secret. Her eyes shone with mischief and intelligence. It had been days since their kiss, but a flush of heat stole through him as she stared at him from her portrait.

Apparently, her presence was not even required for her to twist his desire for her the slightest bit higher. Thank God bedding her would prove to be no hardship. He grinned at the nearly besotted fool she had made of him.

"Your Grace." Evan turned to watch Crenshaw stride into the room. He came over and offered his hand. "It is good to see you again."

"Likewise. I did not catch you at an inopportune time?"

"Of course not. I only regret that Mrs. Crenshaw is out for the afternoon."

Evan nodded. Thank goodness for small turns of fate.

"Would you care to sit down?" Crenshaw gestured to a pair of wingback chairs, and Evan took a seat. "I'd offer you tea, but I prefer whisky. How about you?"

"Whisky is fine." Evan was surprised when Crenshaw reached behind several bottles on a sideboard and produced an unopened bottle of Lochnagar.

"I've heard this was your favorite."

Evan should not have been surprised that the man had researched his favorite whisky. It was common for well-placed families to know the likes and dislikes of their guests to make them feel more comfortable. And while his visit today had not been known, it had been assumed that he would visit at some point. The man was only being a good host by being prepared. What disappointed Evan was how easily things seemed to be proceeding. Beyond one dinner and a brief conversation at Hereford's ball, Evan had not talked to the man extensively. Yet, he seemed willing to offer up his daughter—either daughter—to Evan on a silver platter, complete with a tumbler of whisky on the side.

August was far more precious than that. The man should have been interrogating him on his plans for her future. Instead, he stood proudly as he handed a whisky to Evan. Taking it with a murmur of thanks, Evan enjoyed the slow burn of the liquid across his tongue as he tasted it, but it settled heavy with the guilt in his stomach.

"I admit that I expected you before now, Your Grace." Crenshaw settled himself with all the aplomb of a peacock smoothing out his feathers in the chair across from Evan.

It occurred to Evan that he did not like this man very much. "Why is that, Crenshaw?"

The older man gave him a knowing smile that made his

mustache twitch. "Because I know the value of my daughters, and I think you do as well."

Evan inclined his head, conceding the point. "Ah, but I know the value I bring to a man like yourself. You would not be satisfied with anything less for your daughter." Did the man even care which woman they were referring to? Probably not. The whisky went bitter on his tongue at his own complicity in this.

Crenshaw threw back his head and laughed. "This is what I so enjoy about you. I admire a man who doesn't mince his words, who doesn't try to say one thing while insinuating another."

"Then we should cut through the preliminaries. I am here to seek your permission to marry Miss Crenshaw." He might have asked to court her, but they all knew his goal. Crenshaw was right. There was no need to mince his words.

The smile the man wore was every bit the cat who had lapped up all the cream. "Our August will make a lovely duchess for you, Your Grace. There is, of course, more to discuss in the way of financials. I am sure you understand that I've had your holdings looked into. I am sorry to say that it doesn't look good. However, I am certain we can come to an arrangement."

Evan was stunned at how quickly everything was moving along. While he had not expected the man to put up much of a fight, he had expected something. Some pushback regarding her welfare. Evan nodded. "Of course."

"I don't have the figures before me, but I presume you would require the settlements of your debts with a generous sum to start renovations or what have you?"

"Yes." Evan nodded again, still fairly stunned at the recent developments. "I have had my solicitor, Clark, arrange a meeting . . ." Mrs. Crenshaw's voice interrupted him from beyond the closed doorway a mere second before it was swung open by a footman. The woman came sweeping into the drawing room.

"How lovely to see you, Your Grace. I am sorry I wasn't at home when you arrived." Her face was flushed, and she seemed faintly out of breath.

Had someone gone to retrieve her the moment Evan had stepped into the house?

Evidently, yes. Crenshaw did not appear in the least surprised to see her as he came to his feet and took her hands. "Welcome home, my dear. Isn't it a lovely surprise to come home and find His Grace visiting?"

Evan had come to his feet as soon as she strode into the room. He offered a curt greeting, suddenly feeling like a prime side of beef on display at a meat market.

Once the woman had settled herself on the settee, Evan and her husband followed suit. Then Crenshaw said with a self-satisfied smile, "His Grace has asked for August's hand in marriage."

"Oh?" The way her eyebrows went up in practiced surprise had Evan tossing back nearly all of his whisky. "Thank you so much for the honor, Your Grace." Then she immediately turned her attention to her husband. "Is that why I heard you discussing settlements and debts?"

Crenshaw had the grace to appear sheepish. If it were real or false, Evan could not tell.

"That is hardly appropriate conversation for the drawing room, Mr. Crenshaw. Not at all. Save it for your study."

"Of course, dear." Crenshaw gave her a smirk and diverted a knowing wink at Evan.

Evan managed to keep his voice benign as he said, "As I mentioned, I have arranged a meeting with Clark where we can discuss the finer details. My study at Sterling House is a setting of which I believe Mrs. Crenshaw will approve."

"When would you like the wedding to take place?" asked Mrs. Crenshaw.

Evan shifted uncomfortably at the abrupt change. The conversation had gone better than expected, but it felt wrong, as if they had been lying in wait for him. Sweat prickled out along his brow as he felt the claws of their trap closing around him. Also, he had to admit to himself there was a fair bit of disappointment. It was not winning if August had not chosen him herself. He had done absolutely nothing to win the right to marry her.

Reminding himself that this marriage was indeed a

good and necessary thing, he said, "As soon as things can be reasonably arranged. Sometime in May, perhaps. I would prefer to have Miss Crenshaw offer her opinion on such details."

Mrs. Crenshaw preened prettily and started blathering on about dates and venues. It appeared that it had not occurred to her that he was right. August should have some say, he felt, and yet she would be the last person to agree to any of this.

"Excuse me, but do either of you not care to discuss any provisions for your daughter?" The words were out before he could call them back. The couple looked at him with matching expressions of bemusement. How was it that he, the fortune hunter planning to take their daughter away from them, was the only one concerned with her future? "While we do indeed need to discuss the financials of the match, should we not also discuss Miss Crenshaw's needs and wants?"

Mrs. Crenshaw was the first to smile. "What more could she need? The settlement will be quite generous, I assure you, with a proper annuity." She glanced at her husband for confirmation, and when he nodded, she said, "So she really has no need to worry."

"But as I understand it, she has a position at your firm." This he addressed to Crenshaw, because the wife appeared to not have a strong grasp on who her daughter was. Evan had spent only a fraction of the amount of time with her that her own mother had presumably spent with her, and he knew August would worry about this arrangement a great deal, whether there was need to or not.

"Yes?" prompted Crenshaw.

Evan stifled an exasperated sigh and said, "She will not be content to leave that position."

The man shrugged. "She has always known that her position was temporary at best. She is a woman, and her place is ultimately in the home. We have raised her to accept that. It would have always come to that eventually. So it has come to that a little sooner than she had planned." He shrugged.

Evan's blood pounded in his head as he fought a wave of anger mingled with disappointment. Is this what it had come to? He was forced to take her from her place in the world and shove her into another as if they were interchangeable?

"I know about Farthington's proposal to Crenshaw Iron Works . . . about India and the railways." It was hardly a secret when the clubs were nothing but nonstop talk of politics and money.

Crenshaw nodded. "Yes, it appears the union of our families has already begun to bear fruit."

Evan swallowed against the disgust rising in his chest. He had never despised himself more than he did at the moment, casually discussing August's future as if she were not even a part of it. "I want her to have a stake in that. In the operations here in England."

"Absolutely not," said the man.

"Why, that's the silliest thing I've ever heard, begging your pardon, Your Grace," said his wife.

"Why? Is she not capable in her current capacity in your employ?"

"Of course she is. It's not about her abilities; it's about what is right. How could she possibly divide her time between a professional position and her family? Her children would suffer. *Your* children. Her responsibilities to the dukedom would go unattended to."

Several voices came from the entrance hall. One of them he recognized immediately as belonging to August.

"That will be my problem to address, not yours." He cursed inwardly in anger at not being able to finish this discussion. "It is something we will have to discuss at length. I did not plan to tear her away from all that she knows." Standing when the voices were right outside the door, he said, "Do not announce the betrothal to her. Let me tell her." He was aware that his lowered voice sounded more like a growl, but he no longer cared what her parents thought of him. It was clear that he could be as brutal as he wanted and they would agree to have him as a son-in-law.

Mrs. Crenshaw frowned, but Crenshaw readily agreed

just as the door swung open again. "Oh!" Violet drew up
short with August at her back.

"What are you doing here?" August asked, her eyes
wide with both fear and anger. She glanced at the faces of
her parents as if she had guessed what had happened in her
absence. Not that it would take some sort of genius intellect
to understand why he was here.

"We've been having a fine chat with His Grace," answered Mrs. Crenshaw, turning to greet her daughters.
"Isn't it wonderful that he has finally paid us a call?"

Violet was the first to recover herself, offering a greeting. August, however, still stood there staring at him as if
she could not believe she had come home to this. A woman
wearing a gray gown with no adornments whom he assumed to be their chaperone filled the doorway behind
them, completely oblivious to what had happened in the
room. "My, what a lovely day it turned out to be now that
the rain has passed." She paused, mouth open in shock
when she noticed him.

"Good afternoon, Miss Violet, Miss Crenshaw, madame," said Evan. "I came because I hoped to speak to
Miss Crenshaw."

The word *alone* must have been implied, because there
was a great deal of shuffling about until he was left alone
with her. To her credit, the chaperone had prevaricated,
torn between her duty to a young, unwed woman and the
Crenshaws' obvious desire to leave them alone together. In
the end, Mrs. Crenshaw took her hand and led her from the
room mentioning something about tea.

"You've been plotting, I see." August came farther into
the room, taking a seat on the settee and folding her arms
across her chest.

"No, no plotting. I simply came to ask your father's permission to court you." It was the truth. The way the conversation had so quickly turned to marriage still made his
head spin.

"And he gave it?"

"You know that he did." She wore a walking dress of the
deepest emerald trimmed in black lace. The square cut at

the top revealed only a hint of her bosom, but it was enough to draw his eye. The ensemble was at the height of fashion, reminding him of the letter he had received from Elizabeth the day before complaining about being forced to continue wearing her mourning colors. While the truth was their mother had insisted on a longer mourning period, Evan knew it was because she had not wanted to strain the family's finances by ordering new wardrobes for the girls. Now of age to enter society, their figures had outgrown their previous clothing, not to mention the change of style.

Remembering why he was here, why he was all but forcing this woman to take his name, helped ease the guilt, but only slightly. He had to find a way to make this tolerable to her.

This garnered him a look, and she paused. "Do not pretend to court me. I am not so gullible as that."

"There is no pretense. I want to earn your hand, not simply have it forced."

The corner of her mouth curved up in a smirk. "I would say that you've gone about this all wrong if that's your intention."

"Touché. So I have." The need to touch her was so great, he forced his hands to grasp the fine fabric of the settee as he sat beside her. It had been days since their kiss, but his body had not forgotten. The moment he laid eyes on her, his heart sped and the blood grew heavy in his veins. Her scent had found him, reminding him of how she had felt in his arms. How she had tasted.

"I've looked over the reports my father had prepared on your accounts. I don't think you have time for a proper courtship."

The wariness in her voice was nearly his undoing. "It is the unfortunate state of things."

"So that is why you decided to speak to my parents without me present. You wanted to get their agreement without regard to my opinion on the matter."

He nearly groaned with how he wanted to take her in his arms and kiss away her reservations. Hereford's ball had been an eye-opening experience to say the least. If nothing else, Evan could arouse her, ease her into accepting things as she floated on a cloud of pleasure.

"I want to marry you." He kept his voice low. "Your thoughts and feelings do concern me. They will from now on."

Her breath faltered. They were so close he could hear it skip, could watch her chest fail to rise with it. He moved to reach for her, but checked the move just as quickly, knowing that his touch would not be welcomed.

"What if my feelings are that I do not want to marry you?"

"August, you must know that I have no choice."

She gasped aloud. "You should not call me that."

"Why?" He smiled at her perplexed expression. "You kissed me. I want to marry you. We'll soon be intimate enough that first names will come naturally."

A strangled sound came from her as she got to her feet and rushed to stand before the fire, her back to him. "I will loan you ten thousand pounds to use for your estates."

He could not help but stare and wonder if she meant it. The solemn look on her face was enough to assure him that she did.

She held up a hand to silence him as soon as he rose and opened his mouth. "Before you refuse, let me assure you that I have the funds in an account under my own name. Should you accept, the terms of repayment will be extremely lenient, obviously, given your . . . your situation."

Evan could hardly believe that she meant it. "You have ten thousand pounds? Your own funds?" His own mother did not have that much money set aside in her personal account. She never had.

"In liquid assets, yes. I could likely gather together another five thousand should that be helpful to you, but there would be a short delay. My brother, Maxwell, would have to arrange to sell stocks he's purchased on my behalf."

"How do you have this at your disposal?"

She shrugged. "I draw an income from Crenshaw Iron Works. My brother helps me invest it. I do hold shares in Crenshaw Iron, of course, but I would not sell those. Lately,

I've been speculating a bit in gold and copper shares and have done fairly well."

She said this as if it were the most natural thing in the world to say. As if she wasn't possibly the only woman in Mayfair who could be offering her own funds to save a duke. This woman he planned to marry was quite amazing. "I appreciate your generosity, but you have failed to understand the depths of my . . . need."

Shaking her head, she said, "I don't understand. There are many who could live on that for life—"

"Charrington Manor has over two hundred families alone. Don't forget my other properties. All entailed. There are nearly fifty thousand acres. It won't be nearly enough."

She paused, a strange stillness coming over her face. Finally, she said, "I didn't realize."

"You could not have known. I confess I failed to grasp the enormity of the mountain ahead of me in the beginning."

She nodded, clearly surprised that her generous offer had been rebuffed. He could hardly blame her.

"Thank you for the offer."

"You needn't thank me. It was more out of self-preservation than generosity."

He smiled. "Nevertheless, I thank you."

She sniffed and stared down toward the fire as if the flames might provide an answer for her. When it did not seem as if she would address him any time soon, he took a step closer to her and asked, "Why did you kiss me?"

She startled and glared at him but did not step away. "I wanted to know what it was like." She surprised him by answering honestly. "If it would be the same as I remembered from the fight." Her gaze went to the nick in his hairline. "Speaking of that night, you seem to have recovered from your injuries."

Absently, he raised a hand to the scar that would fade even more in the coming weeks. "Was it as you remembered?"

She flushed, her gaze dropping to his mouth as if by accident before she jerked it away.

When it was clear she would not answer, he took a step

closer. "I am glad you decided to find out. It was indeed as *I* remembered from that night. We are good together, August." He was aware that his voice had dropped intimately, but he could not do a damned thing to stop it. He leaned in a bit forward and breathed in her sweet scent. His skin prickled in response, and desire flamed to life in his belly. Her family was likely just outside the door, and his cock was already hardening with his need for her.

"Rothschild—"

"Evan."

"What?" Her eyes were dilated when they met his.

"My name is Evan. Rothschild was my father's name."

Her lips trembled slightly as he wondered if she would say it. For some reason, he longed to hear her say it. Finally, she said, "The kiss was good." At the pointed look he gave her, she smiled slightly. "All right, the kiss was very good, but it is hardly a reason to marry."

And they were back to this again. "Come visit Charrington Manor. We can tour the property. Speak to my estate manager. I will give you a full accounting of everything we plan to do with the money. I swear it will be put to good use. Just as I swear that you will not regret taking me for a husband."

He hardly realized that he had closed the slight distance between them until she had to draw her head back to meet his gaze. Elation made him feel as if he was soaring when she did not move away. His chest expanded as he slowly, gently brought his hand up to her face. Her soft skin was still cool from her afternoon walk. His fingers feathered across the pale smoothness, nearly as perfect as silk except for a few freckles at the bridge of her nose. Her breath hitched as he dipped his head. This he knew. As long as she let him kiss her then everything would be fine. He could set her fears to rest. He could show her how enjoyable things could be between them.

Her breath mingled with his as her lips parted to accept his kiss. They were warm and soft. He nearly groaned at how good she felt against him, as if he were coming home to a part of himself he had misplaced.

The door flew open, and he jumped back from her. She

whirled to gather herself, and he stepped between her and whomever had dared to interrupt them. It was her mother who stood there with a pleased smile on her face. Her hands had come up to her cheeks as if she could hardly believe how well things had turned out.

"Have you decided on a date yet?" she asked.

The woman had the subtlety of a bull.

"No—"

"What date?" August stepped around him, glaring between him and her mother.

"The date for your wedding, of course." The woman smiled as if she had not just committed irreparable damage to his courtship.

"Wedding? I believe you're getting a little ahead of yourself, Mother. A courtship and betrothal are two different things."

"Of course they are, but your father and I have already agreed to his terms. The rest will be sorted out by the solicitors. We can announce things soon."

If Evan had held out any hope of salvaging things after Mrs. Crenshaw's initial question, she had just shot it full of lead.

"You said you were only discussing courtship." August's eyes settled on him, blazing with fury and accusation.

"We might have discussed things . . . further." He could easily imagine the terrible names she called him in her head if the look she gave him was any indication.

"We don't need to decide on a date today, but we should soon," said Mrs. Crenshaw. "There are only so many venues available in London. Of course, I am certain that a small chapel in Charrington would do as well." She gave a disgruntled sigh. "It's so far from town that many will not come, so I have to admit that I wouldn't prefer that. It should be a big event. Her Grace and Hereford's wedding was the talk of New York. Our dear August deserves that."

The woman continued her blathering, but August merely shook her head in slow denial. If he had not had a war on his hands before like she had promised, he certainly had one now.

There was no way to salvage the afternoon. August would absolutely despise that he had spoken with her father, and it would not matter that he had not meant to settle things so quickly between them.

"Pardon me, Mrs. Crenshaw, but I must be going." Before his mood became any blacker and he strangled the woman for her carelessness.

"Yes, of course, you're right." The woman beamed as if she had no idea of the problem she had caused. "Weddings are better left to the women at any rate, wouldn't you say?"

Ignoring her, he said to August, "We will settle this to your satisfaction. I promise you."

Arms crossed over her chest, she simply glared at him.

Chapter 13

I would have girls regard themselves not as adjectives, but as nouns.

ELIZABETH CADY STANTON

The velvet slippers that had been made to accompany the scarlet ball gown were the most uncomfortable pair of shoes August had worn in her life. For that matter, the gown itself was torture to wear. It was in the new *cuirasse* style that created an elongated bodice that fit down over the flare of her hips, somewhat limiting the length of her steps. It was also so low-cut that it had required a specially made chemise and corset to accommodate it, and she had to fight her own instincts to constantly try to pull it up. Mary had laced her into her corset to within an inch of her life to make certain her modest breasts were shown to their best advantage. Eating anything at supper later would be out of the question.

August had ordered the Worth dress on a whim when they had placed the order for all of their gowns. She had fallen in love with the fashion plate and the accompanying sample of scarlet velvet as soon as she had seen it. Unfortunately or fortunately, depending on her mood, which changed from one minute to the next, the gown that had been delivered to their townhome last week had been far more scandalously cut than she had realized. To make it more shocking, the overskirt was tied back at her bottom to drape in graceful waves to the ground. From the back it was beautiful and elegant. From the front, the tie-back effect only further served to outline the curve of her hips and hint at the shocking fact that she was in possession of a pair of thighs.

Countless scathing editorials had been written on the indecent new style when it had first made an appearance last year. August had hardly paid them any attention. It had seemed ridiculous that anyone would care overly much about the draping of a dress as long as the important parts were covered. Wearing this particular gown had changed her opinion on that. All eyes in the room had turned to her as soon as she and her family had walked into the ball. This had been expected because everyone wondered about her involvement with Rothschild and if a betrothal announcement would be forthcoming. The eyes had stayed on her and wandered over her lower extremities, however, because of this gown. The result was that she felt naked.

Hundreds of voices carrying on conversations around them muffled her sigh of protest as her toes screamed in pain with each step. Her current partner delivered her back to her scowling mother after their dance, bowing dutifully. When he offered to bring her punch, her mother refused on her behalf and only managed to wait until the man had turned away before saying, "Rothschild has yet to make an appearance." Her voice was low, but the tone was such that August wasn't entirely certain it wouldn't travel to those around them. The insinuation that his absence was August's fault was still heard loud and clear by her daughter.

August tried not to smile. Since her argument with Rothschild about the betrothal two days ago, she had made certain that every one of her waking moments was spent outside her home. Even the sanctuary of Papa's study wouldn't save her from him if he deigned to call. Her absence from home also gave her more time to do all the things a socially acceptable wife would not do.

"Have you heard what they're saying about you?" Mother discreetly indicated the room at large.

August could not help but smile a little at that. She had heard snatches of conversation here and there. All true. "What do you mean?" She feigned a mildly curious tone.

Her mother sighed. "You were seen attending a lecture by that woman reformer."

"Barbara Bodichon." It had been an interesting talk about the value of education for women.

Mother gave a firm shake of her head as if the name hardly mattered. "And what is this about Lord Worth? You were seen on his arm in Hyde Park, without your chaperone no less."

"He won a race. I merely congratulated him." And if Rothschild thought he had competition, more the better. She hoped the knowledge would rid him of his tiresome, ever-present smirk.

"You vex me, child. You know how this will appear to Rothschild. He could withdraw his proposal." She kept her voice suitably low, but they had managed to garner some curious glances. "Your exploits were even written about in one of the gossip rags."

August hadn't known ink had been spilled over her, but she wasn't surprised. "If he is so easily put off by a gossip column reporting my interest in social issues and my lack of chaperone, then I am not certain he is worth our concern."

Mother frowned as much as she was able while still maintaining a pleasant expression for the benefit of those around them. The fine lines around her mouth deepened. "You might have at least been home during calling hours. He has come every day to continue the betrothal discussion."

That was rather the point of not being home. To avoid giving her mother apoplexy there in the middle of the ball, she instead said rather gently, "That is a conversation I do not intend to have. I have made my feelings on the matter very clear."

The frustration coming off her mother was nearly palpable. "How dare you do this to us?" She had turned so that she spoke nearer August's ear to keep her voice down. "We have found you a perfectly suitable husband. He is handsome, from a good family, and he has the connections this family needs. What more do you want?"

"I was unaware that you had been so desperate to find me a husband." The bitter words were out before she could stop them. "For one, I would like a little consideration that I might want to have a say in choosing the man I am to spend the rest of my life with." Fixing a smile on her face, she said, "But perhaps now is not the time to discuss this."

Her mother huffed, and the pleasant expression she had managed to hold all this time fell. August searched the room for an escape. If she argued with her mother here, it would be the talk of the evening. As soon as she opened her mouth to excuse herself, an acquaintance she recognized but could not name came up to them. "Mrs. Crenshaw, how lovely to run into you here."

August stayed long enough to exchange pleasantries before taking herself away from the ballroom. She already had her next minor rebellion in mind. While no one had explicitly said to her that card playing at a ball was not done by a woman, she had noticed that very few women traversed the domain that seemed reserved for men. The few who did were older and had been married for decades or were widowed. The women and younger people had their own lounges at these places where various other games and amusements could be carried out. August, however, intended to conquer this sphere that had been held for the men.

Many already whispered about her "mannish tendencies"; well, let them whisper even louder so that Rothschild could hear. He would hardly want a mannish duchess. As she made her way to the suite of rooms one floor down, the noise from the crowded ballroom gradually gave way to the guffaws and jeering of distinctly male voices. A footman stood sentry at the doorway, giving her a faintly horrified glance as she stepped past him and into the salon.

The room itself was rather tastefully decorated in browns and deep reds with heavy brocade fabrics mixed with top-grain leather. It was a very masculine space with lamps and card tables set out about the room. Several tables were occupied with men playing whist. Many of them gave her interested glances, but none of them bothered to question her presence. The wide double doors that separated this room from the next were thrown open to reveal that room to be more crowded and livelier. Men cheered, and dice clinked together, while several people called out bets.

When she reached the doorway, she could barely see any of the tables for the crowd of men around them. Smoke hung heavy in the air, cloying at her lungs as she took a deep breath to calm her nerves. Had she not been trying to make a point to Rothschild, she would have turned around then and there. It was foolish to gamble on a game she knew nothing about, but she wasn't here to win, simply to prove that she was not duchess material.

She steeled herself for rejection and took a step into the room. "Blast and damn, Crenshaw!" The angry but muffled words brought her up short. Her heart jolted in her chest as she stepped back out of the room, looking for the source of the voice. It must be coming from another room off the card salon. The door was cracked open, so she crept closer cautiously.

"Do not complain to me about how things are moving too slowly." The voice belonged to Farthington; she was certain of it even though she couldn't see him. His voice was a deep baritone that was difficult to confuse with someone else's. "I have received your proposal. I can do no more until you do your part."

She stifled a gasp of shock with her hand. They had to be discussing the Indian railway proposal. She had helped her father draft it herself. One of her afternoons out of the home had been to Farthington's secretary to gather preliminary information on the Indian labor and materials market, which she had then stayed up late into the night to compile into a comprehensive report. From that she had drafted an initial proposal that detailed Crenshaw Iron's strengths along with their readily available assets. The more in-depth planning would come once this initial proposal was reviewed and passed on to the next phase. Assuming it made it that far.

Her father spoke too low for her to hear, but she could see half of the back of his head as he sat across the table from Farthington. Several other men were present, fabric rustled, and one cleared his throat, but she could not see them through the crack between the door and the frame.

"Yes, yes, all of that has been made clear to me," Farthington replied. "You must understand that I cannot present the proposal until *you do your part*."

Again her father's voice was low and calm, but she thought she made out the words *these things take time*.

"Yes, well, time is our enemy. Rest assured that we are very clear on your position and your ability. The issue, which I thought I had made very clear to you, is that we cannot open this market up to simply anyone. If your firm were to secure a contract without suitable justification, I would be swimming in harassment as others tried to secure the same favor. No, we cannot have that." He sliced his hand through the air for emphasis. "The proposal cannot go further until a betrothal is announced."

She brought her hand up to cover her mouth, and a sick feeling twisted in her stomach. The expansion of Crenshaw Iron Works hinged on her marriage to the duke. A marriage she did not want and had no intention of committing herself to. She had naively hoped that by drawing out the courting phase they might secure the contract without an eventual marriage.

As if he had heard her naivete, Farthington laughed. "I trust your honor, but I am afraid we need to see more progress on that front before we can move forward."

She crossed her arms over her stomach to help contain the helpless anger and fear that whirled inside her. She trembled with it. If she dared to let go of herself, it might somehow tear her apart from the inside. A sob half escaped her, drawing glances from one of the tables. Holding it in, she hurried out of the salon and back into the long corridor lined with portraits. At the end, a set of terrace doors had been opened to the night, so she headed toward them, needing to get away from everyone. Unfortunately, the corridor passed right by the dice game room, and a man stepped out as she passed.

"Miss Crenshaw?" It was Lord Ware. "By God, are you hurt? Has someone harmed you?" He rushed after her and glanced behind, looking for the perpetrator that had sent her seeking refuge outside.

"No, I am unharmed. I simply need some air." She did her best to keep her composure, but she knew she failed when he didn't look a bit less concerned.

He glanced toward the terrace. "You should not be out there alone." It was dark, but there were gas lamps. She had seen them flickering from the windows of the ballroom on the first floor. "I shall accompany you."

God save her from men who thought she needed them. She wanted to tell him to leave her alone, but that would likely only make him more suspicious. At the very least it would make things take longer, and with every fiber of her being she needed to be out of this house and have a moment of peace.

Balls were not for her, she decided. Terrible things happened at them.

"As you please," she said and swept past him, although he kept pace with her.

The mansion off Park Street was huge, nearly taking up a block, so the garden was larger than the Ashcroft garden. It stretched the length of the house with several walking paths circling the space. She immediately headed away from the noise of the ball into the far corner near the brick wall.

"Where in hell do you think you are taking her?"

The voice belonged to Rothschild. She whirled to see him coming out of another set of terrace doors, walking toward Lord Ware. Both his tone and his stance were menacing. His hands were in fists at his side as if he were prepared to fight the poor viscount on the spot. For his part, Lord Ware stood his ground, but he glanced to her with eyes so wide the whites were clearly visible around the irises. "Miss Crenshaw wished to come outside. I was merely assuring her safety."

"This isn't one of your bare-knuckle brawls, Rothschild. Lord Ware saw that I was in distress and came to my aid."

Rothschild's gaze swept over her from top to bottom and back again, as if he was searching for the source of her distress. He might as well have checked her over with his hands for how breathless his examination left her. She whirled away from him, crossing her arms over her chest as she reached for the anger boiling beneath the surface. He was the reason she was in this mess. She had no business being so attracted to him. He wore the same damned black-and-white evening suit as every man here, so why did the way his coat stretched over the solid breadth of his shoulders look so appealing to her?

"Thank you for your help, Ware." His tone made it clear this was not true gratitude. "You may leave us."

August rolled her eyes. Just once she wanted someone to not jump at his orders.

To his credit, Lord Ware did not move immediately. "Miss Crenshaw?"

Glancing over her shoulder, she saw Rothschild's jaw clenched tight. Lord Ware fidgeted. To put him out of his misery, she said, "Thank you for your assistance, Lord Ware. I will be fine."

He gave her a nod and walked stiffly back inside. Rothschild waited until he had passed through the doorway to come over to her, stopping before her. "What has happened? Are you distressed?"

Refusing to meet his gaze, she hurried around him to follow the path through the rhododendrons. The last person she wanted to talk to was him.

"You are limping."

"Leave me alone."

She knew he wouldn't, and his shoes crunching on the stone told her as much. She did not dare go too far into the garden with the library incident from the last ball fresh on her mind. Instead, she stopped at the turn in the path, far enough away that some of the noise was deafened, but close enough not to appear too indecent. She hoped.

"Here. You must be cold."

She hadn't realized how cold she was until his tailcoat, still warm with his body heat, enveloped her shoulders. The warmth felt so good and welcome that she wanted to accept it, but the need to never accept anything from him won out. She shrugged out of it, and it would have fallen had he not been faster and caught it. The absence of warmth made the chill air even that much more apparent. With him close, the night filled with delightful notes of lemon and bergamot. Her rebellious body savored it, reaching for more of it all while she continued to face away from him.

There was a moment of silence and then, "Will you tell me what has you upset?" His voice was filled with concern.

"As if you don't know." She refused to look at him, but she wanted to see his expression so badly that she glanced briefly over her shoulder. He had looked down, his hands dropping to his sides. The one holding the coat appeared to have a new scab on a knuckle, leaving her wondering if he had participated in another fighting match. In only his shirtsleeves and vest, he somehow appeared even more handsome. When he looked up, she jerked her gaze away.

"I came every day, but you were never at home."

"Someone else might take the hint."

"Why will you not see me?" Soft amusement had replaced the concern in his voice.

"Are you really so daft as that?" She swung around to look at him.

He smiled, and she couldn't help but fixate on the attractive curve of his lips. It forced her to remember the almost-kiss in her drawing room when she had nearly agreed to allow him to court her for appearances before her mother had spilled the truth all over both of them.

"The things you say to me are outrageous. I like you all the more for them."

"You like that I insult you?"

He gave a soft laugh. "No. I like that you are honest with me. Your honesty is one of the things that drew me to you."

Having not expected that bit of flattery, she looked down. Was it even flattery? When most men flattered her, it was always about appearances or other superficial things.

That she was prepared for. This took her by surprise. Was it wrong to like it?

"Something happened inside. Will you tell me?" After a brief pause, he added, "Please."

She hated that the entreaty made her open her mouth. Perhaps it was also because he still stood in his shirtsleeves instead of shrugging into his tailcoat, not caring that anyone might come upon them. His brows pulled together in gentle concern as he waited. "I overheard my father and Lord Farthington talking."

"Ah, the railway."

"You know about that?"

"Of course."

It should not surprise her at all. "Lord Farthington is refusing to allow our proposal to move forward unless a betrothal is announced."

He was silent as his eyes skimmed over her face. "Is that really so very shocking?" he finally asked, his voice free of judgment.

"I suppose not." Lord Farthington had implied as much at the meeting in Papa's study. It was simply a shock to hear it out loud and put so plainly at that. All of a sudden she was overcome by the weight of failure. She had thought of nothing since this whole betrothal business began but how to get out of it. All of it had been for naught. She had never failed at something so spectacularly in her life.

"Have you given any thought to coming to Charrington Manor?"

She hadn't even remembered that he had asked her until this very moment. "Why?"

"It would be good if you could see exactly what you would be agreeing to."

"Why does it matter? Aren't I obliged to marry you regardless of what I see there?"

He took a deep breath, his gaze fixing on hers so intently that she struggled to draw in anything more than a shallow breath. When he looked at her like that, as if he really saw her, something inside her threatened to crack open. It frightened her, because she didn't know what would become of her when it did.

"No," he said softly. "No, you do not have to accept."

"Easy words to say when you do not have as much at stake." A slash of pain crossed his face, and she wished to call the words back. He had good reasons for wanting this marriage; she understood that now even if she couldn't accept it. "I only meant the railway and the deal with Parliament."

"If you refuse me, then I likely cannot help with Farthington. I can, however, help to bring you other opportunities. For one, the new Royal Albert Dock. There are approvals and licenses being held up in government now as we speak. I can make certain that Crenshaw Iron Works is given the contract for the steel if you're willing to set up an office here."

Papa would not be happy about the railway. He would be furious, but if she could offer him something else, it might be enough. When Maxwell arrived, she would talk it over with him, and perhaps together they could help Papa see reason. It wasn't as if losing the railway would cost the company money.

"Why would you do this?" The chill seeped through her skin, and she found herself rubbing her arms. He draped the coat over her shoulders, and she did not refuse him this time.

"Because I want you to give us a chance." He paused and seemed to come to a resolution. "Come for a week."

"And if we find we don't suit?"

The corner of his mouth turned upward. "You know that we suit, August."

She did know. His eyes had softened as they settled on her. She was no more exposed to him than she was to anyone else at this ball, but somehow his gaze saw more. The telltale whisper of butterfly wings moved in her belly. Swallowing, she said, "I will agree to come for a week, if you will agree to withdraw your offer at the conclusion of that week. Tell Papa that you cannot go through with it."

"Come for a week, and if you still believe that you will hate marriage to me, then I will withdraw my offer."

She gasped before she could stop herself, hardly able to believe that it could be so simple. Elation made her smile, but he interrupted her premature celebration.

"On one condition."

She frowned. Of course there was a condition. He needed more wealth than Job, so he would not be willing to part with her so easily. "What is it?"

"You let me kiss you."

It was a strangely benign request for such a major concession. "What? Here?"

He smiled again, shaking his head. "At Charrington Manor. I get to kiss you when I want to."

"Absolutely not. I would not put it past you to have us conveniently get caught. Besides, why would you want to kiss a woman who wants absolutely nothing to do with you?"

"You might not want to marry me, but you do enjoy kissing me, whether you admit it to me or not."

"Fine. You can kiss me once a day at a time and place of *my* choosing. And that's it. One kiss only."

His gaze had settled on her mouth, setting her senses rioting in pleasant agitation. Why did he have to be the one man she desired? It wasn't fair.

"I agree," he said.

She nodded, feeling more in control than she had since first meeting him. "Good. Then I will come to Charrington Manor."

Rising on her toes, she took Rothschild by his biceps and kissed his cheek. He stood still, letting her. His arms were so strong and warm under her hands that she did not let him go immediately. "Thank you. I cannot tell you how much I appreciate this."

His jaw ticked as his gaze lit on her mouth. He was undoubtedly hoping for another kind of kiss from her, but there was no way she was repeating the library incident again. That kiss had gone much further than she had intended, and she still didn't know how it had happened. She had no faith in her ability to control another one.

"You're so certain you'll still reject me," he said, his voice a soft rasp.

Shrugging out of his coat, she handed it back to him. "It's not you I am rejecting. I simply do not wish to be married yet. Surely, you can understand that. If not for your financial situation, would you be seeking a wife now?"

"Not yet, but I would have no choice but to perform my duty and marry eventually. Do you not think you would marry eventually, as well?"

"I have years before I plan to marry. My brother is given his freedom to wait; I prefer the same. My life is full with my work for now."

He appeared thoughtful as he shrugged back into the tailcoat before asking, "Now that we have settled things, can we please stop this pretense of flirting with every man at the ball?"

She smiled. "How do you know about that? You haven't been here."

"I arrived over an hour ago. Long enough to see you cavorting with Lord Smith, and Lord Hadley, and Lord Bunting, and Lord Dillingham, and—"

"That's enough. Yes, I see your point." She could also see that he was jealous. His eyes had gone all fierce and hooded again, just like they had in the library. It was terrible, but she very much liked when he looked at her that way. As if he could eat her up and make her enjoy every moment of it. "I will not have to flirt anymore now to make you leave off."

"You were flirting to make me withdraw my offer?" He sounded incredulous as he gave a mirthless laugh and took a step toward her. "You were wrong. It only made me want you more."

Self-preservation made a flicker of fear ignite within her, but it was accompanied with a healthy dose of what she was mortified to realize she could only describe as lust. She took a step back, and for some reason a laugh tumbled from her throat. "You stay away from me." Her voice shook along with the hand she put out to ward him off. "We will not have a repeat of what happened in the library."

"I rather liked what happened in the library."

His voice held a bit of a soft growl, and he did not stop at all as he advanced on her. Her heart beat low and deep in her belly. How could he reduce her to this without even touching her? It didn't make any sense. She was as needy for him as she had been after his kisses, and he hadn't even touched her.

"You stay back. I will not be caught with you, and I do not appreciate you trying to coerce me."

He laughed. "I only said I would withdraw my offer at the end of your stay. I never said that I would not use every tool at my disposal to get you to say yes."

Dear Lord! What had she gotten herself into? "I am going inside. Alone." With those words she turned and hurried inside as fast as she could in her torture slippers.

Chapter 11

Trifles make the sum of life.
CHARLES DICKENS

E van!"
The excited voices of his sisters filled the entryway a moment before they both came barreling out of the drawing room to greet him. He was dusty and coated in a layer of grime because he had opted to ride his mount from the station instead of waiting for the carriage to transport his trunk. That did not stop either one of them from throwing themselves into his arms.

"Good afternoon, poppets." He could not help but smile when he came home to them. They were like a pair of tawny puppies grappling over each other to get to him.

"You are so very late." Elizabeth admonished him with a proper scowl on her face as she drew back.

"And disgusting!" Louisa wrinkled her nose as she gave him a once-over that clearly found him lacking.

They were very nearly identical with their dark blond hair and blue eyes, coloring that, like him, they had inherited from their mother. The only real difference was that Elizabeth had a faint scar near her mouth from a childhood mischief, and Louisa had a penchant for Cook's sweets that gave her cheeks a pleasant fullness. Also, they were not puppies any longer. They had grown into women since he had last seen them months ago.

"It is very charming to have all of my faults recited to me as soon as I come home."

"Not *all* of your faults. You have a lot more than two," Elizabeth said.

Gently tweaking her nose, he asked, "Have they arrived yet?" He glanced over their heads to see his mother standing in the doorway of the drawing room wearing a concerned smile. The room behind her appeared empty.

"No, dear. Their wire indicated they would be on the five o'clock train. What happened to you?"

Evan had planned to travel with his mother the day before to allow plenty of time to meet with the estate manager before the Crenshaws arrived. Clark had sent him a message that had arrived an hour before he had been due to leave with his mother asking for an urgent meeting. The meeting had been well worth the delay, but it meant he had barely arrived in time.

It appeared he only had time for a bath and would not be able to meet them at the station. That was all well and good except for the fact that he was anxious to see August again.

"Clark believes that the men he hired might have found Father's missing solicitor. I will explain all to you later." The man had disappeared shortly after Evan had inherited and started asking difficult questions. Perhaps he had been too hasty in terminating his employment.

She nodded, but a crease appeared between her brows. "Do you think it will matter?"

"Perhaps. It is difficult to say without questioning him, but I believe he ran off with good reason. If he's hiding assets, then we will find them."

This time her nod was decidedly more confident. "Good. Clark is a respectable man. Should there be anything to find, he will find it. In the meantime"—she glanced pointedly at the pendulum clock that had been in the nook at the turn of the stairs for as long as Evan could remember—"you had best have a bath and get yourself ready. The Crenshaws arrive soon, and 'tis up to us to make a good impression since the house will not."

Truer words had never been spoken. The ancient house was bloody near to falling down around them. Speaking of which. "Why are you not in your mourning clothes?" he asked his sisters. They were in gowns that had been made for them two years ago. Not only were they hopelessly out of fashion, but they were each at least an inch too short, and artfully folded fichus obscured the poorly fit bodices.

"We were tired of black and gray," said Louisa. "It has been over a year."

"Did you expect us to wear mourning the entire visit?" Elizabeth raised a brow.

He sighed. Those were excellent reasons. He actually had no issue with them not wearing mourning clothes, even immediately after their father's death. The man had hardly been a father to them and had seen them so infrequently that he likely could not have picked them out of a crowded ballroom. The issue was more with the state of their non-mourning clothing. They were in desperate need of entirely new wardrobes. Wardrobes he could not even hope to afford. The ever-present knot in his chest tightened slightly.

"No, we should all be finished with mourning." The twins perked up, but Mother's smile was strained. As a widow, she was condemned to wear the black a bit longer to mourn a man none of them particularly missed.

Elizabeth tugged his sleeve. "Did you bring us presents?"

"Of course I did." Reaching into the outer pocket of his chesterfield, he withdrew two gold paper boxes of chocolate wrapped in white ribbon. "One for each of you."

They squealed in delight and retreated with their presents back to the drawing room. His mother's smile turned brighter as she watched their joy. However, the moment they disappeared into the room, she turned back to him and approached, touching his cheek. "Go shave and dress. I had a suit pressed for you. Do you think you can manage without Stewart?"

His valet had been left to follow along with Evan's trunk. "I think I can dress myself just this once."

"The girls and I finished our tea, but I can send a tray up for you."

"No, I can wait for dinner." He was too anxious for the arrival of their guests to feel hungry. He half expected them to turn away on the drive and refuse to come inside.

His glance struck on his sisters unwrapping their chocolates. They had grown up in the past year, so now they looked like young women playing at being children in their too-small dresses. In the corner beyond them, a water stain extended from the ceiling to halfway down the wall, ruining the wall covering. What devil had possessed him to agree to August's terms? He could no more allow her to slip through his fingers than he could make himself not want to kiss her. Without her, every one of their estates would be reduced to crumbling hovels with their insides picked clean by vultures. His sisters would have no prospects for their futures, and his own mother would further become a victim of Father's neglect. His only hope was to marry her.

Charrington Manor was nearly as dilapidated as August had feared. It wasn't crumbling, precisely. The several spires, chimneys, and at least one turret appeared to all be holding themselves erect. However, the ancient stone facade had weathered to various shades of gray, brown, and even black, and ivy covered a good third of the sprawling building. The arching roof was quite Gothic, made even more so by the weather and oxidation, which had given the roof tiles a very unattractive greenish hue. The house looked as if it had begun its life as a castle or perhaps even an abbey but had altered as it had grown over the centuries. No, it was not a ruin, but it was easily only a century away from such a catastrophe if left unchecked. "Oh dear." Violet's whisper did not sum up August's feeling at all. The manor itself would need extensive renovation on the outside alone. A new roof would be exorbitant. She was afraid to see damage the weather had wrought on the inside.

"Well . . . how medieval." Mother forced a smile. "It is rather delightful."

Papa kept a neutral expression. "It appears just as I imagine an ancestral estate to appear. Old and rather ill-used. Thank God he has the London town house."

"Do you . . ." Violet swallowed audibly as the Rothschild carriage, which had met them at the train station, swept around a curve in the long drive so that the facade could be appreciated from a new angle. "Do you suppose it is plumbed?"

No one did.

A line of people had gathered outside the front steps. The servants were wearing the family's royal blue and black livery, but her gaze was immediately drawn to the figure on the top step. His tawny hair and broad shoulders were unmistakable, as was his chiseled visage. August ran her fingertips over the curls that spilled from beneath her hat to frame her face. Mary had insisted on curling the strands that morning. At first, August had declined the offer, but the woman had insisted that it was just the look the hat needed, so she had relented. Now she was glad of Mary's persistence.

Violet glanced at her and muttered, "You look lovely."

August nodded her thanks but silently bemoaned how her sister seemed to know what she was doing. Violet might draw the wrong conclusion. August could want to look nice for him while still not wanting to marry him. The two were not mutually exclusive goals.

The moment the carriage drew to a halt at the base of the wide steps, a groom moved forward and opened the door. A second placed a step down to ease their departure. August tried and failed not to make eye contact with Rothschild as she took the offered hand and disembarked. He made it impossible as he had come down the steps and was smiling at her. "Good afternoon, Miss Crenshaw. I trust your journey was uneventful?"

What was it about the precise tenor of his voice that settled into her like hot tea on a cold and rainy day? "Yes, thank you."

He offered his hand, and she took it more on instinct than any actual thought. After placing a chaste kiss on the back, he said, "My apologies for not meeting you at the station. I was delayed in London on business and only arrived not very long ago."

His eyes were full of regret, and she found herself wondering again how things might have been different for them had he not been a fortune-hunting scoundrel.

She nodded and meant to reply but Papa was faster. "Do not trouble yourself, Your Grace. We were well taken care of by your man there."

Though his gaze lingered on her, Rothschild slowly took himself down the line until he had greeted every member of her family. The duchess stood on the bottom step with a pleasant smile on her face and two young women August could only assume to be her daughters at her side. They looked like younger versions of the duchess herself.

"Good afternoon, Your Grace. It's lovely to see you again." Despite her mixed feelings about the woman's son, August quite liked the woman herself. There was an innate kindness about her face, and a directness in her gaze that was comforting rather than off-putting. It made one feel seen and accepted.

"I hope your journey went well," the woman said. After she had been assured that it had and pleasantries were exchanged with the rest of the family, she turned to her daughters with obvious pride on her face. "May I present my daughters, Elizabeth and Louisa."

The differences between the twins were immediately obvious. Louisa effused warmth like her mother, while Elizabeth seemed more reserved and wary. They would not be her future sisters, because August had already determined how the week would end, but she still felt anxious and hoped that they would like her.

"Come inside," said the duchess. "We have your rooms prepared and waiting. You must all wish to refresh yourselves after your journey. We tend to keep country hours here, so dinner will be served in an hour."

The entry hall was wide and paneled in oak. It might have been dark had there not been a huge multipaned window over the front door that allowed in the weak afternoon sun. It was enough light to illuminate the grand staircase toward the back of the hall lined with paintings. The walls were painted a faded and rather shabby red, and the carpets were worn and frayed. A peek toward the drawing room revealed comfortable but worn furnishings.

She dared not comment on any of it. Instead she bade Her Grace good afternoon as she followed the maid that had been assigned to lead her to her room. The back of her gloved hand still tingled from the light touch of Rothschild's lips. Being near him did strange things to her. Suddenly, her plan for surviving the coming week, namely, ignoring him, did not seem as clear as it once had.

Mary had just finished the intricate knot on the crown of August's head when a knock sounded at the door of the bedroom she had been given. The room was comfortably furnished but, like everything else in the house, faded with time. The walls had once been rose, she was almost certain, but had become a muddled color somewhere between beige and brown.

"That must be Her Grace. Could you answer it, Mary?" August asked and then rubbed a bit of rose-tinted salve onto her lips. The caller certainly wasn't a member of her own family, who would politely knock before barging in.

"Your Grace." Mary went into a deep curtsy, but something about her disposition had August glancing up.

She rose from the bench at her dressing table when she saw Rothschild. "What are you doing here?"

"I have come to escort you downstairs." He grinned, his gaze straying down to take in her clothing. She couldn't stop her hands from drifting down the bodice of her gown, suddenly concerned if he would like the emerald gown with black piping as much as she had. Not that it mattered what he thought. Why did it matter?

"I am perfectly capable of escorting myself downstairs." The words came out harsher than she had intended.

His perusal of her broke off immediately, and she worried that she had hurt him when his gaze went to Mary. Sensing that he wanted a moment alone with her, she said, "That will be all, Mary. Thank you." She really shouldn't send the maid away. His presence was improper even with Mary here, but part of her was too curious to care about propriety.

The maid bobbed a series of curtsies and somehow made her way out the door as she did so. The second her footsteps began to disappear down the corridor, Rothschild came across the room to stand before her.

"Are we back to this again?" Displeasure showed in his every step. "This antagonism. I thought we had come to an understanding, but I can see we have returned to needless baiting."

He was right. She was already regretting her outburst. There was no need for the bitterness, especially since the boundaries had already been established and an agreement made. She could walk away from him after the week was finished. "You're right. I'm sorry." His eyes widened slightly. "You surprised me. I didn't think you would come to my bedroom. On that note, we should really continue this conversation in the hallway so that we are not left alone."

His grin was immediately back in place. "I came because I thought you might need to see me, and I can see I was right," he said, ignoring the part about them being alone.

Immediately suspicious, she asked, "What do you mean? Why would I *need* to see you?"

That infuriating grin only widened. "Because you miss me, or perhaps you even want to kiss me."

She laughed, both taken aback by his insolence and impressed by his nerve. "That is the most ridiculous thing I have ever heard."

"Is it? Isn't that why you feel the need to lash out at me? You find me attractive but that bothers you and makes you bitter. Also, per our agreement, I get to kiss you once each day you are here. I have come to relieve you of the burden of anticipation."

By the time he finished his little speech, she had to forcibly close her mouth. "You have some nerve."

That damned grin reappeared. "I do."

He was deliberately provoking her, and she refused to give him the satisfaction of a response. "Fine. Have done with it, then."

He stepped right up to her until the heat from his body warmed her front. That was no small thing, considering how drafty the place was. She had to fight against her instinct to close the space between them and soak up all the warmth he would give her. Dipping his head, he brought his hand up to gently touch her jaw. The backs of his fingers skated over her skin, sending a ripple of pleasure down her spine. She licked her lips in anticipation, but he hesitated, hovering over her mouth as if he were savoring a cup of coffee that was slightly too hot.

When she absolutely could not take another moment's delay, she pushed upward until her lips touched his. He obliged her by fitting his lips to hers, moving them in a gentle rhythm that had her parting for him. By now his kiss had become familiar to her, though she had no idea how it had happened so fast. She only knew that she anticipated the soft heat of him and his taste in a way that made kissing him feel like indulging in a heavenly slice of the most decadent chocolate cake. He *was* decadent and sinful, and she wanted more than she should.

It was over all too soon and he was pulling back. Why was he stopping when they had only barely started? She opened her eyes to see him staring down at her, mischief in his gaze but something far more satisfying smoldering underneath.

"Shall we go to dinner?" he asked.

She nodded, wishing for a moment to compose herself but not wanting to give him the satisfaction of knowing how deeply he affected her. She took the arm he offered and hoped that the effects of the kiss were not visible to anyone else.

Mother had a distinctive twinkle in her eye when she saw them, but she stayed silent on the point. The duchess inquired about their comfort, and everyone stood around chatting amicably for several minutes until a servant announced that dinner was ready.

Dinner was less formal than the Ashcroft affair. For one, the table had an extension that had been removed for the occasion, making it much smaller for their party of eight. Secondly, the gender order was thrown off with only two males present, so everyone wandered in as a group. There was no awkward dithering over where everyone would sit. Rothschild would naturally take his place at the head of the table with his mother at the other end. Mother had latched onto him the second they began to walk in that direction, and August thought it rather appropriate that he ended up with her. Mother was known for her endless conversation, so he should be suitably entertained all night. The sisters had already engaged Violet in conversation before August had come down, so they sandwiched her sister between them, taking up one side of the table. Her Grace gently took August's arm, saying, "Come sit next to me, child, so we can learn more about each other." Apparently, Rothschild had not shared their agreement with his mother.

The dining room was breathtaking. It had a ceiling that arched gracefully in several places with wooden beams leading toward each apex. The hearth extended out into the room with a beautiful and ornate mantel and a chute facade that soared to the ceiling. It was very dramatic, and the effect was gorgeous. However, the decay of the house was noticeable. Plaster was crumbling and in need of repair before a new coat of paint could be applied. The wood, both in the beams overhead and the wainscoting, was dark and in need of polish. Although some of it might need to be replaced before that could happen, as several water stains were visible. One large water stain ran down the length of one corner of the wall, no doubt caused by the leaky roof that desperately needed to be restored. The whole place held the faint odor of neglect.

"How are you enjoying your stay in London, Miss Crenshaw?" the duchess inquired as she nodded to one of the footmen, who began filling their wineglasses.

August had warmed to the woman immediately in their previous brief interactions. Seeing her with her daughters tonight had only improved August's perception of her. It was no hardship to chat with her, so they spoke until the fish course about London and the amusements they had each attended. Over stewed eel, the duchess turned slightly toward August and said, "I am curious: tell me about your work with Crenshaw Iron. Do you find it fulfilling?"

August nearly choked on the tender bite of eel she had just taken. No one had ever asked her about her work before. August had overheard snatches of conversations where people were obviously talking about it, but no one had ever asked her directly. This phenomenon was not limited to London. It happened back home as well. It was known that she worked alongside her father and brother, but it seemed to be an unwritten taboo for women to ask her about it socially.

After a discreet bout of coughing, she said, "Pardon me. Yes, actually I do find it very rewarding. I quite enjoy the research and the forensic inspection of a financial statement."

"August was nigh this high"—Papa held a hand up to the level of the table—"when she climbed onto the desk in my study and added a column of figures that had been making my head hurt. I allowed her to occasionally help with the ledgers after that. She gradually took on more responsibility as she grew older. She finds the work rewarding, but never fear, she is more than capable of turning that enthusiasm to new projects."

The pride on his face was unmistakable, and August nearly smiled automatically in response before she understood exactly what he meant. He was assuring the duchess that August was perfectly content to give up the career she had worked long and hard to build at Crenshaw Iron.

The duchess gave a tight smile, and her brow raised ever so slightly when her gaze fixed on August. August blinked, and the older woman said to Papa, "What a clever child."

"She is a very clever child," said Papa. "I believe she will be successful in everything she does."

"I do not prefer to give up my work," August said, quietly setting aside her cutlery and reaching for her wineglass.

Papa's lips twitched with a hint of displeasure. Thankfully, the duchess broke the silence. "You do not find the day-to-day tasks of office work tedious?"

Putting aside her earlier misgivings, August said, "Some days can be dull. We cannot always be in the midst of planning a new venture or acquiring a factory. However, there is always a satisfaction in knowing that a day has been well spent in a way that will benefit many."

"Hmm . . ." The duchess made the thoughtful sound as she took a dainty sip of her white Burgundy. "The railways *have* completely changed the way we live."

"Yes, there is that, but I also speak of our workers. I like to think that they are looked after. We provide them with good, gainful employment so that they can support their families. Their families in turn grow healthy and educated to further a productive society."

The duchess nodded and smiled. "Indeed, that sounds rather progressive."

"I think it simply makes good sense by whatever name it is called," August said.

Not to be left out of the conversation, Papa said, "Never to worry, Your Grace, Maxwell and I keep her in line when she becomes too generous with the help. August is not so foolish as to not listen to those who know better."

Her face flamed in both anger and embarrassment. He was doing everything he could to boast of her business acumen with a wink and a nudge that assured everyone not to worry that she was still perfectly domesticated. "I am not some wayward puppy that you must keep in check. I do understand financial constraints and measurements."

Papa laughed. Whether he was putting a good face on things for Her Grace or he did not understand her pique was impossible to say. The duchess ignored him and viewed August with an appraising eye. "August is an unusual name."

Momentarily taken aback at the change in topic, it took a moment for her to answer. "My grandfather was Augustus, and I was named for him."

She nodded as if she had expected as much. "You do him proud, I think."

Warmed more than she had anticipated by the kind words, she said, "Thank you. I enjoy that I am making a difference in a venture our grandfather started with his own hands."

"Yes, I imagine you would."

The woman went back to her eel and then turned her attention to her daughters, which was just as well, because August was still rattled by the exchange with her father. Had he always been insidious with his enthusiasm of her accomplishments and she simply hadn't noticed? Had he always seen her as a child he would humor until it was time to marry her off? If so, how had she been so blind to it before?

Sneaking a glance down the table, she was not at all surprised to find Rothschild engaged in conversation with her mother and Violet. Mother was relating some childhood mishap, and Rothschild laughed when he was supposed to, but his gaze found hers across the table. As if sensing her unease, a crease formed between his brows, and he glanced to his mother before fixing his attention back on her. As the laughter died down, he turned his attention to his sisters and his voice rose to encompass the table. "I am sorry to say, but these two can outshine any mischief your children might have made. Did Mother tell you of the time they locked their governess in the very attic they had convinced her was haunted?"

"No!"

"Evan!"

The twins simultaneously cried out, sending the table into laughter. His concern felt genuine, as did the way he tried to turn the flow of conversation away from her and her family. She appreciated the gesture and felt herself softening toward him again. When he glanced back at her, she inclined her head in appreciation, and he grinned, making her heart pick up its pace the tiniest bit. The rest of dinner carried on in that same vein.

No one mentioned marriage or fortunes.

Chapter 15

*No man ever became great or good except
through many and great mistakes.*

WILLIAM GLADSTONE

The next morning, Evan took the family on a tour of the estate grounds. It had been one of the singularly most unpleasant experiences of his life, akin to baring the ugliest parts of his soul to strangers. Strangers who made a fuss about how quaint and charming it all seemed, the rural and very real decay that decorated their country jaunt.

All Evan could see was evidence of his failure.

When the tour had concluded, he had likely not so graciously bade the Crenshaws a good day while ushering August to the stables. There was more she was entitled to see before making her decision, but he refused to allow her parents the opportunity to come along. Now they were slowly riding their mounts down the drive to a row of nearby tenant farms. August had barely said a word, but she kept glancing at him. He was too ashamed of the mess his father had left and his own inability to clean it up to ask her what she thought so far.

"Do you ride very often?" she finally asked, breaking their self-imposed silence.

"Yes, as much as I can in London. Usually, every morning. You?"

"I have a horse at home, Poppy. She's a beautiful palomino. I ride her as often as I get the chance."

He glanced at her, taking in the easy way she settled into the saddle and moved with the animal. She had a natural grace about her. It pleased him to see her easy manner with horses. He could hardly imagine having a wife who did not enjoy riding. Once more, he was gripped by an urgency to seal this deal. She was nearly perfect for him in every way. Only, more and more, guilt followed on the heels of that urgency. She had an entire life he was taking her away from.

She caught him looking and gave him a smile. "Shall we race?"

"It would hardly be fair. You are sidesaddle."

A line formed between her brows. "Then give me a head start."

He laughed. "You are the last person I would believe would ask for a concession."

"Concessions are needed, dear sir, when the very fabric of the rule is inherently unfair. Change the rule and I wouldn't need one." She clicked her tongue and snapped the reins before he could respond, and she was off racing down the road. "First one to the gate wins!"

His bay perked up his ears and took very little prodding before giving chase. Even sidesaddle, she was fast. His heart pounded as he started closing the distance between them. Her hat appeared very near to falling off her head, and he loved that she didn't care. When she glanced over her shoulder, she appeared much more concerned with winning. In the end, they pulled up to the open gate at the same time before coming to a slow stop to allow the horses to catch their breaths. "You are a very good rider," he said.

"I love horses."

She gave her borrowed filly a few loving strokes that had a strange sort of jealousy coming to life in him. What would it take to make her touch him in the same loving way? Probably calling off this marriage pursuit would be a good start, but Evan could not go that far. Not when they needed her so desperately.

Instead, he guided them off toward the path that went along the river that cut through the estate. Many of the farms bordered the southern part of the estate and made use of the river. It was time to start showing her one of the few things he could offer her. Freedom.

"Have you ridden astride before?"

She nodded. "We have a country house in Connecticut. I usually ride astride there."

"Why am I not surprised?" He grinned.

She smiled over at him. "No one is supposed to know, but I have riding trousers and a special skirt made for the task. Violet does as well."

"I would not mind if you did that here . . . should you agree to become duchess." He glanced out over the gray, slow-moving water to avoid her face. It was the first they had spoken of marriage since the night of the ball. Even now he could not quite say it. He spoke around it, and a queer sort of flicker began in his stomach. It was an agitation he did not care for.

"How magnanimous of you." There was a bitterness in her voice that was softened by the shape of her smile. It drew his gaze to her shining eyes. "Or I could simply stay unmarried and do as I wish."

He gave her a nod. "Or you could do that."

Logic urged him to remind her that she would eventually marry. He might have believed that she was perfectly happy not to marry, if he had not kissed her. If he had not witnessed how her eyes lit up and her body softened to him. She wanted companionship, the kind that only a lover could bring. He was surprised that he also wanted that. Marriage had never been important to him, but it was all he thought of lately by necessity. With her, however, his thoughts took him further. He found himself imagining nights at the theater, days at home with her in front of the fire, surprising her with small things like a necklace or a book. He had noticed a few of those on the desk in her bedroom.

"I have read about the suffrage case before the American Supreme Court."

Her head whirled back to him. "What do you mean?"

"The case for women's suffrage."

"*Minor v. Happersett*?"

"That's it. Have you followed it?"

She gave a small laugh that sounded a bit like disbelief. "I have. I daresay any thinking American woman has heard of it, or at least its predecessor, the Susan B. Anthony case. I'm . . . I'm merely surprised that you know of it, or paid attention to it."

"It is a newfound interest of mine." Very new, considering he had not been bothered to give the issue much thought before her. His world had been very narrowly focused on his own needs, with the occasional thought of his mother and sisters butting in. "Both were unsuccessful in their attempts to gain suffrage equality."

She nodded. "I don't think anyone actually believed that Minor would prevail, but it was a challenge that needed to happen."

Wanting to completely understand her position, he asked, "How do you feel about voting rights for women?"

She had turned forward, but she cut her eyes at him as she spoke. "I think the more pertinent question is: How do you feel about voting equality?"

He could not help but to smile at her boldness. "I believe that it makes no sense that my butcher be allowed the vote but not someone as educated and contemplative as you."

She finally looked at him head-on, and he could see that she was startled. "Then you support women's suffrage?"

"I do, and I also happen to be in possession of a seat in Parliament." He swallowed and plowed forward with his bid for her acceptance. "I could use it to further that cause."

Her lips parted and she visibly swallowed. "Have you been to Parliament this season?" she asked dubiously.

"I go only when absolutely necessary. I can hardly stand to listen to the endless speeches by the pompous, boorish, and self-important men who spend their days there."

"But you would brave those if you had to?"

He gave a nod. "For good reason, yes, I would spend more time there." He hated the idea of it. Politics was something he loathed almost as much as he had loathed spending time alone with his father. But for her, he could take his place there.

"One of our tenant farms." He gestured to a house in the distance. They had passed a bend a while back that made the first farm come into view. Now they were close enough to make out several figures in the far field in the midst of harvesting the winter barley. She had yet to respond to him, and he hoped it meant that she was thinking it over. "This is Harold Armstrong and three of his sons." Harold raised an arm in greeting as they approached. "His family has lived on this estate for over a hundred years."

"Good mornin', Your Grace." Harold took his hat off as he approached, revealing a receding hairline and a generous amount of gray mixed in with the brown. The man was only approaching middle age, but he looked as if he could be sixty, such were the lines and crevices in his face.

Evan introduced him to August. After greeting her, the man turned and introduced her to his sons. They stood like step stools all in a row of descending height from the oldest, who was about fourteen or so, to the youngest, who appeared to be half that.

"What lovely children," August said politely. She could not have missed how their clothing was worn, the leather of their shoes nearly cloth-like in its texture.

"Where is your older boy? Alfred, isn't it?" Evan asked.

"Off to York. Our young want the city life."

"Indeed." He did not need to point out that it was not *want* so much as *need* that had likely sent the boy to a factory position. Young people were leaving for the cities in droves.

They spoke about mundane things for a few minutes—the weather, the harvest—before Evan bade him goodbye and led August back toward the river. He hardly dared to look at her, knowing that her eyes would reflect her disappointment and condemnation of him. Who was he to live like a . . . well, like a duke, when the people in his care were barely surviving?

"Why did you bring me here?" she asked when they were far enough away no one would hear them.

The censure he expected in her voice was not present. It was quiet and pensive, instead. Her face was still, and when he met her gaze, it was unreadable.

"We made a deal. One week. I wanted you to know what you would be walking away from."

August rode in silence for a few moments as she absorbed what Rothschild had revealed to her. Her emotions ran the gamut from anger that he would try to manipulate her into accepting him to grateful appreciation that he was willing to show her unpleasant things about the estate and its troubles. Perhaps not everything, but at least this. She could not stop from thinking about the children in that family. Did they even know how to read?

Deciding that it was best to know, she asked, "Can you tell me more about the farmers? Their plight?"

He gave a curt nod. "Their plight? Yes, I should be happy to. Several years ago, before his death, my brother, William, got it into his head that the farms were faltering. I do not know if he had met with the estate manager or if it was simply observation, but he urged me to take his side in convincing Father to modernize. I did." He glanced at her then, revealing the mischievous glint in his eye along with the self-deprecating smile. "Do not let that excite you. It was no high-minded gesture on my part. I took his side because it meant not taking Father's. No more and no less."

She smiled in spite of herself. "Yes, I could tell you were the obstinate type immediately after meeting you."

Grinning more naturally now, he continued. "William was a scholar. He generally spent his days studying Latin and Greek philosophy, but he set his mind to farming for whatever reason and determined that the world was moving on without us. Did you see the ridges in the grazing fields you passed on your journey here?"

She had.

"Yes. It is called ridge and furrow and is a remnant of

the Middle Ages. It is caused by the method employed to plow the same patch of land every year." When he saw her confusion, he added, "They only cultivate the soil on one side of the plow per pass. Over time, those mounds result as the soil is built up. Our farmers were still employing the use of that plow even though there are more efficient tools that allow better and more thorough tilling. In fact, there are a great many more modern tools that we were not using: scarifiers, rollers, grubbers, clod crushers, reaper-binders." He paused, giving her a self-effacing grin. "I have learned more about farming than I ever wanted to learn. All are machines built to increase the man power of a single farmer. Nevertheless, it was no use. Father refused any sort of modernization at all, even after William and I provided him with evidence of their efficiency."

August had no idea what machines he was talking about, but even she could understand the need to modernize farming techniques. "What happened?"

"He simply refused all of our attempts to make him see reason. He believed that the land had supported these people for hundreds of years, and if it was failing them now, then it was their own burden to bear. It was as if he thought they were to blame for it."

August hadn't spent a lot of time wondering about Rothschild's father, but she had instinctively formed a poor opinion of the man. Now that opinion worsened. "But how could he be so callous? They cannot be blamed for market conditions beyond their control."

"I agree, but he would not be reasoned with. He was very much one of the men who live in the past and refuse to see the benefits of change."

"You are not one of those men?" She could plainly see that he was not, but she wanted him to elaborate.

"I hope not. I very much hope to give them the tools necessary to lead successful lives. Harold's son went to York because he would rather slave in a factory than starve on a farm, and I can hardly blame him."

She had seen all morning how difficult it was for him to visit the estate, but now the bitterness of his words confirmed it. He was embarrassed, and rightfully so. The estate had been mismanaged to the point of negligence from what she could ascertain. "What else would you do differently?"

"Nearly everything. Most of it comes down to educating the farmers. Aside from the mechanized equipment to start, we must embrace the four-course technique in crop rotation, instead of the three-course, which allows for a fallow year. There is no time for years with no harvest, and they cling to it because they fear change and my father so instilled a love of tradition in them. We also must bring in cattle and pigs. No matter how I have stressed the importance of moving from crops, they refuse it."

"Why do they refuse the animals?"

"I am told that genteel farmers do not dabble in animals. They are unclean and undignified."

"How unfortunate. Cattle farming is a prosperous industry in America. The railroads have helped to make it so."

He nodded. "Yes, I have studied your markets, as well as the markets in Britain and all of Europe. If I could get my farmers to cooperate, we could likely move into the nineteenth century before the twentieth century begins."

He took in a deep breath and looked at her again. His gaze caught hers, and the intensity was so great that she could not look away. She had never once seen him this passionate about anything except courting her, and she found that she rather liked this side of him. "The issue is that I lack the funds for the initial investment to ease their reticence and provide incentive. That is the true reason I brought you here. Yes, this marriage would be for financial gain. It seems only fair that you are able to see firsthand what your money would be funding. As I said before, the marriage is not simply for my own selfish gain. There are other lives at stake. Lives that I am responsible for.

"There are families here, families struggling to eke out a living, and your contribution to our marriage would be for them. There are over two hundred of them on this estate alone."

He went silent as they rode on toward the next farm. She had to admit that she had never imagined the need was so great, or that it even really extended past his family. He was clever to bring her here. The Armstrongs had put a face on the very real human need, and it was hard to ignore. It wouldn't make her change her mind about her own future, but it worked to soften her stance toward him. He was no longer a simple fortune hunter. He was a man determined to help the people who depended upon him. It was admirable. He was admirable.

"How did you learn so much about farming? From your brother?"

He shook his head, his eyes fixed on the house in the distance, another tenant farmer and his family out in the field. "I wish I could say that we had not let the matter drop, but we both did. After Father died and I learned the true state of our affairs, I knew that something had to be done. I have spent the past year studying modern farming methods."

"I think you've done an admirable job so far."

He glanced at her in surprise and shook his head again. "No, William would be much more suited to the task."

She opened her mouth to offer some consolation, but he clicked his tongue and urged his horse forward to greet the next farmer, who was already making his way toward them. This meeting commenced in a similar vein as the last. This farm and the one next to it were smaller in scope, and the houses were built close together, so they rode immediately for the next one.

"If these visits are intended to demonstrate financial need, then I believe you have proven your point," she said as they left the last family.

"You have had enough?" His smile was slow, like that of someone who had revealed the worst about himself and come out the other side surprised to still be intact.

She nodded. "We've been gone well over an hour. My parents are possibly worried."

"Possibly, but not likely," he teased.

She laughed, conceding his point. "You're right. They would let you take me to the ends of the earth with barely a complaint. At any rate, I do not need to see more. I am more concerned with the question of your plan to move forward."

He was silent as he guided them to the path that would take them along the river again and back home. Finally, he said, "A plan without funding is no real plan, but yes, I have a plan. Would you like to see it?"

"Yes, I believe I would. I could potentially offer some suggestions. I know little about farming, but I know something of business and investment planning. I could take a look and offer advice."

"By all means. I have an appointment to meet with my estate manager this afternoon. Join us."

She smiled, having anticipated his gracious refusal of her help. "Truly?"

"Yes. I would be mad to refuse."

"Why do you say that?"

"Because while I have been humbled this past year, I have the good sense to recognize someone with sensible business acumen. I would not turn away any suggestions you have."

This was a new sort of flattery and one she was not at all immune to. Her heart flickered like a wild thing in her chest, and she had to take several breaths to calm herself.

"Then yes, I will join you."

The smile stayed on her face the entire ride back to Charrington Manor. By the light of the full sun, the great house had a charm that she hadn't noticed the day before. It was rather Gothic, but in an old-world charm sort of way, rather than the overwhelming intimidation that she had felt the day before. If houses could have personalities, and she was convinced that some could, this one would be a benevolent grandfather who had been quite charming in his day. With a new roof, new plaster, and a good scrubbing, the stones might take on a creamier tone rather than the grimy gray streaked with oxidized green.

"You are smiling," he remarked as they rode toward the stable.

The stable boy came running out to hold her reins steady as Rothschild dismounted and came around to help her down. A little flutter of pleasure in her belly reminded her of her awareness of him when his hands gripped her waist. Using his strong shoulders for leverage, she allowed him to help her down. It was entirely decent but indecent at the same time. Countless stable hands and grooms had helped her dismount before, but their touch had felt cold and distant. Then again, theirs had never lingered on her waist like his.

"Thank you." Her voice trembled the tiniest bit as she stared up at him. There was a new depth to his eyes that she hadn't noticed before. "I am smiling, because I like the idea of helping you."

"Indeed?" His brow raised attractively. "I thought you rather enjoyed the idea of thwarting me."

"Can't one do both?" she teased.

"When one is named August, perhaps she can."

At the use of her name, she automatically looked for the boy, but he had already led their horses inside without her even noticing. Not that it mattered if he heard. Her parents would be thrilled if they knew Rothschild had used her name. Instinctively, she glanced toward the house, thinking to find them watching from a window. However, the stable faced away and was at the peak of a gentle slope, so they were blocked from view. The situation gave her an idea.

"Do you plan to kiss me now?" Lord help her, but she wanted him to. She had decided that she would enjoy each and every kiss that he gave her this week, even if she did plan to thwart his goal of marriage. It was indeed possible to do both.

He smiled, a big one that showed all his teeth and made her fixate on his lips. "Are you wanting to have it done with for the day?" he asked.

"No." She found herself being honest with him. "It simply seemed like something you would do." Not honest enough to tell him that she wanted it. Not here in broad daylight.

His hands tightened on her waist, and he pulled her toward him perhaps a fraction of an inch. She took a deep breath of bergamot, filling herself with him the only way she could. Every nerve ending had come alive with his nearness.

"I will not be kissing you now, Miss Crenshaw."

Disappointment left her feeling heavy and flat. His smile had faded a bit, but it still lingered in his eyes, which had dropped to stare at her mouth. "In fact, I will not be kissing you anymore."

"What?"

A hand came up to gently press against her cheek before his thumb caressed the fullness of her bottom lip. "I have had time to reflect on the deal we made, and I do not think it right and just to steal your kisses from you. They should be freely given."

She was astonished. Even while knowing his kisses were devastating to her state of mind, she had been looking forward to them. Did he know? Was he somehow trying to use that as leverage against her?

He drew away and offered his arm, but the only thing she really wanted to do was have him in her arms with his lips on hers. No. More accurately, she wanted his mouth. The entire thing. She wanted his tongue licking at hers, and his teeth biting at her lips. She wanted her mouth at the mercy of his and whatever he wanted to show her. But nice, well-bred young women didn't want such things, much less did they even think to ask for them.

At a loss for how to proceed, she took his arm and allowed him to lead her back to the house.

"Cook will have prepared a small luncheon," he was saying. "After, we can meet with Hughes, my estate manager."

She nodded her agreement and tried to appear very interested in what he was saying as she convinced herself that these urges toward him would go away.

Chapter 16

How little can be done under the spirit of fear.
FLORENCE NIGHTINGALE

The afternoon meeting with the estate manager had left
August feeling even more confused. Rothschild had
been perfectly amicable to her, responding to her questions
with appropriate interest and listening as she offered suggestions. His gaze had not once lingered on her lips, and he had
made zero suggestive comments. She should feel relieved,
because it must mean that he had given up his pursuit. Instead, she simply felt . . . empty, as if something was missing.

His entirely appropriate and slightly maddening behavior had continued during dinner. He had treated her as he
had every other guest. The same man who had caressed her
so indecently but so deliciously at Camille's ball now
seemed undisturbed by her presence. She did not know
what to make of that.

Was it a trick? If so, it was a damn good one.

That question followed her into the music room where they
had all retired after dinner. The twins were entertaining them
with a performance of *Romeo and Juliet* on the piano. They
took turns playing and were both very good. August tried her
best to enjoy it, but she couldn't help being distracted.

Her gaze kept drifting over to where he sat watching the

performance. The room was arranged so that two sofas were positioned facing the piano in an L-shape with an armchair on either end. He occupied the sofa with her father, while his mother and hers sat in the armchairs. An elderly couple who had been invited for dinner, Sir Henry and his wife, occupied the other sofa. From the settee near the window that she shared with Violet, August was treated to a view of his profile, a very classical and exceptional profile.

Violet hid her grin behind a glass of wine as she leaned over to whisper, "If you keep staring, everyone in this room will know how you really feel about him."

"What do you mean? I'm watching the twins."

A giggle was the only response to that. As they both knew she was lying, it was an appropriate response. "What happened between you this afternoon?" Violet asked after she had sobered.

Glancing at everyone to make certain their whispered conversation wasn't overheard, she said, "It was glorious. We met with Mr. Hughes, and Rothschild allowed me to see everything. All of it. Every ledger with every line item recording every debt."

"Is it terrible?"

"Oh yes, decidedly so." Another glance to make certain they were not being observed. "He's going to need an heiress to save him."

They both laughed, drawing a disapproving glance from their mother. Straightening to show that she was contrite, she waited for her mother to face forward again before saying, "Truthfully, I feel a bit sad for him."

"Sad?" Violet spoke a bit too loudly for comfort. Her brow furrowing, she pretended to smooth the ribbon on her bodice as she waited until the music worked its way toward a crescendo before continuing. "Sadness for the fortune-hunting aristocrat who wears custom suits and owns countless estates?"

"I know how it sounds, but he did nothing to cause his debt."

"He did nothing to *not* cause it," said Violet.

Another glance from their mother sent August to her feet under the pretenses of refilling her wineglass. Violet followed her lead, and they both made their discreet exit from the room and out into the long gallery that held portraits of all the dukes of Rothschild and their progeny. A footman closed the door to the music room behind them.

August's gaze was caught by the Elizabethan-era duke staring down at them with disapproval. His hair was darker than Rothschild's, but he had the same eyes. The same direct way of staring at one. A flutter of awareness awoke in her tummy, and she would have laughed at the sensation if she wasn't so disturbed.

Keeping her voice low, she said, "You are right. He was a reckless fool who spent more than he should have, but I blame his father for not telling the family of their straightened circumstances. That man had the family live on credit and the strength of their good name for at least a decade. Rothschild is not blameless, but I commend him for trying to do something about it."

Violet moved to stand in front of August, her eyes narrowed in concern. "But he's trying to force you into marriage, August. That is not commendable."

"No, it's not. However, I told you about the deal we made. I will walk away at the end of the week."

Violet stared at her with a curious expression. It was almost as if she didn't believe her, and that put August on the defensive. "I was impressed with the plan he had in place to improve his circumstances. He's researched everything needed to make the farms more efficient. From newer strains of grain and corn resistant to mold and pests, to mechanized equipment that would make the farms more efficient, to a plan of annual investment for a small percentage of profits meant to be an insurance against future failures, I can see that he's been busy since his father's death."

Violet watched her quietly as they walked the length of the gallery. Her brown eyes had gone from concerned to thoughtful. "I suppose it's good that he's taking his circumstances seriously," she finally said. "Are all the estates so dire?"

August shrugged. "I believe so, but the extensive records are kept in town at Sterling House where his father resided. Rothschild showed me drafts of similar plans for improvement for each one."

Violet sighed and stopped before one of the portraits to look it over as she ruminated. Finally, she said, "Meanwhile, the tenants continue to suffer."

August nodded. After luncheon, she had shared with Violet the details of the morning, even the fact that he refused the offer to kiss her.

Finally, Violet turned to her again and said, "You believe that Rothschild's plan can save them?" A perfectly arched brow warned that she might be getting at something.

"I do." Before coming to Charrington Manor, she would have answered differently. The past couple of days had shown her an entirely new side of him.

"August . . . don't be angry, but I have to ask. Do you think you could be happy here as his duchess? Perhaps this is an opportunity."

August's step faltered, and she nearly tripped over the hem of her gown. "No, absolutely not."

"Hear me out," said her sister, holding up a hand in a silent plea." You clearly respect him and are impressed by him. You like his"—Violet glanced around to make certain the footman was several yards behind them—"kisses. Perhaps you could make a life for yourself here."

"And leave Crenshaw Iron?"

A crease formed in Violet's forehead. "That is the crux of it, isn't it?"

"Partially, yes, but I have no wish to give up my freedom to a man. Not yet. Do you know that I would be forced to become a British citizen? For all intents and purposes, I wouldn't be American anymore. I would have no right to my own funds or property. It would all fall to him. Rothschild would control everything. My entire life would be in his hands. Even if I am able to stay on at the company, all of my earnings, except a mere pittance, would go to him, even shares and dividends."

"That is a lot to give up." They walked in silence for a while, making the circle of the room. Finally, Violet asked, "But you do want to marry someday?"

August shrugged. "I have always seen myself married. I want to have my own household and children, but I suppose

I assumed that I would have years yet before taking that step." Now that she had tasted the passion Rothschild had shown her, she wanted that, too.

"What if you were ten years older? Would you accept the duke?"

If she were willing to give up her freedom and her rights for some unknown man in some unknown future, would she choose Rothschild to be that man? The answer was surprisingly easy. "I suppose I might."

"Girls!"

They whirled to see their mother standing in the doorway of the music room. Inclining her head toward the door, she whispered, "Your absence has been noticed."

Violet gave her one last glance that asked far too much before she returned to the room. August followed, but she was even more distracted and torn than before.

Evan had not been able to stop thinking about August. Not kissing her yesterday by the stables had been one of the most difficult things he had ever done. And then later, after the musical, August and her sister had bidden the room good night, and her eyes had lingered on him. In that brief moment, they had been hot and needy, asking for more. It had taken all of his self-restraint not to quietly go to her room after everyone had retired and see where another kiss would lead them. Instead, he had been forced to relieve his ache for her by his own hand.

Not that his need for her had been assuaged for long. He had woken up with the very same need, his thoughts consumed by her. Somehow, his time with her had made his desire more intense. He had been forced to bare the extent of the need facing the dukedom to her and had been prepared for her derision. It had not come. She had not sneered at him or made it seem that she could not respect him for failing. Instead, she had given him understanding and thoughtful suggestions on how to improve his plans.

His eyes blurred as he tried to focus on the tenant contracts for properties in Haverford spread out before him on the long table in the library. It was no use. He had read the same passage at least ten times already.

"Oh!" A feminine voice intruded on his dilemma.

August stood in the doorway, and the smile she gave him was completely unguarded and genuine.

"Good morning, Miss Crenshaw." He rose, marveling at how his body nearly vibrated as she stepped into the room.

"I didn't know anyone was in here. I thought you were in your study working."

"I needed to spread them out." He gestured to the unwieldy stacks of paper. The truth was that he had missed her at breakfast and hoped to see her. She was lovely in a plum day dress that seemed to mold itself to her breasts. He had to rip his gaze from the row of tiny buttons up the front.

"Contracts are rather boring, aren't they?" Overcoming her reticence to disturb him, she walked over and glanced at one. "May I?"

"Of course."

She snapped it up and read the first page with remarkable speed. His throat constricted with how unbelievably attractive he found that. To hide the effect, he sat back down, but it only made it worse. Now his face was on level with her bosom, and her scent surrounded him. He picked up another contract and tried to focus on it.

"I don't envy you. You could be here all day," she said, laying the paper on the table and making her way around the room. She seemed to have forgotten him as she perused the shelves.

He mumbled an appropriate reply as he went through the one in his hand, marking out the extraneous penalties for late payments his estate manager had added.

"I am glad to see you are taking my advice," she said, when he was certain she had forgotten him.

"I have made note of all of your suggestions from yesterday." It was true. He had written down every one.

Finished with the paper in his hand, he pushed it aside and snatched up another one, but he could not concentrate. Of course he could not. She was there, hovering in his peripheral, and it was not long before the shape of her back as it narrowed toward her hips proved endlessly fascinating. Or the tender skin of the nape of her neck. Her hair was pulled up in a simple chignon, leaving the graceful arc there exposed. He imagined that would be the perfect spot to kiss her, because he could bury his nose in her hair and fill himself up on her scent.

Grabbing a book off a shelf, she turned in profile as she opened it and momentarily propped herself against the bookcase to skim a page. The small mounds of her breasts seemed to be pushed up higher today than normal, and he remembered how they had looked above the bodice of the scarlet ball gown. And how they had tasted in Hereford's library. Absently, she toyed with a strand of baby-fine hair that had slipped from the knot at the back of her head. His fingers itched to stroke it and then bury themselves in the mass, pulling it free of its pins.

The rustling of paper had him returning his attention to the crumpled contract on the table before him. She gave him an absent smile and turned back to the books, reshelving that one and making her way behind him.

"Could I help you find something?" he heard himself asking.

"No, thank you. The twins gave us a tour yesterday, and I was quite taken with the library. Since it's raining today, I thought it would be a good time to explore. The twins have Violet playing charades, so I have a bit of leisure time alone."

Was it his imagination, or had she put a twist on the word *alone*? As if she meant everyone were busy and they would not be disturbed? He glanced to the door, disappointed to see that she had left it open a bit. Definitely his imagination. "I apologize for them. They rarely have visitors and never anyone close to their own age."

"Please don't apologize. They're lovely. I'm simply more accustomed to having several hours to myself every day. Violet is the outgoing one."

His disappointment grew. Clearly, she meant that she wanted to be alone, and he was twisting the scenario in his mind because he could not seem to get enough of her. From nowhere came the image of the respectable Miss Crenshaw sitting very prim and proper on the table while he knelt before her, pushing her skirts up and—*Cease this at once!* He rubbed his eyes to try to dash the image out of his head.

The soft waft of her scent warned him a moment before she dropped a heavy stack of books down on the table. Dust flew off the leather bindings to settle on the gleaming oak surface. He did not have to read the title on the first cover to know that she had found William's writings.

Thank God William is heir. Evan will amount to nothing. The boy has the brawn of a bull and the brain of one, too.

His father's words had lost the sting they had possessed when Evan had overheard the man say them to his mother, though they were as true now as ever. William would have made the better duke.

"*A treatise on observations of Rhetorica ad Herennium in the grand style as it relates to Greek philosophy* by William, Marquess of Langston." August's voice turned the title into something almost musical. Raising her gaze to him, she asked, "Your brother?"

He nodded, a peculiar lump lodging itself in his throat. "He was something of a scholar."

"I see." She went on to read the cover of each tome aloud. Each more obscure and convoluted than the last.

When she finished, he said, "There is likely another stack or two on the shelf. He wrote extensively on Latin and Greek scholarship."

She picked up one thick tome to flip through it. "My, he was . . . thorough."

"I was in awe of him." Evan opened the next book on the stack, noting the neatly elaborate script and the lack of lines marking out any mistakes. He stopped when he became aware of her watching him.

"I am sorry for his passing." Her voice was far too gentle, its warmth seeping into the cold hollows of his chest.

He shrugged, trying to deny how good it felt, and stared down at the page. "It was years ago."

Her hand covered his, drawing his gaze to her. "Nevertheless, I am sorry. I can see how you cared for him."

Perhaps it was the affection in her eyes, or it could have

been the care in her touch, but something made his throat tighten. It took a moment before he was able to say, "I did. I am quite certain that I hounded him mercilessly when we were children. He was endlessly trying to read while I wanted him to play with me."

"When you love someone, I don't think the passing years mean very much. Yesterday, or several years, the pain of their loss is still there."

The ache came back to his throat, forcing him to swallow several times. When he could finally speak, his voice was a hoarse whisper. "How do you know?"

"I never lost a brother, but I was close to my grandfather Augustus. He died when I was a child, and I still remember the very moment I learned of his death. Despite what Papa says, *he* was the first one to encourage me to work at Crenshaw Iron."

Evan found himself absently rubbing his thumb over her fingers, but he could not compel himself to stop. She only gave his hand a squeeze. Pushing away thoughts of William, he said, "It must have been difficult for you without a champion."

"Maxwell has always supported me, and Papa does, too, though he wavers in his support, but I can hardly complain." She smiled at him, and the simple kindness threatened to break something inside him. It quivered in his chest, like a dam on the verge of giving way.

When Evan was away at school, it was William who had sent him notes of support. Father only ever sent terse replies to Evan's requests, almost all of them pleas for an early allowance, and almost all of them refused. When Father scoffed at the idea of Evan being involved in owning and operating a club for gentlemen, William had silently listened and offered encouragement.

"Rothschild?" Her voice was full of concern as were her eyes.

He glanced away from them and toward the fire. He shook his head as if it were nothing, but the words came pouring out of him anyway. "William should be the one sitting here. Not me." She did not respond but merely leaned against the table, her breath and the sound of the rain pattering on the window the only sounds. "He was always so studious, so prepared. He was meant to be duke."

She put her hand on his shoulder, and he had to close his eyes against the need to pull her into his arms. To turn to her and seek the comfort she offered. If he did that, he was afraid that the dam would open and everything would come pouring out. There would be no better way to send her scurrying away from him than to do that. Instead, he allowed the pain of loss to flow through him with every beat of his heart, absorbing each pulse like a blow.

He admonished himself to be quiet, but the words came anyway. "He would be so much better for the family. I have done nothing but make things worse in the past year. He would have figured out a way to improve the situation."

"Evan." Her voice was wrought with the very pain in his heart.

At his name, he jerked in surprise and met her gaze. To his utter astonishment, her eyes were bright with tears. Before he knew it, she had pulled him against her front, and his shoulders were shaking with the effort of suppressing the ache inside him.

"No," he whispered, but his fists had found their way to her skirts and were not letting her go. He felt like an observer outside his own body.

"Shh . . . it's all right to feel the way you do." Her fingers tightened in the hair at the back of his head, and she spoke against his temple. "It must have been a shock to lose him."

He closed his eyes and allowed himself a weak moment to rest his cheek against her breasts and breathe her in. "He had a heart defect. The physicians believe it was congenital but lay dormant for years." Her fingers stroked the back of his head in a way that felt like heaven. Shivers of pleasure raced down his spine and wound themselves around the aching wound of his heart.

"How terrible," she whispered, her breath teasing his ear as she halfway bent over him. "You are doing a remarkable job in his stead. He would be proud of you."

Evan tried to laugh, but it came out as a sob that he muffled against her breasts. "He thought I spent too much time drinking and cavorting with loose women. He was right."

"Perhaps before, but you have done an admirable job in your tenure as duke. You've had nothing to work with, and yet you've kept the creditors appeased."

He shook his head, unable to speak past the lump in his throat.

"And you will find a way to continue to do so. I do not know very much about him, but I daresay that William would not have fared nearly as well. Scholarly pursuits won't help you when you find yourself in dire circumstances and a flailing dukedom."

He could not look at her for fear that he would lose his composure, but she would have none of that and gently took his face between her hands. "Would he have been equipped to write the extensive plans for improvement as you have done?"

"He was the one to first broach the topic of mechanized equipment with Father." His voice belonged to someone else. He could not recognize it.

"Ah, but your father refused. Correct?"

Evan nodded.

"And I am guessing William did not follow through on his own."

"No, after Father refused, he returned to his books." Evan glanced toward the bookcase filled with every bit of classic literature William had amassed.

She followed his glance and said, "And continued to indulge his passion for antique and expensive manuscripts?"

He nodded.

She smiled tenderly. "Would he have been willing to hunt down his very own heiress?"

Evan gave a soft laugh at the idea of it. "No. He despised London."

"Would he have begun brawling for his dinner?"

Another reluctant smile tugged at his mouth. "William was a scholar, and while he could hold his own in a gentleman's match, he could never have fought the likes of Wilkes."

"Then I think had he lived you might still be the one saving your estates."

He was stunned dumb by that conclusion, because she might well be right in her assessment. He had spent his life looking up to his older brother and knowing that he would never live up to William's example. Never once had it crossed his mind that William might not have been up to the challenges of being duke.

"I miss him." It was the first time he had said that to anyone.

"I know." She leaned down so that their noses almost touched. Her eyes had darkened and become more intent. Something had changed within her. "I cannot say how things would have been different had William lived; no one can. But I can say that you have done well by your responsibility, and I admire you greatly."

The tightness in his chest that had held him prisoner for so long loosened with her words. It was as if she had cut the rope binding him and he could breathe freely for the first time in years. "You . . ." His voice was thick and raw when he spoke. "You admire me?"

"Yes." Her fingers stroked his cheeks. "Very much so."

He had no time to consider what that might mean, because she pressed her lips to his. He opened beneath the soft pressure, greedy for her after having denied them both this simple pleasure. She tasted as sweet and good as he remembered. The soft brush of her tongue should have been a balm to his pain, but instead it made it surge, setting the dam inside him to wavering perilously. She curled her fingers in his hair and made a sweet little sound as she kissed him with all of the pent-up hunger he had been harboring for her and slid into his lap. Salt mingled with her taste. It was only then that he realized he had been crying. He was crying. With the twist of pressure in his chest gone, there was nothing to stop the flood of pain from spilling over the top, sending the dam crashing down.

The swell of sadness inside him was so overwhelming that he let out a gasp. She jerked back as if she was afraid that she had hurt him. "I'm sorry."

"No." He pulled her back to him, taking her mouth as if he needed it for his next breath. "Do not be."

She wrapped her arms around him, and he held her

tight. But the pain would not be held back. It surged to the surface of the kiss to make itself known. Another gasp moved between them, and then another. A sob welled, and he had to break the kiss to hold it back.

"Evan?"

Burying his face in her neck, the sob tore out of him. She gathered him close to her breast and placed small kisses along his hairline while murmuring encouragements. It was only in that moment that he realized he had never mourned his brother. He had gone through the motions, but Father had always been there lurking in the background, waiting to swoop in on some perceived weakness. Evan had opted to hold the pain of William's loss inside, hoping that if he held it long enough, it would dissolve into nothing. And then when Father had died, Evan's life had become a series of obstacles, each more damning than the last, as if the man had designed them as a sort of punishment that would continue long after his death.

"I miss him," he whispered.

She kissed his temple and ran a soothing hand down his back. His muscles rippled beneath her touch, like a cat being soothed by a beloved human.

She held him for a long time, until he had stopped trembling and managed to halt the tears. Taking one last deep inhale of her scent, he pressed a kiss to her neck, then another to her chest, and one more to the swell of her breasts. Her fingers lightly tugged at his hair, drawing him upward. He pressed a soft kiss to her lips, but it quickly burned hotter and hungrier than before. Experienced now, she opened to him, and the bold brush of her tongue only inflamed him more. One of her hands moved down the column of his throat, her thumb gently pressed to his pulse before dipping lower, trying to find its way between the buttons of his shirt to reach his skin. He groaned with the need to touch her, too, and feel the warmth of her skin against his.

"August." He whispered her name as he took a breath. Her mouth chased his, taking another kiss. And then another. She had assuaged the pain so sweetly, there was only fire between them now. He took control of the kiss, seizing her mouth with a need bordering on desperation.

". . . reading, most likely. It's where she normally sneaks off to at home."

Violet's voice came crashing down around them mere seconds before the door was pushed fully open. She stepped in just as August jumped from his lap. Violet's eyes went wide at the sight of them, and she whirled to face the twins, who likely stood behind her, obscured by the door. "Perhaps we should go fetch some cakes before we disturb her. I'm famished."

"Excellent idea," Louisa agreed, and the voices began to fade.

August's chest heaved as she struggled to catch her breath, and her cheeks were flushed. Their kissing would be no secret to anyone who looked upon her. Or him, especially if he stood up.

"I should go before they come back," she said.

He nodded. It was the logical thing, but he wanted her to stay. He wanted to spend the whole rainy day with her. First here in the library, and then in his bed. It was probably the one thing her parents would not agree to allow. Or perhaps they were desperate enough to permit him the indiscretion if it would entice her to say yes to him. A wild impulse to test the theory nearly propelled him out of his chair, but one look at her stopped him.

She stared at him with such beautiful trust and tenderness that he could not act on his dishonorable thoughts. If they went further, it would be because she chose him, not because of her parents or his need for a wife. It would only be because of their need for each other.

"Goodbye." She cupped his cheek, and he turned into the touch, kissing her palm. Smiling, her fingertips traced the ridge of his jaw in a lingering caress as she walked away, leaving him alone.

Evan was left too weak and disoriented to move right away. He leaned forward, propping his elbows on the table and resting his head in his hands, much the way she had found him.

Chapter 17

Truth is such a rare thing, it is delightful to tell it.

EMILY DICKINSON

The rain did not let up that day or the next. It continued in a steady drizzle that turned the world to gray and eventually exposed the cracks and flaws of Charrington Manor. Everyone pretended not to notice that the water stain in the corner of the drawing room had begun to ooze. The pitter-patter of drips was frequently disguised with vigorous piano playing and shrieks of laughter as the twins participated in one game or another. To combat the drafts and cold that seeped in through the stone walls, every hearth roared with the heat of a robust fire.

It was very nearly an idyllic getaway from the city and the endless rounds of meetings and entertaining that had kept August busy since their arrival at the beginning of the month. She was coming to find, rather surprisingly, that she enjoyed it here. For certain the house could use modernizing, but when seated before a fireplace with a lap blanket and a cup of tea, it really was bearable. It helped that she had the memory of the duke's kisses to warm her, as did the memory of how he had clung to her as he had cried for his brother. *Real tears.*

Although she had only seen one male cry—Max when he had broken his arm at fifteen—she had long suspected that they were as capable of tears of sadness as any woman. That was no surprise. The surprise was that Evan had allowed her to see them, and that he had embraced her instead of pushing her away. She hadn't been able to stop thinking about it, or him, ever since.

After the library, at tea and then again at dinner, he had gazed at her with those same warm eyes. He did not treat her with the kind of benign courtesy with which he would regard any guest; there was more there now. The tenderness hinted at a secret fire simply waiting to be released. She shivered as the imagined flames of that fire moved over her in ribbons of heat.

"Do you need another blanket, dear?" Violet smiled at her from behind her teacup.

August had shared with her what happened in the library—the kissing part, not the tears. That seemed too special to share. Violet had been staring at her with that knowing smile ever since. More than once she thought back to the conversation she'd had with her sister. If she were ready for marriage, she knew in her heart that she would choose him. If only choosing him didn't require her to give up everything she held dear.

"I'm fine, thank you."

"Are you certain? You seem to be brooding for a particular gentleman who was called away."

"Stop it, Violet." August could not help but laugh. "I am not brooding. Besides, he was merely called into town. He will return soon."

Violet shrugged and set the cup and saucer down. "Well, something has you looking out that window every two minutes."

August knew Violet was right, because she had caught herself doing it. She was saved from arguing by determined footsteps approaching and the rustle of fabric as Mother stepped into the room.

"Good afternoon, Mother. I thought you were resting. Would you care for some tea?"

Mother shook her head, her expression drawn and firm. "No, thank you. If you are finished, your father and I would like a word."

Unease moved through her, but August managed to keep a smile on her face even though her mother's scowl indicated an unpleasant conversation was ahead.

"Certainly." She exchanged an uneasy glance with her sister, before following her mother from the room.

As they reached the stairs, a commotion from the entry hall had them both turning. Evan hurried inside, handing his dripping hat and coat to a footman. He had left when there had been a pause in the rain, but it had not lasted long. Her heart gave a little thump at the sight of him. He was soaked through, which molded his clothing to him like a second skin, emphasizing the breadth of his shoulders and his trim waist. When his gaze met hers, it was as if an arc of electrical current moved between them. It was only tamped out when he registered that her mother stood beside her.

"Good afternoon, Your Grace," Mother said. She waited only long enough for his polite greeting before taking August's arm and leading her upstairs to the sitting room she and Papa shared.

Papa was nowhere to be seen. Mother closed the door and then sat in a chair near the fire, so August followed her lead. "I wanted to talk to you before dinner."

"Yes?" August feigned a benign interest, but her heart was already beginning to pound.

Mother took an audible breath as if finding her courage. August stopped breathing.

"There has been no sign of a betrothal announcement."

"Mother—"

She held up a hand in a call for silence. "I understand your reticence in this, August. Truly, I do. I was not persuaded in any way to marry your father. He charmed me from the beginning, so I am certain that I cannot speak to how it must feel to have your husband chosen for you."

"No, I am certain you cannot." August regretted the bitter tone in her voice, but it was beyond her control.

Her mother blinked. "Nevertheless, it has been done for generations of women. I know you think you are different, and perhaps you are, but in this your father and I know best. We have chosen this man for you, and we want you to accept him."

August tightened her hands into fists on her lap. "I will not be forced into this."

Mother's expression was as firm as her voice. "That is why we must discuss things."

"Discuss? Discuss?" August could feel the anger flaming to life inside her like a brush fire, and she tried to control it, but it wasn't easy. "This isn't a discussion. You want to tell me what to do and have me agree."

Her mother inclined her head, conceding the point. "You are a bright girl, and I do understand your need for justification. I know how you value your facts and statistics, so here are the facts of the matter. You will have no marriage prospects at home. Your stunts, which were written about in the papers here, will be gossiped about at home."

August laughed. "No one will care that I went out without a chaperone, and they'll forget all about the scarlet dress and the walk with that nobleman."

"Perhaps, but they will not forget that a duke lost interest in you."

"What do you mean? He has hardly lost interest. If anything, I believe he still wants to marry me."

"That doesn't matter at all. You were very close to marriage. Everyone has whispered about it. Everyone knows that we have been guests at his home. Everyone has the expectation that an engagement will be announced upon our return to London. If one is not announced, I am afraid that your reputation will not withstand the gossip. They'll all wonder why he cried off."

"He didn't cry off. I am the one not accepting him."

"That doesn't matter, August, and you know it. The gentlemen in these situations hold all the power. One word from him, and no one will so much as look at you again."

"You are putting a dramatic twist on this that is not true. Evan—" Her mother's eyes widened. August really needed to stop thinking of him by his given name. "Rothschild will not say cruel things about me. He is a true gentleman."

Now Mother's eyes narrowed with speculation. "If he is the gentleman you claim, what is your objection to him? Anyone with eyes can see that the two of you get on well."

Crossing her arms over her chest, August held her ground. "That's true. We are friends now, and I have found things to admire in him. But I do not want to be married now." She wanted to continue working at Crenshaw Iron, and she didn't want this forced on her. Perhaps if she was given time to settle into the idea, but not like this.

"But you would find him acceptable if you did want to be married now?"

August sighed. This was bordering on her conversation with Violet. "Perhaps, but there are so many things to consider. I hardly know him. I believe that for a marriage to be happy, it is important for a couple—"

Mother waved a hand in the air. "I have heard enough. Your father and I have decided that you will marry him, and that's final."

"Final? I don't understand."

Mother took in a breath and gripped her hands together in front of her. "If a betrothal isn't announced by the time we leave, your position at Crenshaw Iron will be eliminated."

Had her mother struck her across the face, the shock could not have been greater. "Papa would never agree to that."

"He already has."

Her blood ran cold and she bolted to her feet. "I don't believe you."

"August . . ." Mother crossed the distance between them but stopped short of reaching out to touch her. "We have grown impatient with your obstinance. We know what is best for you. If you were to walk away from this opportunity, it would be the biggest regret of your life. We cannot allow that to happen."

"You mean this is what is best for you, not me." August had to put a hand out to the mantel to keep her balance.

"This marriage will be best for the family and the business—there is no mistaking that—but also for you. You will have opportunities you cannot even imagine."

"Opportunities? I have all the opportunities I need. Now. With Crenshaw Iron."

Mother shook her head. "Not if you refuse this."

Mother stared at her with the cold indifference of a stranger. No. Not a stranger. It was as if she, August, were the single obstacle in the way of her getting what she wanted, and Mother would rather plow through the hurdle than find another solution.

The door to Papa's bedroom swung open, and he hedged into the room. His gaze went to Mother first before reluctantly settling on August. She knew then that he had deliberately waited, not wanting to deliver the message himself.

August had to speak through a throat gone tight with sadness and anger. "Papa, you cannot mean this."

"Do not look so put-upon, darling." His voice held a gentle, chiding tone. "You are hardly being fed to the wolves. We have investigated this man and found him thoroughly acceptable. Your time at Crenshaw Iron would have come to an end eventually. This is the life you are meant to lead, and it is more glorious than anything your mother or I could have imagined for you. Let Maxwell run the business as he was meant to do, hmm?"

Mother reached out to touch August's shoulder, but August recoiled instinctively. She could not pretend that everything was fine, when they were trying to tear her world apart.

"You've always been strong-willed." Mother sighed. "In time you will come to understand that this is the best thing."

"You both say these things, but what of Camille? Will Camille come to understand that as well?"

Mother smiled and gave a sad shake of her head. "Camille is not nearly as logical as you."

"Rothschild is hardly Hereford," said Papa. "You may feel that your situation is similar but only on the surface. I would not have felt nearly as justified in handing you over to Hereford as I do to Rothschild."

She stared at him, momentarily taken aback by the words *handing you over.* Their accuracy had stolen her breath. How had she fooled herself for so long that she was in charge of her life? All this time, they had simply been humoring her. "But you would have handed me over." It wasn't a question. The answer was written on his face.

"August." There was a sharpness in his voice that she had only rarely ever heard appear. It was reserved solely for those who had stretched his patience thin. "I will not entertain hypotheticals. We are discussing Rothschild and his suitability."

"No, we are not. You are telling me who to marry. You are telling me that the only value I have to you is in which man I can make your son-in-law."

Color rose in the apples of Papa's cheeks. "You are making this into something it is not."

"It is you who are refusing to see the barbarism of your own actions."

"Enough of this, both of you," said Mother, stepping between them. "What does any of that matter? The question of marriage is settled." Turning to August, she continued, "Her Grace mentioned that the duke's business might have him called back to London tomorrow."

Now August understood why her parents had felt the need to have this conversation now.

"I've taken the liberty of having the appropriate documents arranged," said Papa, his voice back to normal. "We can sign them when we return to London."

For the first time in her life, August knew how it felt to want to hit something. To rage at it so that it was forced to absorb all of her anger and heartache. A sob almost escaped her throat, and her shoulders started to shake, but she held them both back. Now was not the time to give in to despair. Now was the time for action.

Turning abruptly, she left them both behind in the sitting room. She had to see Evan now. If this marriage was to be forced on her, she would set the terms herself. Her heels echoed off the walls as she made her way down the corridor. Armed with only a vague notion gained from a tour by the twins of Evan's chamber being in the west wing, she made a turn that took her away from the giant staircase and then another that put her firmly into his domain.

The family's rooms were here. She paused at each door, continuing on if she heard a female voice within. Finally, she heard a male voice muffled behind the thick oak of one of the last doors off the corridor. It wasn't Evan's, but it was possibly his valet's.

Steeling herself, she raised her hand and gave a firm knock. It was a moment, but soon it opened, and the valet stood before her with a very put-upon expression on his face. "Miss Crenshaw?"

"Good evening. I have come to see Rothschild."

"I am afraid that is not—"

She pushed past him, and he was so stunned that he gave way. The room was a heavily paneled affair with sofas and chairs in shades of dark blue. Obviously a sitting room. Her gaze caught on an open door, and she headed in that direction.

"Miss Crenshaw, His Grace is at his bath. I am afraid this is . . ."

She came to an abrupt stop as she had entered a dressing room. Armoires and heavy but well-cushioned furniture was scattered around the room. An open door revealed the heavy brocade of a bedroom beyond them. She would have known this was his room by the seductive smell of bergamot and citrus alone. However, the very naked man in the copper bath was evidence enough.

"August!" He half rose as if preparing for action, remembered his state of undress, and sank back down in the water. But not before she got a very clear view of the hair gathered at his lower belly, tawny but darkened by the water. Her gaze followed the trail up as it narrowed toward his navel and then continued up his flat and ridged stomach to where the muscles began to take shape under the smooth skin of his chest, burnished with a scattering of hair. There was a small indentation where the muscle met that of his shoulder, which flexed as he gripped the edge of the tub.

"Christ, August, what the hell are you doing here?" He didn't sound angry, merely astonished.

She was also astonished. Now that she thought of it, she might have assumed he would be having a bath after coming in from his ride soaking wet. She didn't know what she had thought to find or accomplish by barging into his bedroom. Her anger had guided her.

She opened her mouth to apologize for her bad behavior, but she couldn't seem to find her voice. His nipples were as hard as tiny pebbles, and his pectoral muscles flexed as he shifted to better shield his manly part from her. A rush of heat gathered between her thighs, and her body fairly vibrated with awareness of him. What would his skin smell like when wet? It was the only thing she could think. Some inner strength she hadn't been aware of was all that was keeping her from going to him to find out.

"Miss Crenshaw, please come with me." The valet used his sternest voice, but he stopped short of physically hauling her out.

His presence was enough to shake her from her stupor and get her senses back. She had come to do battle. Best to get it over with. If she retreated now, the show of weakness would mean she had already lost.

"That will be all," she said in the voice she used to deal with difficult vendors at Crenshaw Iron.

Clearly not expecting that, the man stood aghast and stared at her.

"You may leave us," she added in case there was any question.

His eyes widened, and he glanced to his employer for confirmation.

"Leave us," said Evan. "Close the door behind you."

There was a moment of silence, and then the valet retreated, his footsteps muffled on the heavy carpets. Evan's hair was soaked from being washed and was pushed back, so that his eyes shone out brilliantly. The blue was like jewels. The plains and angles of his face were drawn in sharp relief, making her notice anew how strikingly handsome he was.

But that didn't matter now. She had to concentrate. "I came to tell you that I will not be at dinner tonight."

He stared at her before finally asking, "Are you all right?"

"Yes . . . no . . ." His brows drew together in concern. "Physically, yes, I am fine."

Her answer seemed to relax him. He sat back, his arms draped over the sides of the tub. "Something has happened. Tell me."

The position elongated his torso, making her eyes drift downward, taking in the line of hair that trailed down his belly and disappeared beneath the soapy water. The water was cloudy but still reasonably transparent. If she took one or two steps closer, she would no doubt be able to see what he had hiding down there. There was a ripple beneath the water. It was a slight tremor that had her gaze jerking up to meet his.

"Tell me," he prompted, shifting and raising a knee to further shield that part of himself from her. The limb was muscled and covered in tawny curls. She had sat on his thighs, but she had the urge to touch him with her hand and determine if those muscles were as hard as they seemed.

"Right, yes." She closed her eyes and forced herself to turn around. Staring at him made every pulse point in her body throb so that she couldn't think. Turning around was the only proper thing to do and what she should have done immediately instead of standing there ogling him. "I will not be at dinner." She could not bear to face her parents so soon, and if it was true that he was leaving, then she wanted things clear between them before he went. "But I need to meet with you. Alone. Tonight."

He was silent for so long that she nearly turned around. "All right. After dinner, then?"

"No." She shook her head for added emphasis. Her gaze caught on the dressing gown thrown casually over the back of a chair. It was a deep red and decidedly masculine, and she knew immediately that it would smell just like him. "I would prefer that we not be disturbed. Let's plan to meet in the library tonight after everyone has retired for the evening."

She left before he could agree or disagree.

Chapter 18

Generally speaking, it is injudicious for ladies to attempt arguing with gentlemen on political or financial topics.

ELIZA LESLIE

Evan rose as soon as the library door opened late that night. True to her word, August had not been seen after leaving his bedroom. Her mother had made August's excuses at dinner, saying that she had taken to her bed with a headache. Something must have happened between them. Evan would have been a fool not to suspect it was about marrying him. He had wanted to demand answers from her parents but had decided to honor August's request and wait to talk to her. Now that she was here, his body hummed with expectancy.

She appeared in the doorway and gave him a quick once-over as if she half expected him to be nude as he had been in the bath. A tremor of pure desire coiled and tightened low in his gut as he recalled the way she had looked at him as he sat in the tub, obviously curious. She closed the door, and he took in the emerald dressing gown she wore. The velvet hugged the curve of her backside and her breasts, nipping in at her waist. He had never seen her without a corset and had only ever imagined the shape of her natural form. Though she was fully covered from wrists to slippered feet to the buttons that went up her neck, his blood heated and thickened.

As soon as the door closed, her demeanor changed. Her eyes hardened with determination, and her shoulders went back, full of confidence. When she crossed to the table, it was reminiscent of their very first encounter in the Ashcroft drawing room.

"Good evening," he said.

"Good evening." She laid down a single piece of cream parchment that appeared to have come from the desk set in her room.

"Would you care for a drink?" He indicated the tumbler of whisky on the table before him.

She shook her head to refuse, but her lips trembled. "Actually, yes, I will have one."

He nodded and poured her a drink at the sideboard. When he returned, he walked around the table and offered it to her. The tips of her fingers brushed his as she accepted it, sending a tendril of pleasure up his arm. "Will you tell me what happened?"

She shook her head. "It hardly matters. It was simply pointed out to me that the time has come for a decision."

Bloody hell. Her parents had interfered when they should have left it to him. She took a healthy sip and made a face before continuing. "Since my decisions have been made for me, I am left only with my will to negotiate." The bitterness in her voice was unmistakable, and it was punctuated by her deliberate and efficient movements as she set the crystal down and turned her attention to the parchment before her.

Instead of returning to his chair at the other end of the table, he sat in the one near her. "I agreed to allow you to leave at the end of the week if you choose with no further harassment on my part."

She appeared not to listen. Her eyes skimmed over whatever she had written as he spoke.

"August?" He could not resist covering her hand with

his. She was cold, but her skin was smooth as silk and nearly as delicate. "I will not force you to wed me."

She met his gaze then, hers full of a mix of anger and pain. "Lucky for you, my parents are willing to handle that nasty little task."

"Have they threatened you?" Fury roared to life inside him. How dare they attempt to usurp him in this? The marriage was their decision, not her parents' to force and manipulate.

Bitterness twisted her lips, and she moved her hand from beneath his. It appeared all the progress they had made had been lost. "You could say that. I was told that if I don't marry you, then I have no position at Crenshaw Iron. It's funny, because if I do marry you, then I have no position at Crenshaw Iron. How wonderfully that works out for you."

God, no. This is not what he had wanted to happen. Perhaps originally when he had been an arrogant imbecile who had not considered that a woman such as her would not want to marry him, he had thought it would hardly matter how she made her way down the aisle; but now it was very possibly the worst thing her parents could have done. He did not want her to be forced. And then there was the fact that things had been very good between them over the last several days. She had warmed to him, and while she might not have been ready to agree to marriage, he could see that she was considering it in a new light.

"August, believe me when I tell you that I had no part in that."

Her eyes flared. "You had every part in that. Perhaps you did not force my mother to come to me earlier tonight, or my father to issue an ultimatum, but this is all your doing, Rothschild. Had you not forced this entire situation then this would not be happening."

Evan made himself take a breath before answering her. He did not want her to think the anger he felt toward her parents was directed at her. Keeping his voice calm, he said, "I accept responsibility for approaching you and your family about the marriage in a less-than-ideal manner. In hindsight, I would do things differently." Her eyes fairly crackled with fire as she waited for him to finish. "However, I have in no way pressed them for an answer, nor was it ever my intention for them to issue such a devastating ultimatum."

"Your intentions hardly matter, especially when you have received what you set out to attain. I am here and ready to be your wife."

Joy and relief warred with anger and dismay. He could not stop himself from glancing at the paper she had brought in, wondering what it was and how it would have an impact on this discussion. The sheet contained a list. He could make out the words *children* and farther down *jointure*. A marriage negotiation, then.

Fighting that dark part of him that urged him to accept her, to grab her and hold on to her before she could get away, he thrust the slender thread of noble instinct he had left to the forefront. He could not accept her unfairly. "This is not necessary. Whatever they have said to you, I am certain that once I talk to them, things can be smoothed over. I do not want you to lose your position."

She sneered. "I find that difficult to believe, since your goal is to have me as your wife. I could hardly continue my work and still be your duchess, now, could I?"

"But you could." Since their last kiss, he had hardly thought of anything else but of how to allow her to keep a foothold in her family's business.

She stared at him openmouthed before straightening her shoulders again and declaring, "You're only saying that. Everyone knows that duchesses do *not* work. They do a bit of charity work, possibly, but that is all."

"Traditionally, yes, but there is no reason you cannot change that." Christ, the way she stared at him now, as if she would never believe a word he said, was completely his fault.

"And how would your old Eton friends react? What about their wives? Do you truly deceive yourself that they would accept me?"

"August, your being American will be enough to make

half of them ostracize you. The other half will certainly find it objectionable that you work. The lot of them can go hang for all I care. All that matters is you and me."

She stared at him, but some of the anger had drained from her face. Seizing on that, he hurried on. "Perhaps your role would change a bit—after all, there are certain duties that you must carry out as duchess—but I see no reason for you to stop working completely. I believe that once there is an office established in London, you should assume a leadership role there."

"You're lying. Duchesses do not work." Her jaw firmed with the resolve of a prosecutor who had already established the guilt of the accused.

He sighed, hating how she distrusted him and that her parents had forced the matter. Indignation at himself drove him to his feet, where he paced the length of the table and back. Bloody hell, he had well and truly botched this by approaching her the wrong way in the very beginning without any concern for her feelings. "I have seen how effortless it was for you to peruse my ledgers and accounts. To find mistakes and make suggestions for improvements. It comes naturally to you, or at the very least it is a skill that you have honed well in your years of employment. I would not take that away from you.

"In fact, should you agree to marriage, I would like you to also consider taking an active role in the running of the estates. With the agricultural improvements—"

She made a dismissive sound and waved her hand as if she was swatting away an insect. "Estate farming for profit is no longer viable. Your best course of action there is to make the improvements you can and then train your other tenants. Expand your best farms to absorb the vacant land—"

"And invest in industry," he said. She turned her head to look at him with something akin to astonishment on her face. "Manufacturing and machine works. Factories to bring employment to the displaced farmers."

She nodded. "I see you have been listening."

"I listen to you, August."

She blinked and turned back to stare at the sheet before her. "We have established that I am to marry you; there is no need for meaningless flattery."

With a groan of frustration, he sat down again and took her hand. "And if I refuse to marry you?"

She laughed. "Then you would be mad."

"You are right. I would be mad." He stared at her profile earnestly, hoping that she would look at him and they could have a proper discussion and not this adversarial one. "But I want you to accept only when you want this." *When you want me.*

Finally, she did look at him. Anger made the color rise in her cheeks. "And why would I want *this*? It's a crumbling pile of stones that should have been razed a century ago or more. *This* means subjecting myself to endless social engagements where I have to overhear all of the fine people talking about how mannish I am and how I don't deserve to be a duchess. And they are absolutely correct. I don't deserve it. There are at least a hundred other women I have met over the last few weeks who are far more deserving of it than me. They care for it so much more." She rose in her fury and crossed to the fireplace, where she stood facing away from him toward the flames with her back stiff. "I only want to work and continue with the legacy my grandfather left us."

He had lost her before he had even had a chance of holding on to her. Disappointment sat heavy in his stomach. There was no way to refute her argument. Evan followed her but stopped feet short of where she stood.

"You are right. They will call you names and say terrible things." He took in a breath. "But they already do that."

If possible, her shoulders stiffened even more. "You've heard?"

"They already say these things about you, and you have not bothered to care before now."

She shrugged but did not look at him. "I am accustomed to their bitterness. Besides, there is a sort of insulation in being an outsider."

He took another breath, proceeding slowly because he

very much felt as if he was poking at a nest of bees. "Do the people in New York not say similar things?"

There were a few moments of silence before she said, "They do. No one knows what to make of a woman in business."

"No, I suppose they do not. I only say that to demonstrate that it is not so much their censure that has given you reason to shun the title." He paused long enough to allow that to sink in. "What is the true reason?"

"Because I would not have it forced on me, of course." One shoulder shrugged again, and she still did not turn to face him. Her shoulders trembled slightly. Despite her strong voice, she was close to cracking, and his heart ached for her.

"Then go home and live out your life as you had planned. You will continue to work in some capacity—I have no doubt of it—and marry some dowdy professor on your thirtieth birthday."

This made her whirl to face him. Her eyes were wide before she seemed to grasp ahold of herself again. "How do you know that's my plan?"

He grinned. "I know you whether you want to admit it or not. You want someone quiet who will be too timid or too consumed with his own scholarship to get in your way."

She bristled. "You know nothing about me."

"We both know that is not true. I know so much about you now, August." She looked down quickly, and he took that as a sign that he was right. "I know that you are afraid of a man taking away the small bit of power and autonomy that you have been able to wrest for yourself. I also know that the last person you expected to take that from you was your father."

She nodded, and though she still looked down, he thought she must be holding back tears, because her whole frame shook with the effort. Gently, he rested his palms on her shoulders. It was all the encouragement she needed to throw herself into his arms. There were no great sobs, but the trembling increased.

"I feel so terribly betrayed." Her voice was muffled

against his chest. "It's as if he has merely amused himself with me all of these years. As if he doesn't understand or care that I have my own needs."

Evan squeezed his eyes shut as he held her to hold back the anger he felt for her father. There was no doubt that she was right about the man's sentiments. Crenshaw was ruthless when it came to business, and it seemed he merely saw his own daughter as an extension of that. She was to further the family's influence, and if that came at the sacrifice of her own well-being, then so be it. He wanted to punch the man right in his arrogant jaw.

He despised how he had played into this game of adversaries and resolved to proceed fairly. She deserved that. She deserved so much more than that, more than him, but he needed her.

"I would not treat you that way, August." He whispered into her hair as he tightened his arms, savoring the feel of her curves and warmth against him.

She pulled back but did not release him. Her eyes were bright with tears. "I . . . I realize that . . ." She paused and took in a deep breath, her lips trembling with the effort. "I'm sorry I misplaced my anger at my father. It's not your fault. At any rate, I have come to talk to you. I want to negotiate our marriage."

"You wrote down your terms?" he asked, referencing the sheet of parchment on the table.

"Yes, but I expect you to add terms of your own."

"Are you certain this is what you want?"

She shrugged. "I am certain that my trust in my parents is shaken. I think this is the only way for me to get any semblance of what I want."

"And what is that?"

"A happy marriage, though I had planned for that to be far into the future, but it was a goal, nonetheless. Some autonomy. It is actually all in the terms I have set forth." She pulled back then, all business again. "If you will?" She indicated the table.

He paused, disturbed by the fact that he was the villain in her story. "We can have a happy marriage, August."

She gave him a slight nod, as if she did not believe it were true, and then took herself to her chair.

It took some time for August to settle herself at the table. He sat across from her as if this were a true negotiation, and she found that she was reluctant to begin. All her years of thinking of marriage in pragmatic terms and as some looming business transaction in the future, and it turned out she was a romantic. Her idea of a happy marriage— before now—had been two people who tolerated each other for companionship and children. Well, she wanted more than that. The problem was that she didn't know how to define *more*, or how to write it into a contract. Also, she was feeling quite vulnerable after nearly giving in to tears with him. In addition, she couldn't stop thinking about him being naked in the tub. It was an unsettling way to begin a negotiation.

Clearing her throat to give herself some reason for the delay, she picked up the pen. "I have taken the liberty of listing the simple components I believe we both require. Shall I read them?" A glance at his expression showed strain around his mouth and eyes. He nodded, so she continued. "I believe it is desirable to have at least two male children, yes?"

The image of his naked chest rising up out of the water filled her mind, the light dusting of tawny wet hair, the pink of a hard nipple, the strength encased in smooth skin. She would see even more of him to conceive those children. A pleasant flutter low in her belly had her shifting in her chair.

"It is the standard." His tone was closed off and difficult to read.

"Primogeniture being what it is, I have written that two male children is ideal. If, however, we have reached five children without two male issue, then I would want to renegotiate. If we have one son at that time, then I will likely not be willing to bear more children." She paused. The word *son* sat between them, heavy and unwieldy with meaning. One day soon they would have a child together. It did not seem that something so hallowed should be a business transaction, and yet it was. She blinked to bring the words into focus again. "If we have two sons immediately, then I would still like to have a daughter, but again, I believe five children is a good limit. However, and I must stress that all of this is dependent upon my health and ability to—"

"Jesus Christ." He scrubbed a hand over his face and then stared at her incredulously. "I would never force children upon you. Of course your health comes first. That is not something that we must write down to enforce later."

"Unfortunately, writing it down does nothing to prompt later enforcement. I am yours bodily after marriage. I simply wanted things to be understood between us."

He stared at her with a peculiar look on his face. It seemed to suggest disbelief coupled with something she could not name straightaway. "So you agree?" she asked.

"Yes."

"Good." She dipped the pen in ink and made a check mark, forcing herself to move on to the next point. "The next is slightly more delicate but no less important." She had to clear her throat again before continuing. "It concerns you more than me, so I would prefer your honest input." He gave her a single nod. "I am aware that things are done differently here than in New York, and I am willing to concede marginally on this one point." Though it pained her to do so. Even writing the words had caused her an ache that she did not altogether understand. "It is my understanding that it is customary for a man of your position to keep a . . . well . . ." Why was it so difficult to say the word? It was a fact of his world, was it not? She cleared her throat again. "A m-mistress." The word settled between them like a stone plunging to the bottom of a lake. "I would demand that you do not set one up until after we are finished with children."

His voice sounded strangled when he asked, "Does that mean that the physical part of our relationship would be over at that time?"

She nodded and forced herself to look at him. "That is

precisely it. If you would like to consort with someone else, then we would not . . ." Her face flamed and she could not say it. "We would not . . . anymore."

He ran his hand over his face, much as he had on the previous point. "I do not intend to have a mistress."

"We are not a love match. I do understand that you may seek one out. Actually, to be sure, this includes all women, not simply one you may set up as mistress." She stopped talking when he rose and began to pace, his movements jerky and short. His broad shoulders shifted restlessly under the fine wool of his coat.

When she had made the list in her bedroom, the idea of a mistress had been dispassionate and another point on the list. Now, however, being this close to him and having the heated imprint of his hands still on her body, well, it seemed vulgar and maddening. She did not like it one bit and was tempted to strike out the possibility completely. The more she imagined him kissing some other woman as he had kissed her, the angrier it made her. "In fact, I demand that you are not to be seen with any woman. If you have one now . . ."

Where had that thought come from? It had never occurred to her that he might have a mistress. Did he? Had he touched her so intimately in Camille's library only to go to his mistress afterward? Nausea churned in her stomach. "If you have one, then you must give her up immediately."

He looked at her as if she had grown a second head. "You think I have a mistress? Are you mad? I have been too busy of late trying to save my estates to even consider the expense of one."

Some devil made her ask, "But you had one before?"

He shook his head. "I have never felt the need to confine myself to one woman."

It was a reminder that he had never intended to and likely never would confine himself to her alone. Oil trickled onto the seething blaze of her anger. "What of that dancer . . . Madame Laurent . . . She is not your mistress?" The woman was beautiful, had been present at his fight, and had appeared proprietary with him.

"No."

"But she is your . . ." What was the word for a woman a man slept with but was not responsible for? "Lover?"

"Friend. We are friends, and yes, I have known her intimately, but not for several years."

She nodded and pretended to study the paper. However, all she could see was the two of them in bed together. The parchment trembled with her suppressed and unreasonable rage, so she laid it back down. One was not supposed to become emotional during negotiations.

"She attends most of the matches," he explained. "She enjoys them, and the crowd enjoys her. Her presence promotes attendance and betting."

All perfectly reasonable. Only she could not stop imagining them together, the beautiful woman's hand on his shoulder, proclaiming an ownership in that simple touch. It was a claim that August would never have. The black against white of ink on parchment could not give her that. And did she even want it, knowing that the arrangement had been coerced?

Yes! she realized with a start that nearly propelled her to her feet. She wanted it very much. Her anger was rooted in jealousy. She was jealous and possessive of this husband she hadn't wanted. Only now she very much wanted more than a negotiated marriage.

"What else is there?" He was behind her, looking down over her shoulder. "May I?" His brows lifted as he stared at the paper.

"Yes." She moved her fingers to give him an unobstructed view.

"Yes to the jointure. I suppose it is wise that you are considering my early demise, even if it is unsettling." He paused to read the next point. "Yes to the account in your name and the allowance. It is your money, after all. Ah, the fighting matches."

"I believe they're dangerous. You should not put yourself in danger that way."

Grinning at her, he said dryly, "There will hardly be a reason after my accounts are funded. I will still participate in sport matches at the club from time to time."

She nodded, taken aback by the force of his smile so close. It was the same one he had given her that night in the warehouse match. He turned his attention back to the parchment, skimming the rest of the list, which contained everything from provisions about educating the children of the tenant farmers to stipulating that she could visit her family as she wanted. "Yes to all of it."

He reached over and gently took the pen from her. The warmth of his body encased her, and his scent washed over her, taking her back to kissing him at this very table. His grip on the pen seemed particularly harsh as he signed his name with a flourish.

"Do you not have anything to add?" she asked.

"You seem to have thought of everything." His tone was perfectly practical, but his jaw was clenched tight, indicating his displeasure.

She could not help but poke the beast. "Oh, then you are fine with me taking a lover?"

He stared at her as he dropped the pen, leaving an ink blot on the parchment. "You are intentionally provoking me." He paced back to the fireplace.

She was and they both knew it. She wanted him to be as filled with impotent and restless anger as she was. "I am simply hoping to clarify things between us, and I find it odd that you don't prefer to include a provision on my having a lover. What else am I to conclude but that you don't mind?"

"I do mind." He faced away from her, staring into the flames, his voice rumbling with barely constrained emotion.

"I find that difficult to believe. This is simply a transaction to you. You need a wife who comes with significant capital, and I happen to be that woman. I don't know the figure you and my father have discussed, but I have read the papers, and I know the rumors say two hundred thousand dollars—"

He turned toward her, and a sound she could only describe as a growl issued from deep in his chest. Before she could move, he was pulling her against him, one hand at the small of her back, the other delving into her hair to gently cradle the back of her head.

"You are mine, and I will not share you with any man. I want us to be done with this negotiation."

Her instinct should have been to put distance between them, but instead of pushing him away, her hands moved up his shoulders and curved around them. Her body pressed closer to the hard strength of his, thrilled to be held by him again. This was the emotion she craved from him. "No, you wanted this negotiation."

"I want *you*, August." The intensity of his gaze only inches away burned into her. "I want the woman who fought me at every turn. The woman who knows that this entire negotiation is archaic and wrong."

Her heart pounded, but she was afraid to hope that his words meant what she wanted them to mean. That he, too, wanted that indefinable *more* with her. "Archaic and wrong because you believe certain things should not be discussed?"

His breathing came hard, almost as if he had been running. His breath was hot on her lips. Somehow, the inches between their mouths had reduced to a mere fraction. "Because I want us to be more than a business transaction."

His lips crushed down on hers, and she melted into his kiss.

Chapter 19

❖

What draws men and women together is stronger than the brutality and tyranny which drive them apart.

MILLICENT FAWCETT

Kissing him made all of the fury and aggression vanish. They simply slid away like warm honey under the onslaught of such tenderness, for it was not a frenzied, chaotic thing. While the initial touch of their lips had bordered on fierce, he had gentled her, moving to cup her face and take her mouth in a tender and slow caress. The kisses melted one into the next until she was a trembling thing of need. August clung to the lapels of his coat, suddenly aware of the difference in their clothing as her unencumbered breasts pressed against the stiff fabric of his dinner attire. Yet it hardly mattered in her search for the comfort he brought her. The heat of his body became a part of her.

She gasped, drawing in much-needed breath, and squeezed her eyes shut. He moved; whether it was to pull back, she couldn't say, but she grabbed his arms and held him. He made a soft groan, and his hand slid up to cup her head.

"August," he whispered, soft and barely more than

breath of sound. "If I could save you from this, I would. Forgive me for not understanding earlier?" He placed petal-soft kisses along her jaw and neck.

"For not understanding what?" she whispered.

"That I need you for you and not your wealth."

He drew back then but only so far that she could see his face clearly in the firelight and the single lamp that burned on the table. His eyes were tender and full of a dawning wonder. It made the ache in her throat expand. "I want to shield you from this. Let me negotiate with your father. I promise that once we are married, you will not have to worry."

"No." She gave her head a shake because eloquent words had deserted her, and she needed him to understand she meant it. "I don't need a shield."

"How thoughtless of me." A smile curved his lips, and he pressed a kiss to her mouth. "You need someone to fight beside you."

His eyes were serious as he said that, as if he meant the words and was not humoring her. "Do you mean that?" she asked, because she dared not believe he could understand.

"I do. We will do this together."

His hands roved down her back to fill his palms with her bottom. An involuntary gasp escaped her as he squeezed and brought her against the hard ridge contained in his trousers. Molten heat burned low in her belly and throbbed between her legs. Without corset or petticoats, she could feel him all along her front, except the very thickness of his own clothes was in the way. Her hands fumbled their way inside his coat and pushed it down off his shoulders. He released her long enough to shrug out of it and allow it to drop to the floor before reclaiming her. His mouth took hers, tongue delving in to taste her. Her fingers tore at the buttons of his waistcoat as his mouth dragged across her jaw to nibble at ear. An erotic shiver rocked her to her core, and the insistent throb between her thighs grew more intense.

"I love being able to finally feel you." His voice was a harsh rasp as his mouth moved down the column of her neck in hot, openmouthed kisses. She let out a sound of satisfaction as one large hand kneaded her bottom and the other covered her aching breast to shape it and revel in the unencumbered touch. His thumb brushed over the sensitive tip, tugging at the need building inside her. Never had anything felt more gratifying.

Her hips moved against him in an unconscious rhythm, desperate to get closer. He groaned into her neck and held her tight against his rigid length. Tugging his shirttail from his trousers, she pushed her hands beneath to find his smooth skin and the light furring of hair that abraded her palms. It was only then that she realized this groping wouldn't be enough. She wanted to explore all of him.

"I want to see you."

His answer was immediate. He let her go to quickly unbutton his shirt and toss it away. The firelight kissed him, turning his skin a pale gold. She marveled at how his muscles were clearly defined, like a sculpture. Her fingertips explored him with a will all their own, tracing the line that bisected the ridges on his stomach to where it disappeared into the high waist of his trousers. His erection was clearly outlined beneath the fabric, but she wasn't quite bold enough to explore there just yet. Instead, she moved upward to the twin muscles of his chest. She squeezed gently, marveling at how well-formed he was.

He gently took pins out of her hair until it fell in a heavy rush down her back. His fingertips traced down the curve of her brow to take a length of hair and bring it to his nose. He closed his eyes as he inhaled, and her stomach tumbled over itself. The mere scent of him caused her belly to swirl pleasantly. Was it the same with him?

Before she realized her intention, she was talking. "I went into D.R. Harris last week on the pretense of buying my father a birthday gift, but really I wanted to find your cologne."

He gave her a slow grin. "Did you find it?"

"No, and Mrs. Barnes disapproved."

The strand of hair slid out of his fingers as he reached down again, only this time when his hands grasped her bottom, he lifted her against him. "Oh!" His laugh vibrated through her as he walked with her to the sofa before the hearth. Then he sat down and placed her on his lap. He hardly gave her time to get her bearings as he buried his face in her neck and his teeth raked pleasantly against the sensitive skin there as he said, "She would likely faint if she could see us now. Take this off." He tugged at the buttons of her wrapper.

Her fingers went to immediately tug them loose, and when his hand found her breast again, she sighed in near relief. With only her nightgown as a barrier, she could feel the heat of his palm. The soft cambric rasped against her skin as he pinched her nipple in a gentle rhythm that had answering darts of pleasure coursing through her body. The swell of the delicate flesh between her thighs had her shifting restlessly on top of him. Soon, even that wasn't enough. She wanted nothing between them.

Her hands returned to her nightdress, trembling with her need to have him touch her. Gently, his own steadier hands brushed hers aside, completing the task with minimal time and effort. She could only watch as he smoothed the fabric off her shoulders, baring both of her breasts to him. She had never been this exposed to anyone, but watching his eyes darken with longing and need, she didn't feel shy or embarrassed.

He moved slowly and with intention, sliding out from beneath her and pressing her back to lie on the sofa as he leaned over her. As if it existed on instinct alone, her back arched, pressing upward as he leaned down to lavish attention on first one breast and then the other. She didn't even try to stop the soft cry of pleasure that escaped her with the first tug of his mouth. When he shifted, she moved with him, spreading her thighs in the tangle of too much fabric to allow his heavy thigh to rest between them.

The cool air of the room touched her calf as his hand found its way beneath her nightdress. The hem slid higher as he leaned over her, resting a forearm on the sofa above her. She was held riveted by the intense desire in his face as he stared down at her.

"I want to touch you, August." He didn't ask, but the request was there in the slow perusal of his fingers on the inside of her knee.

Her heart pounded in her chest, and she felt as if she couldn't take a solid breath, but she wanted him to touch her. Nodding, she let her foot drop to the floor, opening herself wider to him. He smiled and kissed her the very moment his fingers delved between the lips of her sex. She gasped against his mouth.

The tip of his finger dipped into her, drawing forth the hot need from her body and smoothing the liquid heat over her swollen flesh. She had read about the clitoris before, in a book she had found beneath her brother's bed almost ten years ago. It had taken her all this time to understand what it was that she had read. A tide of need rose within her as his clever fingers moved in a soft but firm rhythm, causing her body to clench around emptiness. "Evan," she whispered.

She closed her eyes and pressed her face to his arm as her hips arched up to his touch. One finger gently thrust into the emptiness, she could feel herself clench around him, but it was almost as if her body was out of her control. It responded on instinct based in pure need. "Please," she said as it moved in and out of her.

He answered her request by pushing in another finger, stretching her with a slightly burning pain. He rested there without moving, allowing her to become accustomed to the invasion, as the heel of his hand put firm pressure on the swollen ache of her clitoris. His mouth lazily moved downward, kissing her ear, the hollow of her throat, her breast. His tongue teased her nipple, circling it and laving it until he growled and took it into his mouth, plunging his fingers into her as he did so. She nearly came apart at the sensation that sent tunneling through her. And this time he didn't stop. His fingers continued thrusting until the slight burn had been replaced by ripples of pleasure that begged to be fed. She moved her hips beneath his touch, searching for more, and when he shifted so that his thumb could brush over her clitoris, she exploded. Waves of ecstasy crashed over her in a seemingly endless tide until she lay limp beneath him.

She had no idea how much time had passed before she became aware of herself again. It couldn't have been long. Her heart still pounded, and she had yet to catch her breath. He held her against his side, and somehow they had shifted so that she half lay on top of him, her leg wantonly thrown over his. She should have been concerned that her nightdress was still up around her hips, or that his hand—the same hand that had brought her pleasure—rested on her thigh. Or she might have been concerned that her breasts were still bare. None of that mattered.

He smiled at her and brushed the tip of her nose with his. "You're beautiful when you come."

Her cheeks flamed. "Is that what you call it?"

"Yes." He shifted, pulling her fully on top of him, and grabbed her buttocks. She started at the intimacy, and the way his hands molded her to him, spreading her, taking control of her. It felt foreign and forbidden, but also exhilarating and visceral. Honest and primal. He bucked upward, pressing the hard ridge of his shaft against her feminine flesh.

While she had been momentarily sated, her curiosity about him was insatiable, and her body answered that need with a fresh wave of arousal. Testing her effect on him, she moved her hips, grinding herself against him. A masculine groan of desire was pulled from deep in his chest.

Surprising herself, she reached between them and laid her palm against his length. He closed his eyes, seeming to savor her touch. "What do you call this?"

One piercing blue eye opened to focus on her. "A cock," he answered in no uncertain terms.

The word itself sounded deliciously vulgar. She might have blushed had they not already done things that were beyond blushing. She squeezed and watched the pleasant sensation wash over his face. She did it again and he gasped, "Christ, August." His breath was heavy on her, but he didn't pull away. As she learned the shape of him, his hips jerked, and he thrust against her hand. His lips parted and then his jaw clenched tight, his hands fisting in the folds of her nightgown as he squeezed his eyes shut and drew taut as a bowstring against her.

Finally, his hand covered hers and his voice was a harsh whisper as he said, "My God, I want all of you." Amazingly, this man who was vastly more experienced than she gazed up at her with an expression of wonder on his face. His free hand brushed a strand of hair back from her face, and his fingertips touched her lips in awe. "We have to stop now."

"But I don't want to stop." Her words surprised them both. However, she knew they were true as soon as she heard them. She didn't want to wait to have him. She didn't want their first time together to be in a marriage bed that had been arranged by her parents' schemes. She wanted it to be now, after the most intimate moment of her life. She wanted it on her own terms.

"There will be time once we are married." He sat up and swung his legs over the side so that he was seated, taking her with him to straddle his lap. His arms went around her, holding her close so that she thought he meant to pick her up and walk with her back to the table, but he simply held her. She was exhilarated to see that his fingers trembled as he cupped her cheek. "You do not have to give me your maidenhead, not until you're ready. Our wedding night, a month later . . . a year later."

"I want to have this night for our own. No families. No negotiations. Only us." His expression seemed to sharpen with need as he understood she was serious. Desire and decorum seemed to be at war within him, the fighter and the gentleman. The two sides she had only begun to discover existed with him. How she hoped the fighter won out in this. To ensure that it did, she kissed him.

He gripped handfuls of her nightdress and wrapper and broke the kiss only long enough to pull them both off over her head in one fell swoop. Then he wrapped his arms around her and held her flush against him as he devoured her mouth. So *this* is how it felt to be naked in his arms. Where he was hard, she was soft, and where he was lightly furred, she was smooth. She moved, testing and liking the way the hair on his chest scraped against her nipples.

He grinned against her lips and plucked a nipple with his thumb and forefinger. Pleasure throbbed from her nipple to her core. "You like being touched. How fortunate, because I like touching you."

Releasing her nipple, his hand molded itself to her as it moved down to dip between her spread thighs and find her wet. She bucked against his hand as he grazed her still-swollen flesh. He played with her until she was writhing and aching for him to fill her again. Only when she reached desperately for the fastenings of his trousers did he release her to help.

His cock sprang free, rising up toward his navel as he shifted upward to push the trousers down. He froze as soon as she touched him. She hadn't known what to expect, but it hadn't been this impossible length of male that felt hot and smooth as silk against her palm. It did not give as she stroked it, holding itself strong and proud.

"August," he whispered in near pain, but he allowed her to finish exploring.

Her thumb traced over the opening at the end, spreading the tiny bit of pearly liquid she found there. He groaned and grabbed her hips, pulling her up. She clutched his shoulders and rose onto her knees to aid him as he shifted, notching the tip of him against her. She shivered in anticipation.

"Ready?"

"Yes." It was hardly more than a breath. She was more than ready; her entire body trembled with need and longing.

Finally, he let her slide down his length, raising his hips in gentle pumps to ease the way. The pleasure was indescribable. Her entire awareness centered on that point of contact. The ache in her had grown so inconsolable that this was the only way to quench it. Yet, as he filled her, he stretched her with a burning pain, and when her body seemed capable of accepting no more, he pushed upward, filling her the last bit until they were joined completely.

She didn't cry out, but instead pressed her face into his neck, letting his scent surround her. His hands moved in slow strokes up and down the length of her back, the touches gradually becoming more sensual until he was kneading her buttocks and lifting her gently and rocking into her. The pain slowly melted into pleasure, ebbing through her in waves that had her moving with him. Her fingers tightened in his hair, and her gaze met his. She had never felt so connected to another person. It far transcended their physical joining.

His name tumbled from her lips as his movements became more structured and controlled. A hand guided her hip, as the other slipped between them, finding her aching flesh and stroking her with each thrust, caressing her from both sides. It wasn't long before the pleasure in her belly was tightening like a spring, coiling and twisting until it had no choice but to explode within her. He gripped her hips with both hands and held her firm against him as he thrust up inside her in several short thrusts before he found his own release.

As they both came back to themselves, he held her curled against his chest, his lips brushing soft kisses along her brow. "Are you hurt?" he finally asked.

"Only a little sore," she whispered, smiling up at him.

He kissed her softly and with much less urgency than before. This new aftermath felt strange and wonderful all at the same time. Her limbs were heavy, and her body was sated, but she didn't want to leave him, even though a new awareness of her nakedness was slowly settling over her. When she shifted, he slid out from under her and adjusted his trousers. The heat of embarrassment swept over her face as she noticed a smudge of pink on the pale skin of his belly. There was probably a reason this was done for the first time in a proper bed.

An arm crossed over her chest as she realized how reckless this had been. The door was closed but not locked. Anyone could have seen them had they come to check why light was shining from beneath the door at this hour.

"Shh . . ." His voice was a strong murmur as he knelt before her on the floor.

She barely had time to register his intent before he pressed a wad of white cloth—*his shirt!*—against the tenderness between her legs, wiping her clean.

"Do you regret it?" His gaze was soft and comforting.

"No," she answered honestly, unable to stop smiling. "Only surprised. I swear I never intended that to happen tonight."

Leaning forward, he kissed her and then sat back on his heels to clean the evidence of her virginity from his skin. She gasped aloud when he finished and leaned forward, placing a kiss on her inner thigh. "Neither did I, but I am glad it did."

Grabbing his face, a face that was quickly becoming beloved to her, she brought him up for a kiss, probably their thousandth of the night. And they would have so many more in their future. A rare feeling of hopeful contentment settled over her. She still had mixed emotions about marrying at this point in her life, but she could finally answer Violet's question with confidence. Yes, she would choose Evan over all other men.

"Me too."

"Come." He rose and offered her his hand. Pulling her to stand, he helped her dress, kissing her breasts before he buttoned her nightdress over them. As she shrugged into her wrapper, he put on his coat and retrieved his shirt and waistcoat. Wrapping an arm around her, he said, "I will escort you to your room."

"What if someone sees?" she asked, mildly alarmed. She'd had visions of them both skulking out of the library at different times to avoid suspicion should anyone be about.

"Let them. We will be married as soon as it can be arranged."

She laughed but quickly covered her mouth to stifle the sound. "We cannot announce what we've done to the entire house."

"Then you should take care to be quiet," he teased.

He would be her husband. They would make love as often as they wanted. It seemed unbelievable, but genuine happiness filled her at the thought. Amid giggles because he persisted in trying to get them caught, they made their way to her bedroom. Thankfully, the halls were dark and there was no one about. It made for a longer trip because he kept stopping to kiss her.

At her bedroom door, she pulled him full against her with their final kiss and spread her palms against his bare chest, reluctant to give him up touching him.

"I wish I could have you again," he whispered. "But you need time to heal, and we will not have long to wait."

She nodded. "I know. I simply feel . . ." How did she explain the sudden dread that had developed when her bedroom had come into sight? What if things between them went back to how they had been? What if this side of him was only a mirage?

Holding her close, he kissed her forehead and then gently touched her chin, urging her to look up at him. "I do want us to have a marriage built on respect and affection. We will have many more nights like this."

"You are leaving tomorrow?" she asked.

He nodded. "I have to. A business matter has come up, and it cannot wait."

"Business? More fighting?" She thought of the horrible man with the spikes on the soles of his shoes.

"There will be another fight next week. Wilkes owes me that much after the stunt he pulled. But I have to leave tomorrow because my solicitor has long suspected that our previous solicitor absconded with funds. He's been found, and there appears to be new information." He gently touched her lips before she could speak and grinned. "Do not get too excited. I am certain whatever he took has long been spent, nor would it be enough to cover my debts."

She smiled at him. "I'm sure you're right. Please be careful with Wilkes. He's a dangerous and likely desperate man."

He kissed her once more. "I will. I promise you, this will be the last fight for money, and then there will only be us to consider."

He was right. They would be married soon. She would be a wife. They would be happy. Her dread was only leftover misgivings and anxiety about leaving her old life behind.

Chapter 20

❧

Life is a flower for which love is the honey.
VICTOR HUGO

E van should have spent the morning focusing on how he
was going to persuade Mercer from calling the loan on
Sterling House. Wilkes's payment had not satisfied the
man's greed and ruthless glee at having a Sterling under his
thumb. In fact, it had seemed to have the opposite effect,
rather like a starving wolf scenting blood. Not only had he
not extended the grace period, but he had demanded the
rest payable immediately. Clark's telegram the day before
had all but expressed his personal despair at the situation,
which had required Evan to book a seat on the noon train
back to London in order to appear before the creditors personally. It had also hinted at new information in the disap-
pearance of the solicitor, but Evan was not inclined to put
much hope in that. His thoughts should have been absorbed
with the upcoming confrontation.

But he was not. August absorbed his thoughts.

He might also have been irate about his brief meeting
with Crenshaw after dinner last night. The man had taken
particular glee in writing out a letter that Evan had been
forced to confess was necessary. The letter was now held
securely in the inside pocket of Evan's chesterfield. It stated

in no uncertain terms that Evan was to be married to the man's daughter in the very near future, date to be determined. The very idea that Evan, a duke of the realm, needed someone, especially an American, to vouch for him was galling. Or it would have been under normal circumstances.

But there was August. The fact that she was there waiting for him at the end of this string of indignities was enough. The events of the previous night still seemed otherworldly. Had Evan not gone to sleep with the smell of her on his fingers, and the memory of how exquisitely her body had joined to his, he might have thought it a hallucination. He had woken up aching for her all over again. Unfortunately, he had yet to see her, because the morning had been spent packing and arranging papers and contracts with the estate manager.

Dropping the last of the contracts into his traveling case so that he could review them on the train, he snapped the leather case closed. At that exact moment, the study door swung open and August stood framed in the doorway. Her cheeks were lightly flushed, and there was a softness about her features, a sort of wonder in her eyes, that he knew must have been mirrored in his own. He drifted around his desk and toward her with the irresistible pull of iron to lodestone.

"Good morning, Evan." Her voice was low but heavy with meaning.

Evan instead of Rothschild. The intimacy of his given name had warmth settling in his chest. He searched her face for some sign of regret or pain, but he only found awe. He felt the same. It was as if they had stumbled upon a secret they had both only begun to suspect existed and it had far surpassed expectation.

"Good morning." His own voice was low and raspy, naked in a way he had never felt with her or anyone.

She laughed, her teeth tugging at her bottom lip to stifle it. He laughed, suddenly aware that neither of them knew how to proceed with this newfound intimacy. But his hands knew just how to touch her. They curved around her hips and settled at the small of her back, and her own hands moved up his shoulders so that her fingers could twist in the hair at the back of his head.

She rose up on her tiptoes and kissed him. Whether she meant it to be a light kiss or not, it took over them both, fanning the flames between them as if they had not had sex only hours before. He kissed her until they both had to pause for air, and then he only let her go a fraction of an inch. "I missed you."

She nodded, her nose brushing his, and she kissed him again, a tinge of desperation taking shape. "I know. Me too."

"'Tis a bloody shame that I have to leave. I want to take you upstairs and bar the door and keep you there for at least a week."

She laughed again, but a pretty blush stole over her features. Her gaze turned mischievous as she said, "I think I would like that very much."

He cupped her face in his hands and kissed her again, this time more gently. "I shall call on you when I can. Your father has already mentioned a marriage contract in the works. I suspect he will send it over soon after you return to London. Have you seen it?"

"Not yet, but I will before he sends it."

"Send me a message if there is anything within it that you find objectionable. I want us to be in complete agreement before we sign."

She nodded.

"You do believe that?" He did not want to do a single thing that would take away the acceptance and affection he saw blooming in her eyes.

"Yes."

"Good. Once everything is finalized, we can announce the betrothal. The rest is up to you. We can marry whenever and wherever you want."

"Shh." Her fingers covered his lips, and he could not resist placing a kiss on her fingertips. "I simply wanted a moment alone with you before you leave. We can discuss the details and contracts later."

Taking her hand, he kissed her palm and then her wrist, giving silent thanks that this woman would be his soon.

"I can't help but be afraid that . . ."

A momentary tremor of unease crossed her features. "Afraid of what?" he asked.

"That with our return to London, everything will . . . go back to how it was."

He smiled. "That is because I was an arse in London. I will endeavor to put that behind me."

She smiled back before becoming somber again. "I, too, was a bit irresponsible."

"But now we know what we can have with a little understanding and perseverance," he teased.

"True."

"Our future together will be what we make of it."

The mischief returned to her eyes. "Then it will certainly include more nights like last night." Her hand moved down his chest, intent on reaching the very evident erection that she could likely feel through the layers of their clothes.

"And days," he said, lifting her against him and eliciting a giggle from her as he swung around to sit her on his desk.

Kissing her, he made short work of moving his hand under her skirt, half considering if they had time to do more, when a sound from the door had him spinning around, shielding August from the intruder.

Elizabeth stood there with her arms crossed over her chest and a knowing scowl on her face. "Mother sent me to find you. She says if you do not leave now you will miss your train." He opened his mouth, but she spoke before he could. "It would be rude in the extreme to make an entire train wait for you."

"What is the point of inheriting a dukedom if one cannot indulge oneself at times?"

Elizabeth laughed, August raised a brow, and he had a startlingly clear vision of his future. For the first time in his life the view was beautiful. "Leave us so that I can finish saying goodbye to my betrothed."

Another storm came through after Evan left, so instead of leaving early they stayed the entire week, while repairs were made farther downtrack. August didn't mind, because, despite its faults, she was coming to see the charm in the old pile of stones. She had found herself wandering through the rooms and viewing them with an eye that was becoming increasingly proprietary. She made checklists in her mind of the refurbishments that would need to be addressed first and even talked to Mr. Hughes about the roof so that he could begin to gather figures for its much-needed replacement.

Each night found her making her way to Evan's bedroom. She wandered through his dressing room to run her fingertips over the varied fabrics and textures hanging in his armoires. They were very masculine fabrics, heavy and thick. She sat on his bed and smelled him there, and imagined that they shared this bed together. Those thoughts always made her feel heated and alive and excited to see him again. Not one part of her regretted what had happened between them in the library.

The feeling of unease, however, had not left her. It stayed with her through the nights in his bedroom and the train ride home. She told herself that it was because she had begun to look at her family differently. Her parents had been willing to force her to marry Evan at the expense of her own needs and wants, and she still did not know how to reconcile that with what she thought she knew about them. But there was more.

August did not know how to identify this new person she would become. Duchess of Rothschild. It was a stranger's name.

These thoughts consumed her when she walked into the townhome on Grosvenor Square. Before taking off her gloves, she hurried to the silver tray on a side table that held correspondence. A quick flip through the various invitations and notes revealed nothing from Evan. Disappointment swelled inside her.

"Maxwell!" Violet's surprised voice rang out as Max hurried down the stairs to greet them. He was dressed as if he had spent the day out.

"Maxwell?" August and her mother echoed.

Violet stopped halfway through tugging off her gloves and threw herself into his arms. "How long have you been here?"

"I arrived yesterday." He greeted each of them in turn,

catching August's eye with a question in his. "I was told that everyone was spending a week at the Duke of Rothschild's estate. How was it?" His gaze then went to August's hand, which was absent a betrothal ring.

"Both dreadful and marvelous if you can believe that," said Mother. "The place is practically falling down around them, but it's so huge. And filled with Rembrandts and Titians and, my God, I think some of the furniture is Georgian, possibly even older." She held a hand to her chest.

"Calm yourself, Millie. You'll give yourself apoplexy," Papa teased. "We have El Greco, Titian, and van Dyck at home, along with, and I cannot say enough how important this next point is, indoor plumbing." He laughed loudly at his own jest.

"Of course, dear. I am simply beside myself with joy." Her gaze narrowed in mock frustration as she turned her attention to Max. "I suppose I don't need to ask what brings you to London." She hugged him and kissed him on each cheek. "I'm afraid to say that your father is right about the lack of plumbing. I've been waiting days to freshen up properly. Give me an hour and then I want to hear all about your crossing. I trust it was uneventful?"

Max nodded. "Very uneventful, Mother."

"Good. I am happy to report that our time here has not been uneventful." She raised a knowing brow at August. "We are expecting good news any day now." With those promising words, she left them and retreated to her bedroom upstairs.

"Is there no news, then?" asked Max. "No betrothal?"

She started to reply, but Papa beat her to it. "Sadly, not yet." He gave her a telling glance that seemed to imply the lack of a formal betrothal was her fault. August had not shared with him the extent of her personal discussion with Evan. "Although the duke has indicated a willingness to begin negotiations, which is promising. I am having a contract sent over today."

"Then I have come in time," Max said with resolve and pressed a reassuring hand to her back, his dark eyes flickering with censure.

His tone caught Papa's attention. "So you have come to save your sister from marriage?"

"I expressed as much in my telegrams. We are Cren-shaws, for Christ's sake. We do not have to sell our daughters and sisters for coin or prestige."

"No one is selling anyone. We are the ones paying him." Papa gave them an antagonistic grin.

"Yes, I gathered as much," Max replied.

Aware that the tension was rising in the front hall and the servants had disappeared, Papa huffed out a final breath and smoothed a hand down his lapel. "I find that I, too, need a few moments to refresh myself. We will continue this discussion in my study. Say a half hour?"

Max gave him a nod of deference, and they watched him in silence as he walked up the stairs and then disappeared down the corridor. "What the hell has happened? Are you all right?" Max turned to her and asked.

"Yes, I'm fine. Come, let's sit in the drawing room and talk." August led her sister and brother to the drawing room and discreetly closed the door behind them.

"It's been so awful," Violet began. "First me, and now poor August." She gave August a pitying glance before launching into the entire torrid history of their parents' matchmaking scheme.

August sat in a chair facing them both and fidgeted. She felt badly that Max had come all this way for her to tell him that she now believed that she did want to marry Evan. But she did like Evan. She liked him a lot. Was that enough for marriage?

It was a good start. Besides, how could she go back to the way life was before this marriage business? How could she trust her parents ever again, especially Papa? Unable to keep still, she rose and paced to the window.

"It seems this duke returned to London with the impression that you were going to marry him. Is that right?" Max asked after Violet had finished the story.

"We spoke privately before he left, and I agreed to his proposal. It's not official until he and Papa sign the contract."

"And you are certain this is what you want to do?"

"I feel great affection for Evan, and I do think that we could make a happy life together." Extremely happy, if she was being completely forthright. Now that she had finally seen past the veil of nobility to the real man, she was certain that he was the right choice. She was less certain that she was ready to make that choice right now. "Besides, even if I said no, things could not go back to how they were. Papa has already said that he will not allow me to continue my work with Crenshaw Iron."

Max rose to stand before her. "He won't get away with that. I have rights in that company. He cannot cut you out that way, not without my say-so."

"I know, but that's not really the issue here, is it? He said what he said, and there's no going back from that." She broke off when her throat closed and turned quickly to face the window when tears threatened to spill down her cheeks. She had never been one to show her emotions easily, but especially not in front of Max or Papa. To show weakness was against everything the Crenshaws stood for.

It was a surprise when Max put his hands on her shoulders. "This is your life, August. Your future. You get to decide. I will stand by whatever you choose."

She nodded and wiped a tear from the corner of her eye. "I've already chosen. I choose Evan."

"Perhaps it is a good thing he was not to be found at Sterling House yesterday."

August whirled to stare at him. He had a faint smile on his face. "You went to Sterling House?"

"I arrived and no one was home. Reginald explained that you had been delayed, so I decided to pay a call and size this Rothschild up for myself."

"Thank God he was not there. I appreciate you coming, and I'm sorry that I pulled you away, but it appears I don't need you to go to battle for me after all."

Max grinned. "Yes, you do. I'll have a look at that contract before it's sent over, and if you do end up marrying this fortune-hunting bastard, I'll have a nice long chat with him first."

She smiled and hugged him. "Thank you for coming, but that won't be necessary. I can manage him fine on my own."

"I have no doubt of that," said Max.

Chapter 21

*But the future must be met, however stern
and iron it be.*

ELIZABETH GASKELL

Several days after his return to London, Evan stepped
into his solicitor's office. Clark came to his feet immediately.

"Your Grace" fell from his lips as he resettled the spec-
tacles on his face. A clerk who had been taking dictation
also rose, dropping his pen in the process.

Afternoon sunlight filtered in through the leaded glass
windows, casting a dreary glow over the confined space.
Stacks of crates lined the wall beneath the windows. Books
and parchments were piled on the floor on one side of the
large desk in the center of the room and on the cabinets that
lined the back wall. The desk itself, however, appeared neat
and organized.

"It was not my intention to catch you unaware. I received
your note at the club and, since the matter was of some
urgency, decided to call instead of driving over to Sterling
House to wait for you there."

"Yes, of course, Your Grace. Excellent suggestion. I
would never have presumed to set a meeting here, but you

are quite right, it is much more expedient." Perhaps without realizing it, Clark's gaze took in the messy office.

The clerk who had shown Evan in hovered in the doorway behind him. His voice cracked a little when he spoke. "Tea, my l—er, Your Grace?"

"No, thank you." Turning his attention back to Clark and the overstuffed office, he said, "It appears you have been busy." Evan had only been here once before when he had hired the man. That visit had been much the same with the genuflection of the clerks surprised by the presence of a duke in their midst, but the office had been nearly sparse then.

Clark indicated that the clerk taking dictation should leave them. The young man, who could not have been any older than Clark himself, presented them with his front as he backed out of the room in a nearly comical display of deference before closing the door.

"What have you told them about me?" Evan asked as he took the vacated chair.

Clark smiled and took his seat behind the desk. "I think your reputation says it all, Your Grace."

Evan smiled, reminded of why he had hired the man. Clark had been the only one to speak to him plainly after the initial show of respect.

"I must thank you," Clark continued and waved a hand toward the papers filling his office. "My fledgling practice has nearly tripled in large part due to your recommendations."

"Due to your competence, you mean."

Clark lowered his gaze in humility. "Nevertheless, thank you. My association with you and Montague has certainly enhanced things." He rose and opened one of the cabinets on the wall behind him. Taking out a box filled with papers, he brought them back to his desk.

His gaze all but pasted to the box, Evan asked, "I assume this meeting is because you have further confirmation?" When he had arrived back in London from Charrington Manor, Clark had met with him at the club with the news that a man claiming to be in the employ of George Sterling, the Duke of Rothschild, had been found in Pleasant Ridge, Montana Territory.

Clark nodded and resumed his seat. "Yes, it's Lichfield. He originally used an assumed name, but our investigator was able to find papers in his rooms that proved him to be Gordon Lichfield."

Evan let out a breath and felt a strange sense of relief wash over him. None of that was a surprise, but it was confirmation that his instincts had been correct. "I assume any funds he took were gone."

Clark gave a funny little laugh and withdrew a sheaf of paper from the box. "Well, that is the interesting bit. You see, it appears that we have uncovered so much more than stolen funds."

Evan leaned forward, fully engrossed now. "How much more?"

"Forgive me for not telling you sooner, but I found it rather unbelievable myself. I had to authenticate the information with the registrar of the territory and then had the solicitor in New York authenticate it to make absolutely certain there was no question of . . . well . . . authenticity. I still can hardly bring myself to bel—"

"Spit it out, man!"

"Yes, yes." Clark shook his head and then nodded as he picked up a yellow paper with printed words. It appeared to be a telegram. "Your Grace, it seems that your father is—was—a major shareholder in the Pleasant Ridge Mining Company, which has operations based in Montana Territory. The shares never appeared in any of the documents pertaining to your father's estate. I believe we can safely assume that is because Lichfield did his best to make certain there was no trace of them. To be honest, I am not certain your father was aware of the value of the claim. From New York, we know that his signature appears on several documents pertaining to the company. I can also confirm that a bank draft was issued in the amount of the cost of the initial shares several years ago. It was recorded in the ledger as funds for capital improvements. I made a visit to the bank myself to research the purchase and have proof of the draft from the bank here."

"That whoreson!"

Clark dug further into the box and produced a piece of paper, but Evan had difficulty focusing on the words. That son of a bitch Lichfield had stolen from them. The man had played the trusted servant and confidant only to steal from the man he had served for nearly forty years. Impotent anger raged through Evan. How unfortunate the object of his rage was thousands of miles away. Perhaps it was very fortunate indeed, because Evan could have happily strangled him.

Unable to sit still, Evan bolted to his feet and paced the cramped office. The need to hit something coursed through him, but he managed to control it. "Have you contacted the authorities? I want him arrested and tried."

Clark stared at him before coming to his senses and nodding. "Yes, he was taken into custody by the local sheriff and handed over to a U.S. marshal. I have requested that he be delivered back to London, but that could take time."

"Why haven't you told me any of this?"

"As you know, I only became aware of his possible existence in Montana Territory before you left for Hampshire last week. There was no hint of the mining company until a few days ago, and, as I explained, I wanted to make absolutely certain that my information was accurate before passing it along to you."

"Yes, of course. That is why I hired you." Evan inclined his head in understanding.

Mollified, Clark nodded. "Your Grace, forgive me, but I think you may be overlooking the bigger issue here."

"Bigger than Lichfield stealing from my dead father?"

"Yes, well, there is the issue of the mining shares. The company has been productive since its inception, which means your shares are worth roughly £1.2 million, but that information is sourced from an outdated balance sheet. I suspect they are worth considerably more now."

"More?"

"More."

"Bloody fucking hell." Evan sank back down into his chair and leaned forward to drop his head into his hands. The figure was unbelievable.

"I am told that Lichfield lives like a king, so I doubt there is room to recover any annuities you might be owed from previous years. But, should you sell your stock, or even a small portion, we could have funds within the week transferred to London."

Clark droned on about stock valuation, annuities, and extradition procedures, but Evan was having a difficult time taking it all in. The only thing he knew for certain was that he was free. Relief made him feel light as if he were rising like a balloon. His tenants would have funds for leaky roofs and new equipment. His mother would not be forced to leave Sterling House. She could buy new dresses. His sisters no longer had to wear clothing they had outgrown. He could fund all of the plans for Charrington Manor and his other estates that he had discussed with August.

August! She was also free. Free to choose not to marry him. She could go back to her life as she had planned it. He had to tell her. She would be ecstatic. He started to rise but sank back down into the cushioned seat as he grasped the reality of that.

She would choose not to marry him. She had never wanted their marriage, so why would she choose him now? Disappointment and sadness drained away every drop of joy. A very selfish part of him wanted to pretend this conversation had never happened or even toss away the mine shares. He wanted the life they had planned in those hours alone at Charrington Manor. But that wouldn't be fair. He had to offer her freedom. It was the one thing he could give her.

"Your Grace? Your Grace?" From his puzzled expression, it appeared that Clark had been trying to get his attention for some time. "There is the Crenshaw matter to discuss. I have made certain to keep the mining news quiet. Not even my clerks know, so the decision is yours to make.

Do you want to move forward with the betrothal contract?"
He withdrew a thick sheaf of papers from that bottomless
box. "I have it here, ready to be finalized."

Evan was forced to clear his throat to speak. "You were
able to receive the concessions from Crenshaw?" The past
several days had seen the contract volleyed back and forth
from Clark to Crenshaw. The man had been nearly belliger-
ent about not allowing his own daughter to stay employed
as a stakeholder in the London-based portion of Crenshaw
Iron, while Evan had insisted her employment be assured
in writing.

"Yes. Yesterday I met with him and his son, Maxwell. It
seems the son was able to persuade him."

"Ah, Maxwell Crenshaw. It is good to see that at least
one of them has sense." Maxwell had left his card at both
Sterling House and the club in an apparent bid to meet with
him. Evan was sorry he had not yet arranged a meeting.
Now it appeared there was no need. An ache opened up in
his chest at how close they had been to having happiness
together. But even then he had to remind himself of his own
selfishness. She had been coerced. There couldn't be true
happiness unless she chose it for herself.

Evan rose and Clark followed. "Do you not want to sign
the contract?" Clark asked.

"To what purpose? I am no longer in need of their funds.
God knows, I loathe the idea of taking a bride who does not
want me."

Clark swallowed. "Yes, I suppose, but he agreed to your
requests. Unless I mistook your earlier conversation, Miss
Crenshaw has provisionally agreed to the match."

Evan smiled. "Are you saying I would be a fool to pass
up such an offer?"

The man flushed. "It is a fine offer, Your Grace."

"It is," said Evan as he took his leave of the office. "But
that choice should be for August herself."

He needed to talk to her. The betrothal ring he had retrieved from the family safe at Sterling House burned a
hole in his pocket. It had been there ever since he had returned from Charrington Manor with thoughts of a brand-

new future before him. At the time, he had been certain it would grace August's finger by the end of the week.

Now he was not so sure. He wanted to give it to her. Now that he had begun to see a future with her, it was impossible to imagine one without her. Especially after he knew her taste and the soft sounds of pleasure she made when he was inside her. He wanted more of that. More of her.

But would she choose him? He had to go see her and find out.

The Duke of Rothschild to see you."

August had been sitting at the writing desk in the family's drawing room in the back of the house when the footman made the announcement. The telegram she had been drafting to direct funds to their newly opened London account was immediately forgotten. Her hands went to her hair, her skirt, and then back to her hair as she rose. Shoving her stockinged feet into her slippers, she said, "Show him in."

The words were barely out of her mouth before the door was pushed open and Evan brushed past the footman. He gave her a long, sweeping examination that traveled the length of her body and back. She found herself nearly preening under his gaze as she remembered the last time she had seen him and the night that had preceded it. A glimmer of awareness came to life in her belly. She had missed him. Her fingers ached to bury themselves in the thick silk of his hair, and she could already anticipate the hard length of his torso pressed to her front. A pulse beat between her thighs, reminding her that his hard length had been there as well. Stubble covered the lower half of his face. It was a few shades darker than the hair on his head and made him seem only barely civilized in his gentleman attire, as if the clothing were only a facade. He reminded her very much of the fighter he had been on their first meeting.

"I shall return with tea," said the footman, interrupting their moment.

"No tea," she said, not wanting to be disturbed, but then thought better of it. "Unless you want some?" she asked Evan.

"Leave us," he said without looking at the man. The weight of his gaze seemed to caress her across the distance.

The footman nodded and left the door ajar, but Evan reached back to push it closed. Her nerve endings came alive at the simple gesture, and the fact that she was alone with him again, delightfully alone.

"Where is your family?" he asked as he crossed toward her, his gaze heavy with charming intensity.

"Out for the afternoon." Mother had all but demanded that August go calling with her and Violet, but August had refused, preferring to stay home and work, though she had actually spent most of her time staring out the window and sulking. It wasn't how she had categorized it at the time, but now that he was here, she knew that she had been moping for him. Despite the fact that she and her family had been in London for several days, he had not sent a message to her as the marriage contract had flown back and forth during negotiations.

"Where have you been?" She almost grimaced at how that sounded. Needy. He had things to do, and she did not want to give the impression that she had been waiting for him, accurate as it was.

He grinned and came to a stop before her. He did not reach for her, but his fingertip brushed over one of the onyx buttons on the front of her dress. "I missed you, too."

Her face burned as she stared down at that long, graceful finger. Remembering how it had touched her and brought her such pleasure made her body prickle in anticipation. Only when she met his gaze again did she see a hint of the uncertainty that lingered there. Days ago he would have taken her into his arms, but not now, apparently.

"Something has happened?"

"My apologies for not coming to call earlier. Some issues have come to light with my solicitor, and I wanted to see them through before I spoke with you. I have come directly from his office." The warmth in his eyes faded with each word.

A fist of dread clenched tight in her belly. This was not the man who had held her and kissed her as if he couldn't get enough of her only days ago. "Is everything all right?"

"Everything is fine. Perhaps we should sit." He gestured to the sofa and waited for her to get settled before sitting beside her. His knee pressed into the fabric of her skirt, reminding her of the weight of his leg on hers. In the days since their night together, she found herself closing her eyes quite often to remember how he felt. "I am glad your family is not here. I wanted to talk to you privately."

He took a breath and her heart tumbled. "Evan, please." Despite her intention to keep herself contained, she reached out and touched his hand. He immediately turned it over beneath hers so that their palms were touching and brought her hand to his lips. His eyes fell closed briefly as his lips touched her skin. An errant lock of hair fell over his brow, and she gently brushed it back. "Tell me what has happened."

He smiled, but there was a distinctive note of sadness in his eyes. "Everything. Everything has happened." There was another pause during which she was quite certain she was going to lose her grip on any pretense of remaining calm. "After his death, I began to question my father's solicitor on irregularities in the reports he presented to me and the ledgers I reviewed. It soon became apparent that he was lying, so I dismissed him. Soon after that, he disappeared. Clark, my current solicitor, believed that he had absconded with funds, though we could find no proof of that. Well, he was recently found in Montana Territory claiming to be an agent of my father's and living like a king."

"I don't understand." But dread was spreading through her like spilled ink.

"It appears that my father owns shares in a mining company that has been very profitable. His solicitor had scrubbed any mention of this investment from the estate, hoping that he could claim it for himself."

"I see . . . So you are not the pauper you believed yourself to be."

He smiled in obvious relief, and his grip on her hand tightened infinitesimally. "Apparently not. The shares were worth over one million pounds last year. Likely more now."

She nearly swallowed her own tongue at the figure. "That is . . . quite a lot."

"It is." He spoke as calmly as she had ever heard anyone speak in regard to that amount. "I have come to release you from our betrothal."

He didn't want to marry her now. Why would he? It had only ever been about securing a fortune for him. Her heart twisted in her chest as she thought back to that night in the library. *We have to stop now. There will be time once we are married.* He had tried to push her away. She had been the one to ask for more. She did not regret a moment of it, but it stung to think that maybe those moments hadn't meant as much to him when they had meant so very much to her.

"August?"

She rose and walked to the fireplace. Her voice seemed lodged in her throat, and she had to force it out. "That is rather unexpected." She hoped she sounded unaffected and lighthearted. If he wanted to be free of her, then she wouldn't guilt him.

The fabric of his clothing rustled when he stood, and the very air around her seemed to thicken as he approached. She closed her eyes to savor the heat of his body along her back, or maybe that was her imagination. He wasn't touching her.

"I did not mean that we *have* to call off the betrothal. Only that we could now . . . if you want." Was he offering the choice to her, then? Did he mean that he wanted the marriage anyway? Hope blossomed inside her, only to be crushed by his next words. "Obviously, if there is a need, I will marry you."

"A need?"

His palm touched her upper arm, the heat warming her

through the sleeve. "If there are consequences of our night together." His voice was soft and kind; something about that tightened the grip on her heart, twisting it more. "I should have taken precautions, but I was too certain of the future, it seems."

He meant a pregnancy. He only meant to do the honorable thing and marry her if she were with child, not because he wanted her as his wife. Her hand instinctively went to her belly. A second wave of sadness washed over her as she realized there would never be a child between them. Those tiny faces that had begun to take shape in her imaginings were gone as quickly as they had been conjured. It was silly to be sad about something she hadn't really wanted to start with, but she was, because it turned out she *had* wanted that without even knowing.

Responding to the gentle pressure of his hand, she turned to face him. She expected to see a glimmer of fear or a hint of anxiety as he waited for her to answer him. A hope that she would relieve him of the burden. But there was only affection and warmth. It made the ache return to her throat, so she shook her head. "No, there is no need."

His brow furrowed. "Are you certain? It has only been days."

"Yes, very certain." She blushed, embarrassed to be discussing such a personal issue with a man. "My *time* has come."

"Ah, I understand." There was the slightest hesitation before he said, "I suppose it's for the best."

For the best. The heaviness inside her sank even lower. *For the best* is how one described a loss that wasn't truly a loss. He didn't want marriage. This entire conversation felt very much as if she were losing him, and while she had wanted that very thing just days ago, now she wasn't so certain. She would be lying to herself if she didn't admit to feeling some relief that her life could go back to how it was before him, but a larger part of her realized that it wouldn't be the life she had been prepared to leave behind. There would be a void now.

"Yes," she said, forcing her voice not to wobble as she gave him what she hoped was a smile. "I suppose there's no need for a ring now."

He paused, studying her face as if he could see every painful emotion tearing through her. It wasn't fair, because she couldn't read his expression at all. Finally, he said, "No . . . No, I suppose there isn't."

"How do you feel about the surprise inheritance?" she asked, needing to move this conversation along. She wanted to be alone to sort things out. This wasn't how things had been meant to go at all, and she didn't know how to properly respond.

His eyes lit up. "Relieved. Despite evidence to the contrary, no one wants a marriage forced on them. And I am happy that I can provide for my family again."

She nodded, swallowing thickly as the ache swelled in her chest. It was easy to forget that their betrothal had been forced on him as much as on her. Of course he would be happy not to be forced to wed. Though they shared an affection, everyone knew she was not the material from which duchesses were made.

"How do you feel?" he asked, his gaze searching hers.

August forced a brightness to her expression. "I am happy for you."

It was true. Perhaps tomorrow she would feel better about all of this. Once the sting of loss had passed, she could go back to her life. It is what she had wanted.

The intensity came back to his eyes as he dipped his head a bit to meet her gaze. "And for yourself?"

A moment of panic took over that he could actually see her torn feelings. Giving a shrug, she gave him another strained smile. "Of course. It will be a welcome change to not have to dodge a fortune hunter with every step."

He laughed and surprised her by touching her cheek. "May I kiss you once more?" He was already moving in, barely giving her time to breathe out a yes before his mouth covered hers. His lips were soft and warm as they brushed hers. The tender ache in her chest expanded until she wanted to cry with the pain of loss, but she refused to do that and dampen his obvious joy. Instead, she took hold of the lapels of his coat and kissed him harder, hoping to convey all that she felt without words. His slight growth of beard rasped over the sensitive skin of her face, abrading it in a way that was unexpectedly pleasant. Unable to stop herself, she tasted him, and he deepened the kiss, his tongue brushing hers.

When he pulled back, they were both gasping for breath, and he wasn't smiling anymore. His eyelids fell closed as he pressed his forehead to hers. "Say we will always be friends."

Say that you still need me.

Instead of giving voice to that, she swallowed and said thickly, "Always."

He pulled away from her, and the moment was over. His voice was normal as was his expression. "My fight with Wilkes is tomorrow night, same place. You should come."

She tried and failed to stomp out the alarm and fear those words evoked. He wasn't hers to be concerned about. "Isn't that a dangerous place for a lady?"

"Not if you are with my men."

"But someone might recognize me."

"I suppose you are right. You see what happened last time someone recognized you there." He teased her.

She wanted to laugh to appease him, but it was impossible. "Please be careful. I don't trust him."

"With good reason. I will be careful."

She nodded and reluctantly said, "You should go before my family returns. I'm certain they'll be upset."

"Then I should stay and deal with them."

That sounded terrible. She wouldn't be able to hold herself together sufficiently to handle them both, especially when she didn't understand exactly what she felt. She should be happy, but she was decidedly miserable. "No, please go. I'd rather do it myself."

"No. You should not be forced to face them alone." He appeared resolute.

"Please, Evan. It'll be easier alone."

He stared at her for a moment charged with meaning.

Finally, he nodded. "I understand." Reaching up, he brushed his thumb across her lips before dropping his hand and turning away. She forced herself to stay where she was instead of following him out. At the door, he said, "Goodbye, August."

She smiled and managed a wave. Words would have hurt too much.

Chapter 22

I never wanted but your heart—that gone,
you have nothing more to give.
MARY WOLLSTONECRAFT

Persuading Max to take her to the fight had not been easy. He had outright refused each time she had mentioned it. It had taken her approaching him in the same cloak Camille had given her when it was time to go to convince him that she was serious. Now that they were in the warehouse awaiting the fight, he seemed to be experiencing an extreme case of doubt. They were not on the riser like last time, having deemed it prudent to stay among the crowd of working- and middle-class patrons to not get noticed. It helped that Max hadn't been properly introduced to Society, so that any who saw him wouldn't recognize him anyway. August kept her hood up just in case.

"Why have we come here again?" Max sounded grumpy as he swiveled his head from left to right to take in the crowd. He had pushed them through the mass so that they were close enough to the ring to have a reasonable view but next to the wall. He stood squarely between her and anyone who might want to get close to her. She thought he was overreacting, but he wouldn't listen to reason.

"Because I want to see him. You should at least pretend

you're here to watch the match. All of that head swiveling is going to get us noticed."

He scoffed. She couldn't see his face, but she could hear it in his tone. "You are here to see the man who cried off and broke your betrothal?"

"Stop. It was mutual, and if you recall, I didn't want to marry him anyway."

Glancing over his shoulder, he gave her a knowing look. She had cried a little last night, so her eyes were slightly red rimmed. Anyone could plainly see that. She quickly turned her attention back to the empty ring. The tears that she had not been able to stop last night had finally convinced her that she cared for Evan. No. More than cared. She loved him and wanted a future with him. It was why she had come, to face her fears and tell him that very thing.

To be fair, she had been uncertain of that fact when he had come to her. It had been much later in the privacy of her bedroom when she had succumbed to her tears that had made things clear for her. She wouldn't be hurting if she didn't feel genuine love for him. As much as she had despised giving up her freedom to marry him, she hated giving him up even more. She missed his touch and his kisses and his quick wit and the way he had of looking at her that made her think he actually saw who she was and who she wanted to be.

Mostly, she missed the life that they had begun to plan out together. After ruminating over that fact all day in her bedroom, she had come to the only conclusion possible. She wanted to continue their courting. No, that wasn't the complete truth. She wanted their engagement. She was ready to marry him as they had planned, but if he preferred, they could take their time. The moment the decision had been made, August had known it was the right one. Something inside her had settled as if all was well with her world again.

She would tell him after the fight. There was no sense in distracting him beforehand. She had not shared any of this with Max, hence his grumpiness. Actually, he had been angry enough with Evan that the knowledge might make him grumpier. She couldn't be certain. The only person she had told was Violet, who had wholeheartedly agreed with her decision.

All at once, the mood of the crowd changed. They became louder and pushed forward. The men guarding the ring were forced to hold out their batons to keep the area around the ring cleared. She and Max were pressed closer to the wall, his body shielding hers from the crush. He cursed under his breath, and she conceded this might not have been the most well-executed plan she had ever devised. They weren't as isolated here as she and Camille had been on the riser.

But her heart was pounding through her chest, and the blood was thrumming through her veins. She would see him again soon. Standing on her tiptoes to see over the head of a man who had moved in front of them, her stomach tumbled joyously when he approached the ring. The same men as before surrounded him, only this time the Earl of Leigh was a part of the escort. He leaned close to say something to Evan, who nodded, and then Leigh went to lean against the riser.

Evan stepped through the ropes and into the ring, raising his fists and drawing a roar of approval from the crowd. His beard had grown in a little more, almost as thick as it had been the first time she had seen him. The pomade darkened his hair, and the beard partially obscured his features, but he was still the most handsome man she had ever seen. Her chest swelled with warmth and affection. His gaze scanned the crowd, and she hoped he would see her, but of course he didn't. There were too many people in front of her.

He was barefoot this time. Perhaps it was a condition of the fight. Her suspicion was confirmed when Wilkes entered the ring moments later dressed only in trousers. He still looked as mean as he had before, with eyes that were mere slashes of menace. His gaze never rose to the crowd. All of his ire was reserved for Evan.

Genuine fear churned in her belly. Why hadn't she tried harder to talk Evan out of this fight? It was completely unnecessary now with his financial troubles solved. A large part of it was for his own pride, she knew, but fighting Wilkes seemed to be an exorbitant price to pay.

Her chest tightened when Wilkes approached Evan. He paid no attention to the fact that the official who was presumably setting the rules for the match had not yet finished speaking. He was angry and out for blood, so the blow was no surprise. Evan managed to move back to avoid it, and the official whirled away, hurrying out between the ropes. The crowd jeered their disapproval, but that didn't stop Wilkes. He lashed out again and this time clipped Evan's chin. August let out a gasp almost as if she could feel the pain herself. Max glanced at her but was immediately drawn back to the match.

She watched the rest with her fingers covering her lips. Evan came back with a fury, landing blow after blow to Wilkes's torso, but the older man appeared to have something to prove. He absorbed each blow and then matched them, walking Evan backward until he was nearly against the ropes. It was an endless back-and-forth, each taking and then delivering his own vengeance.

Finally, Wilkes began to show signs of fatigue. His chest heaved, and he was slower to pivot and swing an answering blow with his fist. To compensate, he crouched low and rammed Evan in the stomach. This knocked him backward, and Wilkes fell on top of him, swinging his fist.

"Dear God," August cried out, and she pushed forward so that she could see if he was all right, but the crowd was too thick, and the men were on the ground. The men who had accompanied Evan rushed forward, but they didn't seem to be entering the ring.

"Stay here!" Max ordered and pushed his way forward. She had no intention of being left behind, and she followed in his wake. The crowd roared again, and Max called back, "He's back on his feet."

Peering around his shoulder, she could see Evan's smirk as he raised a hand in the air. The crowd gave another roar of approval. Wilkes wobbled to his feet and made an attempt at engaging Evan with a fist, but it was easily dodged.

When Evan punched him in the chin, the larger man went down and this time didn't get up. The official jumped between the ropes and checked him. "Wilkes is down!" he declared.

The crowd cheered. Evan jumped, punching the air in victory. Several men hurried into the ring to help an unsteady Wilkes get to his feet, leading him out of the ring and down the path that led to the side door. Able to breathe again, August cheered with the people around them, and even Max smiled.

"Do you want to go talk to him?" he asked, bending to hear her answer among the chaos.

She meant to say yes, but a streak of shimmering pink caught her eye. Madame Laurent was walking toward the ring from her place at the riser next to the earl, a wide smile on her face and eyes only for Evan. She must have come into the warehouse behind him earlier, but August hadn't noticed her. With the ropes between them, Evan put an arm around her waist and leaned down to say something. She laughed and said something back to him, and then lifted onto her toes to place a kiss right on his lips. The men near them howled in encouragement, and she smiled before putting her hands behind his head and deepening the kiss. It seemed to go on forever. When the kiss was finished, Evan stared down at her with the same intensity he had reserved for August. Or August had thought it was only for her. Apparently, he looked at every one of his lovers in that way. He had said he and Madame Laurent were only friends, but obviously that had changed after yesterday. Or perhaps they had resumed their relationship when he had returned from Charrington Manor.

Nausea churned in her stomach, and she wobbled on her feet. Grabbing Max's arm before he could react, she said, "No, I want to go."

Frowning, he glanced down at her and then back toward Evan. "Who is that?"

"It's not important. I want to go home." He opened his mouth to say something, but she spoke before he could. "Now."

Fury burned in his eyes as he cast one last glance in their direction, but then he nodded and took her hand, leading them through the crowd and toward the carriage they had left waiting for them. August couldn't speak right away once they were inside and on the way back to Mayfair. It hurt too much. Her body physically hurt with the pain of knowing that Evan had been so quick to move on from her. Less than a week had passed since they had agreed to their negotiated marriage. Since he had been inside her and they had shared the most amazing experience she had thought two people could share.

What a foolish notion. Men took mistresses all the time, and it meant nothing. She had known that and yet somehow had believed that what they had between them was more. Fighting back the sick feeling in her stomach and her heart, she asked, "When do you leave for New York?"

"The day after tomorrow. Why do you ask?"

"I want to go back with you."

She couldn't stay in London and risk running into him again.

C ongratulations, Hellion. That was a hell of a fight." Gabrielle's voice with the faintest hint of a French accent cut through the din of the crowd.

Evan reached out, snaking his arm around her waist to bring her closer. She had been with him from the very first public match, and the men in the crowd seemed to love her, routinely getting louder and betting harder when she was present. "A hell of a fight for Wilkes," he said.

The cheers grew louder at the embrace, obscuring what she said in answer. She leaned up and placed a kiss on his mouth. It wasn't an unusual display of affection after the win. What was unusual was the fact that she deepened it, her tongue brushing across his lips in an effort to have him open to her. They hadn't been lovers in years, but he might have obliged her and played along if something about the way she had looked at him in the heartbeat before their mouths touched hadn't raised suspicion. Her gaze had been too intent, too full of meaning. This wasn't her usual play-fulness. Then she tugged the hair at the back of his head, curling her fingers in the locks in the same way August did, and it suddenly felt like a mistake. Too intimate and with the wrong person. Placing his other hand on her waist, he gently pulled back. Her eyes reflected a passion he hadn't seen in them since he'd left her bed.

She leaned forward to speak near his ear. "Come home with me tonight, Evan."

Had she asked him after the last fight, he would have said yes. They had drifted apart as lovers to pursue others, but the attraction was still present. She was giving and ad-venturous in bed, and he carried nothing but fond memo-ries of their time together. But she wasn't right in his arms now. She was beautiful and perfect in her own way, but she was thin where his hands expected August's curves, and too tall when his body longed to tuck her against him. She was not August.

He wanted to take August home. To have her soothe his wounds and help him in his bath. Then he wanted to spend the rest of the night with her under him in his bed, showing her all the ways they could find pleasure together.

"What happened with Ware?" he asked.

She shrugged one shoulder, and he caught a glimmer of pain in her eyes. "He wasn't who I thought he was."

Evan could have told her that Ware was a scoundrel and would never return her affection, but he had not wanted to ruin the small bit of happiness she had found.

"Now that he's gone, we could amuse ourselves for a few nights," she said.

Touching her cheek to gentle his refusal, he said, "I am sorry, Gabrielle, but I want August." After their talk the day before, Evan had been willing to let August walk away from him. But that resolve had lasted for all of twenty-four hours. He wanted her in his life, and he planned to try to win her.

"We need to get going. You never know when Wilkes's friends might put in an appearance," said Leigh, coming to a stop beside Gabrielle outside the ropes.

It was true. They made certain to not linger after all of

the public matches outside the club. The environment was largely uncontrollable and very prone to disgruntled gang members lurking to take back money that had been lost.

"Do you love her, then?" she asked.

He shrugged. Perhaps he did. Yes, if living without her made him feel so empty, he did. "Come back to the club with us and celebrate."

She nodded and allowed Leigh to lead her away toward one of the carriages waiting out back. Evan jumped out over the top of the ropes to where his friends were waiting. Thorne clapped him on the back in congratulations and tossed him a towel. As Evan brushed off the layer of sweat and blood, he looked toward the crowded riser. August was not there. He knew because he had looked for her as soon as he had entered the warehouse. Still, he could not help but look one more time, hopeful that he had somehow missed her. Foolish of him, but he had hoped she would come. Disappointment was bitter on his tongue.

"The crowd is becoming restless," said Thorne, nodding toward the side door.

Evan agreed and took a last lingering look before following him. His boots were waiting in the carriage along with his shirt and coat. He would take a bath in his room at the club before joining in the celebration. The truth was he did not feel like celebrating. He should have been ecstatic, and in the moment when Wilkes had fallen, he had been, but the feeling had been fleeting.

The same emptiness that had been present ever since he walked out of August's life had come swirling back. He missed her.

Giving her freedom had been the right thing to do, but his noble instincts only extended so far. He wanted her to be his. That last kiss between them had been telling. She had wanted it as much as he had, and her eyes had shown genuine sadness as he was leaving.

He was a duke who was not in need of a wife but who wanted one. He laughed, drawing Leigh's attention as he swung himself up into the carriage. His ribs ached from Wilkes's blows, but he ignored them.

"Wilkes hit you too hard?" Leigh asked.

Evan could not stop the smile that spread across his face. "I am going to ask August to marry me."

Leigh laughed without mirth and glanced at his brother, who was getting into the carriage. "We should have the physician examine him."

Thorne smiled as he sat across from them, stretching his long legs out before him. "He seems fine to me. Inherit a fortune and then sign the Crenshaw contract as insurance."

"This is not about the contract. I only want her."

Leigh looked at him as if he was mad, but Thorne raised a brow. "Words I never thought to hear you say."

They were surprising to Evan as well, but they were true. The hours he had spent without August had reaffirmed how empty his life had been before her. He had the club, his friends, and now the funds to help his tenants, and he would see to those things even without her. But he would much rather have her with him. She brought a light into his world that he did not want to live without. He refused to consider the possibility that she might actually reject him.

Chapter 23

What greater thing is there for two human souls, than to feel that they are joined for life.

GEORGE ELIOT

W hat in the Sam Hill are you doing here?" Violet's irritated voice sounded throughout the entryway of the Crenshaws' townhome.

Taken unawares, Evan and Leigh glanced up to see the lovely young woman hurrying down the stairs and descending upon him like an avenging angel. Sam Hill? It did not take a bloody genius to understand that now was not the time to question that peculiar turn of phrase. Reginald gave him a stiff bow and slowly backed his way down the corridor as if he knew what was about to happen.

"Now you've done it," Leigh muttered dryly.

"Done what?" Evan asked.

The corner of Leigh's mouth kicked up, but he did not answer. He was too consumed with watching Violet rush toward them in a flurry of creamy silk edged with navy. When Leigh had mentioned joining him to pay his call, Evan had thought the request odd but had been too focused on his intention to put up a fight. Now he understood Leigh's reason for coming along. He wanted to see Violet.

To Violet, Evan said, "I have come to see August, but Reginald has told me—yet again—that she is not at home." Evan had called yesterday afternoon, bruised and with an ache in his head from the after-fight celebrations, and had been told that the entire family was not at home for the rest of the evening. Taking the information as a bit of a reprieve, Evan had gone back to his rooms to make himself fresh for the call today and rehearse the words he had planned to win her over. August liked him well enough, but he knew he was in for a fight when it came to her freedom.

Violet's eyes narrowed as she came to a stop before them. "She is not at home *to you* today or tomorrow or next year. I don't care if you are a duke; you are not welcome here. Leave!" She pointed toward the door, and despite the fact that he had faced Wilkes and any number of dangerous opponents, a trickle of fear raced down his spine.

Something was wrong. This seemed to be about more than their agreement to break off their betrothal. "Are you angry with me because I released August from our betrothal?"

She stared at him much as Leigh had when Evan had admitted he wanted to marry August for herself and not her money. "I am angry with you because you are the most arrogant, inconsiderate, faithless arse of a man I have ever had the displeasure to know. Forget that you ever met my sister and get out of this house."

"I see there is no need for me to expound upon Rothschild's virtues. You've summed them up nicely," said Leigh, amusement lacing his voice.

Turning her wrath to his friend, she asked, "You. Why are you here?"

"Because I like fireworks." Leigh grinned.

The full force of her glare should have singed Leigh where he stood. The color high in her cheeks, she said, "Remove yourselves from the premises."

"Perhaps you should hear him out first," Leigh challenged her.

Violet opened her mouth to release what Evan was certain would be an expletive-laced thrashing, so he stepped between them. "Wait," he said. This had to be about something more. Evan knew that he risked bodily harm with his inquiry. However, he was not leaving until he understood what was happening. "Please. I must talk to her. Is she truly not home?" When Violet merely stared at him as if she wanted to bodily eject him herself, he rushed to the stairs. "August! Please come down!"

Violet hurried behind him and pulled on his arm. "She's not here. Why do you care anyway? You have your ballet dancer or God knows how many other women waiting back at your club."

"Gabrielle? What the devil does she have to do with this?" Evan faced her, vaguely aware of Leigh leaning against the wall to watch them in amusement.

"You aristocrats with your mistresses." She rolled her eyes. "August deserves better than a man who would rather be with his mistress than her."

"Gabrielle is not my mistress. Where did you get that idea? August and I have discussed this." A glance upstairs confirmed that August had not appeared. Reginald had conveniently taken himself off to unknown parts of the house. Evan had a terrible feeling that she was not at home, but he had to make certain. He started to go upstairs but then stopped as a terrible thought occurred to him. Had someone told her about the scene with Gabrielle after his fight? Anyone present could have seen her kiss him, but who would have reported back to August? Had her brother come?

"Fine. Perhaps *mistress* is too strong a word for someone you only occasionally share a bed with."

Someone had seen the kiss. He stormed back down the few steps and faced Violet. "Whomever it was who saw Gabrielle with me at the fight completely misunderstood, and I do not appreciate the interference in my relationship with August."

"August saw you, you dolt! She had Max take her to the fight. You kissed that woman right in front of her. You only have yourself to blame."

The blood drained out of his head, and he had to grab

the banister to keep himself from wobbling. He felt like he had just gotten hit in the face by one of Wilkes's ham-handed punches. A cold flood of unease prickled his skin. "August was there!"

He had not realized he had spoken aloud until Violet said, "Yes, and she saw you kiss her. She had gone because she wanted—" But she abruptly clapped her hand over her mouth as if she had said too much.

"Wanted what?" he asked. His future depended on the answer to that question. "Tell me, Violet. Why did she come?"

Violet shook her head as she backed away. "I'm not telling you anything."

He wanted to shake the answer out of her but managed to calmly put his hands on her shoulders instead. "Please. I have come because I love her. I want to marry her." She opened her mouth to no doubt refute that claim, but he pressed on. "It is true that Gabrielle kissed me. We were lovers years ago, and she asked me to go home with her after the match. I turned her down." Fixing on any point to sway the disbelief in her eyes, he said, "Ask Leigh. He was there and saw it all. He was even with me at the club later. He knows I did not sleep with her."

"It's true," Leigh said in his lazy drawl, pushing himself away from the wall to come stand beside Evan. "Gabrielle was otherwise engaged. He slept alone, though the devil himself knows why."

Her brow furrowed, and for the first time the mask of anger she wore began to crack. "Why should I believe you?"

Leigh grinned again, but this time it was hollow. "You should not ever believe me, Miss Crenshaw." It was a warning heavy with a meaning Evan could not take the time to figure out.

"I love August," Evan said, bringing her attention back to him.

"Is that why you called yesterday?" Violet asked, crossing her arms over her chest.

"Yes, I came to tell her that I want to marry her."

Some of the tension left her shoulders, and she said, "She went to the fight because she wanted to tell you that she still harbors some affection for you. I believe she wanted to continue a courtship."

He laughed and pulled her into his arms, hugging her so tightly that she squirmed away, glaring up at him with a hint of her former fierceness. "My apologies," he murmured. "Where has she gone? I need to speak to her. I cannot bear the thought of her believing that I chose another woman over her."

Violet paled and glanced nervously at the door. "She left with Max . . . back to America." She spoke the last in such a soft voice that it took a moment for Evan to realize what she meant.

America. New York. *Across an entire fucking ocean!*

"Bloody fucking hell," said Leigh.

"Today?" Evan asked.

Violet nodded. "They left for Liverpool this morning, and their ship sails tomorrow."

He could only stare at her, hardly able to believe what she was telling him. August was leaving. She would return to New York thinking he did not want her. "Which ship? What time?"

"You'll never make it."

"I have to try." If he did not reach her in time, he would simply follow her.

"Wait right here." Violet hurried into the drawing room and came back with a sheet of paper. "This is their itinerary. What can I do?"

"I have to go directly to the train station. Send a message to the club that Stewart should bring my trunk." He followed Leigh out but then turned back to her. "Thank you, Violet."

She smiled as she threatened him. "Don't make me regret it."

He shook his head and hurried down the steps to his carriage.

"I can telegram the ship and have a message sent to her once we drop you at the station," Leigh offered.

"Thank you," said Evan, leaning his head back against the seat and closing his eyes against an oncoming headache. He was certain a telegram would not keep August, not if she truly believed he had chosen Gabrielle. If he could make the ship in time, he would spend the rest of his life making certain August did not regret choosing him.

Peering at his friend through one eye, Evan said, "Violet does not seem to approve of you. Do your intentions still lie in that direction?"

Leigh smirked. "Despite your newfound bourgeois attitude toward marriage, a fondness is not strictly required for marriage among our set. You know that."

A laugh tumbled out of Evan, despite the anxiety churning inside him. "You have no idea what you are in for, you fool."

August gripped one of the posts of her bed as the ship swayed, nearly making her stumble. The beast gave a great grumble and groan as it pulled away from the dock and deeper into the harbor. A quick glance at the clock bolted to a side table told her the ship was indeed leaving right on schedule. Somehow she had lost track of time as she and Mary had hurried to put her things into the armoire.

"I suppose we're leaving. Hurry on up to the deck, Mary, I wouldn't want you to miss it."

The woman's gaze went to the window. The movement was slow but steady, making it appear as if the dock and the people waving goodbye were the ones drifting away. "Are you certain, miss?"

"Yes, I don't care to watch us leave, but there's no reason you can't." Max had come in earlier from the suite adjoining hers to invite her to go up onto deck with him, but she had refused him. The last thing she wanted was a final glimpse of the place that had upturned her life. The sooner they left it behind, the better. "I won't need you again until it's time to dress for dinner."

"Yes, miss." She hurried from the room so fast that the door didn't quite click closed.

Several voices in the corridor outside rose as if a group of three or four people were talking all at once. After several nights of terrible sleep, August's eyes felt grainy and tired, and she had been irritable all morning. The last thing she wanted was a disturbance because of noisy neighbors.

She sighed and closed the door, locking it just as the commotion was dying down.

The cabin was small but well-appointed with dark wood furniture and fabrics in emerald green with gold trim. She eyed the bed with longing but opted to do a little work at her desk instead. Papa had been so angry that she was leaving, he had sent a small trunk of tedious reports with her that she was to read through and make recommendations. All of them about various manufacturing interests in the British Isles. She supposed she should be ecstatic that he had not gone through on his threat to cut her out of Crenshaw Iron. She wasn't. She was sad and heartbroken.

She had hardly settled herself into her chair when a knock sounded at the door from the adjoining cabin. Not Max's cabin, but the one on the other side. Thinking it must have been accidental and related to the earlier commotion, she ignored it and picked up the first document. The words blurred on the page. Perhaps Papa had been right and running home had been the wrong thing to do. Perhaps she should have simply ignored Evan and faced Society.

The knock came again, and this time more insistently.

"For heaven's sake," she grumbled. Crossing the few steps to the adjoining door, she said, "Hello?"

A knock was the response.

Irritated with having to deal with inconsiderate neighbors on top of her heartache, she unlocked and wrenched the door open. "This is very inap—" The words died on her tongue. His hair was tousled, and it appeared he had not shaved that morning and might even be wearing his clothing from the day before, but Evan stood before her. For a moment she was too stunned to react. Her heart gave a thump, and it was as if her body came alive for the first time since that night in the library. There was no gray, or gloom, only Evan. The intense joy that coursed through her veins was frightening. How could she be so willing to forgive him? Instead of answering that question for herself, she slammed the door in his face.

"August." It swung so hard that it failed to latch and bounced back open. He stepped into her cabin and closed the door behind him. The room was hardly wide enough to take more than ten steps in any direction. With him in it, it shrunk to half its original size.

"What are you doing here?" In a panic she glanced out the window to see that they had pulled even farther away from shore. Too far to swim if she somehow managed to get him up on the deck and pushed him off.

"I came to talk to you."

"To talk? You've boarded an ocean liner bound for New York!" Did he expect to talk to her and then have the entire ship dock so that he could disembark? *No!* It suddenly became clear to her exactly what had happened. The commotion next door was because he had forced some unknown couple out of their cabin. "You made that poor couple move to another cabin?"

He grinned. "What else was I to do? Besides, they are hardly poor after the amount I was forced to give them to accept second-class accommodations."

"And you wonder why you have financial troubles," she said, crossing her arms across her chest.

He laughed. "God, I missed you, August."

"Don't say that. You hardly missed me when you had Madame Laurent to replace me."

"I know that you saw her kiss me, but I turned her down."

"Lie. I saw how you looked at her." Her heart twisted as she remembered that look. How could it still hurt so badly?

He shook his head and approached her slowly, like a wild, cornered animal. Good. He had hurt her terribly; she wanted him to be afraid. "I do not know what you think you saw. She kissed me and asked me to spend the night with her. I told her I wanted you. No more, no less."

He stared at her with such earnest devotion, she wanted to believe him, but she couldn't forget his mouth on hers.

"I did not come all this way to lie to you," he continued. "After you agreed to break the betrothal, I thought it was because you were relieved. I thought that perhaps I could go back to how things were before we met, a man with no responsibilities. But I am not that man anymore. I want you, August. I want the life we had planned. Every moment I spent away from you was a moment I spent thinking about you, wanting you, loving you."

She gasped at the word and stepped back, afraid to believe because it was so close to what she wanted.

He kept stepping forward, until she came to a stop when her back came up against one of the posts at the foot of the bed. "Are you running from me?" His voice was too damn soft and gentle, intimate in the small space between them. He didn't touch her, but he was so close she could see his chest rise and fall with his breath.

This was almost too much to take in at once. "No . . . I . . . How did you find me?"

"Violet. She told me everything after she called me a few choice names."

August couldn't help but smile at the thought of Violet yelling at him. "You must have won her over."

"I want to win *you* over." He bent his neck to meet her gaze directly. "I want to marry you, August."

"Why didn't you say as much when you told me about the mining interest, then?"

"Because I was afraid you would be too happy to have your freedom back." That admission stole her heart. "If you had said you wanted to keep up our courtship, I would have agreed. I thought that giving you your freedom was what you wanted. I thought it was the right thing to do." He touched a lock of hair that fell in a curl over her ear. Her scalp prickled in pleasure when he gave it a light tug. "It *was* the right thing to do. Did you enjoy your freedom?" His warm breath drifted over her lips. They very much wanted to kiss him. His gaze was soft, but worry lurked in its depth.

She shook her head. "It was miserable."

He gave her a slow smile. "Then the choice is yours. God knows I want you, but if you do not want me, I promise I will do my best to leave you alone for the rest of the crossing."

She kissed him, stifling the soft cry that forced its way out of her chest. "Of course I want you." Taking his face between her hands, she pressed her mouth to his, craving the taste of him.

He crushed her against him, and when they could no longer breathe, he buried his face in her hair. "Thank God." He whispered the words over and over again.

Finally, he rifled in the inside pocket of his coat and pulled out a little velvet satchel. Backing away just enough to bring it between them, he emptied the contents in the palm of his hand. It was a ring. A betrothal ring? He held it up for her inspection. A large emerald-cut ruby set in gold nestled in a cluster of diamonds. "It belonged to my grandmother. My mother's mother," he explained. "I chose it because it reminded me of the ruby necklace you wore with the scarlet dress." He met her gaze only briefly before staring back at the ring, almost shy. "I think I knew I loved you then, because I imagined giving this ring to you to match."

"It's beautiful." It was the most beautiful thing she had seen besides him.

"If you would prefer something else, obviously you can have your choice. When we get to New York—"

She kissed him before he could say any more, hardly able to contain her joy. "I love it. Put it on me." Her hand shook as she held it out to him.

He laughed and pushed the ring onto her finger. The weight settled there, feeling as right as anything ever had. A suspicious sheen coated his eyes. "Let's marry as soon as we reach New York. I do not want to wait any longer."

"We won't have a choice if my brother has his way. He won't like that I plan to spend every night on this crossing in your bed."

He gave a hoot of triumph and picked her up, spinning around until they were both dizzy and weak with laughter. They fell onto the bed, and he rose over her. "I love you, August Crenshaw."

She stared up into his eyes, seeing a future that was so much fuller than one she had ever dared to imagine. "I never thought I would say this, but I love you, Duke of Rothschild, Marquess of Langston, Earl of Haverford, Viscoun—" Her words ended on a squeal as he tickled her and then covered her lips with his.

Acknowledgments

There are many people involved in turning an idea into a book. These are only a few of the people who have helped me create this one, and to whom I owe my eternal thanks. To my wonderful agent, Nicole Resciniti, for believing in this idea from the very beginning, even when I didn't. Thank you for your encouragement.

To my amazing editor, Sarah Blumenstock, you loved this story without even reading it all and took a chance on me. Thank you!

To Laurie Benson, for telling me the story about Consuelo Vanderbilt and inspiring this whole idea. Without you I might have stayed in the Middle Ages.

To Tara Wyatt, for reading this book and all my others, and especially for all the brainstorming sessions. You're amazing.

To Jenni Fletcher, for poring over it with a fine-toothed comb and an eye for Americanisms.

To my Unlaced ladies—Catherine Tinley, Elisabeth Hobbes, Janice Preston, Lara Temple, Nicole Locke, and Virginia Heath (and Laurie and Jenni again!) for always being there with a wealth of knowledge, a shoulder to cry on, and a cup of virtual tea.

To Nathan and Erin, for our Saturday mornings.

To Lisa Kleypas, Judith McNaught, Susan Johnson, LaVyrle Spencer, Johanna Lindsey, Julie Garwood, and all the greats who gave me endless inspiration.

And especially to Joe, Livie, Alex, and my parents, for putting up with me and supporting me. I love you all!

Don't miss

THE DEVIL AND THE HEIRESS

*coming Summer 2021 from Berkley Jove!
Keep reading for an excerpt.*

> *It appears that ordinary men take wives because possession is not possible without marriage.*
>
> —THOMAS HARDY

LONDON, MAY 1875

"Humor me, my lord, and tell me why you wish to marry my daughter." Griswold Crenshaw, American industrialist, sat behind his large mahogany desk, hands arrogantly folded over his stomach, cigar clenched between his gleaming teeth, eyes mere slits of condescension. He was a man secure in the knowledge that he held all the power in this negotiation.

It chafed that the bloody fool was right.

Christian Halston, Earl of Leigh, was accustomed to privilege. It meant that he was never required to answer questions or to even ask them very often. Information was gifted to him like tributes wrapped in golden paper. However, a wise man of privilege knew the benefit of a little humbling now and then, or so he had been told. Actively forcing his jaw to unclench, he said, "I should think that is self-evident. Miss Crenshaw is—"

Crenshaw leaned forward and tugged the cigar from his

mouth. "Beautiful. Cultured. Educated. Pardon me, my lord, but I have met my daughter and I am aware of her many attributes. I am asking why *you* are interested in obtaining her hand."

It appeared the humbling was not over yet. Reasonable when dealing with a wealthy American and his daughter, Christian supposed. To be fair, he found the London Season to be one of the more inane rituals imposed upon modern man. It was all pointless chatter and insincere flattery that ended with men carrying home their brides. The whole thing could be condensed into a week if everyone were honest about the matter. It was a welcome revelation that Crenshaw wanted the truth rather than adulation.

Christian could deliver the truth. "I am rather interested in her fortune."

Crenshaw grinned, and the oxblood leather creaked as he leaned back in his chair, straining the springs. "Now we're making progress." Amber liquid swirled in his tumbler as he picked it up, indicating that Christian should do the same with the identical one he had been provided upon arrival a few minutes earlier. Christian complied and let the drink roll across his tongue.

"What has you in need of funds? Debts, my lord?"

The tone the older man used made it seem very much as if the "my lord" bit was optional. Did Christian even want this man for a father-in-law? No, he bloody well did not. He closed his eyes and imagined Violet. Beautiful Violet with her dark hair, creamy skin, chocolate eyes, and the piles of money that came with her. He could do this. There would eventually be an ocean between him and Crenshaw, after all.

"No debts." Those had been dealt with soon after Christian had inherited the earldom at age twelve. He had happily sold almost everything not bolted down or entailed and had never once looked back. That had taken care of his father's debts. Montague Club, the club he had opened with his half-brother Jacob Thorne and a friend, the Duke of Rothschild, kept him comfortable.

Crenshaw's eyebrows shot up into his hairline. "Astonishing. I was led to believe that most of you aristocrats were . . . insolvent."

Christian stifled a wince at this uncouth talk of funds. The man had every right to believe that, and there was a bit of truth to it. Almost every eligible noble in London had been clamoring for one of his daughters. Rothschild had ensnared the eldest daughter already, though their engagement had not yet been announced.

"I consolidated some years back when I inherited. The family seat in Sussex and my home in Belgravia are in working order." Though they were in desperate need of repairs since the rents at Amberley Park barely covered the minimum needed to keep the place running.

"Well, then, that's commendable." Crenshaw took another sip of his drink. "Might I ask why you require funds?"

"I own a small estate in Scotland. Blythkirk. I inherited it on my mother's side, and it holds sentimental value. There was a fire recently, so it requires extensive refurbishment." Years of practice made his tone sound benign. There was no hint of the fact that the home had been his refuge from a father intent on making his life hell. That its near loss had opened a well of pain that he would rather not face.

The older man grinned as if he did not quite believe a mere estate could be worth a wife. "Her settlement will provide for more than that, my lord."

Christian inclined his head in acknowledgement of that fact. "Indeed, it will. I am certain to make good use of it. While I am not insolvent, my ancestral estate, Amberley Park, drains my income. There are improvements I would make there. Furthermore, there are several investments I am interested in procuring. For one, I have a stake in—"

Before he could elaborate, Crenshaw said, "I am going to stop you there, my lord. As you are aware, I am a man of industry. As such, it is not enough that I find my daughter a suitable match, but that I look out for the interests of Crenshaw Iron Works in the process. To be very honest, there are more men who can fulfill the former than the latter."

Christian stared at the man. The rules of matrimonial negotiations were a bit outside his purview given that he had never considered obtaining a wife before Blythkirk's devastation, having been content to allow the earldom to pass to a distant relative, but he was almost certain that the bride's best interest should at least slightly outweigh those of a business. "Are you saying that you need a candidate who can bring business ventures to Crenshaw Iron Works?"

"That's it precisely. The ideal would be someone who meets with our Violet's approval, of course, but can present opportunities for Crenshaw Iron's expansion. Now that we are in the beginnings of setting up operations here, well, the world is open to us." His hands skated through the air in a smooth glide, mimicking the opening of a presumed gateway to the world. His eyes fairly glittered with greed.

"Like Rothschild." Christian knew that the main reason Crenshaw had encouraged and even pursued Rothschild's interest had been because of his title and the doors that title could open in Parliament. Being related to a duke willing to speak on Crenshaw's behalf would give the company nearly unfettered access to the railways being constructed in India.

Crenshaw's gaze narrowed. No one outside of the family was supposed to know that Rothschild had followed their eldest daughter August to America. Christian, however, had been with Rothschild when he had made his mad dash to the Crenshaw's rented townhome off Grosvenor's Square to propose only to find his beloved ready to set sail. He had followed her to Liverpool and boarded her ship just in time. The ship was still en route, meaning no one knew how that had turned out, though Christian would guess the couple would wed very soon.

"Yes, like the duke."

"I have influence with my seat in the House of Lords," said Christian even as a hollow was opening up in his belly. He did not like the direction of this conversation. Crenshaw was a shrewd man. Access to Parliament granted, he would be looking for another advantage.

"Of course, my lord, and that is not inconsequential." A note of consolation had crept into Crenshaw's voice. The hair at the back of Christian's neck bristled. He was about to be refused. "We are very flattered by your interest."

"But you have another offer." A better offer. Christian clenched his jaw so hard that his molars ached. He did not intend to lose Violet to another man. She had fascinated him from their first meeting. If he was forced to consider a wife, then it would be her.

Crenshaw would have grimaced had he not been so accustomed to tense negotiations. Christian could see the urge lingering there in his expression. The corners of his mouth turned downward a small degree and his eyes sobered. "Nothing has been finalized, but there is a tempting proposal on the table, yes."

"Who is it?"

"Well, now, I wouldn't want to give anything away until things are further along."

Christian searched his memory, trying to remember every man who had ever paid attention to Violet at the various balls he had seen her attend. The list was nearly endless, because she was an heiress and beautiful. Even though her older sister August should have been the talk of the season, and she had gained her share of admirers, it was Violet who had commanded the greater share of attention. Part of that was because Mrs. Crenshaw had been very active in taking Violet to every social event imaginable. Part of it was because everyone knew that August was a bluestocking and more concerned with working in the family business than getting married. In fact, she had publicly claimed to not be interested in marrying soon. Until Rothschild had changed that.

Violet, on the other hand, was more refined, more of what was expected in an aristocratic wife. There was a fire lurking beneath her cool exterior that she hid well. It made most believe she would be biddable. Christian knew that she would not, but he wanted her anyway. Perhaps because of that. He liked the way she met his gaze instead of demurring to him. She would challenge him, and if he had to face a wife daily, then why not rise to that challenge?

"What has he promised you?"

Crenshaw sighed dramatically as if he did not want to reveal more but had been given no choice. He smiled again, a practiced one meant to placate "Mineral rights."

One of the many things Christian did not have to offer. "And you will give your daughter away for mineral rights?"

The smile did not fade, but it cooled so fast that it hardened. "You would have me give her away for less."

Touché. "I would have you present all viable options to her and allow her to choose."

"You believe yourself to be a better option, my lord?"

"Naturally. I understand that I've gained a reputation of sorts. You must have heard the rumors." Women. Deviance in the bedroom. Violent brawls and general debauchery. Christian watched Crenshaw's face closely for any reaction to his boldness in bringing up that subject. There was none. Crenshaw was good at what he did. "The women," Christian elaborated.

Crenshaw gave a brisk nod. "Women can be dramatic creatures. I do not put much stock into their reactions."

"Nevertheless, I would assure you that the rumors exaggerate." For example, the gossips claimed his leg had been broken by an irate husband. That he had been set upon by the husband in a dark alley. As if he would be so careless. "Rest assured, I would never put your daughter at risk."

"I am not concerned with your fidelity. Violet will learn that the state of a husband's personal life is his own affair."

"Then it is purely material gain you are after?" The words were strangely bitter on his tongue.

Crenshaw laughed and rose, placing his cigar on the edge of a crystal dish. "I will be certain to keep your proposal in mind." Which meant that he wouldn't.

Dammit. Christian had no way to counter a bloody business proposal when he had only come armed with a title, charm, and an admiration for the man's daughter. He had wrongly assumed that the business need that accompanied marriage would be resolved now that the elder daughter's union was all but assured.

Christian got to his feet and waited for the predictable

throb of pain that shot through his ankle to pass before gripping his cane and following Crenshaw to the door. "Then at least tell me whom I should congratulate for winning her hand."

Crenshaw tipped his head. "I cannot say."

Christian's grip on the silver hawk's head of his cane became a fist, but he forced a lazy tone. "You cannot say?"

"All right." Crenshaw grinned like a boy who had glutted himself on a treat. "I will merely say that you may visit and admire my beloved daughter later this summer in Devon."

Ware. Pallid and weak. It had to be him, because his family seat was in Devon and he seemed to always be at hand when the Crenshaw sisters were about. The man-child could not hold his own against a mildly strong gust of wind much less an angry suitor bent on having Violet. Unfortunately, the issue would not be decided in a bareknuckle boxing match. More's the pity.

And to add insult to injury, Ware was a mere viscount.

"I shall look forward to it." Christian bid good day to the infuriating man and made his way to the front stairs as if he had not been rebuffed by a man whose recent ancestors had been scoundrels and thieves. There was no doubt in his mind that he would be the better match for Violet Crenshaw. The fact that his lack of resources was the only thing keeping her from being his grated.

Ware was a slug. The man wouldn't know what to do with a woman like her. He'd keep her hidden away on his estate, justifiably afraid that a better man would take her from him. Christian, however, would keep her in the light. He would allow her to host as many parties as her heart desired and enjoy as many theater outings as she wanted. She would dance, and flirt, and everything else that was socially acceptable to a newly married bride, but she would be his, and no man would be foolish enough to overstep. The reputation his fists had gained him would work in his favor there.

His old leg injury flared up on cold, rainy days, but otherwise was a mere annoyance that caused a barely noticeable limp. He carried a cane for the occasions when standing excessively was necessary, or for the random uneven pavement and gravel walkway. Stairs were another problem. No matter how he tried, navigating them was slower than he would like and required the use of a well-mounted handrail. Today, however, he was grateful for the delay as he made his way down. It gave him time to notice the most beautiful and haunting voice he had ever heard. Hearing it instantly helped to dissipate his anger.

He knew immediately that it was Violet. The soft rasp of her voice coming through the closed door was unmistakable. A pleasant chill tingled over his skin and down his spine. By the time he neared the foot of the stairs, it was over to be replaced by light applause. Violet said something, but her voice was too muffled to distinguish the words. Laughter followed. The music room door clicked open and a maid hurried out, leaving the door open behind her.

A decent man would have kept walking and not lingered as he passed the partially open door. He would have smiled at the giggles spilling out of the room and hurried on his way to his next appointment. Everyone knew that Christian was not a decent man. He owned a reputation notorious for indecent things.

He stopped at the gap, arrested by a swirl of pale yellow and an upswept chestnut coiffure that hurried past the open door. The woman's face was not visible to him but, like the voice, he knew she was Violet. She clapped her hands once, rounding up her charges—all debutantes her own age—to have them give their attention to the next performer. He could not see the poor girl who started the next song, but her voice was atrociously high. Pity that she had to perform after Violet might have stirred within him had Violet not come to stand on the far side of the room directly in his line of sight. She stopped everything for him.

In profile, it was obvious that her nose was possibly too strong for her small features, and that her mouth was likely too wide, but taken together they were perfect. Her foot tapped along to the music, making him smile because it was not the least bit proper. The hem of her gown fluttered as the toe of her shoe worked in a steady rhythm. He followed the vibrations of the fabric up to her small waist and the hug of pale yellow over her bosom where it ended in a ruffled collar at her neck. Hungry for another look at her profile, his gaze continued upward, and his heart nearly stopped in his chest when a pair of irate dark eyes settled on his.

Her mouth quirked in displeasure.

He had met Violet twice. The first time they had been introduced at a ball and briefly exchanged pleasantries. He had found her both charming and alluring. The second time had been when he had come to this very house several days ago with Rothschild in his quest to win back her older sister. They had exchanged words then. Unpleasant words.

You, she had said to him here in this exact entryway. *Why are you here?*

Because I like fireworks, he had answered.

It appeared she was prepared to repeat their exchange as she made her way to him. Taking hold of the door, she glanced into the entryway, taking note of the footman at the door before allowing her gaze to fall on Christian. "Lord Leigh," she said, her voice low, giving it a smooth huskiness that rasped pleasantly across his ears. An elegant brow rose in question, and she stepped out of the room, drawing the door closed behind her. "What a surprise to see you here again."

"Miss Crenshaw." He inclined his head. "It would appear I cannot stay away for very long." He teased her simply to see her flush with displeasure.

Her eyes flared in annoyance. "How lucky we are, my lord." Her tone implied the opposite.

She was not above having her feelings known, even if she was refined enough to couch them in polite words. It had been years since he'd felt this spark of interest when talking with a woman. Despite his best intention at keeping it contained, a laugh escaped him.

Violet openly glared at him. "You find humor in that?"

"I was just thinking that I very much enjoy our encounters."

She had the grace to blush as she undoubtedly recalled how angry she had been during their conversation here in this entryway. She had mistakenly believed Rothschild to be unfaithful to her sister and hadn't held back her disappointment. Instead of being a good friend and pleading Rothschild's case, Christian had baited her.

Swallowing, she asked, "Is there something you wanted, my lord?"

You. All of you.

"I am just leaving from a meeting with your father," he said instead.

"Ah, then please do not allow me to keep you."

Swirls of amber flame glittered at him from the depths of her brown eyes. No, he decided then and there, Ware would not have her. She was too good for the likes of him.

Inclining his head, he said, "Good day, Miss Crenshaw."

"Good day, my lord." She opened the door and stepped back into the room.

He crossed the entryway, aware of the weight of her gaze on his back when he had expected her to close the door between them immediately. The footman opened the front door for him, but instead of stepping out, Christian glanced back at her. She was staring at his shoulders, her gaze slowly moving down his back. The glaze of attraction in her eyes was unmistakable.

She flushed when she realized he had caught her and closed the door firmly between them.

He stared at the lacquered wood grain for the space of a few heartbeats. He knew because he felt each of them as his blood rushed through his body. Talking with her always had the effect of making him more aware of himself and less aware of everything around him, except for her.

Finally, the footman made a nervous sound in the back of his throat. As Christian walked out to his carriage, he decided that he would bypass her parents in his bid to win her. They were set against him, so it made much more sense to approach the woman herself. It would not be easy given the unfavorable impression of him she had thanks to Rothschild, or perhaps she had heard murmurs of his past, but he could overcome that. It would be a simple matter of finding her heart's desire and giving it to her. Then she would be his.

Ready to find
your next great read?

Let us help.

Visit prh.com/nextread

Penguin
Random
House